Claimed

TARAH SCOTT

Broken Arm Publishing

BROKEN
ARM
PUBLISHING

This is a work of fiction. Names, characters, places, and incidents are either the product of the author's imagination or are used fictitiously, and any resemblance to actual persons living or dead, business establishments, events, or locales, is entirely coincidental.

ISBN: 978-0692408622
ISBN 13: 978-0692408629

Author's Website: www.TarahScott.com
Facebook: Facebook.com/TarahScottsRomanceNovels
Twitter: @TarahScott
Blog: TarahScott.TarahScott.com

Cover design by Erin Dameron Hill

First Trade Paperback Printing by Broken Arm Publishing: March 2015

10 9 8 7 6 5 4 3 2

ACKNOWLEDGEMENTS

Despite the countless hours a writer spends alone writing a novel, the finished product is, without doubt, a collaboration. Each time I take stock of the wonderful people who contributed to my work, my heart overflows. I am very fortunate.

I must first thank my editor, Kimberly Comeau. Your devotion to make my novels shine never ceases to amaze me. Thank you, Kim. Second, huge thanks to my good friend Sue-Ellen Welfonder. Sue-Ellen, I cannot tell you how much I appreciate your input. I feel secure that all things historical are as they should be. (Any foibles are all my doing!) Next, my beta readers, Tina Hairston and my sister Stooge, Debbie McCreary. Ladies, feedback from honest readers is invaluable. You're both worth your weight in gold. Lastly, thanks, once again, to Erin Dameron-Hill for a wonderful cover. Your art inspired a book beyond what I imagined. (I hear your laughter, Kim.)

DEDICATION

This one is for Tracey Reid and Valerie Cozart. This book reminds me of our day in Queens.

Chapter One

~

August 1291 Scottish Highlands

"YOUR GRANDFATHER AWAITS you at Longford Castle where you will marry Lord Melrose immediately."

Had she heard correctly?

Disorientation at being abruptly roused from a sound sleep combined with disbelief caused Rhoslyn's heart to thud wildly. Pain shot down her left arm as Prioress Hildegard twisted the limb and shoved her hand into the sleeve of a gray, wool dress.

"I am sorry, child," the prioress said, but she didn't slow her hurried dressing of Rhoslyn.

Hildegard pulled the dress down over her body, then grabbed the belt she had tossed onto the pallet. She cinched it around Rhoslyn's waist and snatched up the mantle hastily thrown across a nearby table. Rhoslyn recognized the fur-lined cloak as the one she'd worn the day she arrived at the convent fourteen months ago. The prioress swung the garment around Rhoslyn's shoulder.

"Hildegard, please," she began as the nun fastened the clasp at her neck.

Hildegard grasped her arm and started toward the door. "We must go. Your grandfather's men wait outside."

Rhoslyn stumbled over the hem of her skirts and barely righted herself as they passed through the doorway and into the convent's narrow hallway.

"I must speak with Abbess Beatrice," Rhoslyn demanded.

"She sent me." Hildegard made a hard right around a bend, her grip firm on Rhoslyn's arm.

They reached the front entrance, where three nuns stood at the open door.

"Where is the abbess?" Rhoslyn asked.

Hildegard pulled her through the door into the fog that hung in the lit bailey. Shock dug deeper at the sight of men-at-arms, a dozen—no she realized, more, at least two dozen—up ahead. Was her respite at the convent truly over?

The prioress hurried her toward the men who waited near the gate.

As they approached, Sir Ascot, who held the bridle of his horse at the front of the company, dropped to one knee. "My lady."

"Rise, Knight," she instructed. "Quickly, tell me what has happened."

He came to his feet, then reached inside the front of his mail shirt and produced a missive that he extended toward her. Her gaze caught on the broken seal—the Great Seal of England. She jerked her gaze to the knight's face in shocked question. He said nothing and she took the document.

Rhoslyn unfolded the parchment and her heart beat faster at sight of the boldly scripted salutation addressed to her grandfather from "King Edward I, Lord Superior of the realm of Scotland," she read out loud.

"God save us," Hildegard breathed.

Rhoslyn snapped her gaze onto Sir Ascot. "How did King Edward come to be Lord Superior of Scotland?"

"Forgive me, my lady," he glanced at the nun, "Sister. I assumed ye knew."

"Knew what?" Rhoslyn demanded.

"The Maid of Norway is dead."

Rhoslyn felt as if a horse had kicked her. Their future queen dead? "How?"

"She drowned in Orkney on the way to Scotland."

Hildegard made the sign of the cross.

"She was but seven," Rhoslyn breathed. Tears pricked her eyes. "When?"

"Eleven months past," he said.

"Eleven months?" Only a few months after her arrival here.

She couldn't think, couldn't fathom all the consequences of Margaret's death. Why hadn't her grandfather told her? Because, she realized with a rush of emotion, it was like him to protect her. He had been protecting her since the death of her parents at age five. Then he rescued her again after the death of her husband…and son.

"More than a dozen claimants to the throne have come forward," Sir Ascot went on. "The Guardians fear civil war between the Bruce and Balliol's supporters, so asked King Edward to arbitrate."

Rhoslyn snorted. "He used the unrest to demand sovereign lordship of Scotland." And the Guardians acquiesced. The pea-brained men had no sense. She forced her eyes back to the missive, ashamed to find that her hands trembled. Her heart stopped cold at sight of the royal command for her to—"Marry Sir Talbot St. Claire." She pinned Hildegard with a stare. "Ye said I was to marry Lord Melrose."

The nun looked helplessly at Sir Ascot.

"Aye, my lady," he said. "Your grandfather has arranged for ye to marry Melrose before St. Claire can obey his king's command."

"What? That is madness." To defy Edward at any time was dangerous, but to do so when he had such power was suicide.

Why St. Claire, a mere knight? A knight born in sin at that, despite the fact Edward legitimized him after their return from Wales. She was the daughter of a baron, widow to a wealthy earl. Her noble lineage stretched back two hundred years. Her mind spun and she wished she could return to her cell and bar the door against the world.

"My lady," Ascot began, but she waved him off, tilted the parchment toward the light, and read on.

Edward commanded them to recite the vows a month from now. The letter outlined the details of the contract, which endowed her grandfather with property in England. Anger pricked at seeing the properties her husband had bequeathed her listed as part of her dowry to St. Claire—with Castle Glenbarr, the wealthiest of the properties—at the head. The castle abutted Dunfrey Castle, she realized with a flash of clarity. Edward had given Dunfrey Castle to St. Claire after he quelled a revolt in Wales three years ago.

Her property combined with St. Claire's would make him a force to be reckoned with. But she couldn't forget—and she was certain Edward hadn't forgotten—her grandfather's property would come to her upon his death. Combined, the lands would make the knight one of the most powerful lords in the northern Highlands. Here was why the king had chosen him. Only a man like St. Claire could defend and keep the land should the need arise. And the need would arise. Edward knew it. So did she.

Yet all this wasn't enough, she read with mounting anger. Edward also demanded a year's salary from these properties. How much of her dowry would pay the debts for his past military campaigns? She gave a grim smile. He generously allowed her grandfather two years to pay. No doubt Edward had already sent word to his money-lenders that they could expect a large payment in the coming months. How many other Scottish nobles were paying Edward's debt—a debt he incurred long before he achieved power in Scotland?

The sovereign had planned well. The English estates he bequeathed her grandfather would pass to St. Claire upon her grandfather's death, and her Scottish property would pass from the house of Seward to St. Claire...and his liege lord, King Edward. Her stomach roiled. The bastard knight would even inherit her grandfather's title as Baron Kinsley. She pictured the knight rising from their marriage bed 'ere his seed dried inside her to take possession of Glenbarr. Her heart twisted. She had intended the castle as part of her stepdaughter's dowry.

Aye, Edward knew his business, she thought bitterly. This was the king to whom the Guardians had handed Scotland.

"Forgive me, my lady." Sir Ascot's voice interrupted her thoughts. "We must make haste. Your grandfather awaits us at Longford Castle."

To prepare her future husband for battle, no doubt. St. Claire was well known for ruthlessness in battle. He would not take well the news that his newly awarded prize had slipped through his fingers. The slight to him—and his king—would not go unanswered.

"We flee in the night like cowards," Rhoslyn muttered.

Wasn't that exactly what she had done fourteen months ago? Her heart clenched with memory of her son, not two months old, laid to rest in the cold ground. When he had died two weeks after his father, Rhoslyn begged her grandfather for time in a convent. The guilt she had submerged beneath long hours of exhausting work now resurfaced. She had left her stepdaughter Andreana in her grandfather's care.

Rhoslyn thrust the letter back toward Sir Ascot. "My grandfather cannot have thought this matter through."

He took the letter with a deferential cant of his head. "Sir Talbot arrived a week ago, and Lord Melrose returned from Edinburgh tonight. Your grandfather could no' act before now. But he wishes as much leeway as possible before Sir Talbot discovers ye are married."

Shock reverberated through her. Her grandfather hoped Melrose would get her pregnant before Sir Talbot learned he had been tricked. Sweet God, her grandfather had gone mad. Melrose was an honorable man, but he was sixty-five.

"How does my grandfather expect an old man to sire a child?"

Sir Ascot shook his head. "Ye are to marry Jacobus Auenel. The old earl is dead."

"Dead?" She was to marry Lord Melrose's son?

Her pulse sped up. Was it possible to become wife and future mother in a few days' time? Disgust displaced the hope that surged through her. Jacobus Melrose was but twenty-one. A pup. A pup would have no trouble siring a child. It was Rhoslyn who might not conceive. Rhoslyn twisted the wedding ring she still wore. She wanted neither child *nor* husband.

Damn the sovereign to hell. He interfered where he had no business. And her grandfather was still trying to protect her. In the process, he would get himself and young Melrose killed. This she could not allow.

Rhoslyn faced Hildegard and gave her a fierce hug. "Thank ye."

The prioress' gnarled fingers tightened on her shoulders. "May God keep ye safe, lady."

They drew apart.

"Beatrice…" Rhoslyn began, a lump in her throat.

Hildegard smiled gently. "You will see the abbess again in God's time."

Rhoslyn gave the nun's hand a final squeeze and turned to Sir Ascot. He helped her mount one of the horses and she kept her gaze straight when they passed through the gates. In the dark mist beyond the convent Rhoslyn saw only Edward's bold script commanding that she marry Sir Talbot St. Claire.

TALBOT OPENED THE door to the bower and took in the slim figure seated on the bench in front of the fire. Beautiful dark hair hung unbound about slim shoulders. Canny blue eyes met his stare. Beside her stood a tall warrior at least ten years Talbot's senior, but fit as any man Talbot's age. Firelight glistened off the polished hilt of the well-used broadsword at the man's hip.

Talbot paused inside the doorway and returned his gaze to the woman. "Lady Finlay, I am honored to meet you. I understand you wanted to see me."

She rose. "Will ye enter and close the door?"

Talbot flicked a glance at her protector.

She said, "So long as ye do no' harm me, he will not harm you."

"So long as he stays at his side of the room, there will be no misunderstandings," Talbot replied.

"He will do as I bid. Please, Sir Talbot, time is short." She nodded toward the door. "I canna' risk prying ears."

Talbot closed the door, crossed his arms, and waited.

"I have news concerning your betrothed."

He tensed, but kept his expression cool. "What news could you possibly have concerning my wife?"

Her mouth twitched in indulgent amusement. "Calling Lady Rhoslyn your wife will be meaningless if a priest blesses her union with another man."

"Are you saying an illegal marriage has been performed?"

The amusement reached her eyes. "Until Lady Rhoslyn is in your home—and your bed—there is some doubt as to your claim."

"I make no claim, madam. She is my wife by order of King Edward."

"Then let King Edward come here and enforce the decree. But that would be doing things the hard way. As Abbess of St. Mary's convent, I can simplify things."

"Abbess of St. Mary's?" he repeated.

"Abbes Beatrice," she said. "Forgive the deception. I could no' risk anyone here knowing my true identity. It is best that Rhoslyn—and everyone else—never know I was here." She paused. "I am a good woman to have as friend. Do ye wish me to be your friend?"

Talbot had found the church befriend no one but the church.

He canted his head. "I am always at the disposal of the church."

"A wise man. I expect something in return for the favor I am about to bestow. This is no small matter, Sir Talbot. I am ensuring that your marriage to Lady Rhoslyn does not go awry."

"That sounds like nothing short of a miracle." And he didn't believe in miracles.

"God works in mysterious ways," the abbess said. "Are we agreed? A favor for a favor?"

"I give no favors that betray my king."

She nodded. "Good. I do no' like traitors and I trust them even less. Lady Rhoslyn has spent the last fourteen months at St. Mary's mourning the death of her husband and son. Tonight, her grandfather's men arrived to take her to Longford Castle where she will marry the new Earl of Melrose."

Talbot feared something like this. Upon his arrival at Castle Glenbarr a week ago, he'd visited her grandfather with the betrothal contract. The old baron read the decree, then promised to bring Lady Rhoslyn from her convent. No blustering, no rejection of the marriage terms, not so much as a cross word. Aside from the fact he refused to name the convent, the whole affair had been too easy.

"Seward cannot be fool enough to think I will not take her by force," Talbot said.

"Dinna' be dense," she replied. "He plans to hold up in Longford Castle until she bears Jacobus a child."

"Castles can be razed to the ground."

"More easily said than done," she said, "and at what cost? The castle is a veritable fortress. Lady Rhoslyn's grandfather can wait you out."

"Where is she now?" Talbot demanded.

"We are agreed?" the abbess pressed.

"Aye. We are agreed. But beware, Sister. I honor my word, but I will not commit murder any quicker than I will betray Edward."

Her brows rose. "Murder is your way of life, Knight. But fear no', murder is *not* God's way. I will not ask anything he would not ask."

That frightened Talbot more than anything man could ask. But he had no more intention of allowing God to force him into anything than he did man *or* woman.

"By now Rhoslyn is on her way to Longford Castle," Beatrice said. "I had the prioress delay her departure. I pray we had an hour head start, and Rhoslyn and her grandfather's men willna' have been able to ride as fast as we did."

"You will not countenance betrayal in me, but have no compunction about betraying Lady Rhoslyn," Talbot said.

She lifted her brows as if surprised. "It is no betrayal to carry out God's will."

A WARNING SHOUT at the rear of the company caused Rhoslyn to snap her head toward the murky form of Sir Ascot, who rode beside her in the thickening fog.

The knight drew his sword. "Ride, my lady."

After they'd left the convent, Sir Ascot had given her a dagger and instructed her to flee with two of his strongest men should they be discovered. She hadn't thought there any great possibility that would happen, so hadn't voiced the thought that she wouldn't leave her father's men at the mercy of Sir Talbot.

"Do not lose your head," she ordered. "It is far more likely we have encountered robbers than St Claire. He cannot possibly know I have left the convent."

Ascot lifted his sword and Rhoslyn realized his intention. She turned her horse's head, but not quickly enough to avoid the flat side of his sword smacking her steed's rump. The beast leapt forward and the men parted before her as her horse shot through their ranks. As planned, Aland and David broke into a gallop alongside her.

She pulled on the reins, but her horse gave a cry and sped up when Aland slapped his reins against the beast's neck. David drew closer on the other side, hemming her in. The fools were in league against her.

"I shall strip you both of your knighthood," she shouted.

"Aye, my lady," Aland replied. "But your grandfather will hang us if we do not deliver ye to him safely."

Another, more distant shout went up amongst the men, this one followed by a clash of steel. Was it truly St. Claire who accosted them? Anger whipped through Rhoslyn. The death of her grandfather's knights would be on Edward's head. He would pay. Oh, how he would pay.

The sounds of fighting faded. She could make out the murky shadows of trees alongside the road, but didn't know where they were. The pounding of her protectors' horses' hooves beside her should have given comfort. Instead, she knew the sound would haunt her forever. It was the sound of cowardice. The sound of defeat.

A large silhouette abruptly appeared in front of them.

"My lady!" Aland cried.

He tore to the right and Rhoslyn followed while David galloped left. She heard a thwack, but couldn't guess the source, and forced her horse back onto the road. She pulled on the reins. A man's grunt sounded and a horse gave a shrill cry. Rhoslyn turned her mount toward the sound and one of the knights appeared nearby.

"Aland, is that you?" Or was it David?

He brought his horse up beside hers. Something struck her as odd, but before she could understand what, an arm snaked out and around her waist. She yanked the dagger from its sheath and drove the blade downward toward the arm gripping her as she was dragged from her horse. The blade snagged on her attacker's armor and he muttered a curse as she slammed into a wall of muscle protected by chainmail.

Fear sent a wave of dizziness through her. She raised the knife for another blow, but iron fingers clamped around her wrist. She cried out in pain and her grip faltered. He shook her wrist hard and she dropped the dagger.

Her legs dangled against the horse's flanks and she gave a vicious kick to its ribs. The beast started forward, then the arm around her tightened as its owner pulled back on the reins. She kicked again—

harder—and the horse reared. Her attacker crushed Rhoslyn between his chest and arms as he leaned forward in an effort to force the animal's front hooves back onto the ground.

She gasped for breath through crushed lungs. The horse's hooves hit the ground so hard her teeth jarred. Rhoslyn clawed at the arm that pinned her. Her fingers slipped on a warm, slick substance, and satisfaction surged through her at the realization that it was his blood. She must have cut him below his chainmail. His hold, however, did not weaken, despite the wound.

With a grunt, he seized her arms and trapped them against her body. He threw a leg over her thighs, pinning them against the horse's side, before the horse shot forward. Tears of rage stung her eyes even as she arched and twisted. Her grandfather's men had died for nothing. Aland…David, had died without ever seeing their executioner.

Rhoslyn's legs cramped and she struggled harder. She would plunge the first knife she found into the heart of Talbot St Claire. He was a fool to have acted so rashly. He would not have her, her lands, or the goodwill of his king. Nay. He would die.

Minutes passed in growing agony before her captor at last slowed his horse's pace. Rhoslyn couldn't deny her relief when he released the pressure on her legs. He shifted her bottom across his hard thighs, and she straightened, stretching her legs. One large hand pressed her thigh in what she knew was a warning not to incite the beast again.

Pinpricks of light dotted the foggy darkness ahead. Was this Dunfrey Castle? She hadn't seen lights to indicate they had passed Castle Glenbarr. So her captor had wisely circled around her home to avoid detection. Once they reached Dunfrey Castle she would become a prisoner. Dunfrey Castle, nicknamed 'Dragon's Lair' by the Highlanders who had competed against St. Claire in the *tainchel*, the Great Hunt, was smaller than Castle Glenbarr, but no less fortified. St. Claire would defeat any who attacked him, just as he had his competitors in the games. Truly, the castle was appropriately nicknamed Dragon's Lair, for the knight, like the mythical dragon, decimated his enemies.

They drew closer, and an eerie yellow glow haloed the torches in the fog up on the battlements. Despite her resolve, her belly clenched with fear. She mouthed a silent prayer to Saint George for strength to bind her dragon as St. George had his a millennia ago.

The keep loomed, a shadow in the fog that became a visible wall when they stopped. Something familiar niggled at her.

"'Tis I," her captor shouted, in a cultured English accent.

No simple man-at-arms had been sent to collect her. Only a knight of the first order would do to kidnap Sir Talbot St. Claire's wife.

"Open in the name of peace," he called.

Peace? St. Claire represented anything but peace.

Fury swept through Rhoslyn. "Ye speak of peace when you kidnap innocent women and slay men in the dark? Neither you nor your master shall know peace the remainder of your days."

Her captor gave a low laugh that sent a chill down her spine.

"What man knows peace when he takes a wife?" he said.

Rhoslyn stiffened. The man was a dog. How fitting that a dog should serve a dragon.

Wood creaked as the gates began a slow swing inward. He spurred his horse forward when the opening was barely wide enough to accommodate entrance. The fog obscured their surroundings. He stopped and hugged her close as he swung his leg around the pommel. She threw her arms around his neck for fear of falling as he slid from the saddle. Rhoslyn jolted when his feet hit solid ground. Another warrior appeared beside the horse as her captor strode away from the animal.

"Put me down," Rhoslyn demanded.

He lengthened his stride in response.

"Did ye hear me, Knight? I am Lady Rhoslyn Harper—"

"St. Claire," he cut in.

"What?"

"Lady Rhoslyn St. Claire."

"How dare you?" She slapped him.

They reached the castle. He stopped short and she tensed. Would he strike her back? Did his master countenance the abuse of women?

Her heart pounded. "Have ye something to say, Knight?"

"What should I say, my lady?"

"Put me down," she ordered.

He pushed through the door and Rhoslyn drew a sharp breath upon realizing why she had experienced the sense of recognition. They weren't at Dunfrey Castle. This was Castle Glenbarr.

"What thievery is this?" she demanded. "Your master has no right to claim my property. We are not yet wed." But she knew the vows—and consummation—were a mere formality. Edward's decree held as much power as did the priest's benediction. Still, that gave him no right to occupy her home before even meeting her.

The monster carrying her gave no answer. She had expected none. He was an Englishman, and Englishmen considered their women chattel. St. Claire would soon learn that Lady Rhoslyn Harper, granddaughter of Sir Hugo Seward, Baron Kinsley, daughter of Ihon Seward, was no man's property.

At the far end of the room burned a low fire in a large hearth. Flickering tongues of flame cast light across the room, revealing the forms of warriors sleeping on the floor. English men-at-arms, she would wager. Where were her men? Had there been a battle? Rhoslyn thanked God she had sent her stepdaughter to stay with her grandfather while she resided at the convent. The girl would have been terrified if she'd been at Castle Glenbarr when St. Claire took possession.

Her captor crossed left, to a narrow staircase. Rhoslyn expected to be put down on her feet, but he threw her over his shoulder and took the stairs two at a time.

"Beast," she muttered, but kept still for fear of hitting her head in the narrow space.

He reached the second level and ascended another set of stairs to the third floor where lay the too-familiar private quarters. He took several paces, then pushed through a door that opened upon her late husband's bedchambers. Rhoslyn was abruptly tossed from his shoulder. She cried out and tensed for impact with the stone floor, but bounced on a mattress.

The bed's thick canopy curtain closed behind her. Surprise immobilized her for an instant, then the tread of boots on stone penetrated her stupor. Rhoslyn scrambled to the edge of the bed and threw back the curtain. She drew a sharp breath at sight of her abductor's broad shoulders. His large body had nearly crushed her, but seeing him, she now understood how he had dispatched her protectors so easily—and why St. Claire sent him. He was even larger than the Dragon was rumored to be. That didn't mean she would allow him to leave her in the bed where her husband died.

Rhoslyn leapt from the bed and stumbled before catching herself, then lunged toward the door. The knight reached it several long strides ahead of her and passed into the hall. He slammed the door shut behind him and she collided with the wood.

Chapter Two

A HARD RAP on the solar door alerted Talbot to his captain's return. "Enter."

Baxter D'Angers stepped into the room as Talbot splashed water on his face from the bowl on the table then grabbed a clean cloth to wipe his face.

Baxter crossed to him. "I am gone three days and everything goes to hell. Alexander tells me your bride fled her convent." His attention caught on the bloodied cloths scattered about the table, then his eyes shifted to the bandage Talbot had wrapped around his wrist. "What in God's name happened?"

"Lady Rhoslyn decided Melrose would make a better husband than me."

"Melrose?" Baxter blurted. "What the devil? He is a supporter of Balliol. Seward openly supports Bruce—perhaps even William Wallace, if gossip is to be believed. He cannot possibly want to ally himself with a Balliol supporter. Seward's support of Bruce is one reason Edward chose her as your bride."

Talbot lifted a brow.

"I am not an idiot. Even I can see the obvious." Baxter shook his head. "Is Seward fool enough to defy Edward—or you—and think he can succeed?"

"Had his granddaughter reached Longford Castle it would have been very possible. I understand the castle is well fortified and could likely survive a siege until Lady Rhoslyn bore him a child."

Baxter shook his head. "Kinsley is a fool. Edward's edict cannot be disputed. You have even taken possession of this hellish place."

"Glenbarr Castle is no more hellish than Nightwell Hold."

"Nightwell Hold is in England," Baxter replied. "I told you the old baron was not to be trusted. How did you know—"

A knock at the door interrupted Baxter, and Talbot bid them enter.

Thom, one of his men-at-arms, entered and stopped just inside the room. "Her men are on the way here, including her two escorts. Three died in the fray."

Talbot tossed the clean rag on the table. "Seward will have to explain to their wives why his treachery got them killed."

"We lost one of our own," Thom said.

Talbot cut his gaze to him. "Who?"

"Valance."

Talbot wanted to find the old baron and beat him senseless. "Valance had a young wife. Seward will pension the widow."

"You might take it out of his granddaughter's hide," Baxter said in a rare flash of anger.

Talbot was inclined to agree. "Inform me when the men arrive," he ordered Thom.

Thom nodded, then left.

Baxter nodded at Talbot's wound. "Which of his men wounded you?"

Talbot gave a harsh laugh. "Not a one. It was the lady."

Baxter looked taken aback. "She was willing to go so far as kill you?"

"Aye, and she came closer than I care to admit."

"A month chained in the dungeon will give her time to remember her wifely duties."

"She will be chained, but to me, not the dungeon. She is in my bedchambers awaiting the priest who will officiate the vows."

"Your bedchambers?" Baxter blurted.

Talbot nodded. "I sent word that Seward can attend us this week—at his leisure—for the wedding feast."

"You are playing with fire."

"With that woman?" He snorted. "Aye, that I am."

He remembered his surprise—and shock—when her blade sliced the flesh of his wrist. He also hadn't forgotten the feather-light weight of her body across his thighs. He hadn't met her before tonight, hadn't cared if the sight of her shriveled his bollocks to the size of peas. She represented the possible end of constant warring, the birth of sons, and daughters he would have to heavily dower if they, too, turned out to be horse-faced like their mother.

But Rhoslyn Harper wasn't horse-faced, and her body—her body belonged to a woman who hated him. He would have no trouble consummating the marriage, but he would have to tie his wife's hands to the bedpost to keep her from plunging a knife into his back while he drove into her. He felt himself harden at the thought and grimaced. It might not have been as pleasurable if she had been horse-faced, but it would have been safer.

"Is the king's favor worth allying ourselves to such vipers?" Baxter's voice disrupted his thoughts. "She will cause you misery all your days. I would not ask it of you. No one would."

Talbot crossed to the table near the hearth where a pitcher of ale sat and poured two mugs. He returned to his friend, handed him a mug, and motioned for him to sit on the bench in front of the fire.

They sat and Talbot took a long, fortifying drink of ale before he said, "My marriage is not about incurring favor, as you well know. I can no more ignore Edward's command than Lady Harper can ignore her duty."

Though she had done just that tonight. That was unfair, he realized. What Scottish noblewoman would willingly marry an English knight, and a bastard knight at that, even if he had been legitimized?

Lady Rhoslyn Harper was not stupid, as he had learned tonight. Clearly, she didn't agree with the pervading Scottish sentiment that the extended period of relative peace between Scotland and England meant that Edward wasn't trying to bring Scotland under his rule.

Baxter finished his ale and set the mug on the bench beside him. "You have enough land and wealth to live well the remainder of your days. You no longer need please Edward."

Talbot took a draw on his ale. His wrist ached. He would need several mugs to ease the pain, but not so much as to dull his wits when he was finally alone with his bride. He glanced at the door connecting the solar to the antechamber that led to his bedchambers. He had expected more shouts when he'd slammed the door in her face. She was too quiet. Had she accepted her fate? He snorted. Not that one.

He took another gulp of ale, then said, "You are naive if you believe Edward will ever release me from service." Talbot flashed a tired smile. "I have made myself too valuable."

"And this is how he rewards you? Exiled in this God forsaken country."

Talbot stretched his legs toward the inviting fire. "God forsaken, perhaps. But also far from the certain trouble brewing in England."

"And if the Guardians cannot maintain peace in Scotland?" Baxter demanded. "How much peace will there be here, even this far north? Wallace has no intentions of letting Edward rule Scotland, even if the Guardians are fool enough to let him seize power."

Talbot sighed. He could always count on his captain to name the worst of his fears. "The Guardians chose Edward to arbitrate because he can break the deadlock, and he has the power to enforce his decision. No one wants war in Scotland. Not the Guardians, not Edward—nor I. You put too little faith in our king."

"I *know* our king," Baxter shot back, but with no real malice.

"No matter," Talbot said. "Any rebellion that breaks out here is preferable to war with Wales or France."

Or England, for that matter.

If Talbot could maintain order, here in Buchan, Edward was unlikely to call him to service for anything short of a large campaign. He tired of killing. Seventeen years was enough.

"Let us pray the problems here in Scotland remain small," he said.

Baxter regarded him from the corner of his eye. "Your betrothed tried to kill you."

Talbot barked a laugh. "Women are troublesome."

Baxter gave him a sidelong glance. "I have often wondered that he doesn't worry that your mother's Scottish blood might sway your allegiance."

"Edward believes that I will be accepted *because* my mother was Scottish. I never knew her. I am no more Scottish than you are Flemish."

"I am loathe to admit it, but the place suits you," Baxter said.

"And the rest of Lady Rhoslyn's property will suit me as well."

Whether the lady liked it or not.

RHOSLYN FACED THE room St. Claire thought was her prison. *Fool.* She knew this castle as well as the one she grew up in. A sudden chill threaded through her. There was but one reason St. Claire would lock her in his bedchambers. He intended to skip the wedding vows and consummate their marriage.

So why hadn't he forced himself between her legs when he captured her? The contract was solid enough that no priest need validate their union. The marriage would stand. Another—more devastating—truth hit. He need not lay a hand on her. The mere fact she was in his bedchambers was enough to seal her fate.

Rhoslyn hurried to the bed. She stuffed the pillows beneath the blankets, then arranged them to look like a sleeping body. She lit a taper from the fire in the hearth then slid to the right and groped about the paneling for the hidden latch. A small click sounded and the panel opened to a secret passageway leading to a guest bedchamber on the far end of the castle's west wing. Stepping inside, she pulled her mantle close around her and drew the panel shut.

Candle extended before her, she navigated the narrow passage. Anger coursed through her. Two men she had never met controlled her life: King Edward and his puppet knight Sir Talbot St. Claire.

Knight.

The word echoed in her mind on a wave of disgust. What did a man like St. Claire know of honor, truth, or loyalty? Loyalty. Aye, perhaps he did understand that precept. Loyalty to a king who would fill his knights' coffers with coin dripping with blood—Scottish blood, if need be.

What a fool she'd been to spend fourteen months grieving. He hadn't said it, but she'd read the worry in her grandfather's eyes when he agreed to her request. Before he died, he wanted a grandson to inherit the home and land that had been passed down in his family for generations. She'd been too grief-stricken to care about the future. Her selfishness had lost them everything, including, she realized, her stepdaughter. St. Claire would replace her grandfather as their protector, and would decide who Andreana married. Another English knight, no doubt, who would secure more of her dead husband's wealth for his English king.

Perhaps Andreana's future alone was worth fighting for. Was not her own fate worth fighting for? How many good Scottish men would have to die to keep what was theirs from Edward's greedy fingers?

Fear squeezed her heart. If only she had reached her grandfather. She needed his strong shoulder to cry on, his reasoning to assure her they could keep what was theirs without throwing their clans into a war against England.

How had St. Claire learned she was fleeing the convent? Did he know she intended to marry Lord Melrose? Sir Ascot told her that only he and her grandfather knew of her escape. Even their trusted men-at-arms hadn't been told of their destination.

Rhoslyn reached the end of the passageway and eased open the panel an inch, then listened for any sounds in the room. Silence. She stepped inside, and stopped. Where could she go? How many hours before dawn? Getting a horse was impossible. Even if she managed to reach the stables, St. Claire's guards wouldn't allow her through the gate. Her only choice was to leave through the passageway leading from the chapel to the rear of Castle Glenbarr and outside the walls.

Longford Castle was three quarters of an hour's ride. Walking would take hours. She'd have to keep to the forest to avoid the men St. Claire would send in search of her. Fraser Bell worked the farm nearest Castle Glenbarr. He would help her. No. She couldn't ask his help. St. Claire would punish anyone who aided her. A mental picture flashed of Fraser's two daughters weeping over their father's grave. Instead of asking Fraser's help, she would steal one of his horses.

Rhoslyn forced her thoughts to slow. She needed a weapon. Three jeweled daggers lay hidden in a locked room beneath the castle, along the passageway leading to the dungeon. Only she, her grandfather, and Alec's cousin Duncan held keys. Here was stored a chest filled with coin, a lifetime's wealth saved for lean times or, God forbid, the financing of wars.

Did St. Claire know of the room? She imagined King Edward's long fingers sifting through the coins. Anger tightened her insides. The money and valuables stored there didn't belong to him or St. Claire. Rhoslyn forced a slow breath and concentrated on how she would reach the room undetected, then she realized something terrible; she had to return to Alec's bedchamber for the key.

THE FOG WASN'T lifting. Instead, it had thickened in the minutes Talbot had lingered in the bailey with Baxter and the man who informed them that Baron Kinsley was besieged at Longford Castle by local chief Aodh Roberts. Talbot cursed. He hadn't expected settling in Scotland to be easy, but neither had he expected to find himself in the middle of a family feud.

Talbot glanced at the light that penetrated the fog from a third floor window. Lady Rhoslyn was locked there in his bedchambers. He was cold and tired and had looked forward to a few hours' sleep before rousing the priest to perform the benediction that would solidify their marriage. No man would dare defy the king—or Talbot—after that.

Talbot sighed and fixed his gaze on Iain. Light from the nearby wall sconce illuminated his intense gaze. Iain had been Seward's captain for over twenty years. His loyalty to the baron could cut the fog. There would be no rest tonight.

"Is Melrose prepared for a battle?" Talbot asked.

"He is no' his father," the Highlander replied.

Talbot nodded. "I heard the old earl was a seasoned knight."

"He was," Iain said.

"I suppose you must aid Seward," Baxter said. "Even if the matter has nothing to do with you."

"It has everything to do with ye," Iain interjected. "Until now, Roberts wouldna' dare defy Seward. He knows Lady Rhoslyn would kill him herself."

"God forbid I do any less," Talbot said. "It is Seward that Roberts wants, then, not Melrose?"

"Roberts doesna' love Melrose—he and the old baron fought constantly over cattle—but he hates Seward and I believe he is counting on ye being pleased when he is dead."

Talbot nodded. "What does Roberts hope to gain by killing him?"

"Revenge. He wanted to marry the Lady Rhoslyn, but Seward married her to Harper instead."

Talbot wagered it was the lady who refused. He also suspected Roberts had more than revenge in mind.

Iain pinned him with a hard stare. "These are your people now, St. Claire. You must protect your own, or no' a single Highlander will follow ye. I have fifty men waiting outside Castle Glenbarr willing to follow you. It is a start. Dinna' throw it away."

Talbot knew he had to prove himself. But even if he saved all of Buchan, the one fight the Highlanders might not aid was the effort to drag his wife from one of their kinsman's bed, especially if she carried that man's child.

Frustration lashed through him. Even if Melrose got Rhoslyn with child, Talbot wouldn't annul their marriage. He wouldn't be the first man to raise as heir a son that wasn't his. Before this night ended, Seward would understand that.

Talbot considered having the priest perform the marriage ceremony before marching to Longford Castle. He relished the idea of surprising Seward with that news once Talbot rescued him. Though there would be no consummating the union before he left. Lady Rhoslyn certainly expected more than a three-minute introduction to his skills as a lover.

He addressed Baxter. "Gather a hundred men and send them to

Longford. Have Ross lead them with Iain and his men. Let us see what Harper's captain is made of. You ride out, meet the men bringing Seward's men-at-arms, and take them to Longford. Stay west of the castle in the forest, until I arrive. Send scouts to assess Roberts' men. Sunrise is another three hours. If luck is with us, we can end this before daylight."

He experienced an uncharacteristic hesitation. With the hundred men he was sending to deal with Roberts, Castle Glenbarr would be less well guarded than he liked. He had yet to discover who were his friends and who were his enemies. Then there was the lady to consider. God only knew what she would attempt while he marched to save her grandfather.

What could she possibly do locked in his chambers? One of her friends in the castle might aid her escape. She wouldn't need help, he realized with a start. Castle Glenbarr had been her home for eight years. She must know every door, window and passage—including any passageways from the lord's bedchambers he had yet to discover.

"Have Ross go on ahead," Talbot told Baxter. "I will join you soon."

"What if Roberts attacks before ye arrive?" Iain demanded.

"Then kill him."

RHOSLYN SLIPPED INSIDE the room where slept some of the maids. She wanted information and hoped that one of the girls might have a knife, and so save her the risk of going to the storeroom. Embers burned red in the hearth, casting dim light across the room's four beds. The two beds closest to the fire were empty, but the blankets were rumpled.

"Who is it?" a female voice demanded from one shadowy corner.

Rhoslyn recognized the voice emanating from one of several shapes huddled on the bed. "Sheila, it is I, Lady Rhoslyn."

"Lady Rhoslyn?"

The girl jumped from the bed and hurriedly lit a candle from the hearth, then crossed to Rhoslyn. Her hand flew to her mouth, then she grasped one of Rhoslyn's hands.

"My lady, thank God you are safe."

Three more figures rose and crowded behind Sheila.

"Is something wrong?" Rhoslyn demanded. "Have St. Claire's men abused you?"

"Nay. We are all treated well. But we have been afraid this last week."

The Dragon had been there a week? "Did the Dra—er, St. Claire speak with Duncan?"

Sheila nodded. "They had a long meeting the day after he arrived."

Of course they did. St. Claire would want to inform the steward that he was the new laird of Castle Glenbarr. But that didn't mean Duncan had shown him the storeroom. Duncan was the steward, but Rhoslyn kept the rolls. Each month, she and Alec put a little aside that wasn't included in the accounts the tax collector saw. The accounts that accounted for *all* profits remained locked in the storeroom. Rhoslyn couldn't ask the women if St. Claire had visited the storeroom, for they knew nothing of the room's existence.

"Is it true, my lady? Are ye and Sir Talbot married?" Sheila asked.

Rhoslyn gritted her teeth, unwilling to acknowledge the questions, but the more she thought on the matter, the more she wondered how they would pry St. Claire out of Castle Glenbarr.

"How many men does he have?" she asked.

"At least a hundred and fifty," Sheila said. "And I hear talk three hundred more are on their way."

"Four hundred and fifty?" Rhoslyn said. She envisioned their savings gone inside a year.

"Sir Talbot stocked the barn with cattle," Shelia said.

Her cattle? "Have you a knife?" she asked.

Sheila's eyes widened. "Nay."

She would be forced to go to the storeroom. Truth be told, she burned to learn if St. Claire knew of the room.

"How fares the rest of Castle Glenbarr?" Rhoslyn asked. "Mistress Muira? St. Claire has not overworked her in the kitchen?"

"Oh no," Lorna, a younger maid, interjected. "Muira warned him that she will no' tolerate misbehaving from the men. She threatened to cut off the bollocks of any man that touched the women. Sir Talbot told her that if any of his men harassed us, he would hold the dog down while she used her knife."

"He did not say that?" Rhoslyn blurted.

Sheila nodded. "He did."

"He is handsome," Lorna said. "Very handsome."

Rhoslyn gave the girl a critical look. "Your father would not be pleased to learn you are lusting after an English knight."

The girl hung her head.

"What of Duncan?" Rhoslyn asked. He could help her escape. She had elevated him from steward to lord in her absence.

"He was very angry," Sheila said. "We feared he would challenge Sir Talbot, but when he read King Edward's letter saying you and he were to wed, he left."

Duncan gone? "Where did he go?"

"To your grandfather at Banmore House."

So the craven turned tail and ran. Her grandfather wouldn't be pleased.

"Return to your beds," she ordered the maids.

They obeyed and Rhoslyn headed for the storeroom.

TALBOT EYED THE form beneath the blankets on the bed. Lady Rhoslyn hadn't even troubled herself to make the pillows look much like a sleeping person. It had been longer than he could remember since anyone underestimated him. He grunted. She hadn't underestimated him. He foolishly left her alone in a room that she had escaped in the time it took her to shove pillows beneath a blanket. He should have tied her to his bed. His cock pulsed at the thought. There lay just as dangerous a road as did her escape.

He scanned the room. The door had been locked from the outside. Either someone helped her and was wise enough to lock the door when they left, or there was a passageway in the room. Talbot crossed to the hearth where the wall on each side was paneled wood, and immediately noticed the panel to the right was slightly misaligned. He slid a fingernail into the seam, drew open the panel, and peered inside. A narrow passageway disappeared into darkness.

He got a torch from the hallway, then returned to the passageway and examined the floor. The dust revealed small footprints. Talbot started forward, grimacing when his broad shoulders brushed the walls several feet inside. He reached the end of the passageway to find himself in an empty bedchamber. He recognized the room as one in the west wing. A hint of candle wax scented the air but he saw no candle.

Where would Lady Rhoslyn have gone from here? The stables? Another hidey hole? Was there another passageway in this room, or had she doubled back to this wing, where a secret passageway led from the chapel to a concealed door in the castle's wall. No. Lady Rhoslyn cared too much about her possessions to leave just yet. Which meant there was one place she would go before leaving.

Chapter Three

~

RHOSLYN HURRIED THROUGH the solar door into Alec's bedchambers and stopped short at sight of the secret passageway's open panel. She had closed the panel. She crossed to the bed and pulled back the curtain. The blanket still covered the pillows. Rhoslyn released the fabric and turned. Who had been here? She shifted her gaze to the door. She had no key to Alec's room, so had returned through the hallways and solar so that she wouldn't have to detour to the far side of the west wing through the passageway. Was the hall door locked?

She crossed to the door and eased it open a crack. Her heart pounded. Whoever had entered the room found the secret entrance and—Did St. Claire know of the secret passageway? Why leave her here if he knew? Because, she realized, he hadn't known, but had discovered her gone, then deduced the truth and found the panel.

Her heart fell. She had hoped to be gone before she was discovered missing. Should she leave without the dagger? Nay, traveling without a weapon was foolish, and she had to see if St. Claire had raided their savings.

Rhoslyn went to the left corner of the room near the window and knelt at the wall. She wiggled the bottom left stone free from the wall and breathed in relief to find the key lying in the dust. She took it and replaced the stone, then hurried from the room.

When she at last neared the bottom of the stairs leading to the kitchen, she slowed her descent. Light bathed the half dozen remaining steps. The housekeeper kept a low fire banked in the kitchen hearth, but this was more than the meager dance of light from embers. She crept to the last stair and peeked around the corner. Light spilled into the kitchen from the great hall. Two men stood at one of the work tables.

She glanced at the scullery, which lay ten feet straight ahead. The men's backs faced her. Could she reach the room without being noticed? Rhoslyn drew back and waited a long moment, then peeked around the corner again. The men were still there. They couldn't tarry long.

Shouldn't they be searching for her instead of foraging for food?

Another man appeared in the doorway. "Baxter awaits us at the gate."

"I plan to run a sword through Roberts myself," one of the men at the table said.

His companion grunted. "After I shove my blade up his arse."

"I imagine Sir Talbot will do that for us," the first replied as they started toward the door. "He is not pleased the bastard is threatening Lady Rhoslyn's grandfather."

Rhoslyn barely stifled a gasp. Were they speaking of Aodh Roberts? How could he—understanding flashed lightning fast, followed by a fury so hot she envisioned thrusting a dagger into Aodh's gutless heart. He hadn't forgiven her for refusing his offer of marriage, and now that King Edward had married her to an English knight, he believed she would have no way to avenge her grandfather's death. The coward must believe St. Claire would welcome her grandfather' death, for that meant he would take possession of all his land.

A thought stopped her. The warrior had said that St. Claire wasn't pleased that Aodh was threatening her grandfather. Was the knight going to help her grandfather? There had to be something she didn't know. The man who had sent the brute that kidnapped her was not an honorable knight. But—she shook her head to ward off confusion. None of this mattered. She had to get to Longford this night. Not Longford Castle, she realized with horror. If Aodh was there and St. Claire was on his way, it was too dangerous for her to go there. She would go to her grandfather's castle. She would be just as safe there as Longford.

Rhoslyn eased forward and peeked around the corner. The men had gone. Lifting her skirts, she hurried down the last few steps and pulled a torch from a wall sconce. She held her breath as she quickly lit the torch from the small flame in the hearth, then hurried into the scullery. Along the far wall, she pressed a panel that opened to steep, narrow stairs. Rhoslyn took the first few steps, turned, and pulled the panel closed behind her.

Carefully, she descended the stairs to the first level where she turned left. A lone door was located on the far wall. Rhoslyn grasped the door handle and held her breath as she pressed the latch. Locked. She closed her eyes and released the breath while sending up a prayer of thanks to Saint George for protecting their valuables.

Rhoslyn pulled the key from her belt pouch, quickly unlocked the door, then slipped inside. A cupboard stood against the far wall near the left corner. Swords, axes, crossbows and shields were mounted on all visible walls. Additional weapons leaned in corners. A chest sat against the left wall, filled with larger valuables, including the dagger she sought. The coin, however, lay hidden in a smaller chest inside a secret panel.

She crossed the room to the wall on the right and knelt. Deftly, she ran her fingers along the bottom of a stone until she felt the latch. She pressed and the stone clicked open. Relief flooded her when she found the chest unmolested.

"I wondered if there was a hiding place where more coin was hidden," said a male voice behind her.

Rhoslyn shot to her feet and whirled. The beast who had kidnapped her stood, shoulder leaning against the cupboard. Where had he come from? She had closed the door behind her. He couldn't have entered without her knowledge. She cut her gaze to the corner behind him. It was the only place he could have possibly hidden. How had he wedged his broad shoulders between the cupboard and wall? How had she missed him there?

His eyes dropped to the chest. "Is that money entered into the accounts?"

"Ask your laird," she retorted.

His gaze jerked up to meet hers, surprise in his dark eyes, and Rhoslyn realized her mistake. Her eyes flew to his right arm, covered with a linen shirt and chainmail, where was rumored to be painted a picture of St. Claire's sister who had died as a young girl.

Rhoslyn lifted her gaze to his face. "*You.*"

He didn't reply, only stared at her with intense brown eyes. A strange flush of heat reached her cheeks. She startled upon realizing his attention lingered on her mouth.

"*You* murdered my grandfather's men—then kidnapped a defenseless woman," she said.

His gaze lifted to hers. "Defenseless? You stabbed me."

"Ye are a common thief."

"Have you counted the coin?" he asked.

She frowned. "What?"

"I wonder that you can call me thief when you have yet to confirm that a single silver coin is gone."

"It matters not if every piece is here. Ye will spend it when and how you please—despite the fact the money is mine."

"It was your husband's, I wager," he replied.

"As much mine as his," she shot back, remembering the countless hours spent buying and selling goods, saving, counting, hording money and valuables against the storm that had brewed in Scotland. But her efforts had been in vain. The storm had come to her. She suddenly remembered the dagger she'd come for—and her grandfather. "What has happened with my grandfather?"

"Aodh Roberts intends to settle a score."

"Aodh is a bitter man, who takes what he wants rather than work for it."

"I have yet to meet him," St. Claire replied in an even voice, but Rhoslyn was certain she detected a hint of amusement.

"You will meet him tonight at Longford Castle."

"Who said I was going to Longford Castle?"

"I overheard your men say so, and your chainmail tells me ye plan for battle."

He nodded, but said nothing. Rhoslyn realized he didn't appear surprised that she had escaped from his bedchamber, and he had clearly known where to look for her.

"You have made yourself comfortable in my home," she said.

"My home," he replied.

Anger knotted her stomach. "King Edward is not a priest, and our marriage has no' been officiated or consummated." Sweet Jesu, she must sound like a madwoman.

He straightened. "You are right." He reached her side in three steps. She was forced to tilt her head back to maintain eye contact. He grasped her arm, but she pulled free and retreated a step.

"What are you doing?"

"Do you plan to stay here the night?" he asked.

She glanced at the chest.

"Never mind the chest," he said. "We will lock the door when we leave."

He didn't wait for an answer, but grasped her arm again and drew her toward the door. She wanted to protest, wanted to return the small chest to its hiding place—more than anything, she wanted to grab the dagger from the larger chest—but wants would not help her at this moment.

He stepped into the hallway, then pulled the door shut and waited.

She lifted her chin. "You must have a key. Lock the door yourself."

He shrugged.

Rhoslyn cried out when he pulled her against his side. "What are ye doing?"

"I have no wish to be conked over the head or stabbed in the back while I lock the door." His tone was mild as he opened his palm to reveal the key he'd been holding.

"For pity's sake, release me," she said. "I dinna' plan to kill you by stabbing ye in the back."

His arm tightened around her waist as he inserted the key and she was suddenly aware of his fingers pressing into her stomach and her arm wedged against the hard muscle of his chest. Her heart picked up speed. He turned the key in the lock and his fingers flexed when he withdrew the key and straightened.

"So you intend to look me in the eye when you kill me?" he asked.

"Aye," she replied.

He drew her down the short corridor without loosening his hold. "I am gratified my wife has some honor."

"I am no' your wife."

"Aye, you are."

They reached the stairs and he urged her up ahead of him. In the kitchen, he grasped her arm and led her into the great hall. Men stood in half a dozen clusters about the room. Rhoslyn caught sight of a priest sitting with his back to them at the table nearest the hearth.

"Why is Father Crey here?" she demanded, but knew the answer. Her head whirled. What was she going to do? How could she stop this? *Could* she stop this? "Were ye no' on your way to help my grandfather?"

"Aye."

"Then how can we have a wedding?"

He looked down at her. "Even by your Scottish law we are already wed. I am willing to say the vows simply to please you."

Rhoslyn understood. "Ye will help my grandfather only if I say the vows. Along with being a murderer and kidnapper, you are an extortionist."

"You forgot thief," he said.

"I have forgotten nothing."

They neared the priest and he rose.

"I will help Seward because he is your grandfather. Is that not enough?" St. Claire asked.

"And if I do no' say the vows?"

He shrugged and she wanted to scream.

"Then you can await me in my bedchambers until I return—or your bedchambers. I imagine there is no secret passageway in the lady's room as there is in my chambers. I will bring your grandfather back with me and then come to you."

Rhoslyn stared openmouthed.

"Fear not, lady. I am not so uncouth as to come to your bed straight from the battlefield. I promise to bathe first."

"If ye dare come to my bed I will cut off your bollocks," she snapped.

His brows rose. "I see you have been talking with Mistress Muira."

LADY RHOSLYN WAS not what Talbot had expected. She was beautiful. A fact that might be more pitfall than windfall. Auburn hair hung to her waist in a thick braid that begged to be unraveled and spread in a halo atop white sheets. He would never wonder what this woman thought. Every emotion appeared in her dark eyes like a rolling tide. And in this instant her eyes conveyed distrust. But he didn't read in them that she would refuse the vows.

"I will not repeat the vows," she said.

Leave it to a woman to prove him wrong.

Talbot shrugged.

"Sweet Jesu, shrug one more time, St. Claire, and I will drive a blade through your heart."

He started to shrug again—a habit he had to confess his father's wife disliked as much as Lady Rhoslyn seemed to—but he managed to check the action.

Talbot looked at the priest. "You have read the contract, Priest?"

"I have."

"It is binding?"

The man's mouth thinned. "Aye, it is binding."

Talbot looked at Lady Rhoslyn. "As far as the law is concerned, we are man and wife. If you care nothing for holy blessings, then you may go to bed."

She cast a helpless appeal to the priest.

"I am sorry, Lady Rhoslyn. It is true, you are legally married. King Edward has decreed it."

She cut her eyes to Talbot. Anger had darkened them. "Then I imagine we have no need of a priest."

"But ye do," Father Crey interjected. "For when the bairns come."

Her cheeks reddened, but it was the anguish in her eyes that caught Talbot's attention. He recalled the newest headstone in the family cemetery. Dougal Harper. The child had been two months old when he died.

"There is always the chance your husband will not survive the battle tonight," Father Crey said. "If you have my blessing, should he die, then no one can dispute that his lands are yours."

Lady Rhoslyn glanced at Talbot.

"Beware what you wish for," he said. "The next man Edward marries you to might not be as generous as I."

"Generous?" she retorted. "Ye have taken over my home, your men eat my food, burn my wood."

"I have paid for my men out of the money I brought with me. I will spend none of Castle Glenbarr's money until I have studied the household rolls."

"Ye will deal with me *and* my grandfather if you take anything that doesna' belong to you. And lest you wonder, he will deal with *you* concerning the slaughter of his men."

"That he will, for he is responsible for the death of one of my men."

"One of your men? By God, you have bollocks. Ye slaughter his men, yet have the audacity to be affronted when *one* of your men dies in the battle?"

"There was no slaughter," St. Claire said. "Only three of Seward's men were lost. The rest are on their way here."

"What? I do not believe ye. I heard the fighting."

"When they arrive, Lady Rhoslyn, you may see for yourself."

Her eyes narrowed. "Three were killed?"

"Aye."

She pursed her lips. "You feel no' one wit of regret for killing those men."

"You may speak with your grandfather concerning their deaths. It is he who chose to defy law and secret you away in order to perform an illegal marriage. I merely protected what is mine."

Surprise flitted across her face, quickly replaced by ire.

"Do no' delay," the priest urged. "If Sir Talbot dies and your union hasna' been sanctioned by the church, Edward can seize Sir Talbot's land, as well as yours."

The truth of what he said flared in the lady's eyes. She looked at Talbot. "I will no' marry ye unless you bring my grandfather back safe."

Talbot canted his head. "I vow to deliver him tonight. Until then, you will await me in your chambers."

Her eyes narrowed. "I will wait where I please."

"Nay, lady. My men are well trained, but I will no' risk your safety while I am gone." Talbot shifted his attention to Father Crey. "We will need your services tomorrow."

"The wedding is a month hence," Lady Rhoslyn said.

He shrugged. "As you wish. We can repeat the vows now or a month from now, but when I return, we will live as man and wife."

Chapter Four

R HOSLYN ASCENDED THE stairs ahead of St. Claire. He kept two steps behind, but she could still feel the heat from his large body. They reached the second floor and she glanced left. A blanket-covered figure slept in the shadows of the balcony overlooking the great hall. Movement and a guttural groan emanated from the blanket. She slowed and squinted into the shadowy corner, then veered toward the balcony. Rhoslyn yanked the blanket from the figure. She gasped. A man lay atop a woman. Her legs wrapped his waist. St. Claire muttered something and brushed past Rhoslyn. He grabbed the man by the arm and yanked him up and off the woman. Rhoslyn caught sight of the man's sculpted body and healthy erection.

"Do no' hurt him, laird," the woman cried.

"Alana?" Rhoslyn took a step closer and the woman shrank deeper into the corner, covering herself with the blanket. "Alana, have ye lost your mind?" Rhoslyn demanded. She whirled on the two men. "You let your men abuse my women, St. Claire?"

"She does not look abused," he replied.

"Daniel wouldna' harm me," Alana interjected.

"I do not want a brood of bastards running about Castle Glenbarr," Rhoslyn snapped.

"Bastards have their uses, my lady," St. Claire replied.

She rolled her eyes. "You are too sensitive. I meant that these women will be left with fatherless children to raise."

"You cannot stop human nature," he said.

"I can enforce rules. Your men must understand that their actions carry consequences."

"You mean marriage?"

"Or prison."

"Sir Talbot," Daniel began.

"Beware, Daniel," St. Claire warned, "you might find yourself in prison this very night, or worse—" Rhoslyn thought she detected a hint of amusement when he ended with, "married."

"Get up, Alana," Rhoslyn ordered. "As for ye," she said to Daniel, "be gone."

"Nay, my lady," Alana cried, but the man made no such protestations. He grabbed his clothes and rushed down the stairs.

Alana leapt to her feet. "Nay," she wailed.

"The man sported with you, nothing more," Rhoslyn said in exasperation.

"He might have wanted more if ye hadna' interfered."

Rhoslyn pinned her with a hard stare. "You forget yourself, Alana. I am mistress here."

The girl's eyes dropped. "I havena' forgotten."

"Put on your clothes and go to bed," Rhoslyn ordered.

Alana grabbed her dress from the floor and with the blanket around her shoulders, hurried down the hallway ahead of them.

"Keep your men away from my women," Rhoslyn told St. Claire as they started forward.

"As you wish, my lady."

Something in his voice caused Rhoslyn to look up at him. He lifted a brow, but she read nothing more in his expression than curiosity. But this time she was sure she had heard it: Amusement.

RHOSLYN TOSSED IN bed, stomach churning. Sheila stirred in her sleep beside her and Rhoslyn stilled. The maid quieted. Rhoslyn stared up at the canopy in the near darkness, willing her mind not to picture her son's crib beside her bed. How long had she lain in bed? Two hours? Longer? Try as she might, she still heard only Dougal's ragged breathing in those moments before he breathed his last while cradled in her arms. The weight of his small form pressed against her arms. She'd told herself a thousand times it was her imagination, but he'd seemed lighter in that instant after he'd died. Did the soul have substance?

Rhoslyn forced back a sob. Fourteen months in the convent and the pain still cut like a knife. She was so certain it would lessen by the time she returned. *Lies!* She fled to the convent with the intention of never returning. Wasn't that why she planned to dower her stepdaughter with Castle Glenbarr? A rustling caused her to start before she realized that their guard merely shifted on the bench near the hearth.

Oh Dougal! Dearest Alec. You left without seeing your son buried.

Neither had Rhoslyn seen him buried. She'd simply left him to be lowered into the cold ground without the comfort of a mother.

She fisted her hands. *Why, God, did I not die instead?*

Curse King Edward for interfering in her life and curse St. Claire for bringing her to Castle Glenbarr.

A knock sounded on the door and Rhoslyn bolted upright in bed. Had St. Claire returned? Her stomach turned a somersault before she realized he wouldn't knock. He would enter unbidden through the door that connected to the solar. She drew back the bed curtain and watched her guard as he reach the door.

Hand on sword hilt, he called, "Who goes there?"

"Mistress Muira," the housekeeper replied.

The guard opened the door. Rhoslyn slipped from bed, fully dressed, and hurried toward the housekeeper.

"Mistress Muira." Rhoslyn embraced her.

The old woman gave her a hug, then drew back.

"Ye are looking well," Muira said.

"And you," Rhoslyn said. "All is well? You have not been ill-treated?"

"St. Claire has been fair. You have a visitor, my lady."

"A visitor, so early? Who?"

"Dayton St. Claire."

"Dayton St. Claire is here?" the warrior said. "What business has Sir Talbot's brother with Lady Rhoslyn at this time of morning?"

Rhoslyn wondered the same thing. "Show him into our private solar," she said. "You may join us there, Knight." He opened his mouth, but she cut him off. "With you and Sheila present, Sir Talbot canna' take issue with his brother visiting me. Go, Mistress Muira. 'Tis early, but if ye would send up mead, I would be grateful."

Rhoslyn and Sheila sat in the solar with the guard standing near their bench when the door opened and Mistress Muira entered. The man who followed was as different from Sir Talbot as the sun was from the moon. Where Talbot was fair, this man was dark. Talbot's hair hung to his shoulders, but his brother's hair covered only his ears. His dark beard gave him the look of the pagan god of Mars, though softer, gentler. More than the physical differences, was the warm demeanor and cordial light in this man's eyes. Sir Talbot struck her as hard, distant.

Sheila hurried to the table as Muira set down the mead and goblets. Dayton St. Claire reached the bench where Rhoslyn sat and grasped her hand, then fell to one knee, and she recalled Sir Ascot's actions at the convent. Her heart twisted to think of the knight dead, then she remembered St. Claire saying only three men had perished in the fight. Was Sir Ascot one?

"Lady Rhoslyn," Dayton St. Claire murmured against her hand.

Rhoslyn glimpsed the distrust that narrowed their guard's eyes. "Rise, sir, and sit with me."

He obeyed and Sheila offered them goblets filled with wine. She gave the third goblet to their guard, then hurried back to the table as Mistress Muira left.

"To what do I owe the honor of your visit?" Rhoslyn asked.

"I have come to celebrate my brother's marriage." He took a drink of mead.

She laughed. "The wedding is a month away. You are early, sir." Not to mention, he need not have asked for an audience in the early morning in order to celebrate his brother's marriage. Clearly, their guard agreed, for he stiffened.

"Forgive me, Lady Rhoslyn," Dayton said. "I could have waited until tomorrow to meet you. The truth is, I bring a gift for you, one I fear my brother might object to you receiving."

Their guard took a step forward.

"All is well, Knight," he said to the man. "I speak of a horse. An Arabian brought from the Holy Land."

"How could ye have known to bring a wedding gift from so far away?" Rhoslyn asked, and also wondered why the man was truly there. This, too, could have waited until tomorrow.

He grinned. "I confess, I did not know. I bought the beast for myself. When I heard Talbot was to marry, I knew the horse should be my wedding gift."

"I am an able rider. I am anxious to see the steed."

"That must surely wait until tomorrow, my lady. To take you from the comfort of your chambers so early is a sin Talbot would not forgive."

And one he would not allow, Rhoslyn privately acknowledged.

"I do not deny that I was anxious to meet you," he said.

"Were you?" Rhoslyn sipped her wine.

"I wondered what kind of woman would eventually capture Talbot's attention."

"I believe 'twas King Edward whose attention I caught," she replied.

He laughed. "Aye, but Talbot is one to go only where he pleases."

Rhoslyn thought the opposite was true. He obeyed his king without question.

Dayton finished his wine and rose. "Would you like more wine, my lady?"

"Sheila will fetch it for us."

"Perhaps your guard would like more?" He turned toward the man.

Dayton's arm shot out. Sheila cried out as his fist rammed into the guard's jaw. The man's head snapped back. Rhoslyn leapt to her feet. The knight reared back, fist raised, but Dayton was quicker, and rammed a second fist into his belly, then another into his ribs. The guard swung. Dayton sidestepped and brought his clasped hands down with all his might across the man's back. He slumped to the floor.

Rhoslyn whirled toward the door as Sheila screamed. Iron fingers seized Rhoslyn's arm and yanked her back against a hard body. She twisted wildly in an effort to break loose.

"Lady Rhoslyn," he said, "I swear, this is not what it seems."

Sheila screamed again.

"Silence, woman," he hissed to her, then said to Rhoslyn, "Please."

His hold remained firm. Sheila would provide no help. The girl now whimpered. Rhoslyn stilled, breathing heavily, and nodded. He released her, but stepped between her and the door.

"This was the only way," he said.

Rhoslyn backed up two paces. She wished she had secured one of the daggers from the storeroom. "Only way for what?"

"Edward commanded you to marry Talbot so that he could pay his debts with your money," he said.

"What is that to you?"

"The king's favor has turned my father's attention to Talbot. Talbot even took my father's name after Edward legitimized him. He is the elder brother, but that does not matter. He is a bastard. He has no right. I will not let my father disinherit me in favor of Talbot."

"Your family problems are not my concern," she snapped.

"But it is. Talbot's marriage to you is what captured my father's interest. He wants a grandson to carry on the St. Claire name."

"So give him grandsons."

His expression darkened and his handsome features twisted in resentment. "My father does not approve of the woman I would marry. He threatens to disinherit me if I defy him."

Rhoslyn felt a stab of compassion. "I am sorry, but I do no' see how that concerns me."

"If you do not marry Talbot, my father will be forced to relent. I am here to help you escape."

"What? St. Claire's guards will never let us pass through the gates."

"Surely, there is a secret passageway that leads outside the walls?"

There was, but Rhoslyn hesitated to say so.

"Tell me you wish to stay here and I will leave you in peace," Dayton said.

Was this not what she'd wanted? She had planned this very thing before St. Claire caught her in the storeroom. Rhoslyn couldn't help a glance at the doorway that led to her chambers. She would give anything not to have to return to that room. How could she live here...sleep in that room where the ghost of her son couldn't possibly have come to peace yet with death?

"Decide, quickly," Dayton said. "I have no wish to kill your guard, but if he awakens, I will have no choice."

"We must go directly to Banmore Keep," she said.

"Your grandfather's home?" he said. "You will be safe there?"

She wasn't sure. Longford Castle would be better, but the battle between St. Claire and Aodh made that impossible. In truth, she feared her plans would be for naught. Short of Jacobus getting her with child, Sir Talbot could enforce the marriage. All that aside, something bothered her about Dayton St. Claire. The gentle light in his eyes when he first arrived had been replaced by a feverish look that bordered on desperation...or was it insanity?

If she delayed or didn't agree to go with him, would he kill Sheila? Might he kill her? That would solve his problems. Why didn't he simply kill his brother? That too would end his problems. Was he capable of such treachery? Either way, she had to get him away from Sheila and the unconscious guard. There had been enough killing for one night. She could take him through the castle on a route that would get them discovered.

"I will be safe in my grandfather's home," Rhoslyn said, then told Sheila, who cowered beside the table, "Fetch my cloak."

The girl rose slowly. "My lady, are ye certain you should go?"

"Do no' argue" Rhoslyn snapped. "Fetch my cloak from the chair." She faced Dayton. "It is early yet. The servants should not yet be here to the third floor, but this night has been a strange one. Look and be sure no one is in the hallway."

He turned and started to the door. Rhoslyn took two steps to the fallen warrior and quietly slid his dagger from its sheath and slipped it into her cuaran along the inside of her ankle. She glanced at the warrior, then gave a prayer of thanks that his chest rose and fell with even breath. She rose and stepped away from the man. He would have a headache when he woke, but likely nothing more.

The creak of the door sounded behind her. "There is no one in the hallway," Dayton said. "Come, we must go."

Sheila stepped up, swung the cloak around her shoulders, and tied the cord.

Rhoslyn grasped her shoulders. "Say nothing of this, Sheila. Do ye understand?" The girl nodded, wide-eyed. Rhoslyn pulled her into a hug and whispered, "Wake the knight when we leave." She drew back and said, "Hurry back to my bed and stay there until someone comes. Say you do not know where I am."

Rhoslyn whirled and hurried to the door.

THIN CURLS OF fog swirled about three approaching horsemen. Talbot assumed the one in the lead was Aodh Roberts. Of the two men who flanked Roberts, one carried a white flag of truce, the other a torch. Talbot shifted his gaze beyond the riders, past Roberts' warriors, to the battlements of Longford Castle. Seward and the young Earl of Melrose must have watched Talbot's approach, seen his and Seward's banners. Each banner-man carried a torch to ensure the banners were recognized—a risky move, but he didn't relish the idea of getting shot by a *stray* arrow if mistaken for one of Roberts' men. There was, of course, the possibility they would shoot him on purpose.

Roberts neared, then came to a stop a few feet from Talbot.

"I am surprised to see ye here," the Highlander said. "I expected you to wait at Castle Glenbarr for the good news that you are the new Baron Kinsley."

"Go home," Talbot said.

Roberts grinned. "So ye wish to kill the old man yourself."

"Kinsley is my wife's grandfather. You will not harm him."

The Highlander's brows snapped downward. "What? Ye should be glad to rid yourself of the old man." He snorted. "Save those words for your wife. *She* might believe you."

"Beware trying to deduce my thoughts, Roberts. Now, leave peaceably so my two hundred men may return to their beds."

Dawn inched across the horizon, but it was the torchlight that allowed Talbot to read the shock on Roberts' face.

"Ye have no right to interfere," he snapped.

"Think," Talbot said. "Even if I allowed you to kill Seward, the Earl of Lochland would hang you for murder. He is your lord as much as Seward's."

"Hang me? God's teeth. Have Englishmen no bollocks? Here in Scotland we take what we want."

Lady Rhoslyn was right. Aodh Roberts was a man who would rather take what he wanted than work for it, laws be damned.

"And ye have it wrong, St. Claire." Roberts' tone turned friendly. "Lochland will welcome you as the new baron. He understands you are Edward's man."

Talbot suspected it was Roberts who hoped to ingratiate himself into Talbot's—and Edward's—good graces. Lochland wouldn't be so eager to trade a willing Scottish vassal for an English knight.

"Leave," Talbot said.

Roberts urged his palfrey so close that Talbot's horse snorted and sidestepped. Talbot tightened the reins to still the animal.

"Lochland willna' interfere." Roberts locked gazes with him. "Neither will you."

Talbot lifted a hand over his head and made a 'come forward' motion with two fingers. He didn't have to look back to know that a hundred of his men separated from the shadows of the trees.

Roberts' eyes narrowed. Then he reached for his sword.

Talbot had his sword out and had slapped the flat of the blade across Roberts' shoulder before the Highlander's sword left its sheath. He tumbled from his horse. His two men drew their swords in unison with Talbot's men.

Talbot leapt from his horse and pointed his sword at Roberts' face. "Hold," Talbot ordered the men. Then to Roberts, "You dare draw a weapon under a white flag?"

The man's face mottled with rage. "Are ye daft, man? Think what you have to gain by joining forces with me."

"What have *you* to gain?" Talbot demanded.

"Longford Castle."

That was probably the most honest thing the man had said all night.

"Then take it when Seward is not there." Talbot sheathed his sword and stepped into his saddle. "You have until I return to my army to leave before I attack." Talbot whirled his horse toward the trees.

ROBERTS LINGERED A few minutes before leading his men past Talbot and his warriors. It was the Highlander's way of saving face and letting Talbot know he wasn't cowed. But leave he did. Talbot waited until the last of the men filed past before taking Iain and leading a dozen of his men and all of Seward's men to the gates of Longford Castle under his and Seward's banners.

"Call up to your lord," Talbot instructed Iain.

"Kinsley," he called up to the battlements, "'tis I, Iain. St. Claire is with me. He is a friend."

A moment later, the gate opened and Talbot led the men inside. They were met by half a dozen men, Seward, and a young noble Talbot assumed was Melrose. Talbot swung his leg over his horse's rump and stepped to the ground.

"What are ye doing here, St. Claire?" Seward demanded.

The baron was a large man, almost as large as Talbot, still well-muscled and more vigorous than many men half his sixty-two years. Talbot liked the man, and respected his desire to marry his granddaughter to a Scotsman. Seward understood King Edward's power grab. None of that changed the fact that the old baron had miscalculated in defying *him*.

"You are damned lucky I came," Talbot said. "Especially given that you went behind my back to try and marry my wife to this pup."

Surprise flashed in the old man's eyes. The younger man reached for his sword.

Kinsley's head snapped in the boy's direction. "Keep your sword in its sheath, Jacobus." He then said to Talbot, "Where is Rhoslyn?"

"Where she belongs, at Castle Glenbarr."

"Ye devil. You have no right to take her."

"Take her? A man does not *take* his wife. I made sure she was delivered safely to her home. I did not take you for a fool, Seward. What did you hope to accomplish?"

"What do ye think?"

Talbot nodded. "She is my wife. Nothing will change that."

Seward studied him. "You could have left me to fight my own battle. Why interfere?"

"Because my wife would hate me if I did not help you."

"Your king would have been better served if ye had left me to my fate."

"It is short sighted to believe that your money has greater value than your life," Talbot replied.

"'Tis more likely ye wanted my gratitude by appearing to save my life," Seward said.

Talbot grunted. "I imagine I could arrive with a heavenly host and not receive your good graces. If you wish, I will send Roberts back to resume his attack."

Kinsley snorted, then turned his attention to his captain. "I suppose I have ye to thank for interfering?"

"Roberts had another fifty warriors on their way," Iain replied without hesitation. "'Tis my duty to see to your safety."

"'Tis your duty not to conspire with the enemy."

"Are you truly set on pitting yourself against your granddaughter's husband?" Talbot asked.

"I was set on you not being her husband."

At least the man was straightforward. "I *am* her husband. Nothing will change that. You know that as well as I."

"I have no intention of dying anytime soon," Seward said.

"I am sure Lady Rhoslyn will be relieved to hear that."

"You dealt easily enough with that dog Roberts. Did ye threaten to bring down the entire English army on his head?"

"He was caught between my men and yours. He was wise enough to recognize the weaknesses of his position."

Kinsley glanced at his warriors, who remained mounted. "Three of my men are missing."

"They died defending my wife. One of my men died as well. I expect you to pension his young wife."

"I am no' obligated—"

"You will pension his wife or I will take the money from your grand-daughter's store of silver, then find a way to replace it with a large piece of your hide."

"Ye will spend Rhoslyn's money anyway," Seward shot back.

"I do not spend hard earned money unless necessary. I pray no necessity arises anytime soon."

Seward stared for a long moment. "If ye harm my granddaughter in any way—"

"She is my *wife*," Talbot repeated forcefully. "I will protect her, not harm her."

Chapter Five

R HOSLYN HOPED THEY would get no farther than the great hall before someone discovered them. Surely, some of Sir Talbot's men had gone back to sleep there.

Dayton stopped when they reached the dimly lit second floor. "Where is the passageway?"

"In the scullery, there are stairs leading to the dungeon. From there, a passageway opens outside the walls." She had never been a good liar. Did he believe her?

"Act naturally," he said. "We do not want to attract attention."

"This is a dangerous plan." She feigned fear.

"Aye, but I see no other way. You must escape before Talbot has an opportunity to consummate your union. Unless—he has not yet bedded you?"

"He had to ride for Longford Castle. My grandfather is under attack," she said, then wished she hadn't answered so quickly. He might not have been so insistent upon helping her if he thought his brother had already consummated their marriage.

"So I heard. I am surprised that he left any ends untied."

Was she an *untied end*? Even Sir Talbot's remote manner didn't make her feel so cold.

Dayton frowned. "Perhaps it is best you not wear a cloak. Anyone we encounter is sure to wonder why you are dressed as if to leave."

"You are right." She yanked the tie loose and swung the cloak from her shoulders, then tossed it near the wall. Cool air enveloped her and she shivered.

"I will see to your comfort once we are away." He pressed a hand to the small of her back and urged her forward. "You need not fear, my lady."

Rhoslyn realized her hand trembled. Curse her nerves. She had spent too much time in the peace and safety of the convent and her courage now flagged.

"Are you well, Lady Rhoslyn?"

His question startled her. Had she given away the truth in her expression? Surely, he couldn't read her face in the meager light? Nay, but the man wasn't stupid.

"Forgive me, I am no' accustomed to fleeing in the middle of the night."

"Aye, lady, I understand."

Rhoslyn heard in his voice the same charming smile he'd worn upon his arrival. That smile had gotten him far in life and he knew it.

When they reached the stairs leading to the kitchen, Rhoslyn mouthed a prayer to Saint George that either someone worked in the kitchen or she could break free and reach the great hall.

Dayton grasped her arm. "I am sorry."

She looked up at him. In the near-total darkness, she still couldn't discern his expression. He shifted and her heart jumped. In the next instant, the back of his hand struck her cheek with mind-numbing force. Pain splintered across her face. She jerked with the force of the blow and fell forward. She crashed into a hard body and arms closed around her as the world went black.

POUNDING PAIN PENETRATED the darkness. Rhoslyn groaned, then winced at the way the sound reverberated against her skull. Where was she? What had happened? She couldn't focus.

"Do not move. It will be easier."

Rhoslyn jerked at hearing the deep voice and snapped open her eyes. Light bore into her eyeballs like a needle and she jammed her eyes shut with a cry. A hand grasped and gently squeezed her shoulder. The pounding in her head intensified. She gritted her teeth until the roar subsided to the duller sound it had been a moment ago.

"Where—" she swallowed against a dry throat, the simple action difficult. "Where am I?"

"Safe in bed."

Bed? She struggled to remember what bed and why she felt as if she had run headlong into a stone wall. Rhoslyn touched her face and winced at the tenderness in her cheek. She released a shaky breath and slowly opened her eyes. Light pierced her vision, but with less severity than a moment ago. She turned her head away from the direct light and blinked the unfamiliar room into focus.

"Where is this place?"

"A cottage near Stonehaven," the man said.

"What?" she said in confusion.

The hand on her shoulder gave another squeeze. "There was no other way."

Then she remembered. Fear rammed through her on a wave that brought the prick of tears. She turned her head to face Dayton St. Claire, who sat on the bed beside her. She shoved his hand away from her shoulder. Pain ricocheted off her skull.

Rhoslyn winced. "Why? I agreed to leave with you."

"You know why."

"Why not slay me at Castle Glenbarr?" she demanded.

His brows drew down in shock. "I am not a barbarian."

Her heart pounded in tandem with the thud in her head. He intended to lock her in a dungeon? Ransom her? Nay, that didn't make sense. If he intended that, she would not be laying on a soft feather bed.

"Then why am I here?" she asked.

"You will marry me instead of Talbot."

Shock washed over her. Sweet God, it *had* been the light of madness she'd glimpsed in his eyes. "My grandfather will never allow it. If I have learned anything about your brother, neither will he."

"Until I present our sons to them, they will not know where you are."

"Sons?" Panic sent a tremor through her. "Sheila will have alerted someone."

Sorrow filled his gaze. "I am sorry. She and your guard were dead five minutes after we left."

She drew a sharp breath, ignoring the jolt to her head. "No."

"I could not risk them telling anyone that you left with me."

Rhoslyn fought panic. "Mistress Muira knows."

He gave a small shake of his head.

Rhoslyn lunged at him. "Bastard." She landed a blow to his nose before he seized her wrists. "Mistress Muira was a second mother to me." Tears streamed down her cheeks as she struggled to wrench herself free of his iron hold. "Sheila had yet to know a man. Ye craven whoreson." Her stomach pitched and she gave a great sob, collapsing back onto the pillow, panting hard. His grip loosened and she yanked free. "I will not submit."

"I pray you will, lady. I have no wish to force you. Think, once your belly swells with my babe, resistance will be pointless."

The room spun. *Breathe*, she told herself, *Breathe*. She hadn't allowed herself to consider the possibility of having another child. How could she fathom this man's child growing inside of her?

He shifted and she jerked.

"Lady Rhoslyn," he said in a gentle voice, "I offer you a good life. I will be a better husband than my bastard brother. Mayhap you believe his Scottish blood makes him more desirable, but you are wrong."

"What of the woman ye love? Was that a lie?" Rhoslyn demanded.

"Never mind her."

Rhoslyn couldn't believe it. "You intend to keep her."

"You think Talbot will be any different?" he sneered. His expression cleared. "Do you not see? I will give you the life you want. Once you bear me sons you may even return to Scotland, if you like."

Panic escalated with the pounding of her heart. "They will find me."

"Nay," he said. "They will not."

Rhoslyn did a quick calculation. Kildrum lay sixty miles from Stonehaven. That meant they had ridden into early afternoon. A slight thump caught her attention and she started at the realization that the sound had come through the floorboards. They weren't in a cottage as he claimed. *An inn*, her mind raced. If he left her alone, she would be able to get help.

"Forget my brother," Dayton said. "My father will sanction our union and will press Edward to decree our marriage valid."

He leaned forward. She shrank back against the pillow. He meant to kiss her! Rhoslyn rolled toward the far side of the bed. He yanked her back and swung a leg over her hips, then again bent to kiss her. She raked her nails across his cheek.

He seized her arms, shoved them above her head and kissed her. Rhoslyn bit down on his lip. He bolted upright, shock on his face. For an instant his confusion seemed to paralyze him. Then he dabbed at his mouth with his shoulder and looked at the blood that smeared his shirt.

His eyes returned to hers. "Do not make me hurt you."

She emptied her lungs in a scream. He clamped a hand over her mouth, grabbed a cloth from the table and stuffed it into her mouth. Rhoslyn gagged and raked her nails across his face. He grunted and tightened his thighs painfully around her ribs. She wheezed and pulled at his wrists while he tied another cloth around her mouth.

"You leave me no choice," he said.

He clasped both wrists in one hand and grabbed another cloth from a stack on the nightstand. On a surge of panic, she bucked with all her might. He lost his balance and tumbled from the bed. Rhoslyn gagged against the cloth in her mouth, but yanked up her skirt and seized the knife hidden in her boot. Dayton leapt to his feet and threw himself on her. She drew back the knife, but he glanced over his shoulder and twisted aside so the blade only grazed his outer thigh.

Dayton seized her wrist, wrenched away the knife, and threw it across the room. Once again, he straddled her and grabbed her wrists. She yanked, but he snatched up the cloth he'd dropped and wound it around her wrists in a flash, cinching the knot so tight she cried out. He grabbed another cloth, forced her arms over her head and tied her to the right post.

"This is your fault, Lady Rhoslyn. I begged you not to force me to hurt you."

He pushed off the bed, unfastened his belt buckle, then tossed the belt onto the bench at the foot of the bed. He pulled his shirt over his head, then his tunic, and shoved his braies and hose down his hips. Her stomach roiled at sight of his full erection. The burn of bile rose in her throat and she swallowed for fear of choking. He stepped toward the bed. Rhoslyn screamed through the gag and kicked at him, landing a blow to his hip. He grabbed her ankles. She twisted. The bindings cut into her wrists, but she ignored the pain and twisted so hard that her arms felt as if they ripped loose of their sockets. He slammed her body back onto the mattress, yanked her legs apart, and fell on top of her.

His face was so close his breath filled her nostrils. "I will do this every day until you are with child."

He dragged her skirt up. In a frenzy, Rhoslyn bucked, but his weight pinned her to the mattress. When his cock butted the soft flesh between her legs, her head swam.

"Next time, you will obey me," he said in a strained voice.

Saint George, she silently screamed. *Help me.*

"THE HORSES CANNOT keep this pace any longer, and we're still an hour from Stonehaven," Baxter shouted above the pounding of hooves.

Talbot ignored him.

"Talbot," Baxter called. "You will maim our horses and we'll be left afoot."

He was right. Talbot pulled on the reins and slowed to a trot. His horse gave a great snort, its breath curling in the evening chill. Baxter shouted a command to slow, and the men behind them obeyed.

Rhoslyn's guard and maid were missing, and Talbot knew with certainty his brother had murdered them. It was the housekeeper, found unconscious, who, when revived, told them Dayton was behind her disappearance. Twelve hours had passed since Dayton kidnapped her. She had been at Castle Glenbarr less than a day—less than half a day—under Talbot's protection.

Two years after Talbot had been sent to train under Sir Hugh, their father sent Dayton to the knight, as well. For the sake of their father, Talbot endured Dayton's envy, jibes, and cruelty in those years before Talbot left to fight. But a father's protection wouldn't save Dayton now. Talbot would kill him.

A rider approached. Another moment, and Talbot recognized Cullen, the scout he had sent ahead, and Ross, Alec Harper's captain. When they met, the men fell into a trot alongside Talbot.

"Their tracks enter Stonehaven," Ross said, "but dinna' leave it."

Talbot gritted his teeth. "He intends to leave by ship." Would Dayton attempt to marry Rhoslyn before or after he left Scotland? Talbot had immediately realized his brother intended to marry her. At least that meant he wouldn't kill her.

"I spoke with the harbormaster." Ross said.

Talbot jerked his gaze onto the man. "I did not give you leave to speak with anyone. If you alerted Dayton—"

"Dinna' lose your temper, English," Ross cut in. "I know how to be discreet."

"I advise you to remember that I am your lord," Talbot snapped.

"I advise ye to remember that you are in Scotland," the man replied without rancor—or fear, Talbot noted. "The old harbormaster is more likely to talk to me than you, English. You might also remember that I have known Lady Rhoslyn since she was a lass of fifteen. I do no' intend to let an Englishman steal *her* away from her home."

So there were those who knew the story of his father's Scottish mistress, and how he took her and their son away to England.

"What did you learn from the harbormaster?" Talbot asked.

"A man booked passage for himself, two other men, and a woman. They leave tomorrow morning. Though the man does no' fit the description of your brother, he is the only Englishman to sail. There are two inns near the harbor and one other reputable inn on the road leaving Stonehaven."

"Did you inquire at the inns?" Talbot demanded.

"We stopped at the inn on the road and had a wee drink. That establishment is so busy, no one took heed of us. The cook is a talkative woman and I learned that no English passed their way in the last day. The inns near the harbor house are for those booking passage or for travelers with more money to spend than most who stay along the road. I wager your brother is in one of the two. 'Tis better, I think, for us to separate your men and make inquiries. Ye want numbers to ensure he doesna' escape."

Talbot nodded. "He will not escape."

"DINNA' LOSE YOUR temper," Ross warned Talbot forty-five minutes later, as they dismounted at the inn nearest the harbor. Talbot had sent Baxter with a dozen men to the inn west of the harbor and the dozen he'd brought with him waited among the trees, alert for his signal. The remaining five quietly searched the harbor for signs of his brother and Lady Rhoslyn.

"Let me do the talking," Ross said. "Not all Scots like the English."

They entered the tavern and Talbot scanned the crowded room.

Ross headed toward the bar, where a large man placed ales in front of two men. "Are ye the proprietor?" Ross asked the man when they reached the counter.

"Who be asking?" the man demanded.

"I am looking for a friend who might be staying here," Ross said. "Large man with a dark beard."

"That describes half the men here," the man replied.

"Aye, but this one is English and he is with a gentle born lady."

Talbot caught the glint of interest in the man's eyes before he said, "'Tis not uncommon for such folk to be here."

"I am willing to pay for the information," Ross said.

The man's eyes narrowed. "I dinna' want trouble."

Ross nodded. "Aye, but if I find out ye know something and you do no' tell me, there will be trouble."

The man's gaze shifted onto Talbot. "Who are ye?"

"I am the lady's husband."

"English," the man said in derision.

"Aye," Ross said. "And a powerful English knight who will kill ye if he thinks you are lying to him. Then there is the matter of the lady's grandfather, who will feed whatever pieces of ye that are left to the dogs. Now, be a good lad and tell us what you know."

The man studied them for a moment. "How much?"

Talbot took a silver piece from the pouch at his side and tossed it. The man caught it mid-slide across the counter.

Talbot grabbed his wrist. "Where are they?"

"Mayhap this man is no' the man you are looking for," he said. "Said the woman was wife and he warned us to ignore any cries from her room. Said she isna' right in the head."

Chapter Six

～

S WORD IN HAND, and Ross behind him with his own sword drawn, Talbot turned the knob on his brother's door. To his surprise, it turned without resistance. He looked over his shoulder at Ross and gave a quick nod, then threw open the door. Nothing prepared Talbot for what he saw. His wife, the woman he had yet to touch, lay on the bed, arms tied above her head, and a gag tied around her mouth.

Fear tightened his chest. She wore the same simple gray dress she had worn on her trip from the convent. The skirt lay bunched around her thighs and thick strands of hair framed her face in tangled disarray. Yet she stared at him, chin held high, eyes aflame with fury. He recalled thinking that when he bedded her he would have to tie her hands to the bedpost, and guilt unlike any he'd ever known rolled over him.

"Sweet God in heaven," Ross murmured.

Talbot sheathed his sword and reached the bedside in three strides. He was aware that Ross had turned back to guard the door—Talbot guessed, to spare Lady Rhoslyn her dignity. That was a kindness he would not forget.

He noticed a faint discoloration on her cheek that hinted at a bruise. Talbot tamped down his fury as he drew her skirt down over her legs, then pulled the knife from the hilt on his belt. No fear shone in her eyes when he inserted the point into the knot of the gag and carefully cut the fabric. He yanked the cloth from her mouth and she spat out a rag and coughed. He cut the bindings that bound her to the post. She bolted upright, coughing into her bound hands. Talbot gently grasped her wrists. She jumped, her eyes snapping up toward his face.

"Be still," he said, and inserted the knife blade between the cloth and her wrists, then sliced the cloth in one clean cut.

Talbot glanced around the room, saw a pitcher and mugs on a small table against the left wall, and hurried to them. He sniffed the contents and the strong, fresh smell of ale filled his nostrils. He filled one mug, then crossed back to the bed. Rhoslyn stood, gripping the short post at the foot of the bed for support. She wavered and he grasped her elbow to steady her.

He offered her the mug. "Drink this."

She reached for the mug with her free hand and he saw the violent tremble of her fingers.

"Sit, lady," he urged.

She shook her head. "I will never again touch that bed."

The fury that had been eclipsed by the sight of her tied to the bed rushed to the surface with a violence unlike any he'd experienced. Then he saw the blood on the sheets.

"Where is he?" Talbot demanded.

Rhoslyn's head jerked up and, from the corner of his eye, he saw Ross turn. She stared for a long moment, and he noted that her eyes were red with crying.

"Where is he?" Talbot repeated.

"I do no' know."

"Ross," he said, "see to Lady Rhoslyn." Talbot strode toward the door.

Ross met him halfway across the room and grabbed his arm. "Ye might consider taking care of your wife first, lad."

Talbot looked at him. "Did you see the sheets?"

Ross' gaze shifted from Talbot to the bed. Ross cursed under his breath and released Talbot.

"'Tis no' my blood," Lady Rhoslyn said in a hoarse voice.

He swung to face her. "What?"

The fire in her eyes had rekindled. "It is your brother's blood."

He followed her gaze and saw a dagger lying on the floor between the foot of the bed and the hearth. She looked back at him, a challenge in her eyes, and Talbot realized she was unsure how he would react to the fact that she had tried to kill his brother.

"If it pleases you, my lady, I will bring him here, tie him to that bed, and let you finish the job."

Her mouth parted in surprise and he was shocked to see her eyes shimmer with tears. The tears were gone as quickly as they appeared and she nodded. The burgeoning respect that had begun to form when she defended herself against him on the road swelled in his chest. How was it possible that he had been betrothed to a woman of such mettle? How was it possible she had been in his care less than a day and she had come to harm?

She took a step forward and gave a small cry. Ross started for her, but Talbot reached her as her knees gave way. He caught her and swept her into his arms.

STRONG ARMS GATHERED her close and Rhoslyn wanted to collapse against the solid wall of warmth, but realized that St. Claire was headed for the door. It was enough that he and Ross had witnessed her shame. She could not bear for strangers to see her raw wrists and the hair falling from her braid in a tangled mess about her head. They would discern at a glance what had taken place in this room.

"I will walk."

"You are safe with me, Lady Rhoslyn," St. Claire said. "No one will ever again harm you."

She snapped her head up, startled by the harshness in his voice. The hard line of his mouth was set in the granite of his face.

"Put me down," she whispered. He didn't respond. "St. Claire!"

He halted and looked at her.

Ross reached his side and laid a hand on his shoulder. "Lad, mayhap we can find a more discreet exit. If ye carry your wife out the front door there will be talk. 'Tis best for Lady Rhoslyn if we avoid gossip."

St. Claire stared down at her, intense eyes filled with an emotion she didn't understand. The need to cry nearly overwhelmed her.

"I will walk," she managed in a shaky voice.

He hesitated, then lowered her feet to the floor. The tremble in her stomach reached her legs and she feared her knees wouldn't hold her weight. She couldn't deny that she was thankful he kept a strong arm around her back.

"There must be a servants' entrance, Ross," St. Claire said.

He nodded and left. Rhoslyn realized she was alone with the man whose brother had violated her. Her husband. Suddenly, she wanted to be as far away from him as possible, as far away from anyone as was possible.

"You do not know where he went?" St. Claire asked.

He spoke soft and low, but Rhoslyn discerned the ice in his voice. "He did no' tell me," she replied. "Though I believe he wanted to speak with the captain of a ship."

St. Claire's gaze sharpened. "Which ship?"

She shook her head.

"He gave no hint of anything?"

Oh, he gave a great many hints; said too many things. A noise in the hallway caused her to start. St. Claire laid a hand on her arm. She jumped back.

"No one will ever harm you again, Lady Rhoslyn," he said.

Ross appeared in the doorway. "There is a servants' entrance, just as ye said. But we must make haste."

St. Claire took a step toward him. "Has Dayton returned?"

"Nay, but Seward has arrived."

"Damn him," St. Claire cursed in unison with her "Sweet Jesu."

"He must no' know—" Her voice broke.

St. Claire hesitated.

"Please," Rhoslyn begged. "My grandfather can never know what happened here."

He nodded. "Ross, take Lady Rhoslyn out the back way and go to the inn on the way out of town. I will deal with Seward and meet you there."

"He will want to see me," Rhoslyn said.

"Leave him to me. By the time we meet again, you will be—" his mouth thinned "—more rested. Lust for my brother's blood will distract him once I assure him you are safely away." He looked at Ross. "Engage a room for Lady Rhoslyn. See to it her room is guarded at all times. No one save myself or her grandfather is allowed in."

She fought the sudden desire to cry. Ross nodded. Rhoslyn sent up a prayer to Saint George for strength to get through the day.

IT TOOK EVERY bit of willpower Talbot had to turn left down the hallway, while Ross and his wife turned right. He wanted to settle her on his horse in front of him and keep her close until they reached Castle Glenbarr. Instead, he must preserve her dignity. Seward wouldn't settle for hearing news of his granddaughter from anyone save him.

Talbot neared the bottom of the stairs and Seward's heated voice met his ears. "I know my granddaughter is here. Either tell me where she is or get out of my way before I knock ye on your arse."

Talbot stepped off the bottom stair and turned left toward the modest sitting room. Seward looked past the man he threatened and met Talbot's gaze.

The old man pushed past the man and reached Talbot as he entered the room. "Where is she, ye dog?"

"What are you doing here?" Talbot demanded.

"Dinna' think to put me off with your highhanded ways," he shot back. "I know Rhoslyn is here."

"She is not."

Seward's eyes narrowed. "I will kill ye, St. Claire, King Edward be damned."

Talbot motioned with his head. "Come where we can speak in private."

Suspicion appeared in his eyes, but he preceded Talbot out the door and halted in the street. When he turned, Talbot said, "First, I will tell you, my wife is well."

"Where is she?"

"She is safely away from here. For now, that will suffice. Who told you she was here?"

"If ye are asking how I knew your brother kidnapped her, that makes you a fool. I have known those at Castle Glenbarr as many years as ye have been alive. They wouldna' dare keep such news from me. As to how I knew she was here, the innkeeper's wife told me there was an Englishman whose wife was mad." He shrugged. "I took a chance. What happened?"

"My brother hoped to wed Lady Rhoslyn in my place."

"Craven bastard," Seward cursed. "Where is he?"

"When I arrived, he was gone. Lady Rhoslyn believes he went to the docks to secure passage from Scotland."

"Where is she?"

"On the way home. But we shall meet her on the way. Will you help me search for my brother?"

The old man snorted. "If I find him, I will kill him."

"Nay," Talbot said. "*I* will kill him."

ROSS TOOK RHOSLYN to a quiet inn and they were seated in a corner of the inn's tavern. Rhoslyn prayed she looked nothing more than a bedraggled traveler. Ross cast her another of the dozen furtive looks he'd already sent her way. Even in the dim candlelight, she couldn't miss the worry in his eyes.

The innkeeper approached and she released a silent breath when he said the room was at last ready. They climbed the steep stairs to the third floor, Ross following the innkeeper and Rhoslyn following Ross, with one of St. Claire's warriors bringing up the rear.

They entered a surprisingly large room, where a maid bustled about. Rhoslyn guessed this room to be one of the most expensive in Stonehaven. To the left, a small desk sat in an alcove, and on the same wall a few feet ahead, a short-postered bed filled another alcove. A small chest and table sat on the right wall. But Rhoslyn had eyes only for the tub sitting before the blazing fire. Washing and drying cloths had been laid out on a small table beside the tub and a kettle of water hung over the fire. St. Claire had spent a small fortune to ensure her comfort. She fleetingly wondered if he'd spent her money, then flushed with guilt. He had saved her, then made sure she was cared for.

"'Tis the best room I have," the innkeeper said. "I hope it pleases ye, my lady."

"The room is lovely."

The maid turned from pouring wine in a mug at the table, hurried forward and curtsied. "Maggie, here, can see to your needs," the man said.

"I will not need her," Rhoslyn said.

"I can help you undress, my lady," the girl said. "Surely, ye need help washing your hair?"

Rhoslyn shook her head. "I will do well enough on my own. Thank you."

The girl looked at the innkeeper.

"Go along, Maggie," he said.

She left and the innkeeper asked if Rhoslyn needed anything else. It was all she could do to keep from shoving everyone out the door, but she politely declined and the man left.

Ross followed him to the door. When the innkeeper descended the stairs, Ross looked back, "Ye will be safe here, Lady Rhoslyn."

"Thank you, Ross."

"I will be outside your door."

Heat crept up her cheeks and the urge to cry rose too close to the surface.

At last, he closed the door and the noise from the tavern below cut to a murmur. Rhoslyn almost tripped in her haste to reach the door. She grasped the key sticking out of the keyhole and turned it. Heart beating, she pulled the key free, then hurried to the tub. Tossing the key on the small table beside the bathing cloths, she yanked the ties of her bodice free, then shoved the fabric down her shoulders and arms. She scooped the dress from the floor and threw it into the fire with such force that sparks sprayed across the hearthstone. She lifted the kettle from the fire and set it atop a cloth on the table nearest the tub.

Her hands shook as she gripped the side of the tub and stepped into the water. Rhoslyn forced herself to ease down, instead of dropping and dunking her head, desperate to remove the feel of Dayton St. Claire's sweat and blood from her flesh. When the water covered her breasts, she scrubbed her belly and thighs with a cloth until they were red, and washed the place between her legs until she was sore.

She poured the kettle of hot water into the cooling bathwater, ignoring the uncomfortable heat as the steam curled in thick ribbons around her body. Back against the tub, she slid downward until her face submerged. When her lungs neared bursting, she shoved upwards, gasping for air. Despite the blazing hearth fire, gooseflesh raced across her shoulders. She pulled her knees up to her belly and wrapped her arms around her legs, then sat until her teeth chattered so violently that her jaw ached. Still, she did not move. A thunk outside her room jerked her from her stupor.

St. Claire.

Rhoslyn scrambled from the tub, losing her balance and nearly falling in her haste to grab the drying cloth and wrap it around her body. Silence came from the other side of the door, yet she stood several long moments before accepting that no one was going to enter the room. Then she remembered the key on the table. She crossed to the small table near the window, poured a mug of mulled wine, and drank the contents in several large gulps. After refilling the mug, she went to the bed and slipped beneath the blanket, back against the wall, gripping the mug close to her breasts.

How was she ever going to remove the feel of Dayton St. Claire from inside her? What was she going to do when St. Claire eventually claimed his husbandly rights? How was she going to be wife to the brother of the man who had violated her? Rhoslyn recalled her first sight of Dayton St. Claire, how the two brothers were as different as the sun was from the moon. They shared the same father, but not the same mother. St. Claire had forcibly taken her from the safety of her father's men—and had threatened to avail himself of his husbandly rights. But he had left her unmolested and had, instead, gone to lend aid to her grandfather.

She mouthed a prayer to Saint George. God had forsaken her, and her supplications to the saints had gone unheeded these last two years. What had she done to so displease her Lord? Was it possible to atone for an unknown sin?

Rhoslyn took another long sip of wine. The liquid sent a ripple of warmth through her body. She took another sip. She longed to return to the convent. But if answers lay there, why had God allowed her to be ripped away before she found peace?

The walls at Saint Mary's hadn't closed in on her as did the current silence. There, she could turn her mind to God. Staring at the wall of the inn, all she saw was a child with dark hair like Dayton St. Claire's. What would Sir Talbot do if his brother's seed had taken root in her? Could she become pregnant so easily when it had taken nearly seven years of marriage to conceive Alec's son?

Alec's kindness hadn't concealed his disappointment. He loved his daughter, but he wanted a son to carry on his name. Daily, Rhoslyn prayed to Saint Anthony, the patron saint of infertility, and Saint Anne, mother of the Virgin Mary, and begged to conceive. At last, her miracle happened, and she missed her flux. Rhoslyn dedicated the next month to prayers and supplications, and didn't miss a single mass. The second month came and no blood appeared.

Alec joined her in daily prayers, and when the child at last moved inside her, she allowed herself to believe she was going to give her husband the son he so wanted. Then six weeks after she gave birth to a healthy baby boy, Alec became ill and died within a fortnight. Then Dougal began to cough and developed a fever. Nothing the doctors did helped the child, and Rhoslyn's prayers went unanswered. Tears trickled down her cheeks. The months she'd spent in the convent melted away and she again sat in her chambers, desperately rocking Dougal in her arms, while his breath rattled. And then stopped.

She held him for hours, washing his face with her tears, while the hearth fire burned to ash and the room chilled. As sunlight seeped through the closed shutters, Mistress Miura entered the room, summoned the doctor, and then sent for her grandfather.

Rhoslyn didn't fight when the old housekeeper took the babe from her arms. She allowed herself to be led to the bed and the covers pulled up over her shoulders. When she finally awoke, she called for her grandfather and begged to go to Saint Mary's. She had gone ere' her son was laid in the ground. She had yet to visit his grave in the family cemetery at Castle Glenbarr.

Rhoslyn drank the last of the wine and set the mug on the shelf beside the bed. Her brain muddled and the room blurred. She considered refilling the mug, but the weight of her body sagged against the mattress and she couldn't muster the strength to move. Perhaps if she rested just a moment...

Chapter Seven

NEAR MIDNIGHT, A sudden downpour ended their search, but by then Talbot knew Dayton had eluded him. Talbot's anger mingled with bitter frustration. He would have to chase Dayton into England and, likely, challenge their father's protection of the cur.

The walls of the inn came into view up ahead and Talbot allowed his shoulders to relax a fraction. The security its walls afforded meant the establishment was of a better cut than the one where they'd found Lady Rhoslyn. He slowed and Seward followed suit, as did the men riding behind them. They passed through the gate into the courtyard and Talbot spotted one of his men sitting on a bench near the door. The man rose as they brought their horses to a halt in front of the inn.

The door opened just as Talbot dismounted. A murmur of voices spilled into the courtyard as a lad emerged, and he glimpsed men inside the tavern on the ground floor of the building.

The lad stepped up to Talbot. "Can I take your horses?"

"Aye," Talbot replied. "Have you accommodations for my men in your stables?"

"Ye can speak with John. Your men can come with me."

"Blair," Talbot called to the man at the head of the company, "you and the rest of the men sleep in the stables. The boy will show you the way." The boy started around the building and the men spurred their horses to follow.

"All is well?" Talbot asked the warrior who had been seated.

"Aye. Ross himself guards your lady wife."

"What room is she in?" Talbot asked.

"Third floor, second door on the left."

Talbot nodded, and Seward followed him inside the tavern.

Talbot stopped a young maid as she passed a nearby table. "Have you another room?" he asked.

"I think so. I will fetch the innkeeper."

A moment later a tall, lean man in his thirties entered from the hallway. "Good evening. Brae tells me ye are looking for a room."

"Aye, my wife, Lady Rhoslyn is here," Talbot said. "Her grandfather, Baron Kinsley, needs accommodations."

"Lady Rhoslyn, yes. She is in our finest room on the third floor. I have a vacant room at the end of the hall on the second floor, the baron can have. 'Tis a good room, though no' as fine as the one where I put your wife."

"That will do," Talbot said. "I have sent my men to your stables. See to their dinner." He turned toward the stairs.

"I expect to see my granddaughter first thing in the morning, St. Claire," Seward said.

Talbot started up the stairs. "I will tell her."

RHOSLYN'S EYES SNAPPED open. A stifling heat washed over her. The glow of firelight penetrated her blurred vision. The convent was on fire! She threw back the covers and leapt from bed. She took two steps before realizing she was naked. She swung toward the fire. There was no hearth in her cell. The events of the last day crashed in around her. Rhoslyn gasped and swayed with the spinning room.

Strong arms caught her against a wall of velvety steel warmth. She snapped her head up and saw a masculine face looming over her. Her mind propelled back to Dayton St. Claire on top of her, his stubbled jaw harsh against her neck as he—Rhoslyn shoved the man's chest.

"No!" she screamed.

The arms tightened around her. "Lady Rhoslyn."

She beat his chest.

"It is I—"

Rhoslyn thrashed.

His arms tightened. "Rhoslyn, it is I, Talbot."

She froze.

Shock rolled over her and tears became sobs. Rhoslyn felt herself lifted from the floor, then her body settled against hard thighs. Her mind told her to break free, but wracking sobs shook her shoulders and she could do nothing but allow the hot tears to flow.

At last, she heaved a long, stuttered sigh, too spent to shed another tear. Too tired to care.

"Are you thirsty?"

St. Claire's voice reverberated through his chest and Rhoslyn remembered she was naked. Fear gave way to an embarrassment that sent a tremor rippling through her stomach. In truth, she wasn't afraid. His gentle touch surprised her and, despite the fact he wore no shirt—and she was certain she felt a bulge beneath her bottom—he made no move to force or seduce her. She was however, uncomfortably aware of her breast flattened against his chest and the warmth of his muscled arms against her flesh.

"Are you thirsty?" he asked again.

Very thirsty, she realized. Her mouth felt like sand. "Aye," she rasped.

St. Claire slid her from his lap onto the bed, then rose. He surprised her by keeping his eyes straight ahead and didn't so much as flick a glance at her naked body. She pulled the blanket from the bed and wrapped it around herself. Her hair was still damp. The long, thick tresses would be impossible to manage into a braid in the morning. She might be forced to allow the maid to help her.

St. Claire turned and crossed back to the bed. When he handed her the mug, she caught sight of the markings on his arm. The face and upper body of a girl no more than thirteen years of age covered his flesh from shoulder to bicep. Long hair rippled along the sculpted muscle.

He unexpectedly grasped her chin and tilted her head up toward his. His mouth thinned and she realized he was studying her bruised cheek. He released her and sat on the bed beside her. Rhoslyn fingered her cheek and found the flesh even more tender than it had been when she went to bed.

"Does it hurt?" he asked.

She startled. "'Tis only a little sore." She took a drink of the wine. "How is your wound?"

"Healing well."

"Is it deep?"

"Little more than a scratch," he replied.

Rhoslyn took another sip of her wine. "You should no' have attacked me."

"You should not have tried to marry another man."

"What was your sister's name?"

"Lilas," he replied without looking at her.

Rhoslyn's gaze caught on the room key still sitting on the table near the tub. "How did you get into my room? I have the key."

"Ross had another."

She should have felt annoyed, but couldn't muster the strength.

"Can you tell me what happened?"

Rhoslyn stiffened. "What do ye think happened?"

He looked at her now. "I am asking how you came to be with my brother."

"I did no' go with him willingly, if that is what ye mean."

"It would make no sense to do so," he replied. And she heard the unspoken thought, *No more sense than to try to marry another man.*

"He killed Sheila and your guard." Her chest tightened. "And Mistress Muira."

"Not Mistress Muira."

Rhoslyn startled. "But he said—"

St. Claire shook his head. "She was found unconscious. I assume her would-be killer was interrupted before he could finish the job."

Tears stung the corners of Rhoslyn's eyes. She took a long, slow drink of wine in an effort to gain control. "Muira took me under her wing when I married Alec," she finally said. "Taught me about herbs, how to manage a kitchen." Her voice hitched. "She was more mother than housekeeper. I thank God he spared her." But could she forgive Him for taking the other two lives? Even as the thought formed she knew it wasn't God's doing, but her own. She had neglected her duty and left herself and those who depended on her vulnerable. *Forgive me,* she mentally prayed.

"She said my brother arrived not long after I left," St. Claire said.

Rhoslyn nodded. "No more than two hours later."

"That is early to receive visitors."

"He was your brother and I had a guard. I had no idea I had anything to fear."

St. Claire nodded. "Still, I would prefer that you not entertain in the early hours of the morning."

Ire flared. "We are no' truly wed and already ye are giving orders."

His expression remained calm. "I do not think it is too much to ask that a wife allow her husband to protect her."

Her heart began to beat fast. What she would have given for his protection when Dayton yanked up her skirt. The shock and anger on St. Claire's face when he saw her tied to the bed came to mind and the urge to cry nearly overwhelmed her.

She dropped her gaze. "I am sorry."

"You are not to blame."

She jerked her gaze back to him. "But you just said I should no' entertain at night."

"That does not mean you are at fault. I should have left you better protected."

"Or not gone at all?" she asked.

A hint of a smile played at the edges of his full mouth. "You would not have forgiven me if I did not help your grandfather."

"That is true," she admitted. "How is he? You didna' tell him everything?"

St. Claire shook his head. "He is well, and sleeping here at the inn. You can see him in the morning."

Anxiety knotted her stomach. Could she face him so soon after what had happened? Another thought struck and her insides began to tremble. "What of your brother?"

The humor on St. Claire's face vanished and his mouth thinned to a hard line. "We did not find him."

She drew a sharp breath.

St. Claire met her gaze. "He will never again harm you."

Rhoslyn nodded.

"I swear, Rhoslyn, I will find and kill him."

"He is your brother."

"You are my wife."

She studied him. "Why would you kill your brother for a woman you do no' know, much less care for?"

"I will do that and more, my lady."

Her breath caught at sight of the intense light in his eyes. She was afraid to ask what the 'more' included.

"What happened with Aodh?" she asked.

St. Claire rose. She noticed a long scar on his right side before he turned toward the hearth. Another, longer, scar slashed across his left shoulder blade, and yet another small scar marred the flesh above the waistband of his hose. He set his mug on the table beside the tub and continued to the hearth. The fire had burned down considerably.

He knelt on one knee and stoked the fire. "Roberts left with little trouble."

St. Claire grabbed a log from the stack beside the fireplace and tossed it onto the burning coals. Rhoslyn couldn't tear her gaze from the play of muscle in his back. She estimated him to be about thirty-three years old, yet his body was better muscled than many men ten years his junior. That's what came of a lifetime of war.

"How did you know I left the convent?" she asked.

"Your grandfather made the mistake of sending two dozen men to escort you. Then he went to Longford Castle. News of such a large company of men travels fast."

"How could you know the men were coming for me? He could have been sending them elsewhere."

He twisted his head and met her gaze. "Somewhere else? Such as?"

Nothing came immediately to mind. She had been sequestered in the convent for fourteen months. She knew nothing of current politics. He went back to tending the fire and she found that his quick dismissal piqued her pride. The man was too sure of himself.

His attention fixed on something amongst the coals. Rhoslyn followed the turn of his head and spied a piece of gray cloth—a fragment of the dress that hadn't burned. Mortification washed over her. She tensed in anticipation of his question, but he jabbed the fabric closer to the coals so that it caught and blazed beneath the logs. He leaned the poker against the stone, then rose.

"Mayhap you should return to bed."

For an instant, she pictured herself naked beneath the blankets and him climbing into bed beside her. Fear slashed through her.

"I have work," he said.

Rhoslyn frowned. "What?"

He pointed to the desk in the alcove near the door. "I have work. You need not worry about me coming to your bed."

What work could he possibly have? But she decided she didn't want to know. He approached and took the mug from her. She nodded thanks, then crawled across the mattress and lay atop the remaining blanket. He strode toward the desk and disappeared from view.

Blanket still wrapped around her, she closed her eyes.

Chapter Eight

~

TALBOT COULD SCARCE believe Dayton hadn't fled Scotland. If what the man told Talbot an hour ago was true, he would find his brother at this Stonehaven port tavern. Talbot scanned the crowded room. His gaze snagged on a dark-haired man near the stairs. The man's back faced Talbot, but he could be Dayton. Talbot still half-believed the messenger was lying in hopes of collecting the ten pieces of silver Talbot had placed on his brother's capture. Talbot shouldered his way through the crowd. He got five feet when the man turned and looked straight at him.

Dayton.

Angry scratches across his brow bore testament to Lady Rhoslyn's struggles against the rape. Rage howled through Talbot. He plunged through the men. Dayton whirled toward the stairs. He reached the staircase in three paces and bounded up. Talbot's foot hit the first stair as Dayton swung around the second floor balustrade.

Talbot reached the hallway to see Dayton disappear into a room at the end of the hallway. A feral growl burst from Talbot. He yanked his sword from the scabbard and ran down the hallway. When Talbot burst into the room, he found it empty and the curtain blowing at the open window.

He raced to the window and swung over the sill. Air born for an instant, he tensed, then landed on soft ground in a crouch. The pounding of footfalls bounced off the buildings in the narrow alley. Talbot shoved upright. Visible in the morning gloom, Dayton raced toward the street. Talbot broke into a run. Dayton stopped at the other end of the alley and looked back at him, then dashed right.

Heart pounding, Talbot pumped his legs faster. Seconds later, he shot out of the alley onto a narrow street, veering right. After several paces, he slowed, drawing in heavy breaths while scanning the nearly deserted street. Two men stood outside a tavern across the street and sounds of male pleasure grunts echoed between buildings as he passed. Talbot sheathed his sword. His brother had to have ducked into one of the taverns or buildings on this street.

A door swung open to his right and bawdy laughter erupted as a man stumbled from the tavern. Talbot sidestepped him, then turned back and entered. Like the other tavern, kilted Highlanders and local Scots dressed in breeches filled the room. He scanned the crowd, but didn't see Dayton. His gaze caught on a door in the back of the room. Talbot worked his way to the rear where a man behind the counter handed two ales to a barmaid.

"I am looking for someone," Talbot said.

"Who?" the man asked.

Talbot pulled a silver coin from the pouch strapped to his belt. "My brother."

"Is he English like you?"

"Aye."

The man grunted. "I havena' seen another Englishman tonight."

Talbot detected no dishonesty and laid the coin on the counter. He made his way back toward the door. A hulking figure stepped in his path. Talbot sidestepped the man, but he followed suit, blocking Talbot's way.

"Do I know you?" Talbot asked.

"Ye hear that, David?" the man said. "He wants to know if we are friends."

Another man, almost as large, joined the first man. "Ye think we would be friends with an English dog?"

"I have not caused you any trouble," Talbot said. "Stand aside and let me pass."

"Ye cause trouble by coming here and marrying our women…then taking them off," the large man said.

Talbot tensed. "I do not know you. But it seems you know me."

"Sir Talbot St. Claire," David said. "Bastard knight."

"What do you want?" Talbot demanded.

The big man crossed his arms over his chest. "Leave on a ship tonight and we will not harm ye."

"Move out of my way and I will not kill you."

David reached for his sword, but Talbot yanked his sword from its scabbard and dug the point into David's throat before his blade cleared its sheath. The room went quiet. The big man shifted.

"Move and I kill him," Talbot snarled. Pent up fury strained against his control. "Remove your hand from your sword."

The big man didn't move.

"Do as he says, Morris," David hissed.

David's eyes shifted to something behind him. Talbot leapt aside, whirling in time to miss a knife slash through the air. David and Morris drew their swords. Talbot sliced his blade down the front of David's shirt, drawing blood. He pivoted and blocked a blow from Morris' sword and threw his weight into throwing the man off balance. Morris stumbled backwards. Talbot drove his sword into Morris' shoulder. Blood gushed.

From the corner of his eye, Talbot glimpsed the flash of another sword and spun as the newcomer's steel clashed with David's sword. The newcomer parried, left, then right. Another sword swung toward Talbot's head. He deflected the blade and drove his sword into the man's belly. Another man lunged, but a third man jumped in and swung his sword, slicing the man's hip.

Talbot turned. The first Highlander who had given aid was being attacked by two others. Talbot rammed his sword into the side of the closest attacker. The Highlander helping him forced his opponent back two paces before slicing a long cut along the man's arm and wrist. His opponent bellowed, but the Highlander brought down a blow so heavy the clang of steel hurt Talbot's ears. The blow broke the man's grip on his sword and he dropped to his knees.

The onlookers nearest the fight stepped toward them.

"We must leave," the first Highlander who had helped Talbot shouted.

The second Highlander backed up alongside Talbot, sword ready. Talbot retreated with his two comrades. When they neared the door, they whirled and burst through at a run. Men piled out of the tavern and gave chase. Talbot followed his companions down a zig zag of narrow streets until the shouts of their pursuers died. Talbot's comrades finally stopped on a quiet lane in front of run-down cottages. The three men collapsed against the nearest wall and drew in deep breaths.

"Ye have a way of leaving an impression," the man who had first helped him said.

"I was minding my own business when those brutes got in my way."

The sun had lifted in the horizon, and Talbot got a good look at his rescuers. Both men were tall and broad shouldered. The one who had jumped into the fight first had red hair with a beard, the second was dark and clean shaven.

"I am surprised you aided me," Talbot said.

"Ye mean, you are surprised we aided an Englishman," the second man said.

"Aye," Talbot admitted.

"I canna' abide an unfair fight," the first man said.

"'Tis no' sporting of them," the second agreed.

"I am Talbot—"

"St. Claire," the first man interjected. "Aye, we know."

"It would seem the bounty I set on my brother's head has made me more popular than him," Talbot muttered.

"That is one way of putting it," the first man said. "I am Ingram Berclay."

"Ralf Wardwn," the second said.

"I would offer to buy you a drink, but I fear it would be our last," Talbot said.

Ralf laughed. "I know a place."

Talbot followed them to a quiet inn farther from the docks. They sat in a corner of the inn's tavern and when ales arrived, Talbot said, "My brother is just as English as I am. I would think my attackers would be glad to collect a bounty of silver on any Englishman."

Ralf grunted. "If he was a dead Englishman, aye. Though, I suspect if those characters knew where your brother was they would collect the money, then kill ye both."

Talbot nodded and took a draught of ale. "I suppose neither of you have any idea where my brother might be?"

They both shook their heads.

"Probably halfway to England by now," Ingram said.

"So I thought," Talbot said. "But I saw him tonight. That is what brought me to the tavern where I met you."

"He was there?" Ingram said in obvious surprise.

"I lost him in the streets. I went into that tavern looking for him."

"Are ye sure it was him ye saw?" Ralf asked, and Talbot detected something more than curiosity behind the man's question.

"It was him."

The two men exchanged a glance.

Ingram leaned forward on the table. "There are those who would prefer to see your brother wed the Lady Rhoslyn, instead of you."

"What makes you think my brother wishes to marry my wife?"

"Ye put the bounty on your brother's head because he kidnapped her. It doesna' take much intelligence to know why."

Talbot nodded. "Why is my brother preferable to me? He is less disposed toward Scotland than I."

Ralf snorted. "Ye dinna' expect us to believe that the Scottish mother ye never knew will sway your passions for Scotland."

"No," Talbot replied. "But Dayton never cared for anything save his own pleasures. I, at least, want to live in peace."

"That will no' make any difference to the lot out there," Ingram said. "They are willing to sacrifice Lady Rhoslyn if it means King Edward's interests are tied up in a family feud."

"You realize Edward will uphold my marriage to Lady Rhoslyn, whether she is here or not?" Talbot said.

"Aye," Ralf replied. "But that will no' matter if ye are in England chasing after your brother and wife."

Talbot realized they were right, and silently cursed. He had already considered how to secure Lady Rhoslyn's safety before he left on what he believed would be at least a month-long journey to catch his brother.

"Ye do know he is claiming he and Lady Rhoslyn are married," Ralf said.

"Married?" Talbot blurted. "God damn him to hell. I will gut him."

Ingram grinned. "That would solve your problem."

Talbot studied the two men. He liked them. Aside from their willingness to jump into a fight that wasn't their own, they had a direct manner he appreciated.

"Would you two be interested in entering my service?"

"If ye are asking if we will find your brother and kill him, nay, I am not interested," Ingram said. "I canna' speak for Ralf."

Before Ralf could answer, Talbot said, "Nay. My brother will die by my hand and no other. However, I would pay handsomely to find him."

"I have no interest in going to England," Ingram said.

Ralf actually shuddered and Talbot laughed. "I would not ask that of you. I only want to know if he is still in Stonehaven. I must escort my wife back to Castle Glenbarr in the morning. All I ask is that you make inquiries and keep your ears open—and, if you hear anything, send word."

"Then your brother and Lady Rhoslyn are no' married?" Ingram asked.

"It would be hard for them to be married when she and I were already wed," Talbot said.

"Have ye said the vows?" Ralf asked.

Talbot took a drink of ale. "Nay, but that is a mere technicality."

"Ye are in Scotland, man. 'Tis more than a technicality. Your king may make all the commands he likes, but if Lady Rhoslyn says the vows with another man, ye will have a problem on your hands."

"Edward is more than just my king," Talbot said. "He is the Sovereign Lord of Scotland."

Ralf laughed. "Let him come to Scotland and enforce his sovereignty. We will kick his arse back to England."

"I have fought with Edward. You are mistaken."

Both men grinned.

"Aye," Ingram said, "but have ye ever fought a Scot?"

"I have been fighting Scots all night," Talbot said. "I will fight more, if necessary, and will not be sent back to England."

"Ye can thank your mother's Scottish blood for that," Ingram replied without rancor, and Talbot laughed again. So his Scottish heritage might work to his advantage after all.

"Do we have a bargain?" he asked.

"I have nothing better to do." Ralf lifted his mug in a toast, and Talbot clinked his mug against Ralf's. Ingram joined in. They finished their ale and called for another.

RHOSLYN WAS IMMENSELY relieved when she woke to find St. Claire gone from their room. A sky blue linen dress lay draped across the foot of the bed. She washed her face and donned the dress, then worked through the tangles in her long hair. At last, she went to the door and opened it. As expected, Ross stood guard.

"Ye look well, Lady Rhoslyn," he said.

She nodded. "Where is St. Claire?"

"He received word that his brother was seen at the port and has gone to find him. Are ye hungry, my lady?"

Rhoslyn started to say no, then realized she was quite hungry. "Aye, perhaps a little bread and cheese."

"We can eat downstairs, if ye like."

She agreed, and they went downstairs where they were given a quiet table. The food arrived and she had taken two bites when St. Claire entered. He scanned the room. Her heart picked up speed when his gaze stopped on them. He stood for an instant, staring, then strode across the room. Rhoslyn was struck with how even his walk bespoke a man of action. She recalled his gentle touch, despite his barely suppressed rage, when he'd cut her bonds. She reached for her wine and realized her hands were shaking. St. Claire reached the table, and she carefully lifted the mug to her lips and sipped.

He sat in the seat nearest her. "You look well, my lady."

Rhoslyn set her mug on the table. "I am much refreshed."

He nodded but she noted the uncertainty in his eyes.

"You do no' look like a man whose quest was fruitful," Ross said.

"I did not find him."

Rhoslyn found herself unable to speak. What was wrong with her? Dayton St. Claire was nowhere near her. But the knowledge didn't stop the tremble in her limbs. A hand unexpectedly covered and squeezed hers. She yanked her hand back before realizing it was St. Claire's hand.

"Forgive me," he said. "I did not mean to startle you. I only wanted to assure you that Dayton will never again come near you."

She nodded. "Thank ye. I know."

"I am surprised he is still in Scotland," Ross said.

"As am I."

"Will ye remain to search for him while we return to Castle Glenbarr?" Rhoslyn asked.

She couldn't decide whether she wanted him to stay or return. If he stayed, that gave her time to reconcile herself to the…kidnapping *and* her marriage. But she couldn't deny the fear that edged through her at the thought of him not being present for the return trip. Stupid, he had a company of two dozen men, and her grandfather had brought men, as well. Nothing could possibly happen.

"I will return with you," St. Claire said. "I have spoken with the sheriff. If they apprehend Dayton, he will notify me."

From the corner of her eye, Rhoslyn saw her grandfather enter the tavern. He strode to their table. When he reached them, he pulled her up and studied her. His gaze lingered on the bruise that darkened her cheek before sending a penetrating glance St. Claire's way. Then he pulled her into his arms and she relaxed into the warmth of his familiar embrace. It took all her will not to break down into blubbering sobs. She was thankful when he declined the morning meal and said he would rather start for home as soon as she was ready to leave.

A DAMP MIST hung in the air all day, which fit Rhoslyn's mood. They stopped twice at taverns for drink and food. She feigned fatigue, but feared her grandfather would guess the truth. As the day wore on, her fatigue became real.

"We should stop for the night," her grandfather said when the sun dipped in the horizon. "There is a village up ahead. We can take shelter in a barn, if need be."

Rhoslyn shook her head. "Nay. I want to reach Castle Glenbarr to-night."

"Lady Rhoslyn," St. Claire began.

"Tonight," she said.

He stared for a long moment, then nodded.

Night fell and with it came a light drizzle. Rhoslyn wrapped her cloak more tightly about her, but as the darkness deepened, so did the chill. Her teeth began to chatter, which helped keep her awake.

Rhoslyn woke with a start when she realized she was falling. She cried out and grabbed for the pommel, but found instead that her fingers closed around warm muscle.

"You are safe," came a male voice.

St. Claire.

His warm thighs beneath her buttocks reminded her of last night when he'd held her. She had fallen asleep and he had pulled her from her horse. Unexpectedly, panic swept her.

She shoved at his chest. "Release me. I can ride."

"You nearly fell from your horse," he said.

"I can stay awake," she insisted.

"We're two hours from Castle Glenbarr," he said. "You will ride with me or we will stop and you will rest." She didn't immediately answer and he added, "We will rest until I am certain you can safely ride."

"Do no' think ye can order me about, St. Claire. I am a grown woman and I can think for myself."

"Then use your brain," he said. "If you fall and hurt yourself that will delay us."

"Ye are no' as logical as you believe yourself to be," she muttered. But she couldn't deny that she had already begun to relax in his arms.

"Take this," her grandfather said.

Rhoslyn felt a cozy warmth settle around her and realized a plaid had been draped over her. St. Claire tucked the blanket more tightly around her and she burrowed closer to the warm wall of his chest.

TALBOT SNAPPED ALERT at the pounding of hooves on moist ground.

Seward's horse let out a snort when the old baron pulled back on the reins. "Ye hear that?"

Talbot slowed beside him. "Two, maybe three riders." He twisted and looked over his shoulder, but discerned only dark shadows beyond the darkness where their company of men ended.

Seward called out a quiet order for his men to face the riders. "Ride with Rhoslyn," he ordered Talbot. "I will deal with these men."

Talbot spurred his horse into a gallop and Baxter joined him with their men riding behind. Rhoslyn stirred in his arms. He felt tugs on the blanket that encircled her.

"What is happening?" she murmured.

The last hour with her rounded bottom pressed snugly against his cock had been torture. Now, her sleep-filled voice made the erection pulse with a vengeance.

"We are nearly home," he said.

She pushed against his chest to straighten, the shift of her weight pressing down on his erection with such force he had to grit his teeth against the exquisite pain.

"Why are we galloping?"

The force of her body jostling against his groin with the gallop of the horse made him wonder—and almost wish—that he would spend himself in his braies. He hadn't desired a woman this badly since the age of nineteen. Then again, he hadn't denied himself having a woman he wanted as he had Lady Rhoslyn this last day.

"St. Claire," Rhoslyn demanded.

"We heard riders approaching from behind," he replied.

"Surely, ye dinna' expect your brother to follow us?"

"Nay, but that does not mean we will not encounter robbers."

"Give me a dirk," she said.

He snorted. "I have yet to recover from the last time you had a knife while sitting on my lap."

"I do no' intend to use it on ye." She sounded genuinely affronted. "If we encounter brigands, I would like protection."

"*I* am your protection," he replied.

The words were barely out of his mouth when riders shot from the trees onto the road in front of them.

Talbot cursed, and drew his sword in unison with his men drawing their swords. "In Scotland less than a week and this is the third battle I have fought," he muttered.

"Three?" Lady Rhoslyn said. "I will want to hear the other two tales. For now, give me a dirk."

"Who goes there?" Baxter demanded as Talbot urged his horse toward the edge of the road and away from the newcomers.

"Prepare yourself," Talbot told her in a low voice. "If I must push you from the saddle—"

"St. Claire," someone called, and Talbot paused, "'tis I, Ralf Wardwn."

"Ralf?" Talbot nudged his horse past his men to the rider and saw that it was Ralf. "I should send you to your maker. What are you doing rushing onto the road like that?"

"I took a short cut to reach ye. Forgive me, Lady Rhoslyn. I hope we didna' scare you. There was no other way. I did not want to shout and alert anyone along the way."

"Including me," Talbot said. "Who is that with you?" He nodded to the rider behind Ralf.

"This is Simon. Ingram and two other men are searching for ye on the road behind us. We broke up so that I could search ahead in case we had missed you."

"You have news of my brother?" Talbot asked. He was sure he felt a tremble in Lady Rhoslyn's body and tightened his arm around her.

"Nay," Ralf said. "I wish it were so. I am here to tell you of a plot to accost ye on the road and kill you."

"Friends of the men in the tavern?" Talbot asked.

"Aye, only meaner."

"How fortunate," Talbot muttered. "We are but an hour from Castle Glenbarr. Why wait so long?"

"The plot was hatched last minute, the result of ale and misguided passions."

"Dayton?" he asked.

"'Tis what we suspect, but we didna' hear for ourselves. Once we got wind of the plan we set out after you."

"You went to a lot of trouble to warn me."

"Ye know how much I hate an unfair fight."

"I believe this is a clue to one of the battles ye mentioned," Lady Rhoslyn said.

"Too long a story for now," Talbot said. "I wager Ingram is who Seward encountered behind us. Baxter," he called, "send a man back to see what goes with Seward. I want to get to Castle Glenbarr as quickly as possible. If it is Ingram who caught up with them, invite him to Castle Glenbarr." Talbot returned his attention to Ralf. "Will you ride with us as well? I can offer food and shelter, and we can talk."

"Aye," Ralf replied. "Glen will come, too."

"Good." Talbot started to turn his horse toward home.

"I should ride," Lady Rhoslyn said. "We can ride faster if I am riding my own horse."

She was right, but he didn't like it. "You will do exactly as I say," he said.

"Beware giving too many orders, English."

"I will brook no argument, Lady Rhoslyn. You will do as I say or ride with me."

"What is your command?"

Her voice was calm, but he heard the steel. He had steel of his own.

"At the first sign of trouble you ride with me and Baxter to Castle Glenbarr as fast as possible."

"The last time I left a fight I was captured by you."

"Then you need not fear," he said, "for I am not the one chasing you this time."

THEY REACHED CASTLE Glenbarr without incident, but Talbot knew the trouble had only begun. Seward knew it as well. He and Ingram arrived half an hour later, and they sought out Talbot in the great hall where he sat with Ralf.

"The vows are not yet said, and ye already have enemies," Seward said in greeting.

"Sit down," Talbot said, then ordered a waiting lad to bring ale before returning his attention to the old baron. "I had enemies before I ever set foot in Scotland."

Seward sat down. "Is the wealth my granddaughter brings to the marriage worth living among enemies?"

"A few enemies is paltry in comparison to war campaigns," Talbot replied.

The old man grunted. "Ye underestimate the Highland temperament. These men have a great capacity for hating you."

Talbot shrugged. "I would find no less if I lived amongst my own."

The boy brought two mugs of ale and a pitcher. He set them before the two men, then stepped back, awaiting further instructions.

"Then it must be your sweet nature that makes ye so loveable," Seward said.

Despite the sarcasm, Talbot detected grudging respect. "About as loveable as you," he replied. "Only yesterday, Aodh Roberts was ready to send you to your reward."

"I should have dealt with Aodh years ago, but I grew up with his cousin. They wouldna' forgive me if I killed him."

"You are a fortunate man to be surrounded by so many relatives."

"They are your relatives now, too," Seward replied.

Talbot laughed. "Do they see me as a relative?"

"They will when they want something from ye. God help you when that happens."

"I have a feeling that is exactly what is about to happen."

"Aye. Ye can begin by telling me who your new friends are." He nodded to Ralf, Ingram, and the other two men who set across from him.

Talbot recounted the story, ending with, "They tell me that Dayton claims he and Rhoslyn are married."

"Married?" The old man's eyes narrowed in anger. "I will kill him for what he did to my granddaughter."

So Seward had guessed that Dayton raped Rhoslyn. Talbot wasn't surprised. The man wasn't stupid. "You will not have the chance," he said. "I claim the right to kill him."

"Ye canna' follow him to England. 'Tis too dangerous to leave Rhoslyn unprotected."

"I would think you could protect her while I am away," Talbot said. "I would also think you would be happy to see me go."

Seward grunted. "If I thought I could get rid of you *and* the rest of your kind, I would tie ye up, send you to the Far East, then marry

Rhoslyn off to Melrose. But your brother's actions give me pause. Edward will no' so easily give up the taxes he'll receive from the Kinsley fortune—and your brother knows it. I wager he gambled that Edward would overlook his methods in ensuring his part of that fortune. If anything happens to ye, Edward is likely to uphold your brother's claim that he and Rhoslyn are married. If I must choose between two devils, I choose the least evil of the two."

"I am flattered," Talbot replied.

RHOSLYN LOOKED UP from the list of goods she was verifying against the wagon filled with vegetables and fruits from the village. Her grandfather and St. Claire approached with determined steps she knew meant they had come in search of her. She had risen early and thrown herself into work in an effort to put the last two days behind her. She didn't like the united front the two men presented. It couldn't bode well for her.

"This will do, Williame," she said to the merchant standing beside her. "Have your men unload the goods in the kitchen." She took a bag of silver from the pouch belted to her waist and handed it to him.

"Thank ye, my lady."

The merchant climbed into the seat beside his son, but not before Rhoslyn caught the glance he cast at her grandfather and St. Claire. His curt order to his son to go to the postern door told her that he, too, knew the men had something on their minds. The cart lurched into motion. Rhoslyn stepped back. Once the cart passed, the two men closed the final distance between them. St. Claire's eyes narrowed on her face and she touched the tender spot on her cheek before checking the action.

His gaze sharpened. "Are you well?"

A strange tremor rippled through her. She hadn't seen him since last night and had hoped to avoid him as long as possible. "I am fine," she said. He continued to stare, and she added, "The bruise isna' so bad."

"Bad enough," her grandfather growled.

"It is over and I am well. That is enough." she said.

"You are a fool if ye believe that, and I didna' raise a fool."

Irritation surfaced. "I had no' expected to see ye. I thought you would have returned home."

"Nay, we need to speak privately with you." He grasped her arm and started toward the castle.

St. Claire fell into place alongside her and she felt as if she were being escorted to the gallows. They reached the front door and, minutes later, entered their private solar.

She seated herself on the bench in front of the hearth and her grandfather said, "Ye and St. Claire will marry tomorrow morning."

Of all the things she might have expected to hear come out of her grandfather's mouth, this wasn't one of them. "But why? Edward commanded we wed a month from now."

"Dayton is claiming you and he are married."

"Married?" It made perfect sense, but that didn't stop the feeling that a horse had rolled across her. "Ridiculous," she said, then cursed the tremor in her voice. "We didna' see a priest, nor was there even the hint of a handfasting."

"It isna' as simple as that, and ye know it," her grandfather said.

Rhoslyn looked at St. Claire. "You claimed Edward's command that we marry was unimpeachable. We are, in effect, already married."

"True," he said. "But Dayton might use the fact you and he were alone to make a claim."

"Is that how ye would have seen things if I had reached Longford Castle and been *alone* with Lord Melrose?"

"Nay. I would have razed Longford Castle, then brought you back to Castle Glenbarr."

Anger tightened her belly. "Yet you fear your brother can claim me?"

"It is my duty to ensure your safety. The church's blessing on our union makes his claims more difficult to pursue."

"King Edward will never uphold your brother's assertions."

"Not as long as I am alive," St. Claire replied.

Rhoslyn gasped. "Surely, your brother would no' go so far as to kill ye?"

"I would not have thought he would dare kidnap you." His expression was impassive, but Rhoslyn felt sure she read the thought, *Neither did I conceive of the possibility that he would dare lay a hand on you.*

"And what will ye do if you bear a child in nine months, Rhoslyn?" her grandfather asked.

Rhoslyn went cold.

"Dayton will say the child is his," he went on. "Especially if there is any question that you and St. Claire havena' lived together as man and wife."

St. Claire remained silent, but Rhoslyn felt his stare. She wanted to argue, wanted to retreat to the solitude of her chambers—or even better, the convent—but could think of nothing to halt the inevitable. As much as she wanted to deny it, they were right. If she bore a child within the next nine months—especially a son—Dayton very well might rally his father and even petition Edward with the allegation that her child was his.

When she'd risen this morning, she had gone to the small chapel near their chambers and prayed to the Virgin Mary herself that she not be pregnant. Her stomach churned, for even while she'd knelt on the stone floor, she had planned how she might obtain penny royal and sage to induce bleeding before St. Claire lay with her.

Chapter Nine

~

RHOSLYN SET THE last egg in the basket, then recorded the total number of eggs on the small parchment she'd brought to the kitchen. Twenty-three eggs in this basket alone. She had always marveled at how Mistress Muira was able to coax so many eggs from her hens. In the past, they had surplus enough to share with the villagers. However, it was likely they would have to purchase more hens just to feed St. Claire's men.

She stepped to the left where a fourth basket sat on the counter and began counting. Rhoslyn reached twelve before her thoughts turned to the wedding ceremony planned for tomorrow morning. A tremor rippled through her stomach. In less than a day, her marriage to Sir Talbot St. Claire, a man she'd known for two days, would be blessed by the church.

Nay. She *met* him two days ago, and had spent less than a day with him. She knew him not at all.

Perhaps, that wasn't wholly true. She knew he was strong of body *and* mind. Physical strength was expected in a knight deserving of his king's favors. Wasn't that what she was, a favor bestowed upon a man for loyal service? Despite knowing such things were the way of the world, the thought galled her.

She'd married Alec because her grandfather believed he would be a good husband. His wealth, she had to admit, was no small consideration, but he'd been a good man who died too soon. She sent up a silent prayer of thanks that he had died before their son. He would have been devastated to know his son had lived only two months. Sadness poked at her heart and she ruthlessly pushed it aside. She couldn't give into sorrow. She had retreated to the convent in sorrow, and look where that had gotten her.

Mistress Muira gave a small cry and Rhoslyn looked up from the eggs. Her stepdaughter Andreana entered the kitchen and stopped a few paces inside. Rhoslyn set the egg she held back in the basket and rushed forward. When she reached the girl, she threw her arms around her. Andreana stiffened. Rhoslyn's heart squeezed. It had been too long since she'd seen her stepdaughter. Rhoslyn drew back and Muira crowded in to give Andreana a hug.

"Och, ye have grown in the two months since I last saw ye." the housekeeper said.

The other half dozen women working in the kitchen crowded around and each hugged her as well, then Muira shooed them back to work and Rhoslyn grasped Andreana's hands and looked at her. In the fourteen months she'd been gone, Andreana had gone from being a gawky girl to a young woman. Her hair had softened and grown lustrous, her face had lost its roundness, appearing longer, with more pronounced cheekbones, and her breasts accentuated a small waist.

"Ye are beautiful," Rhoslyn said.

Andreana's eyes fixed on her face and Rhoslyn detected uncertainty. Ah, so along with the woman's body had risen a woman's uncertainty. And Rhoslyn had been absent during this crucial time when the girl who had known her as her mother entered this new phase of life.

"Why just look at your hair," Rhoslyn said. "So long and soft. I do believe 'tis a darker shade of black than it was when I left."

Andreana's eyes brightened. "Grandfather says it is darker than a raven's feather."

Rhoslyn drew back and studied her hair more closely. "He is right." Rhoslyn held her at arm's length. "And ye have grown into a woman's body."

A blush crept up the girl's cheeks.

"I am so glad to see you," Rhoslyn said. "Who brought ye?"

"Grandfather." She hesitated. "He said it was time I returned home."

"He is right," Rhoslyn said, although she would have given anything not to be there herself.

St. Claire and her grandfather entered, with Sir Baxter close behind. Rhoslyn pulled Andreana aside.

"Andreana," her grandfather said, "this is your mother's new husband, Sir Talbot."

Something strange stirred in Rhoslyn's stomach at hearing St. Claire referred to as 'her husband.'

Andreana gave a pretty curtsy. "Sir Talbot."

He acknowledged with a nod. "Andreana."

Rhoslyn caught the appraising look Andreana gave him from under her lashes, and read the appreciation in her expression. St. Claire seemed oblivious to her inspection, but Rhoslyn had the feeling he simply pretended not to notice. That, she grudgingly admitted, spoke well of him. No doubt, Andreana had broken a heart or two in her absence, and it was no small matter for any man not to respond to a beautiful young girl's admiration. So St. Claire wasn't one to rob the cradle—at least not the one at home.

"This is Sir Baxter, Sir Talbot's captain," Rhoslyn's grandfather said.

"Lady Andreana." Baxter gave a slight bow.

Andreana's eyes shifted onto the knight and Rhoslyn was startled to see a blush creep up her cheeks. Sir Baxter gave no indication he noticed Andreana's reaction, but he wouldn't. St. Claire wouldn't allow it.

Muira stepped up beside Rhoslyn. "Mayhap Andreana would enjoy helping with preparations for tomorrow's wedding celebration?"

Rhoslyn started. "Wedding celebration?" She swung her gaze onto St. Claire. "We only just agreed to have the wedding tomorrow. How can there already be plans for a celebration?"

"Once we decided, I asked Mistress Muira to make the arrangements."

Panic started her heart to beating fast. "But a day is no' enough time to plan a proper celebration. Surely, we need more time? What of your father?"

"I sent word to my father, as well as Edward, that we will say the vows tomorrow. My father can come at his convenience, if he likes."

"Ye dinna' waste time telling Edward," Rhoslyn's grandfather said.

St. Claire shrugged and Rhoslyn wanted to box his ears.

"He will want to know," St. Claire said.

"Did you inform him of your brother's actions?" Rhoslyn demanded.

"I did. It is best he is prepared in case Dayton pursues his claim that you and he are married."

Rhoslyn's heart fell, though she couldn't say why. Whether now or a month hence, it made no difference when the marriage celebration took place. Except, she realized in a moment of honesty, that the celebration announced to the world that she was well and truly married to this man. And, he would claim his husbandly rights.

"Can I really help with the preparations?" Andreana said.

Rhoslyn nodded. "Aye. Though I canna' think we can do much in less than a day."

Andreana's eyes lit. "I can do much." She looked at Rhoslyn's grandfather. "Can I plan as I please?"

"St. Claire is who ye must ask now, lass. Not me."

Andreana shifted her gaze onto St. Claire and smiled shyly. "What would ye have me do, laird?"

"You and your mother may do as you please," he replied.

"Dinna' forget the hunt planned for the day after the celebration," her grandfather said.

"Hunt?" Rhoslyn blurted. She looked at St. Claire. "Ye are planning a hunt?"

"It was your grandfather's idea."

She sent a narrow-eyed look at him. "You are full of surprises."

"I havena' been in a good hunt in too long. I hear your husband is a skilled hunter." He looked at St. Claire. "Mayhap a wager would make things more interesting."

"I never wager with my money," St. Claire said, and Rhoslyn wondered how much of *her* money he would wager.

"I dinna' need your money," her grandfather said. "I saw that beautiful destrier ye rode when you came to Longford Castle. I could use a horse like that."

St. Claire's brows rose. "When have you need of a war horse?"

Her grandfather scowled. "I am no' in my grave yet. I have a fight or two left in me. Are ye game or no'?"

"I am very attached to that horse."

"Then ye are willing to admit defeat before the hunt even begins?" her grandfather said.

"I am willing to admit that fate is sometimes cruel. There are any number of challenges that could arise, none of which are a reflection of my skill."

"Bah! Either ye have the bollocks or no'. Which is it?"

"Spoken like a true Highlander," St. Claire said.

Her grandfather lifted a brow. "Aye, for we know what we are capable of."

"What do you have that I could possibly want?" St. Claire asked.

"Ye already have what I value most." Her grandfather cast a glance at Rhoslyn.

She rolled her eyes.

"Aye," St. Claire's eyes shifted onto her. "What more could I want?"

Rhoslyn startled at the intensity of his gaze, then something fluttered in her belly.

"There is Grandfather's claymore," Andreana said.

Everyone looked at her.

St. Claire crossed his arms over his chest and Rhoslyn forced her gaze from the sight of his muscles bulging against the linen of his sleeves.

"That idea has merit," he said.

Rhoslyn's grandfather scowled at Andreana. "Ye are no' helping matters, lass."

She blushed.

"Afraid?" St. Claire said.

"It is a bet," her grandfather replied.

St. Claire nodded. "You thought you would marry your granddaughter to another man. You were wrong then, too." With that, he strode from the room.

TALBOT HAD INSISTED the vows be spoken, but he wished mightily they could delay a week. Lady Rhoslyn appeared pale as a ghost. She was well in body, of that he was sure, but her spirit had been damaged. However, she would be far more damaged if Dayton's plans came to fruition.

Morning sun streamed through the chapel's small window to the right of the Christ. Talbot stood alongside Rhoslyn in front of the dais, with Seward beside her—his determination thick enough to cut—and

Baxter flanked Talbot—his distrust in equal measure *and* opposition to Seward. English and Highlander crowded the hallway outside the chapel to witness the final blessing, Ralf and Ingram in the forefront.

Father Crey instructed Talbot to place the ring on Rhoslyn's finger. When he grasped her hand, the ruby wedding ring she still wore glinted in the sunlight. Her eyes flew up to his, apprehension and regret mixed in her expression. Talbot smiled gently and covered her hand with his while discreetly slipping the old wedding ring off her finger.

Compared to the ring Alec Harper had given her, the band Talbot placed on her finger was modest: blue topaz and green peridot inlayed on a thick silver band.

Rhoslyn looked up at him, eyes wide. "I have no ring for you."

Her grandfather leaned close and whispered, "Of course ye do." He took her free hand, placed a ring in her palm and closed her fingers around it.

She frowned. "Grandfather—"

"Put the ring on your husband's finger," he urged.

She seemed uncertain, then nodded and grasped Talbot's left hand. Her cool fingers felt almost fragile against his larger ones, but he found them pleasant. Roped carvings decorated the gold band she fitted to his finger. Rhoslyn pushed it down, shoving the ring past the knuckle.

Talbot grasped her hands with both of his and the priest pronounced them man and wife. To his surprise, Rhoslyn didn't drop her gaze, but looked him directly in the eyes as he bent and brushed his lips across hers. Still, he detected a tremble in her body and tasted the salt of tears on her lips. Desire rose to fold her in his arms and assure her all would be well. But how did a man restore a woman's trust?

Talbot slid an arm around Rhoslyn's waist and turned. Cheers went up and the guests parted before them as they walked down the aisle.

At last, they reached their private chambers, and Talbot closed the door on the well—wishers in the hallway. Lady Rhoslyn crossed to the stool at the small table near the window where she kept her accounts and sat down. She absently fingered the wedding ring.

"This is not what I had planned," he said.

She lifted her face to meet his gaze. "You come here at the behest of an English king, take possession of my home before meeting me—you even kidnapped me. What did ye expect?"

He studied her for a moment. "You want me to believe that had I awaited your pleasure at Dunfrey Castle you would have come to me of your own accord? Or perhaps I should have gone down on one knee to your grandfather and begged him to accept an English king's decree to marry his granddaughter to an English knight?"

Her mouth thinned, but she shrugged. "At the very least, you could have gone to Dragon's Lair instead of Castle Glenbarr."

Dragon's Lair. So she knew the name the Highlanders called Dunfrey Castle.

"Who knows what might have happened had you spoken with my grandfather?" she said.

"I did speak with him—though not on bended knee."

Her brows dove down in a frown, then she shot to her feet. "So he tried to marry me to Jacobus. What did ye expect? Sweet Jesu, you took possession of my home before even meeting me."

"That is not why Seward tried to marry you to Melrose," he replied. "Nothing I could have done would have changed things for the better. You know as well as I that had I not reached you in time, Edward would have viewed your marriage to Melrose as a defiance that could not go unchecked."

"So your brother kidnapping me was to be expected?"

"Nay. I had no idea he was even in Scotland. Had I known..." Talbot released a breath. "Perhaps over time, you will be able to forget, but I do not expect you to forgive me."

Her mouth parted in obvious surprise.

"Aye, Lady, I know this is my fault."

"I-I didna' say that," she whispered.

"You did not have to."

She sat back down, and he caught the flick of her eyes toward his chambers. She worried he was about to claim his husbandly rights. That was something he had yet to deal with. Thankfully, a hard rap on the door interrupted.

"Enter," Talbot called.

The door opened and Baxter stepped into the room. "Lady Rhoslyn has a visitor."

"Another visitor? Who?" Talbot demanded.

Baxter's gaze cut to Lady Rhoslyn. "Her intended husband."

"Speak of the devil," Talbot murmured.

"Jacobus?" Rhoslyn asked.

"Aye," Baxter replied. "The Earl of Melrose. You remember him, the man you tried to marry while you were married to Talbot?"

"You will remember that Lady Rhoslyn is my wife, Baxter," Talbot said.

Baxter's eyes jerked onto him. His mouth thinned, but he gave a brusque nod.

"What does Melrose want?" Talbot asked.

"He is demanding to see Lady Rhoslyn. Her grandfather is with him in the great hall."

Rhoslyn rose. "I will speak with him."

"*I* will speak with him," Talbot corrected.

"I do no' want him harmed," she said.

"As long as he causes no trouble, he will not be harmed."

She heaved a sigh. "I am in no mood to argue."

"Good."

She shook her head. "Ye misunderstand. I am in no mood to argue, but I doesna' mean I will take orders. Jacobus came peaceably through our gates. I will see him."

Talbot started to point out that she had said the same thing about Dayton, then stopped. She knew Jacobus Auenel, and he was, after all, just a pup.

They went to the hall. Many of the people who had witnessed the marriage blessing milled about the room, along with Highland and English warriors. Preparations for the evening's party were underway and women bustled between the great hall and kitchen, cleaning and preparing food.

Seward, Ingram, and Ralf, stood with Melrose at the hearth. The two Highlanders had made themselves at home, Talbot noticed. Baxter separated from Talbot and Rhoslyn, and continued on his way to the wall to check on the men as Talbot had ordered. Ingram and Ralf lifted quizzical brows when Talbot and Rhoslyn approached. Young Melrose's gaze latched onto Rhoslyn like a lost dog. By God, he really was nothing more than a boy, and a lovesick boy at that, despite his twenty-one years. Talbot remembered himself at that age, already under Sir Hugh's tutelage for thirteen years and knighted.

"Lady Rhoslyn," Melrose said when they reached the group. "Are ye well?"

Talbot read genuine concern in his tone and a grudging sliver of respect surfaced.

"I am fine," she replied.

"You would never say otherwise." The boy turned his gaze onto Talbot. Ire flashed, which revealed more backbone than Talbot thought the lad capable of. "Less than a day under your care and she comes to harm. Ye dinna' deserve to look her way, much less marry her."

He had a point. Still…

"Yet we are married with a priest's blessing," Talbot said.

Shock registered on Jacobus's face and he looked at Rhoslyn. "My lady, say it is no' true."

"When I didna' reach Longford Castle, ye must have guessed, Jacobus."

"I had hoped that when his brother kidnapped you that meant—" His eyes cut to Talbot. "Ye dirty dog. You have no right to marry her after what happened."

For an instant Talbot thought Melrose knew the truth, then realized he was referring to Rhoslyn being kidnapped, which was, in truth, sufficient fuel for his anger.

"Ye canna' blame the lad for being right," Ralf said.

Talbot shot him a dark look, but Ralf only grinned.

Rhoslyn intervened. "Why are you here, Jacobus?"

His mouth thinned. "I wanted to be sure you were well."

"I just said I was well," she replied.

But Melrose clearly wasn't convinced, for his hand fell to his sword hilt.

Chapter Ten

~

"JACOBUS," RHOSLYN CRIED.

She stepped forward, but St. Claire yanked her back and behind him as the remaining men drew their swords. The nearest warriors leapt to their laird's aid. St. Claire lunged and drove a fist into Jacobus' belly.

"Hold," St. Claire shouted to the men as Jacobus doubled over, then dropped to his knees, wheezing loudly.

St. Claire seized his sword, yanked it from its sheathe then threw it to the floor. Metal clanged against stone in the now silent room, and rushes kicked up as the claymore furrowed a path across the floor, then skidded to a stop.

Her grandfather sheathed his sword. "Have ye lost your mind, Jacobus? You are lucky I dinna' run my sword through your belly just to teach you a lesson."

Jacobus shook his head and drew another pained breath. "I dinna'—" he wheezed again "—understand."

"Then you deserve to die," St. Claire said in a flat voice.

The other two men sheathed their swords, and the surrounding warriors followed suit.

"Damn fool," her grandfather muttered.

Jacobus shoved to his feet, still grasping his stomach. "What did I do?" He looked from one to the other of the men, but they only stared.

Rhoslyn stepped forward. "Surely, your father taught ye never to lay hand on your sword hilt unless you mean to use it?"

His brows dove down in a frown, then understanding dawned on his face. He swung his gaze onto Talbot. "I would no' attack an unarmed man. If I intended to kill ye, I would do it in a fair fight."

"Fair fight?" Her grandfather snorted. "St. Claire would slaughter you." He motioned to St. Claire. "Mayhap ye are the better choice, after all—English king and all."

Jacobus looked at her grandfather, hurt in his eyes. "I would protect her. I *will* protect her, if she but asks."

Rhoslyn groaned inwardly. *Sweet God in heaven, save me from the stupidity of youth.*

"St. Claire's fist is but a taste of what ye will receive if you continue this idiocy," her grandfather said. "Go home, Jacobus—and I suggest you spend some time under the instruction of a knight. You are too old to start learning, but mayhap someone can keep ye from losing your damn head before your next birthday."

Jacobus' face reddened. His eyes narrowed on St. Claire, who met the boy's gaze squarely. For an instant, Rhoslyn feared Jacobus would make some sort of foolish challenge, but he whirled and strode to where his sword lay. He scooped up the weapon, then left.

"Dinna' let that go to your head," her grandfather said to St. Claire when the door closed behind Jacobus. "Just because you are more of a man than the new Earl of Melrose doesna' mean I want ye as my granddaughter's husband."

"Fortunately, your opinion is not the one that matters," he replied.

A gleam entered her grandfather's eyes. "Nay, but Rhoslyn is a Seward. She has as much backbone as I do."

"She is now my wife, a St. Claire," St. Claire said, "and if you interfere in our marriage, you will go the way of that boy." He faced her. "Lady Rhoslyn, I would ask that you do not entertain any male visitors without my knowledge."

Ire piqued, but Rhoslyn was all too aware that she stood poised at a crossroads that could drive a permanent wedge between the man who was now her husband and her grandfather.

"I will make sure ye know of any *male* visitors—who are no' family," she said.

He surprised her by chuckling and saying, "That could be the whole damn village."

RHOSLYN EXITED THE castle through the kitchen door and headed for the gate. The day was still young, but not so young that she dared waste a moment. Any chance she could abort a possible pregnancy before her new husband claimed his husbandly rights would be gone after tonight. If she became pregnant immediately after St. Claire bedded her, she would never truly be sure whose child she carried until it was too late.

Too late? What did that mean? Would love turn to hate if she someday discovered the child she loved belonged to Dayton instead of St. Claire? She certainly wouldn't be able to end the child's life then as she planned to now. Her stomach cramped. God have mercy. What was she doing?

"Lady Rhoslyn."

Rhoslyn paused in her walk and turned. She blinked against morning sun to see St. Claire striding toward her. After the altercation with

Jacobus, St. Claire had sequestered himself in his chambers with Ralf and Ingram, plotting—she assumed—to catch his brother.

He reached her side. "Mistress Muira tells me you are going to the village."

"Aye."

"Until I deal with my brother, I do not want you leaving the castle alone."

"Do ye really think he will return to Buchan, much less come anywhere near Castle Glenbarr?" she asked.

"He has done many things I would not have thought him capable of. I will not risk your safety a second time."

He feels guilty, she thought. Rhoslyn glanced at the gate. She needed to go to the village. Even a small chance that she could obtain the pennyroyal… Was St Claire's interference divine intervention?

"I am only going to the village. No one will dare harm me there."

"I will send men with you."

She nodded, despite uncertainty. "Any strangers unlucky enough to enter Kildrum will probably get run through with a sword before they can deny any crime."

St. Claire nodded. "Step even a foot outside the village without my men, and I will lock you in your chambers until my brother is dead."

Rhoslyn blinked. "What? I didna' argue with you, St. Claire."

"I want to be sure we understand one another," he said.

Words failed her. He hadn't waited even a day to draw yet another line in the sand. "Aye, we understand one another, ye arrogant—"

"Good," he cut in.

He turned and strode toward the castle.

Rhoslyn stared for an instant, then broke from the shock and started forward after him. She stopped. She had won this skirmish—if by accident. Tomorrow was another day, and only God in his ultimate—*male*—wisdom knew what lay ahead.

RHOSLYN'S FEAR WAS realized. She wasn't going to be able to obtain pennyroyal from her local healer. Not that she'd had high hopes. Asking for the herb was too great a risk of exposure. But it mattered not, for Rhoslyn hadn't seen the herb amongst the others in the woman's store. She had obtained oregano, along with several other herbs, but oregano was mild compared to pennyroyal. She trudged along the lane in the village, heart heavy. It was possible the healer had the herb in a safe place, but Rhoslyn couldn't chance sending someone to inquire. That would be damning evidence that she carried Dayton's child, and the villagers had already begun speculating as to what had happened after he kidnapped her.

She didn't yet know if she was pregnant. Her flux wasn't due for another week, and it could delay as much as a fortnight. But she didn't want to wait that long before drinking an herbal brew. The desire to cry rose, as it seemed to every hour. After seven long years of yearning to conceive with Alec, she wouldn't have thought it possible that she wouldn't want a child. What were the chances she would conceive so quickly? She had asked herself that question a thousand times. The chances were small, but what would she do if forced to bear a child that had come to her as a result of rape?

Emotion stirred in her breast. She hadn't considered the possibility of another child. In truth, she had avoided the idea of marriage altogether. Could she so easily end a life, even one born of violence? Whatever sin she had committed that had brought God's wrath down upon her husband and son would surely be multiplied a hundredfold if she took the life of an innocent child.

A woman's scream yanked Rhoslyn from her thoughts. From the corner of her eye she glimpsed a blur of movement between the cottages across the lane. Her hand went to the dagger strapped to her belt before the blur shot out into the lane and she recognized the billy goat belonging to the elderly Christine. The goat had a green dress between its teeth. The fabric billowed above him like a banner.

A girl raced out into the lane in pursuit of the animal. Rhoslyn blinked. Was this Mary Boghan? Only fourteen months ago, Mary had been a slim, petite girl. Now she was...plump.

"Stop the goat!" Mary shouted. "That is my wedding dress."

A boy exited one of the cottages. He stopped and began laughing. The animal neared Rhoslyn and she jumped into the middle of the lane with the intention of turning him back toward Mary. The goat darted right. Rhoslyn lunged for him, but he feinted left, then went right, and loped past her. She whirled as Mary raced past her.

"Bloody animal," Mary screeched.

Rhoslyn yanked up her skirts and gave chase, easily passing the girl. The goat let out a loud bleat that Rhoslyn felt sure was laughter. He dodged between two cottages. Rhoslyn pumped her legs faster and closed in on the animal. She was close enough to grab the dress. She made two swipes and missed, then dove for the animal as they reached the far lane. He veered left instead of right, and Rhoslyn's arms closed around air. She hit the ground and got a nose full of dirt.

Rhoslyn shoved to her feet and whirled in the direction the animal had run as Mary's curses sounded behind her. Two boys had joined the chase, and Rhoslyn shot forward after them.

After a few seconds and another loud bleat, the goat disappeared down another narrow lane. Rhoslyn made a quick right with the intention of cutting him off with a short cut. She zigged and zagged down two lanes and came out on the lane she'd seen him take. He was headed straight for her. She hurried to the middle of the lane and widened her stance in readiness to grab the animal. He raced forward, a dozen people in pursuit, the dress furled in the wind, and Rhoslyn couldn't help laughing. He neared her, spurred on by the crowd. Rhoslyn was sure he'd never enjoyed so much attention. It seemed his gaze locked onto hers.

He let out another loud bleat and tried to dodge right. Rhoslyn whirled and seized his tail. They tumbled through in the dirt in a tangle of fabric and spindly goat legs. He managed a kick to her thigh, and she gasped but held tight. Strong fingers closed around Rhoslyn's arm and she was yanked upright, coming face to face with St. Claire. The goat bleated and took off again, the dress now tangled in its horns.

"Now look what ye have done," Rhoslyn cried.

She broke free of St. Claire and lunged after the animal. The dress fluttered across his face, and he slowed. He was blinded by the fabric Rhoslyn realized with a thrill. She dodged left and grabbed for the dress but missed. The pounding of booted feet sounded close behind and St. Claire came into view running alongside her. He flashed a smile, then passed her with ease.

He was going to catch the goat—and with very little effort—after she had so worked hard to catch him! She ran faster, heart pounding. St. Claire reached the creature and grabbed the dress trailing from his horns. He would tear the dress, Rhoslyn realized with horror.

Mary must have agreed, for her shout of "Nay," went up behind them.

Rhoslyn reached them, and shoved St. Claire while they were still in motion. The dress whipped across her face in a stinging snap. She jammed her eyes shut and felt fingers seize her arm in the instant before she fell chest-to-chest on top of a hard body. The air rushed from her lungs and she struggled to drag in a breath.

Rhoslyn shoved upright to find herself straddling St. Claire's hips. She jerked her gaze onto his face and he lifted a brow. Heat flushed her cheeks. Muffled laughter caused her to look up. The crowd chasing the goat stood staring at them, knowing grins on each and every face. She swung her gaze back to St. Claire. He shrugged. Rhoslyn's heart pounded.

The bleating goat broke the quiet. She started to shove off St. Claire, but he grasped her waist and lifted her off. He sprang up and she staggered back a step as he sprinted after the goat. The crowd surged after him and Rhoslyn stumbled forward in their wake.

St. Claire reached the goat. Rhoslyn was sure the animal would elude St. Claire as he had her, but the goat darted left and St. Claire lunged and seized the horns. St. Claire dropped to his knees, bringing the goat down onto its side. He swung a leg over the goat, straddling him. The goat gave a loud bleat of protest, but St. Claire held him fast and began to untangle the fabric from its horns.

Rhoslyn and the crowd reached him as he pulled the last of the dress free, then rose and stepped away from the goat. The creature jumped to its feet and trotted off with a recriminating bleat.

Mary stepped forward and took the dress from St. Claire. "'Tis ruined," she wailed. "Ruined! I am to marry tomorrow, but now I have no wedding dress."

"Surely, it can be fixed?" he said.

Rhoslyn took the dress from Mary and examined it. The bodice gaped open clear to the waist, and the hem was torn in several spots where mud caked the fabric.

She shook her head. "Nay, the dress canna' be salvaged."

"I will kill that goat and make Christine pay for the dress," Mary snarled.

"Ye canna' blame Christine for what her goat did," a lad said.

"Aye, she can," a woman rebutted. "That goat is always causing trouble."

A murmur of agreement went up amongst the onlookers and Rhoslyn feared the crowd would recapture the goat and slaughter it on the spot.

"Leave the goat to me," St. Claire said. "And Lady Rhoslyn will replace the dress."

"She will?" Mary said, the surprise in her voice mirroring Rhoslyn's.

"What say you, Lady?" he asked.

"Aye," she said. "I will replace the dress, so long as ye agree to leave the goat be, Mary." The girl hesitated, and Rhoslyn added, "I must have your word, else you will wear your work dress when you wed."

The girl's lips pursed, but she nodded.

"And the rest of ye," Rhoslyn said. "Do you agree?"

A chorus of 'ayes' followed.

"Then I will speak with Christine. But she is old, and everyone know she loves that goat."

ONE MAN'S LONELINESS was another man's solitude. Talbot sat alone at the head of the largest table in the great hall. Laughter, music, and loud voices echoed off the walls of the great hall. The wedding celebration was a success—despite those that didn't accept him as the new lord of Castle Glenbarr. His own captain harbored a grudge. Baxter haunted the large hearth while nursing an ale.

Yet, Talbot had never felt more at peace.

Rhoslyn chatted with Ralf, Ingram, and their two companions near the far end of the table. Color had returned to her cheeks and her spirits seemed higher than they had been this morning during the wedding ceremony. Her red mane blazed in a weave of braids that hung past her shoulders. Her olive green, velvet dress befitted her station, but he recalled her grimy face and the dusty dress she'd worn when she chased the goat, and thought her just as beautiful then as now. When she'd straddled him her exquisite weight on his cock made him wish the villagers far away. That memory would keep him awake tonight.

He reached for his mug and took a drink as he watched Rhoslyn's mouth curve upward in a laugh. Ralf grinned back and her smile broadened. Talbot read no womanly wiles in the action, but couldn't help wishing she would smile at him with that much ease. But why would she? In the four days she'd known him, she'd been kidnapped by him *and* his brother, and Dayton had done far worse than move into her home.

In truth, had he considered for an instant that he might feel anything more than and perhaps affection for his wife he might have...might have what? Begged Seward not to marry her to another man—then wooed her? Nothing Talbot could have said would have changed the old man's mind. In fact, Talbot would have done the same were he in Seward's place.

He took another long draught of ale. Rhoslyn now spoke animatedly with the four men. Talbot recognized the male appreciation in Ralf's eyes. He couldn't see the other men's faces, but he wagered they found her just as enticing. Rhoslyn, however, seemed oblivious to their thoughts.

He half wished she had turned out to be the horse-faced woman he'd expected. A man had to choose his battles, and Lady Rhoslyn was the sort of battle he wasn't accustomed to fighting. She had already proven to be a distraction—and not just for him, by the looks of things. He chuckled. If he were to leave tomorrow with Ralf and Ingram, he would have to worry as much about who might bed his wife as he would about Dayton showing up at Castle Glenbarr to abduct her a second time.

His mood sobered. Ralf and Ingram had others searching for Dayton in their absence. Tomorrow, they would return to Stonehaven to continue the search themselves. Talbot had reminded himself a dozen times that going with them was out of the question. Aside from ensuring Rhoslyn's safety, he had yet to deal with consummating their marriage. A task that carried with it more than the weight of finalizing their union. He wanted her, and badly, but the taking would be far more perilous now that Dayton had wreaked his havoc.

The postern door opened and Talbot shifted his gaze to see Duncan Harper enter. Talbot expelled a slow breath. So the fox had returned to the henhouse. What kind of trouble might he stir up?

Duncan pushed his way through the crowd on a direct course for Rhoslyn as Baxter reached Talbot.

"You see Duncan Harper is here?" Baxter said.

Talbot nodded. "And he is going directly to Lady Rhoslyn."

Baxter sat in the chair to Talbot's right and refilled his goblet with ale from the pitcher in front of Talbot. Baxter hung an arm over the back of his chair and leaned into one corner.

"How are you enjoying your new home thus far?" he asked.

Talbot leveled his gaze on his captain. "If you cannot be civil to even me, then perhaps 'tis best you return to England. Edward, no doubt, would be pleased to have you lead his men."

Surprise flickered in Baxter's eyes, then he studied Talbot over the rim of his goblet as he took a drink. He settled the goblet on his thigh. "You would not manage so well without me."

"I am loathe to lose you, but I grow tired of your brooding."

"I am always brooding and you never complained before."

"But your foul moods never affected me directly—nor were they *directed* at me and mine."

Baxter nodded. "Nay, they were not." A moment of silence passed before Baxter said, "What do you think the weasel has in mind for your wife?"

WHEN DUNCAN STEPPED up beside Rhoslyn, she hoped St. Claire couldn't see the furrow of Duncan's brow and grim set of his mouth. If the knight was as intelligent as she thought, he was sure to recognize the trouble that brewed in Duncan's heart.

"I am relieved to see ye," he said without preamble.

Rhoslyn caught the raise of Ingram's brows and the glance that passed between him and Ralf. It wouldn't matter whether St. Claire had detected anything amiss. Ralf and Ingram would share their misgivings concerning her dead husband's cousin. The two Highlanders had taken to St. Claire as if they were long-lost brothers.

She introduced them and their companions to Duncan, then the four men took their leave. Duncan pulled her from the crowded area near the table to a quiet section of wall near the kitchen. Rhoslyn cast a glance at St. Claire. He'd been sitting at his place at the table, but he now stood, his back to her, talking with Sir Baxter and two guests.

"Fourteen months, Rhoslyn," Duncan said in a low voice masked by the revelry. "Have ye lost your mind?"

She probably had, and Duncan would be the one to point it out. "I lost a husband and child in a fortnight. I am only a woman. It was more than I could bear."

He gave her an appraising look. "Are you well? Did that English dog harm ye?"

She wasn't sure which 'English dog' he referred to, and had the distinct feeling his idea of harm wasn't the same as hers, but said, "I am well."

"I canna' see how with that devil as your husband."

"I am not the first Highland woman to marry an Englishman," she said.

"Aye, but that doesna' make it any less devilish," he shot back. "God's Blood, Rhoslyn, anyone would have been a better choice than him. *I* would have been a better choice."

"You?" she blurted.

"Dinna' look as if I sprouted horns. I may not be rich, but I managed Alec's affairs for twenty years. I managed Castle Glenbarr in your absence, and made as handsome a profit as you do. I am as good a man as Alec."

No, he wasn't.

"Ye never said a word," she said.

"How could I when ye ran off without a word. Why did you not tell me you were leaving—at least tell me where ye were going?"

A serving girl emerged from the kitchen and turned their way. Rhoslyn quieted. She glanced at St. Claire. He stood with two men, his back to her.

The maid passed, from earshot and Rhoslyn said to Duncan, "I didna' tell anyone I was leaving."

"Except your grandfather."

"Of course," she said peevishly. "If I simply disappeared, he would have turned the countryside over in search of me."

Duncan's mouth thinned. "And you think I didna' want to do that? I begged him to tell me where you were."

Rhoslyn was at a loss. This was insane. She had no idea he felt this way, and wanted to say it wouldn't have mattered. She wouldn't have married him, but good sense—and the strange fervor in his eyes—stopped her.

"It makes no difference. I am married."

His eyes narrowed. "Ye almost sound glad."

"'Tis simply the way of kings and men. I had no choice."

His gaze turned shrewd. "What would you do if ye could choose?"

"Sweet Jesu, Duncan. I willna' torture myself with useless questions."

He glanced around, then leaned closer despite the fact the nearest guests stood too far away to hear them speak above the din, and said, "If ye are no' happy, we can change things. Ye are married but a day. If St. Claire was gone, you could marry another man and no one would know—or care—if a babe was born nine months hence."

Rhoslyn realized with horror that he meant. "Are ye saying murder—"

"For God's sake, be quiet." He glanced around, then cupped her elbow and urged her along the wall to the hallway. He stopped after a few paces into the hall and swung her around to face him.

"Do you want to be rid of him or no'?"

"Have ye gone mad, Duncan?" But she realized insanity wasn't the sickness he suffered. "You would kill a man in order to be laird of Castle Glenbarr."

His face reddened in rage. "I served Alec faithfully all these years. I have more right than does St. Claire."

"More right to be my husband? Or more right to assume Alec's place, take his land and possessions as your own?"

"Ye have no reason to accuse me of being a power monger."

"Aye, I clearly have every reason, for a man who is willing to murder an innocent man—"

"Innocent?" he cut in. "St. Claire wasna' born innocent."

Rhoslyn scowled. "Sir Talbot has no' lifted a hand against even a dog here at Castle Glenbarr. Why do you hate him so? Is it because he is

English, or because he took what ye believe is rightfully yours?"

"Me hate him? Ye are the one who should hate him. He took possession of your home 'er he met you. He took what was rightfully *yours*. He has no right to Castle Glenbarr, or any of Alec's property—you included."

Rhoslyn stiffened. Even St. Claire hadn't treated her as mere property. "You go too far, Duncan."

"Do I? Alec coddled ye. Before that, your grandfather." He gave a harsh laugh. "He still coddles you, letting you run off as he did."

"You forget your place. You are no' my father *nor* my husband."

"Nay, for if I was, ye would not have run wild as you have all your life."

"Then I count myself fortunate not to be your wife."

"You prefer that English bastard over a Scot?" he snapped "Edward will tax us into poverty. Why do ye think Edward gave him Dunfrey Castle? Edward planned all along to marry him to you."

"Sweet God," she breathed. "Ye are insane. Edward could no' have known Alec would die. Edward has done what any king would have done by marrying me to one of his own. Our own leaders marry us to the English without thought for what we want—and some have taxed us into near poverty." A fact she conveniently ignored when she sequestered herself in St. Mary's. Duncan wasn't completely wrong on that score.

"Is that so?" he said. "I wager the men Edward forced to hand over control of their royal castles would no' agree that he is like any other king."

"What are ye talking about?" Rhoslyn demanded.

"While you were in that convent, the high and mighty King Edward declared himself Lord Parliament of Scotland and, only two months ago, ordered every Scottish royal castle be put under his control. Temporary, he said, but he has yet to return the castles to their rightful owners."

Rhoslyn stared, unable to speak.

"Ye think that was enough?" Duncan went on. "Nay. Every Scottish official is to resign his office and be re-appointed by Edward. Two days later, the Guardians and our leaders swore allegiance to Edward as Lord Parliament of all the Scots. But even that wasna' enough for the power hungry bastard. Only a month ago, he ordered all Scots to pay homage to him personally or at one of the designated centers. Your grandfather went."

"Grandfather?" she whispered.

Duncan nodded. "Now do ye still think Edward is doing what any other sovereign would do?"

She could find no reply.

"He has no right to rule us," Duncan hissed. "And St. Claire has no right to even a fistful of Scottish soil."

The feverish light in his eyes snapped her from her shock. "None of that means I will countenance murder."

His eyes narrowed. "Ye would side with St. Claire after everything I just told you?"

"I will side with honor," she shot back. "And I will not have *you* interfere in my business. I warn you, Duncan."

His mouth curved upward in disdain. "You pretend to be as hard as a man, but ye are still a woman."

"A woman who is capable of killing you. Dinna' doubt it."

He sneered. "What would Alec do if he were here?"

"He would kill ye for speaking to me this way—cousin or no."

"Alec understood the meaning of loyalty."

Rhoslyn nodded. "Aye, and you show no loyalty to me or Alec by threating my husband. I warn ye, Duncan, if so much as a hair on St. Claire's head is harmed, I will not ask any questions. I will kill you. And, in case ye might wonder, my grandfather will bury your remains."

Chapter Eleven

〜

RHOSLYN WHIRLED AND hurried from the hallway into the great hall. Her mind raced. Her grandfather had said nothing about swearing fealty to King Edward—or any of the other recent political changes. He had taken an even greater chance than she'd realized by trying to marry her to Jacobus. If Edward learned that Baron Kinsley had conspired behind his back, he would imprison him.

She paused, scanned the crowded room, and spotted her grandfather near the small hearth on the left wall where a minstrel played a harp. She brushed through the crowd, but stopped when she came face to face with Lady Davina.

"Lady Rhoslyn, at last we have a chance to speak with you." She startled Rhoslyn by pulling her into a hug, then drew back and surveyed her. "Ye look drawn. Are you well?"

Rhoslyn knew what she meant was, 'What did Dayton St. Claire do to you?'

She hadn't missed the looks Davina and other woman had cast her way throughout the evening. The other three ladies in her group murmured their agreement that she looked tired, and Rhoslyn replied, "A wedding and celebration in less than two days is taxing."

"'Tis more than the work." A knowing light entered Davina's eyes. "We heard what happened. For a man whose brother is challenging his marriage, Sir Talbot seems oddly at ease."

"Lies," Rhoslyn replied. "If Dayton's claim had any substance, he would be here under the authority of Edward. Sir Talbot has the written command from his king that he and I are married." In truth, Rhoslyn was relieved to have gotten St. Claire instead of his brother, but to hear the words from her own mouth tightened the knot in her stomach. She couldn't, however, let these women see her fear. She shrugged. "Dayton is jealous of his brother and thought to use me as a pawn." All the truth, and easily deduced.

"But he was alone with ye for a day," Davina said.

Spiteful bitch, Rhoslyn fumed. It wasn't the villagers who spread malicious rumors, but those of her own social station.

Rhoslyn frowned as if confused. "What are ye saying, Davina?"

"I am saying nothing," she replied. "I understand the way of things. King Edward betrothed you to Sir Talbot, and ye canna' ignore his command, nor can Sir Talbot. But not everyone knows you as I do. If a child is born nine months from now—"

"If a child is born nine months from now, that will only prove that St. Claire is a lusty man," Rhoslyn cut in.

The other women tittered and Davina lifted her brows. "He is a bonny man. I can well believe he is lusty."

A nervous flutter skittered across Rhoslyn's insides. He was her husband in the eyes of the law and God, and could exercise his husbandly rights anytime he pleased, which meant she would soon learn just how lusty he was. She had known no other man save her husband. And Dayton St. Claire, she realized with a jolt. The weight of his body on hers as he shoved inside her suddenly pressed down on her as it had three days ago.

"Rhoslyn?" Davina said.

Davina's face snapped back into focus.

"Ye looked as if you were somewhere else." Davina exchanged a knowing glance with the other ladies. "You were no' by chance remembering how *vigorous* your husband is?" Heat flooded Rhoslyn's cheeks and before she could form a response, Davina added, "In truth, no one will dare gainsay the Dragon's word, so it will not matter when your babe is born. In fact, the sooner the better."

"Dinna' call him the Dragon," Rhoslyn snapped, then whirled, *the sooner the better* ringing in her ears. She steered around a crowd and halted when she nearly collided with Lady Elizabeth Broune. Rhoslyn blinked, startled to see her old friend.

"Elizabeth," she blurted.

"Dinna' look so pleased to see me," Elizabeth said.

Under normal circumstances, Rhoslyn would have been ecstatic to see Elizabeth. But she hadn't seen her since Dougal's birth. Aside from her grandfather, Elizabeth was the person who knew her best. There would be no hiding from Elizabeth what had happened with Dayton.

"I-I am very pleased to see ye," Rhoslyn said. "I am surprised, is all. What are ye doing in Buchan?"

"Iain had business. I came so that my son could visit my parents."

"Son?" Rhoslyn repeated. A pang of sadness pierced her heart, but she said, "That is wonderful. How old is he?"

"Almost six months now." Elizabeth's expression sobered. "I am sorry about Dougal, Rhoslyn. I never had a chance to tell ye."

Leave it to Elizabeth to address a mother's concern before worrying about being married off by an English king. Might Elizabeth obtain the pennyroyal for her? Elizabeth had been her most trusted friend her entire life. If there was anyone she could trust… Nay. She loved Elizabeth like a sister, but this was a confidence that even a sister might betray.

A whisper rose from the darkest regions of her mind, *She will remind you that you are murdering your baby.*

Elizabeth's attention shifted past Rhoslyn, and Rhoslyn started when she entwined her arm with Rhoslyn's. Elizabeth cast her a curious glance, then led her past a group of guests. A serving girl passed and Elizabeth stopped her and took two mugs of wine from her tray.

She passed one to Rhoslyn, then took a sip of hers before saying, "Why did ye leave without saying goodbye?"

"Because you were far away up north and I was too grief stricken to think clearly."

Elizabeth nodded. "You could have told your grandfather to at least tell me where ye were. I would have written."

"I was no' allowed correspondence. Only my grandfather could communicate with me."

Elizabeth dipped her head to take another sip of wine, but not before Rhoslyn caught the hurt in her friend's eyes. "What would you have done?" Rhoslyn demanded. "Have ye any idea what is it like to lose a husband and a son in a fortnight?"

"Nay."

"Then ye cannot judge me harshly."

Wasn't that what everyone was doing, judging her? Andreana, Duncan, Elizabeth, probably even her grandfather. He must believe if she hadn't stayed away so long, she wouldn't now be married to St. Claire.

"Forgive me," Elizabeth said. "I didna' mean it that way."

Guilt rolled over Rhoslyn. She'd known Elizabeth her entire life. They'd seldom had more than a childish squabble. Elizabeth was one of the kindest women she knew.

"What of your new husband?" Elizabeth said. "I have yet to meet him."

Rhoslyn shrugged. "He is English."

"Is he terrible?"

Rhoslyn looked toward the head of the table, where St. Claire and Baxter sat in conversation. "See for yourself." She nodded in his direction.

Elizabeth turned. "Sweet Jesu. He is very large and very…handsome."

Frustration pricked. "So everyone keeps saying."

Elizabeth's attention returned to her. "Is he cruel?"

Rhoslyn barked a laugh. "Do ye call kidnapping cruel?"

"Are you speaking of his brother?" She laid a hand on Rhoslyn's arm. "Did he harm you?"

"I am well," she said too quickly.

It seemed as if Elizabeth would comment, but to Rhoslyn's relief, she nodded.

"I must speak with my grandfather," Rhoslyn said.

The hurt returned to Elizabeth's eyes. "Mayhap we can talk tomorrow? I will be here for another week. 'Tis fortunate I was here. I would no' have known of your wedding celebration, otherwise."

"I told St. Claire there was little time for anyone to attend, but he was determined to hold the celebration immediately."

Elizabeth smiled. "Men do like to have their way."

"Some more than others," Rhoslyn muttered.

Elizabeth frowned. "What has he done, Rhoslyn?"

"Nothing." And it was true. He'd done nothing—nothing terrible, that was. Aside from waylaying her when she'd fled the convent, he had been kind and even caring. She would rather he had been someone she could dislike. Someone like his brother, perhaps. A chill crept up her spine. Nay, not like Dayton. There was a difference in disliking a man and hating one.

"I must speak with my grandfather. It was good to see ye, Elizabeth." Rhoslyn turned and pushed through the guests milling about the middle of the room. Her grandfather still stood where she'd last seen him. When she reached his side, he stopped talking and turned to her with a raised eyebrow.

She greeted his companions, then said to him, "Have ye a minute to speak with me?"

"Aye." He nodded to the men and they left.

Rhoslyn drew him to the other side of the hearth, a little ways away from the musicians. With the music playing and the laughter and gaiety surrounding them, there was little chance of being overheard.

She leaned close and said, "You didna' tell me that ye swore fealty to King Edward a month ago."

He shrugged. "So?"

"If he discovers you defied him, you will end up in an English prison."

Her grandfather snorted. "I did not succeed. He will warn me no' to try such a thing again."

"What better reason to seize your wealth than because ye disobeyed a royal command?" She shook her head. "And you call me naive."

He released a heavy sigh. "Leave it be, Rhoslyn. What is done is done. I would have done it one way or another. I did no' want ye to marry St. Claire."

"Ye certainly have accepted him," she said.

"Fate favored him. At the very least, he does protect his own, and ye are his. I can hope for the best."

"The best?" she repeated. "Has Edward returned ownership of Banmore Castle to ye?"

"Aye. As well as all my other estates."

"What of our nobles? Duncan told me Edward has yet to return ownership of their castles."

"That is true of many," he replied. "But Edward married you to St. Claire, and it was good business for him to ingratiate himself into my graces."

"He is only grabbing power."

"Aye, as are Bruce and Wallace."

"But they want power for Scotland.'

"And themselves," he said. She opened her mouth to rebut, but he stopped her. "Aye, they are our nobles and have Scotland's interest at heart, certainly more than Edward. But they are working hand in hand with him. They fought amongst themselves like children. Someone had to step in and bring order. He made more progress in these last months than our leaders have in a year."

Rhoslyn couldn't believe her ears. "Ye sound as if you agree with him."

"I agree with putting someone on the throne in Edinburgh. Not Edward," he said quickly. "You underestimate our leaders, Rhoslyn. Do ye think they will let Edward dictate to them any more than I did when he ordered me to marry you to St. Claire?"

"Lot of good your rebellion did," she muttered.

"Luck was not with us. Though how St. Claire knew ye were on your way I canna' say. Did he say how he knew?"

She shook her head. "Nay. I would like to know that, as well."

Her grandfather grunted. "I wouldna' be surprised to learn he made a pact with the devil."

"Just as you did with Edward," Rhoslyn said.

"Dinna' fash yourself over Edward, Granddaughter. Once he has settled the matter of the true successor to the crown, we will deal with him."

"And how will you deal with my English husband?" she demanded.

"You really dinna' know?" he asked.

Her pulse jumped. Was he in league with Duncan? "Ye cannot mean murder?" she said in a low voice.

He laughed. "I would consider it, but, nay. There is a simpler way."

"And that is?"

"Fire up his Scottish blood."

Rhoslyn stared. "*That* is your plan?"

"Scotland is a siren, and no Scot can resist her song."

"God save us," she muttered.

Before Rhoslyn could say more, she spied St. Claire. He stood now, casually looking down at Lady Isobel Herbert, and still managed to radiate danger. Rhoslyn wondered if it was the shoulders that filled out the mid-thigh length surcoat he wore, but realized it wouldn't matter whether he wore chainmail or lawn. St. Claire didn't look dangerous. He *was* dangerous.

Isobel laughed at something he said and laid a hand on his arm. Rhoslyn's gaze riveted onto her fingers, small and elegant on the sleeve of his shirt. St. Claire seemed not to notice her touch, but Rhoslyn knew he did. He noticed everything. Yet he didn't step away.

"Ye had best beware, Granddaughter," her grandfather said. "Women like Lady Isobel have no compunctions about warming a married man's bed."

"I never had to worry about such things with Alec." She silently cursed the tremble in her voice. What was wrong with her?

"Alec was no young man," her grandfather said.

Neither was Isobel's husband, which was one reason she had no qualms about seeking her pleasure elsewhere.

"I would no' give St. Claire a reason to bed another woman," her grandfather said.

"Men like him do no' need a reason."

"Ye canna' condemn a man for being a man, nor can you condemn him before he has committed the crime."

"He is not rejecting her advances," Rhoslyn said.

He unexpectedly looked up from Isobel and met Rhoslyn's gaze. He said something to Isobel, then started toward Rhoslyn. Her heart pounded. She felt Isobel's eyes on her and returned the woman's bold appraisal. Rhoslyn thought she discerned a slight smile on her face and was startled when jealousy stabbed at her. St. Claire approached and Rhoslyn caught sight of his stare.

Her grandfather leaned close and whispered. "Does the man ever simply look at a body?"

Rhoslyn wondered the same thing. It seemed as if his eyes pierced to her very soul.

He stopped in front of Rhoslyn. "Seward." He nodded at her grandfather, then said to her, "I am pleased to finally see you, Lady Rhoslyn."

"I have been here all evening," she said.

"Aye, but you have been so busy with the guests, we have had no time together."

That had been her plan.

"You look beautiful."

From the corner of her eye, she saw her grandfather's brows raise. Warmth crept up her cheeks. Alec had told her she was beautiful. No, not beautiful. Lovely.

"Thank ye," she said.

"Will you sit with me?" He didn't wait for an answer, but said to her grandfather, "Forgive me, Seward, but I have had no time with my wife."

"I can remedy that problem." Her grandfather grasped Rhoslyn's arm. "Come along, St. Claire."

Her heart jumped at the thought that he meant to announce that they were leaving the party to consummate the marriage. "Grandfather." She choked out the word, then nearly sagged when he started away from the staircase that led to the upper floors. Seconds later, he veered around a group of women with St. Claire at his side, and she realized he was headed toward the musicians.

"Grandfather," she said under her breath. "Ye will make a spectacle of

St. Claire."

They reached the musicians and Rhoslyn pulled free of him. "I am too busy for this nonsense."

Her grandfather nodded to the man playing the lute, then leaned close to him and whispered something. The musician continued to play, then nodded when her grandfather straightened.

He turned to them and said over the music. "Do ye dance the reel, St. Claire?"

"Of course, he doesna' dance the reel," Rhoslyn cut in. "He is not a Scot."

"We do dance the reel in England," St. Claire said.

Rhoslyn looked at him in horror. "Do you realize what ye are saying? My grandfather intends us to dance."

"'Tis tradition for the newlyweds to dance during the wedding celebration," her grandfather said. "And St. Claire said he hasna' had any time with ye."

"Dancing is not spending time together," she snapped.

Her grandfather lifted a brow. "Ye prefer to retire to your husband's bedchambers?"

"Mind your own business, Grandfather."

The music ended and the musicians struck up a reel.

"There is no sense in fighting," St. Claire said. "It is best we follow tradition." He extended his right arm and Rhoslyn wanted to box his ears.

"We canna' dance just the two of us," she said.

"Others will join once you begin," her grandfather said.

She shot him a fulminating glance before placing her hand on St. Claire's arm. He led her forward, and the guests parted. He stopped, took two steps away from her, then bowed as if he truly was in King Edward's court. Rhoslyn curtsied, then rose as he grasped her fingers in time with the music. He surprised her by turning in a tight circle, then gliding gracefully to the left. St. Claire released her and they danced several steps right as if skirting other dancers. Guests took the hint and three couples joined them, Lady Isobel being one of the ladies.

Rhoslyn stepped back from St. Claire and the women fell into line alongside her with the men opposite. Lady Isobel, Rhoslyn noticed, had placed herself at the far end where, Rhoslyn estimated she would pair with St. Claire for a dance down the center of the other dancers.

They all danced forward to within inches of one another, then back. Rhoslyn glided to the middle where the man to her opposite left met her and grasped her fingers as they turned a tight circle. The ladies faced one another and bobbed around each other, back to back in a circle, then fell back into line. The men did the same and Rhoslyn caught St. Claire's eye. A corner of his mouth ticked up and he shrugged. She couldn't help a laugh and the smile reached his eyes.

A nervous flutter skittered across the inside of her stomach. This man was the Dragon. The dragon Duncan said would aid his king in bleeding Scotland dry. The same dragon who only this afternoon chased a goat and rescued a peasant's wedding dress. Rhoslyn startled at the unexpected memory of his hips between her thighs when she'd straddled him.

Her stomach flipped as the men fell into line. St. Claire and Lady Isobel stepped back on opposite sides when the rest of the dancers clasped hands and began circling. From the corner of her eye, Rhoslyn glimpsed Isobel's gaze pinned on St. Claire. Ire whipped through her. She took a step too wide, causing the dancer to her right to stumble. The woman righted herself, and they came to a stop full circle, then separated into two lines.

St. Claire grasped Isobel's hand and they skipped down the center of the aisle formed by the other dancers. Isobel looked up at him from beneath her lashes as they separated in front of Rhoslyn and the man opposite her. Isobel's gaze remained on him. Rhoslyn stuck out her foot beneath Isobel's swirling skirts. Isobel pitched forward with a cry. St. Claire whirled amidst screams and scooped her up before she hit the floor. The other dancers rushed to surround them as Isobel wilted against him. St. Claire started toward the nearest table.

"Are ye all right?" one woman asked.

"Poor thing," Margery Kincaid said. "That was well done, Sir Talbot. She would have had a nasty fall if no' for ye."

Rhoslyn stared, stunned at her actions, and furious with Isobel—and St. Claire—all in one. What had gotten into her? A woman brushed past her and hurried after the group. Rhoslyn forced her legs into motion and followed. St. Claire stopped at one of the tables. Isobel looked like a small, fragile bundle in his arms. Her sky blue dress a soft contrast against his frame. He surely couldn't help but notice the dainty fingers that fisted his shirt.

He lowered her into a chair, but she shook her head and clung to him. Rhoslyn rolled her eyes. Isobel was acting as if he had saved her from falling off a cliff instead of a tumble to the floor. He settled her on the chair, but she didn't release his surcoat and he was forced to crouch beside her. He pulled back and she looked at him with tear stained eyes.

Rhoslyn hurried to the far end of the table where sat pitchers of ale. She filled a mug, then pushed through the crowd gathered around Isobel and St. Claire.

Rhoslyn wanted nothing more than to splash the ale in Isobel's face, but instead, thrust the mug toward the hand that gripped her husband's shirt.

"Drink," she ordered.

As expected, Isobel released St. Claire and reflexively grasped the mug with both hands. St Claire rose and Isobel's gaze jerked up to Rhoslyn, eyes stormy. Recognition flickered and the pique vanished.

"Thank ye, Lady Rhoslyn." She took a tiny sip of ale and Rhoslyn had to refrain from rolling her eyes.

St. Claire stepped back and the ladies closed ranks around Isobel, cooing as if she'd been snatched from death's door. Rhoslyn turned and found St. Claire beside her. He slid an arm around her waist and started walking. Rhoslyn hoped he couldn't hear the pounding of her heart.

"Are ye sure Lady Isobel will be all right?" Rhoslyn asked.

"She is well tended by the ladies," he replied.

Rhoslyn snorted. "The ladies' attention isna' what she wants."

"What does she want?" he asked.

"Dinna' be naive," Rhoslyn said.

"She does like the attention of men," he commented.

"And they do no' mind," she shot back.

"Lady Rhoslyn, you sound jealous."

"Jealous? Bah! I am sickened by such behavior. This is our wedding celebration, yet she fawned over ye as if you were a stable boy for the taking."

"I would not go that far. Though I am pleased you remember this is our wedding celebration." He navigated around a cluster of men. "Did your cousin remember that as well?"

Rhoslyn snapped her head up to meet his gaze. "What?"

St. Claire looked down at her. "Did he wish you well in your marriage?"

"He isna' happy with the match." There was no use denying the obvious.

"He was not happy when I forced him to vacate Glenbarr Castle," St. Claire replied.

Rhoslyn stopped walking. "Ye forced him to leave? This has been his home for twenty years."

"Would you have me keep an adder in my home?"

What had Duncan done to reveal his true feelings to St. Claire?

"You are very free with calling my home yours," she said.

"Our home, then. Would you rather he lived here at Castle Glenbarr?"

The truth was, she wouldn't. She had never been overly pleased to have Duncan living with them when Alec was alive. But, as he'd said, he'd helped manage Alec's affairs. Given his hostility toward St. Claire, she would have send him on his way if St. Claire hadn't.

"He would no' be happy," she said.

St. Claire started forward again. He pulled Rhoslyn close and squeezed between two groups of men. "I imagine he would like to kill me."

Rhoslyn stumbled. His hold around her waist tightened and she caught herself.

"Are you all right?" he asked.

"Aye."

"I hit the mark, then?" he said.

"Hit the mark?"

"Duncan wants to kill me."

It wasn't a question. The man was too discerning. "If ye suddenly died, he would no' shed a tear." Rhoslyn caught sight of Andreana seated at the main trestle table and surrounded by several of St. Claire's men. "I told ye that I didna' want your men taking up with my women. That includes Andreana. A pack of your dogs have her cornered."

He slowed and his gaze shifted to the group. Rhoslyn expected him to shrug off her concerns, but his eyes darkened and he steered them toward the group.

They reached her, and the men stepped back.

St. Claire released Rhoslyn, and said to the men, "You have better things to do than speak with Lady Andreana. Remember that in the future."

The men scattered. Rhoslyn sat on the bench beside Andreana. St. Claire sat beside Rhoslyn. She glanced sharply at him, then turned her attention to Andreana.

"You should no' be spending time with St. Claire's men."

St. Claire began pouring ale into three mugs. Discomfort sent a ripple of awareness along Rhoslyn's arm when his arm brushed hers.

"They were only talking to me," Andreana said. "We sat in plain sight of all your guests."

St. Claire set ale in front of Rhoslyn, then Andreana. "Your mother is right."

Andreana frowned. "They did nothing untoward."

"Aye, they did," he said. "They know it is improper to approach you. Not a one of them is in a position to win your affections."

"Because they are mere knights?" she asked.

He laughed. "Most are not even knights, Lady. They are simple men-at-arms. They should not deign to look in your direction."

"There are some who say the same of you and Lady Rhoslyn."

"Andreana," Rhoslyn cut in, but St. Claire interrupted.

"When a king bestows land upon one of them and then betroths him to you, I will agree he is worthy."

Andreana frowned.

"You will not encourage them," Rhoslyn said. "Do you understand?"

"I gave them no encouragement."

"A smile is encouragement enough for any man," St Claire said.

His mouth twitched with amusement and he looked at Rhoslyn. She smiled before realizing the reaction and his smile broadened.

He returned his attention to Andreana. "A simple smile, my lady. Nothing more is needed."

Chapter Twelve

I T WAS TRUE. A woman's smile was enough to encourage a man to commit even murder. Tonight, however, Talbot was fortunate that Lady Rhoslyn's smile had simply haunted him, which was enough to make him once again curse his brother to hell. If Talbot knew where Dayton was, he would ride an entire month to lay hands on him, then kill him. Talbot gave a private laugh. It would seem her smile had incited him to murder after all.

The reverie showed no signs of abating as Rhoslyn disappeared into the kitchen. She remained animated and busy, clearly intent upon staying up until the very last guest retired. But Talbot recognized the fatigue in the corners of her eyes and knew he was the reason she hadn't sought her bedchambers.

He wondered if she might try to avoid the hunt tomorrow and sleep while he hunted with the guests. That he wouldn't allow. Neither would he allow her to be so exhausted she fell from her horse.

Talbot finished the last of the wine he was drinking, then rose. He skirted the guests until he reached the kitchen, and went inside. The bustle in the room came to a halt and Rhoslyn looked up from the platter she was filling with meat.

Her brow furrowed. "Is there something ye need, St. Claire?"

"Aye." He came to her side and cupped her elbow. "It is time we retired, Lady Rhoslyn."

Her eyes widened, then her brows dove down in ire. Talbot easily guessed she wanted to tell him to go to the devil, but she was a highborn lady, and such ladies didn't bare their feelings before servants…feelings that included the memory of a man who had violated her days before.

Mistress Muira entered from the pantry. She took the room in at a glance, then said in a clipped voice, "Back to work, lasses."

The room jumped to life and Talbot plucked a piece of pork off the plate Rhoslyn had been filling and popped it into his mouth.

"Are ye hungry, St. Claire?" she asked.

"Nay. It just smelled too good to resist." He shifted his gaze onto her. "Like you, my lady."

To his surprise—and satisfaction—a pretty blush crept up her cheeks.

"Ye may go to your bedchambers, if you like," she said. "I will join you there later. We have many guests still celebrating. I must see to them."

Talbot poured a cup of wine from a pitcher. "You must see to them?"

"Of course. It is my duty."

He emptied the glass and sat it on the counter. Then he pulled her close. Her head snapped up and Talbot bent and brushed his lips across hers in a gentle kiss. When he pulled back her eyes smoldered with fury.

"Come along, Lady Rhoslyn. Mistress Muira is capable of handling kitchen tasks." He looked at the older woman.

"Aye, laird. I have things in hand."

"Please send up wine to my chambers, Mistress." Arm still around Rhoslyn, he led her across the room to the servants' stairs.

He caught the furtive glance she cast at the women who, though bustling about their business, kept one eye on her. They reached the stairs and he urged her ahead of him. She marched up the stairs. Aye, he would never have to guess what this woman was thinking. There was some comfort in that knowledge.

Minutes later, they reached his chambers and she whirled on him. "What sort of barbarian are ye to maul me like that in front of the servants?"

He closed the door with a soft click. "Forgive me if I embarrassed you, my lady. I thought it best we assure everyone our marriage is not affected by your kidnapping."

She frowned. "Ye could have said something."

"Servants, maids in particular, can hear through stone walls," he said. "I could not chance any of them overhearing."

"There was no need for us to retire so early."

"Early?" He lifted a brow. "Dawn is but three hours away."

"Oh," she said.

She stood as if rooted to the spot, and he had the suspicion she would stand there all night if it meant they didn't have to share a bed.

A rap sounded on the door. Talbot put a finger to his lips and hurried across the room to the bed. He sat down and called "Enter," as he began tugging off a boot.

A maid entered with a pitcher and two mugs. She set them on the small table near the hearth, then hurried out.

"Would you pour us some wine, Lady Rhoslyn?" he asked as the door clicked shut.

She remained frozen for a moment, then jerked into motion and crossed to the table. A moment later, she appeared beside him and extended a goblet. He dropped his second boot on the floor and took the wine. Rhoslyn took a quick step back and then crossed to the window. She opened the shutter and gazed outside.

"It is a beautiful night," he said.

"Aye," she replied, her voice wistful.

Talbot wondered how receptive she would be tonight if not for Dayton. He finished the last of his wine, set the goblet on the table beside the bed, then stood and unfastened his belt. He tossed it onto the bed, then pulled off his surcoat. Rhoslyn glanced his way, but said nothing. His shirt and undershirt followed, and she finally faced him.

Her gaze shifted to the markings on his right arm.

"How old was your sister when she died?"

"Fourteen," he replied.

"I am sorry. How did she die?"

"A fever." He crossed to the table with the wine and refilled his goblet.

She joined him and he froze when she lifted a hand and traced a finger over the picture of his sister on his arm. Her light touch sent a skitter of gooseflesh along his skin.

"It is so smooth," she said. "The skin isna' marred at all." She looked up at him. "It is as if the picture is a part of you."

"It is," he replied.

She stared for a moment before tearing her gaze from his and taking two steps back. "I have no sisters or brothers," she said. "It canna' be easy to lose a loved one."

"You lost two loved ones."

She nodded and took a sip of wine. "How long ago did your sister die?"

"Ten years," he replied.

Her eyes lifted to his face over the rim of her goblet "Do ye ever forget?"

"Nay. But the pain does ease."

"The shock has subsided," she said as if speaking to herself.

"That is a start," Talbot said.

"Do you still miss her?"

"Aye." More often than he liked to admit. Talbot finished his wine in two big gulps and set the goblet on the table. He went to the door that adjoined the solar. "I will see you in the morning, Lady Rhoslyn."

She frowned. "Where are you going?"

"To sleep in your bed."

"But I thought..." She glanced at the bed, then frowned. "Are you going to leave your clothes strewn about your room?"

He shrugged. "What better way to make your maids think we were occupied with consummating the marriage?"

"But they will see my mussed bed." Her mouth twitched in amusement. "St. Claire, you willna' get a wink of sleep in my bed."

"Why is that?"

"Because ye are very large—too large to sleep comfortably in my bed." Her amusement vanished and he was startled when pain flared in her eyes. That emotion, too, disappeared as quickly as it had come, and she said, "Mayhap I should sleep in my own bed."

Talbot recalled the cradle that had occupied a corner of the room when he'd arrived and remembered thinking the room had seemed oddly unused. Suddenly he understood. The babe had died in this room. In all likelihood, her husband had taken his last breath in that bed. How in God's name was he to bed a wife in the very room where she had lost husband and son? How did a man bed his wife after his brother had raped her?

"As you wish," he said. "Sleep in your own bed."

She crossed to the door connecting to their private solar, then stopped and looked at him.

He nodded in the direction of the door. "Go, Lady. Rest well."

Her brows drew down in uncertainty.

Talbot met her gaze steadily. "I may be English, but I am no barbarian."

RHOSLYN AWOKE TO a tap on her door. She burrowed deeper into the bedding. The door opened and she discerned the light pad of feet on the stone floor, then the carpet. The scrape of metal across stone followed, and she yawned at realizing one of the maids was tending the fire, which meant it was morning. She didn't want to rise, but cracked open an eye anyway. Today was the hunt, which meant she couldn't dally in bed. She looked through the open curtain at the foot of the bed, surprised the curtain was open. Hadn't she pulled it closed last night?

Alana tossed two logs on the embers, then rose and faced the bed. She smiled, her gaze moving to Rhoslyn's right. Rhoslyn followed her eyes and started at seeing St. Claire beneath the covers, his exposed back to her. For an instant she could only stare at the broad expanse of muscled flesh, beautiful, despite the scars, then Alana giggled and Rhoslyn jerked her gaze onto the girl. She grinned, then scampered from the room. When the door closed, Rhoslyn braced her feet against St. Claire's back and shoved.

"You will have to push harder than that to shove me out of bed."

His deep voice, gravelly from sleep, startled her, and she froze, her feet still flat against his back.

"What are ye doing in my bed?" she demanded. "You gave me the scare of my life."

"A bigger scare than the night I grabbed you from your horse as you fled your convent?"

Ire flared. Rhoslyn shoved at his back with all her might, but it was as if she pushed a stone wall. She grunted with the effort.

"A little lower, Lady Rhoslyn. You were right. This bed is too small. I have a kink here." He shifted his hips.

Rhoslyn gave a frustrated growl and shoved harder—to no avail—then shoved the curtain aside on her side of the bed and leapt to her feet. "Are ye insane?"

He rolled onto his back and shoved his hands behind his head. Her breath caught at sight of his chest. Feather light hair trailed from his belly button to disappear beneath the blanket at his hips. Even in the shadows of the curtained bed, she could discern the ripple of muscle across his stomach. Alec hadn't looked like that.

She yanked her gaze onto his face. "I thought ye were going to sleep in your own bed."

"I did. But early this morning I crawled into bed with you. It will not do for the servants to talk about how we spent our wedding night apart."

Her mind whirled with the thought of a true wedding night with this man. The long, hard length of him beneath her bottom when he'd held her on his lap at the inn was just a hint of what she could expect. He would be nothing like Alec. Her husband had been kind, gentle, and...and what? Not young, like St. Claire, that much was certain. Guilt and shock dropped in the pit of her stomach like lead.

"Ye didna' say anything last night about getting into my bed," she said.

He shrugged and Rhoslyn was torn between wanting to box his ears and wanting to stroke the markings on his arm again. She hadn't forgotten how the muscled arm felt beneath her fingers. Her gaze shifted of its own volition to his right arm where his sister's face was visible above the blanket.

Then her mind came to a screeching halt at the realization that his sister's face reminded her of someone.

THEY RODE OUT of Castle Glenbarr two hours later, a company of forty-five people and two hounds. A company befitting a king. Twenty of St. Claire's guardsmen surrounded them. Six spearmen, five archers, one kennel master, her grandfather, eight guests, Andreana, St. Claire, and Rhoslyn. The dogs barked excitedly and the guests called to one another above the tramp of horses' hooves.

She had never been on so fine a hunt, and wished she wasn't on one today.

She, St. Claire, and her grandfather led the hunt, along with Lord Kinnon, riding at St. Claire's right. She cast a furtive glance at St. Claire, who talked in low tones with the earl. He sat straight in the saddle as if born to it, which he probably had been. The chevaler strapped to his side and the bow slung over his back seemed almost a natural part of him. She could easily envision him pulling an arrow from the quiver tied to his saddle and felling a large buck before her grandfather could let fly his own arrow.

Years of training had refined his lean frame into a wall of muscle so that his shoulders looked impossibly broad in his red and gold jerkin. His shirt sleeves couldn't hide the play of muscle in his arms. Rhoslyn unexpectedly recalled the strength of those arms around her when she rode with him on the way home from Stonehaven. Heat rippled through her at the memory of her bare bottom across his thighs—and his hard length flush against her thigh. He hadn't acted upon his lust, as too many men would have.

A mental picture of Dayton St. Claire poised over her intruded upon the recollection. Her stomach knotted. Lust hadn't driven him, at least not lust for her. Greed was what hardened his cock. A wave of revulsion pitched her stomach.

Rhoslyn gazed left, at trees that blanketed the hills ahead. St. Mary's lay east, beyond the trees. How she longed to return. Frustration surfaced. The herb garden at the convent was Abbess Beatrice's pride. There, Rhoslyn could find pennyroyal in abundance. Shame caused her to lower her head. God would surely punish her for thinking of using anything at the convent to end her child's life. And if Abbess Beatrice could read her thoughts…

"Is something amiss, Lady Rhoslyn?"

Rhoslyn started at the sound of St. Claire's voice. The baying of the dogs and murmur of conversation brought her back to the present and she looked at him. He stared, brows drawn in concern.

"Nay," she said. "Should something be wrong?"

"You appeared deep in thought."

She shrugged. His gaze sharpened and she felt certain he thought she was mimicking his annoying habit of shrugging when asked a question. Her mouth twitched with an unbidden smile, but she managed to restrain the impulse. He lifted a brow. Rhoslyn shrugged again, then returned her attention straight ahead. From the corner of her eye, she saw him study her for a moment before returning his attention to Lord Kinnon.

"I hear the rebellions in Wales are spreading," Lord Kinnon said. "Does Edward plan another campaign there?"

"Edward does not confide in me, but I doubt it," St. Claire said. "The uprisings are not serious."

Lord Kinnon grunted. "I suppose he is busy enough as arbiter and Sovereign of Scotland."

"I imagine so," St. Claire replied. "He has no easy task in that regard."

"Edward knows what he is doing. He will choose wisely."

Her grandfather snorted, but said nothing. Rhoslyn easily read his thoughts. By 'choose wisely' Lord Kinnon meant 'John Balliol.' Lord Kinnon was a supporter of Balliol, and she suspected he hoped to become one of St. Claire's newest and closest friends in order to ingratiating himself into Edward—and Balliol's—good graces.

"What think you of Edward as Sovereign of Scotland, Lady Rhoslyn?" St. Claire asked.

She jerked her head in his direction. He stared, eyes intense—as always—but she detected something in his expression. Rhoslyn blinked. Was that mischief? It was. What trouble did he intend to make? Then the truth dawned. He, too, suspected Lord Kinnon was a Balliol supporter, and he knew she wasn't.

"I think Edward would be wise to stay in England and leave Scotland to sort out her own problems," she said.

"A dream, Lady Rhoslyn," Lord Kinnon interjected. "Our leaders quarrel amongst themselves to the point that we canna' decide who will lead in a single battle."

"I imagine Wallace or Bruce would decide that without hesitation," she said. "And our squabbling doesna' mean an English king should be dictating to us."

"Have ye a better idea?" he asked.

"Anything would be better than English interference." She thought of Duncan and was glad he wasn't here to hear her echo his words.

"Anything?" St. Claire interjected.

She met his gaze squarely. "Aye."

"I suppose, then, I should be thankful my mother was Scottish."

Rhoslyn couldn't believe her ears… Everyone knew he never spoke of his mother, and considered himself every inch an Englishman, not a Scot.

"No' Scottish," her grandfather corrected, "a Scot. Ye didna' say anything about being a Scot when Edward gave ye Dunfrey Castle. You flew the English banner—even at the Highland Games."

"Where I believe I won every match I competed in," St. Claire replied mildly.

Rhoslyn hadn't attended the games that year, for Andreana had been ill and Rhoslyn refused to leave her side. But for months afterward, stories were told of St. Claire's prowess as a soldier and his loyalty to his king…and, she recalled, the fact that he didn't dally with the Highland women.

LUCK ELUDED THEM that morning, and St. Claire called a halt in a small clearing three hours later when they hadn't sighted a single deer. He was at Rhoslyn's side as she brought her horse to a stop. He startled her by grasping her waist and lifting her from the saddle. She braced her hands on his shoulders and his eyes locked with hers as he lowered her. Her knees felt as weak as apple pudding when her feet touched the ground.

His fingers flexed on her waist and she suddenly realized her waist wasn't as trim as it had been when she'd been Andreana's age. Birth and the passage of time had rounded her curves. St. Claire couldn't miss the difference between Andreana's youthful beauty and Rhoslyn's fuller curves—especially given how dazzling Andreana looked today in her dark green linen dress.

Rhoslyn couldn't halt the flush of embarrassment that warmed her cheeks. St. Claire's gaze sharpened. He hadn't released her, and her embarrassment grew more acute when she glimpsed Lady Isobel glancing their way. The kennel master knelt, tying the hounds to a tree near a large boulder to their left and the rest of the party had moved a discreet distance away.

"Seward insists there is game aplenty here in Buchan," St. Claire said.

Rhoslyn nodded. "My grandfather always returns home with game." Why didn't he step away?

"Did you lay a wager that he would beat me?"

"I did not."

"Then you wagered that I would beat him."

She shook her head. "Nay."

"If you wager on me I will work doubly hard to win," he said.

"I think you had better work doubly hard not to lose your horse."

"I do love that horse," he mused. "If you will not lay a wager on me, would you give me a favor?"

She frowned. "We are no' at court in London."

"True, but I am an English knight and you are my wife. It would please me to carry something of yours."

"I have nothing."

"The scarf in your hair is perfect."

She had forgotten that scarf. Was Lady Isobel still staring? How could she not be? How could all of them not be staring? St. Claire stood so close she almost tasted his breath. If she gave him her scarf everyone would talk. Wasn't that what he wanted? He released her and before she could step away he began unfastening the scarf from her hair.

"St. Claire," she protested. "My head will be bare if you take the scarf."

"This is the first time I have seen you cover your hair," he said, his attention on the scarf. "You have beautiful hair. Why hide it now?"

He freed the scarf and she froze when he brought the fabric to his nose and breathed deep, eyes closed. Her heart began to pound. There was no way their guests could have missed a single thing that passed between them, and this…

He opened his eyes. "I will treasure this small gift, my lady."

Rhoslyn tamped down on the urge to yank free. Gossip would follow if she were seen fleeing her husband. St. Claire grasped her hand and brought it to his lips. His mouth, warm and soft against her flesh, sent a prickle of awareness up her arm. He released her, then slipped the scarf between his mail shirt and shirt.

"Are you hungry?" he asked.

"Aye," she replied, though she didn't think she could swallow a bite.

He tied the horses' reins to a nearby bush, then slid an arm around her waist and turned toward the rest of the party. Some guests sat on rocks, others on fallen branches and the ground. They talked in low tones and ate the bread and cheese that had been packed for them. Rhoslyn wished she didn't have to face them. Alec had been attentive, but other than a chaste kiss to her hand and the occasional endearment, he didn't make public displays of affection. Affection? Nay, what St. Claire did wasn't affection. It was to forestall any questions about the kidnapping.

They reached the picnickers and Lady Isobel called, "Lady Rhoslyn, sit with us." She patted the large rock upon which she and Andreana sat.

Isobel was the last person Rhoslyn wanted to sit with, but she smiled and said, "Thank you, Lady Isobel."

St. Claire released her and she joined the women. He gave her some of the bread and cheese. She accepted and couldn't prevent her gaze from straying to him as he lowered himself onto the ground beside Lord Kinnon and two other guests.

The sun warmed Rhoslyn's face. Her heart had slowed and the food had revived her so that she felt that the remainder of the day might not be so bad, after all.

"Will you walk with me?" Isobel asked. "We face several hours in the saddle, and I would no' mind stretching my legs."

"Aye." Rhoslyn looked at Andreana. "Will you come?"

She shook her head. "I will stay here."

Rhoslyn stood with Isobel and they strolled toward a cluster of daisies growing at the edge of the clearing. She squatted to pick a few while Isobel continued on. The horses nickered and Rhoslyn glanced up. Her palfrey skittered away from St. Claire's horse and whinnied. The stallion snorted and shifted restlessly.

St. Claire rose and strode to the horses. He ran a gentling hand along the mare's neck and she stilled. He turned to his horse and—the dogs began barking. Rhoslyn jerked her gaze onto them. They strained against their leashes, snarling. Then Lady Isobel screamed.

Rhoslyn surged to her feet as a large blur shot from the trees. Andreana's screams mingled with the men's shouts. The boar charged Isobel as she scrambled up the high rock near where the dogs strained against their leashes, snarling and growling. The boar bellowed and turned toward Rhoslyn.

She couldn't reach the rock Isobel had climbed. Rhoslyn fell back two paces, scanning wildly for another rock. She spotted the kennel master racing past toward the dogs. The boar veered toward him. The man skidded to a halt, then whirled back toward the group as Rhoslyn stumbled toward a tree fifteen feet away.

An arrow whizzed past her. She glanced over her shoulder. The boar suddenly turned her way again. A spear sailed through the air and grazed the boar's back. Blood spurted from the wound. He bellowed, lowered his head, and charged.

"Duck, Rhoslyn!" her grandfather shouted. "We canna' shoot him with ye—"

Her toe snagged on something and she crashed to the ground. Pain splintered through her shoulder. She rolled onto her back, the snarls and growls of the hounds deafening. The boar leapt into the air. Rhoslyn screamed and brought her arm up. An arrow pierced the beast's heart. He squealed. Another arrow tore through his hind quarters as he dropped like a stone onto her legs. His hooves scored the ground and he growled low. Two more arrows whizzed over her, stirring the hair on the boar's neck and disappeared into the grass.

Rhoslyn started to push up, but movement in the corner of her eye jerked her gaze to the right. St. Claire stood, bow aimed as an arrow jettisoned from the weapon toward her. She jammed shut her eyes. The boar jerked and she snapped her eyes open. The arrow protruded from the creature's skull, a hair's breadth from her thigh.

Her grandfather dropped down beside her and shoved the boar off her legs. He seized her and pulled her upright. Her legs gave way beneath her and St. Claire caught her and swept her into his arms. Rhoslyn buried her face in his chest and the tears fell as if a dam had broken.

Warmth enveloped her and a low, deep voice whispered incomprehensible words. She went limp in St. Claire's arms and cried until, at last, her sobs subsided and she became aware of the low murmur of voices, as well as the hilt of the sword pressing against her leg. St. Claire breathed deep and the solid wall of warmth her cheek rested against rose and fell with the action. Rhoslyn released a stuttered breath.

"Rhoslyn. Rhoslyn. Are ye all right?"

Rhoslyn recognized Andreana's voice, and the tremor that made it sound as if she hovered on the verge of tears. Rhoslyn couldn't find her voice, so simply nodded. The shock had worn off, and embarrassment set in.

"If you can ride, we will return home." St. Claire's voice reverberated through her.

"We need not return home," she spoke against his chest.

"Nay, lady. I would prefer you return home."

Her shoulder ached and she realized she did want to go home. Rhoslyn nodded He gathered her closer and started to stand with her in his arms. She pushed upright. As expected, everyone surrounded them. Her cheeks burned.

"I can stand, St. Claire."

"Let him carry ye." Andreana said.

"Andreana—"

"Please?" Tears shimmered in her stepdaughter's eyes.

Rhoslyn sighed. "Aye, he can carry me."

Andreana grasped her hand and pressed it to her cheek. A lump formed in Rhoslyn's throat. How lonely and scared had Andreana been all those months Rhoslyn deserted her? Andreana released her and St. Claire stood. He called out an order for one of the men to pick up the boar while the rest prepared to leave.

"There is no need for everyone to return," Rhoslyn said. "The day is young. Send a few of your men with me, and the rest of you continue the hunt."

He shook his head. "Our guests may continue, but you ladies will return with me and my men." They reached the horses and St. Claire lifted her onto the saddle. He turned and said to Lord Kinnon, "What say you, my lord, would you prefer to continue the hunt?"

A hard gleam appeared in his eyes. "I suddenly have a taste for wild boar—lots of wild boar. If you can spare your spearmen, I would see if there are any of that boar's kinsmen in the vicinity."

St. Claire nodded. "I will leave the archers with you, as well."

Lord Kinnon smiled.

Minutes later, the party split up, and Rhoslyn rode alongside Andreana and Lady Isobel surrounded by fifteen of St. Claire's guardsmen with him at the lead.

Chapter Thirteen

~

"I WAS SO afraid," Andreana told Rhoslyn after they'd been riding for a short time. "The archers could not get a clear shot of the boar because ye kept getting in the way." She glanced at Rhoslyn. "I couldna' bear to lose you."

A lump lodged in Rhoslyn's throat. How selfish she'd been. She lost a husband and son, but Andreana lost father and brother. Then Rhoslyn left her. She grieved just as Rhoslyn did. Rhoslyn had told herself she was going to the convent just long enough to clear her heart of grief, but if not for King Edward's command to marry she would still be there. Perhaps her betrothal was God's punishment for deserting her family. She started. If marriage to an Englishman was divine justice, how much more was her punishment to bear a child conceived in violence?

"God's avenging angel," Andreana said.

Rhoslyn looked sharply at her. "What?"

Andreana stared at the men ahead. "Sir Talbot. I have never seen the like. When he notched his bow…"

"Not a hint of emotion moved on his face," Lady Isobel finished for her. "He has ice in his veins."

It did seem as though he was made of ice. Rhoslyn recalled how he stood forty feet away. Too far to reach her before the boar. Close enough for her to discern the intense concentration in his expression—and the determination. A contrast to the fury that had flashed in his eyes when he'd rammed his fist into Jacobus's belly after the young man laid his hand on his sword hilt. But St. Claire hadn't let his anger control him even then. The dispassionate tone of his voice had belied the flash of his eyes.

"The tales of his skill as a hunter didna' do him justice," Isobel said. "All three of his arrows found their mark."

Rhoslyn looked at her. "The three arrows that felled the boar were St. Claire's?"

"Aye," Andreana said. "Ye ran in an erratic line. As I said, the archers and spearmen couldna' shoot for fear of hitting you."

"Some did shoot," Rhoslyn said. "I saw the arrows, and a spear."

Andreana nodded. "But if you hadna' been in the way, they could have felled the boar with a dozen arrows. It is fortunate Sir Talbot stood beside the horses. He had a clear vantage point."

"The man isna' human," Lady Isobel said.

Isobel's voice held a hint of fear, but interest lit her eyes. Rhoslyn turned her face away in disgust. Only last night St. Claire had saved Isobel just as he had her. Maybe that gave Isobel reason to think he wanted her. Though he had immediately deposited her onto a chair and tried to disentangle himself. But then, all their guests looked on. To have settled Isobel on his lap would have been a direct insult to Rhoslyn.

She was fooling herself. Men seldom turned from a beautiful woman's attentions. Alec hadn't kept a mistress, but he was no young man. He had been good to Rhoslyn, attentive and caring, but his passion had diminished greatly over the years. St. Claire, on the other hand, was clearly a passionate man. Though he had made no attempt to bed her yet. Why?

Rhoslyn cast a furtive glance at Isobel. Her eyes remained on St. Claire's back. Rhoslyn would wager a full harvest that the woman was envisioning the glow of firelight off his naked body, slick with sweat after making love to her. His large hand slid along her ribs to the curve of her waist then hip. Rhoslyn's pulse skipped a beat when his fingers brushed her thigh, then traced a line upward to the curls between her legs.

Mortification jarred her from the fantasy. Sweet Jesu, how had her mind gone from knowing what Lady Isobel was thinking to seeing her own naked body pressed against St. Claire's arousal? A strange emotion flitted across her insides and she found herself even more disturbed by the desire that stirred between her legs.

She swallowed against a dry throat. He was exceedingly handsome. She didn't half blame Isobel for lusting after him. No doubt, most women did. But he had sworn fealty to a king who intended to rule Scotland by the might of knights like him. He was, in fact, Scotland's devil, the enemy that would destroy them from within. How much easier it would be to hate him if angry horns jutted from his head, and his eyes blazed red with hellfire. Nay, she added after conjuring the image. Even as a demon he would be beautiful.

Rhoslyn's attention snapped onto St. Claire when he reached for his sword. The snap of a twig beneath horses' hooves sounded within the trees. The scrape of steel followed as the guardsmen drew their swords. Riders shot out from the trees on both sides of the road. St. Claire released his sword hilt, deftly unslung his bow, and pulled an arrow from the quill strapped to his saddle.

In an instant, Rhoslyn counted twelve men, swords drawn. Half a dozen of St. Claire's guardsmen broke from the circle and met their attackers head on. The remaining nine men closed ranks so closely around them that Rhoslyn was forced to keep a tight rein on her horse to prevent it from shying. Andreana's horse gave a shrill cry and started to rear. Rhoslyn seized the reins and yanked them downward.

"Hold her steady," Rhoslyn ordered as steel rang against steel.

An arrow flew from St. Claire's bow. The arrow found its target even as a second arrow flew, then another. Rhoslyn's heart thundered. All three arrows felled an enemy. An enemy warrior notched an arrow for a shot at St. Claire.

"St. Claire!" Rhoslyn shouted, but he had already turned, another arrow pointed, and let the shaft fly.

The man's arrow flew through the air, missed St. Claire, and sailed past. A attacker reached him. A scream stuck in Rhoslyn's throat when the man swung his sword toward St. Claire's head. St. Claire yanked his sword free of its scabbard in time to block the blow. He parried, his blade moving in a blur as he drove the man back. Suddenly, he kicked his horse forward. The animal lunged and Talbot drove his sword through the man's belly.

Her heart leapt into her throat when another enemy warrior shot past him, sword swinging. St. Claire wheeled his horse around so quickly that Rhoslyn could scarce believe it when he thrust the blade through the man's back.

Andreana screamed. Rhoslyn jerked her gaze onto her. A nearby guardsman fell from his steed as an enemy warrior yanked his sword from the man's neck. The man who had killed him charged the guards nearest Rhoslyn. Another barreled down on them to her left where Andreana sat atop her horse.

Rhoslyn's heart pounded. The guardsman surrounding them edged closer to the three of them. The double attack was sure to break their line of defense and she, Andreana, and Isobel would be vulnerable. Sweet God, why hadn't she brought a dirk? She hadn't thought with all the men St. Claire brought that she would need a weapon.

"Lady Isobel," Rhoslyn said. "Have ye a dagger?"

"If I had a dagger I would kill at least one of those bastards."

The men reached them and two of the guardsmen met their steel with ferocious swings of their swords. One of St. Claire's men landed a blow to his opponent's neck that sent the man flying to the ground. Hope surged through Rhoslyn, but in the next instant, another half dozen enemy riders poured from the trees. She glanced at Andreana. Her step-daughter stared wild-eyed with fear. One of the riders bore down on them. Rhoslyn scanned the road. The fighting surrounded them. They wouldn't ride ten feet before an enemy caught them, but they had to try.

"Ride!" Rhoslyn hissed.

Lady Isobel gave a sharp nod.

Rhoslyn tightened her grip on the reins. "Andreana," she began, then broke off when St. Claire shot into view, sword raised.

One of the men bearing down on them jerked his head in St. Claire's direction, but too late. St. Claire swung his sword and slit his throat in one clean cut. Blood spurted across his arm in the instant before the man toppled from his horse.

"Sweet Mother of God," Isobel breathed.

St. Claire turned his horse, leaned forward in the saddle and galloped after the second rider. The man glanced over his shoulder, then veered right, narrowly missed two fighters and headed toward the trees.

Rhoslyn's horse sidestepped, bumping Andreana's horse. Rhoslyn tightened her grip on the reins, her gaze fixed on St. Claire as he swung his sword in an arc that caught an enemy warrior across his back. The man's scream rose above the clash of swords. Her heart raced. The rumors of St. Claire's ruthlessness in battle were true—and more. Ice did flow through his veins.

He whirled his horse toward one of the guards who was losing ground to his opponent, reached the fighters, and drove his sword through the attacker's ribs. The man's head snapped around and he slashed at St. Claire's midsection St. Claire's sword descended upon the man's wrist, severing his hand.

"We must ride," Rhoslyn shouted.

St. Claire's horse skittered aside, and St. Claire turned him full circle. "Rhoslyn," he shouted, "stay here. Others may be waiting in ambush." He whirled back to the fight.

Panic caused her heart to race. St. Claire felled another warrior, then another. Rhoslyn gasped when one of the enemy landed a blow on his arm. St. Claire jabbed with his blade, piercing the man's mail. The warrior retreated, tried to parry St. Claire's assault, then wheeled his horse and raced down the road.

St. Claire shot past one of his warriors and drove a fist into the side of his opponent's face as he raced by. An enemy warrior dashed through an opening between their guardsmen and Andreana. She shrieked. Lady Isobel forced her horse up beside them and lashed at the man's face with her reins. He backhanded her across the cheek. She jerked to the side, but stayed on the saddle.

Rhoslyn kicked her mount's ribs and the palfrey lunged forward. She did as Isobel had and lashed her reins across the man's face as he grabbed Andreana's arm. One of their guardsmen whirled and plunged into the circle and slashed at the man's face with his sword.

A hand seized her arm and yanked. Rhoslyn's grip on her pommel slipped. She snapped the reins across her attacker's face. The leather cracked like a whip and blood sprang up in a line across one cheek and eye. He howled, and his grip loosened.

Rhoslyn kicked her horse's belly and the beast lunged forward. She dodged left to avoid one guardsman, but slammed into an enemy's horse. Rhoslyn jarred, and began falling from the saddle, but hung on. The enemy warrior retreated in his parry against one of the guardsman, and the guardsman drove his sword into the man's neck. She turned her horse around and gasped when another man came up behind Andreana and grabbed her.

"Andreana," Rhoslyn shouted.

St. Claire shot into view, sword slicing across the back of the man's neck. The man toppled to the ground and seconds later, the last of the enemy raced away from them.

Andreana burst into tears. Rhoslyn urged her horse past the guard, dismounted, and helped her from her horse. The girl collapsed into her arms. She held Andreana close while Isobel knelt beside one of St. Claire's men.

Rhoslyn glanced around at the fallen men. At least two dozen of the enemy lay dead or wounded. Not wounded, she realized. If any of the fallen men lived, it would be nothing short of a miracle.

WHEN RHOSLYN ENTERED their private solar, Talbot shifted his attention from Seward. The shock had disappeared from her expression, but her eyes were drawn at the corners. Seward stood, and she crossed to him without a word and nearly fell into his embrace.

"Stay strong, lass," he said after a moment.

She nodded and pulled back. He led her to the bench near the fire where Talbot stood and they sat together.

"Did the hunt fare well?" she asked.

"Lord Kinnon shot a deer," Seward replied. "And there is the boar. Mistress Muira is looking forward to carving him up."

Rhoslyn gave a small smile. "'Tis a shame ye lost your wager with St. Claire."

Seward cut him a glance. "Your life is worth the loss of my sword."

"I did not win the sword fairly," Talbot said. "We will save the wager for another day."

Rhoslyn looked at him. "How far do ye think your brother is willing to go in order to have me?"

"As far as he has to. Today is yet another example of that."

She nodded, but her eyes flicked from his and he knew she wasn't certain Dayton was responsible for today's attack. She believed—or at least wondered—if Duncan was responsible.

Anger had radiated off Duncan in waves last night—anger and the sense that he'd been cheated out of what was rightfully his—Lady Rhoslyn included. But would he stage an attack? Talbot suspected Duncan would take a more direct and easier approach. Poison, a knife in the back, maybe. It took money to induce men to risk their lives. Two dozen skilled warriors wouldn't come cheap. Their attackers wore breeches, which made Talbot suspect they'd come from Stonehaven. More oft than not, the locals near Castle Glenbarr wore Highland kilts. The evidence pointed at Dayton. But Talbot had learned even the greatest fool could be dangerous.

"St. Claire and I think it is best if ye stay at Castle Glenbarr until we catch his brother," Seward said.

"What?" Rhoslyn cut her gaze to Talbot. "That could be months, maybe longer."

"He will not wait long before striking," Talbot said.

"I will no' be a prisoner in my own home."

"I will catch him."

"What if he was no' behind the attack?" she asked.

"Who else could it be?"

She hesitated.

"Perhaps your cousin?" he asked.

"Duncan?" she blurted.

"Why would Duncan attack you?" Seward asked.

"Ask your granddaughter," Talbot said.

The old man frowned. "What is this about, Rhoslyn?"

"He is angry St. Claire forced him to leave Castle Glenbarr."

"Duncan can be an ass," Seward said, "but he isna' capable of orchestrating such an attack."

"You know your kin better than me," Talbot said. "But to rule out other possibilities when nothing is known is a fool's mistake."

Seward snorted. "It isna' that he is not capable of hating ye enough to do it. The truth is, he does not command enough respect among men to gain their loyalty, and he can no' afford to hire mercenaries. Look for something more underhanded from Duncan."

So Talbot had been right.

"Grandfather," Rhoslyn admonished. "Duncan was loyal to Alec. He never stole a single silver piece from us."

Seward laughed. "Only because he believed he would one day be master of Glenbarr."

"That is ridiculous," Rhoslyn said. "Alec and I had a son, and there is Andreana. At the very least, the castle would pass to her."

"And her husband," Seward said. "But that doesna' matter. Duncan wants you."

Rhoslyn's eyes widened. "He told you that?"

"He didna' have to say it," Seward said. "He was more anxious than he should have been to know where ye had gone. It does not matter. I do not believe he was behind today's attack, but it doesna' matter. You will not leave Castle Glenbarr until Dayton St. Claire is dead."

"I will not remain in the castle," she shot back.

"Aye, lady, you will," Talbot said. "I will take no more chances with your safety. You will remain at Castle Glenbarr until I say otherwise."

She opened her mouth to reply, but Seward spoke in an obvious attempt to quiet her. "'Tis a shame none of your attackers survived. Ye might have learned something."

Talbot agreed. But he didn't regret killing every last one of the bastards.

MINUTES LATER, ST. Claire left Rhoslyn alone with her grandfather. It would take some time to wash the grime and blood off his body.

The door clicked shut behind him before she asked her grandfather, "Do ye not think you are making too much of this?"

He gave her a thin-lipped look. "Men died today."

Guilt crashed over her. She hung her head.

"Your husband is right. His brother willna' wait to try and abduct you again. He will grow more desperate with each passing day."

"Use me as bait. Lure him to us," she said.

Her grandfather snorted. "If St. Claire allowed that I would kill him. But I dinna' think he would."

Rhoslyn didn't think so either.

"I see why Edward chose him to marry ye."

"You do?"

"Not since your great uncle Liam have I seen such an archer. What was he like in battle?"

"Fearsome," she said, and recalled the cold detachment with which he wielded his blade. Then she remembered the fury on his face when he'd discovered her tied to Dayton's bed. The contrast between cold and hot sent a shiver down her spine. Was this the same man who had chased a goat in order to save a wedding dress?

"I wish I could have seen him," her grandfather said.

"Ye may yet get a chance," Rhoslyn replied. Then remembered what she wanted to ask. "Have you seen the picture of his sister on his arm?"

He shook his head. "Nay."

"The girl's face is familiar. Ye remember Lady Peigi?"

He nodded. "Cailin Kenzie's daughter."

"Aye. The picture on St. Claire's arm is the spitting image of her."

Her grandfather shrugged. "There are often resemblances between strangers."

Rhoslyn shook her head. "Nay. When I say she is the spitting image, I do no' exaggerate. I was young, but I remember when she returned to claim her father's title after his death. She created quite a stir when she claimed the title."

He gave a short laugh. "She did do that. He hated her for leaving and swore he would outlive her. Many thought he would succeed. He lived to eighty-two."

"Do ye remember that Lady Peigi's mother is no' Scottish?" Rhoslyn asked.

"Aye, Kenzie brought her to Buchan from Galicia. He met her while on pilgrimage to Santiago de Compostela."

"Her features betrayed her heritage," Rhoslyn said. "Her face is longer and her eyes more slanted than ours."

He nodded, eyes unfocused as if remembering. "She was very beautiful, even as she aged."

Rhoslyn leaned closer. "I am telling you, the face is the same. Do ye no' think that strange? Perhaps, if they looked very much the same, and had been of Scottish descent, it would not be so odd. But how is it St. Claire's sister looks like a woman who is also not of pure Celtic blood?"

"It does seem strange," he agreed. "I would like to see this marking. Can ye arrange some way for me to see it?"

"Perhaps if he works outdoors he will take off his shirt." The thought sent a shiver through her. What had come over her? She couldn't once remember experiencing a shiver at the thought of Alec's naked chest.

Chapter Fourteen

~

R HOSLYN OPENED HER eyes and lifted them to the Virgin Mary in the nook of the small chapel. "Four more days have passed and still my flux has no' come. Please, Holy Mother, beg your Son no' to punish me in this way." Desire rose to obtain the herbs to abort the possible pregnancy and guilt twisted her belly. "Forgive me," she whispered while a voice inside her cursed her grandfather and St. Claire for imprisoning her in Castle Glenbarr. They were right, it was too dangerous to leave. Four of St. Claire's guardsmen had died in yesterday's attack. She couldn't ask more men to die to protect her. But being confined meant she had no chance to find the needed herbs.

"Is it so wrong not to want this man's child?" she asked, but silence was her only answer. "Have you also deserted me, good lady?"

Fear stabbed soul deep. She as much just told the Holy Mother she was beyond God's grace. Sweet Jesu, God was sure to punish her further if he found her guilty of sloth. She racked her memory. What was the prayer for forgiveness for committing one of the seven deadly sins?

Rhoslyn prostrated herself on the stone floor and began to pray.

At last, Rhoslyn tore herself away from the chapel. If St. Claire noticed how much time she spent praying, he might ask what was wrong. She started across the bailey toward the storeroom and caught sight of her grandfather striding from the stables. He slowed and they met near the stables.

"We need to talk," he said without preamble.

Unease prickled down her spine. "Is something wrong?"

He turned her back toward the castle and began walking.

"I was going to the storeroom," she said.

"Later." He waited for a group of men to pass, then said, "Ye are not living up to your wifely duties."

Rhoslyn stopped short and stared. Two women passed carrying baskets and Rhoslyn started forward again, but waited until she was certain they were out of earshot before saying, "I wonder not only how you came to this conclusion, but what emboldens you to think ye have the right to speak to me of such personal matters."

"I am your grandfather. That gives me the right. As to how I came to the conclusion, I have eyes. I can tell when a husband and wife are no' sharing a bed."

"If you doubt that St. Claire slept in my bed, ask Alana. She saw him there."

"Sleeping in a woman's bed isna' the same as bedding her. The man doesna' strike me as being anything like his brother. But if ye tell me he is cruel to you, I will kill him and face Edward's wrath."

"I think you have interfered enough, Grandfather."

He barked a laugh. "Are ye saying that because I took you from the convent, your troubles are my fault?"

"Nay," she grudgingly replied. "But you havena' helped matters, either."

"I disagree," he said, "but that does not matter. What matters is now. Do ye despise him for what happened?"

"Nay."

"Then why has he not bedded ye?"

"This is none of your affair," she warned.

"Aye, it is. Since we are stuck with the man, I want great grandchildren while I am still able to teach them what it means to be a Highlander."

Her heart twisted. She wanted that was well. What if it was Dayton St. Claire's son she bore instead of Sir Talbot's? Would her grandfather reject the child? They reached the postern door. He opened it and motioned her to enter. He followed and she veered right, toward the table at the far end of the great hall. He grasped her arm and steered her toward the stairs.

"We are no' finished," he said, and urged her up the stairs.

They reached the third floor and entered her private solar. "Why are ye doing this?" she asked when he closed the door. "You were the one who was most against the marriage. You even tried to marry me to Jacobus."

"Aye, but that opportunity passed." He met her gaze. "I know Dayton St. Claire did more than kidnap ye. I saw it in your eyes the day I met you in the inn."

Rhoslyn startled, but managed to check the panic that shot through her.

"St. Claire has accepted you as his wife and he wants ye," he said.

"What do you mean?" she blurted. "That is ridiculous."

"Is it? I see the way he looks at ye."

Her heart beat painfully fast. "All men see is lust."

He grunted. "I am still vigorous enough to understand *and* recognize desire when I see it."

"*Grandfather!*"

"Dinna' act like a thirteen-year-old virgin. Ye were married eight years, and I made sure ye understood the reality of life from the time you were a child. He wants you, which is to his credit. Many men would blame a woman for what happened to ye *and* hold a grudge. 'Tis not so with St. Claire. What will ye do if you find yourself pregnant with his brother's child?"

Rhoslyn drew a sharp breath before catching herself.

Her grandfather's eyes narrowed. "Ye are no' already carrying his child, are you?"

"I am no' pregnant," she snapped.

"Have ye had your flux?"

She stared in horror. "That is none of your business."

He gave a succinct nod. "Just as I thought. 'Tis time ye got down to the business of bedding your husband."

"Business? Is that how ye see my marriage?"

"In this case, yes. You did no' marry the man out of love." His expression softened. "I say this for your own good. You canna' allow what happened to paralyze you. You could have done worse than Talbot. Ye could have gotten a man like his brother."

She shuddered. Worse, his brother could have succeeded.

WHEN RHOSLYN NEARED the stables that afternoon, male laughter coming from the side of the building caused her to slow.

"Go on, lad, you can catch her," came a deep English voice she didn't recognize.

Another round of laughter went up, even more boisterous than the last. She crept forward and peered around the edge of the building. St. Claire and several of his men stood facing the far side of the building. Sounds of a scuffle ensued, and St. Claire threw back his head and laughed. Rhoslyn startled at the sound of his rich laughter amongst the guffaws of his men. Although she watched him in profile, she noticed a softening of the normally hard lines of his face. He looked ten years younger.

His broad shoulders shook with laughter. "Have you not the bollocks to tame her, lad?"

"Is that how you let a female treat you?" a third said, and more laughter erupted.

"She willna' obey me," a young male voice replied.

Rhoslyn recognized John Forster's voice, eldest son of the most prominent freeman who worked their land.

"You cornered her," a large man said. "Now you must bring her to heel or she will never obey you."

"Show her who is master," another said.

"Give her a good swat on the rump," one said. "That will teach her you mean business."

"That never works," another said. "Mount her, lad. Do not give her a chance to get away."

A hard bump against the wall was followed by a woman's cry.

"Ina, I didna' mean to hurt ye," John said. "Hold still, damn you."

The sound of a body knocking hard against the wall came next. Rhoslyn froze.

Some of the men darted from view around the building.

"You have her, John," St. Claire said. "She cannot get past us."

"Want me to hold her?" another said.

John grunted, then shouted, "I did it."

Was he panting?

"You would think he cornered a lion," one man said.

St. Claire chuckled. "She did put up a fight."

Rhoslyn broke from shock and lunged forward, nearly tripping in her rush to reach them. St. Claire's head snapped in her direction. Amusement seemed frozen on his face. In that instant, his unguarded expression confused her, and she couldn't reconcile the man who had tenderly freed her from the bed where her rapist had tied her with the man who cheered on a wisp of a boy while he raped a woman. The look vanished and she jarred from her confusion when his eyebrows dove down in a fierce frown.

He started toward her. "What is it, Lady Rhoslyn?"

She pushed past him and around the building, then stopped cold at sight of John with—

Iron fingers closed around her arm and swung her around. "What is amiss?" St. Claire demanded.

"I—" She cut her gaze back to John.

"Rhoslyn."

She looked back at St. Claire. "I—"

John halted in front of her, gripping the reins of the horse their stable master had recently broken. Ina sat astride the animal.

"Look, my lady," Ina said. "John has given me this horse. He is teaching me to ride."

The young man blushed, for he was sweet on Ina and everyone knew it.

No one laughed or teased him this time. They all stared at her. St. Claire's gaze sharpened and she read understanding in his eyes.

He released her and said to John. "Lead the horse around the bailey for your lady's first ride, John. Let them both grow accustomed to the saddle."

The boy's blush deepened and he started toward the courtyard.

When John had passed, St. Claire turned to her. "Will you walk with me, Lady Rhoslyn?"

Inwardly she cringed. But she nodded and they began strolling in the direction John had gone.

Once they were well out of earshot of his men, he said, "Do you really think I would stand by and watch a man abuse a woman?"

Shame flushed her cheeks. "I am sorry."

"I have not gone in pursuit of Dayton," he said.

The abrupt change of subject startled her.

"I wanted—want—nothing more than to look under every rock in Scotland for him. But I made the mistake of not protecting you as I should have and I feared…" His words trailed off, and Rhoslyn found she couldn't speak. He looked down at her. "Mayhap my not going gave you the impression—"

"Nay," she cut in. "I never thought that."

"Until now."

She lowered her eyes. "I truly am sorry."

A group of men approached and St. Claire cupped her elbow and steered her around them. His gentle finger pressure sent a strange heat through her and she nearly snatched her arm away once they passed the men.

"I do know ye are no' the kind of man to allow anyone to harm a woman," she said.

Odd that he should be so gentle with her, and such a ruthless killer at the same time. She had known other warriors. Few men survived who had not killed in their lifetime. But St. Claire killed as easily as most men breathed. Yet she saw no cruelty in him. Not even brutality. He killed…efficiently—and without emotion. Was that how he made love? She startled at the thought and snapped her head up to meet his gaze. He stared down at her expectantly.

"I can do nothing more than ask your forgiveness," she said.

His expression softened. "You need not ask forgiveness. You are allowed doubts."

Hers had been more than a doubt, but she was grateful for his kindness. "I have no' seen Ralf and Ingram today. Have they left?"

He nodded. "I sent them back to Stonehaven to continue the search for my brother."

They were halfway across the bailey when a woman and three men rode through the gates.

"Elizabeth," Rhoslyn murmured.

"Do you not wish to see her?" St. Claire asked.

Rhoslyn released a breath. "She is a childhood friend."

He chuckled. "She is a rival, then?"

"Nay. She is a friend." Rhoslyn said no more and felt his eyes on her, the question still hanging in the air. "I had better greet her," she said.

"We might as well greet her together."

She started to disagree, then realized a husband and wife greeting guests was natural. Her stomach began to churn. Husband and wife. Their marriage still seemed like a dream. St. Claire, however, was no dream. He was a flesh and blood man walking alongside her.

They reached Elizabeth as one of her escorts helped her to the ground.

"Rhoslyn." Elizabeth embraced her and gave her a squeeze. She pulled back, brows drawn. "I heard what happened. Are ye all right? Andreana, she is unharmed? And Lady Isobel, she was with you, as well. What of her?"

"We are all well," Rhoslyn replied.

Elizabeth turned toward St. Claire. "Sir Talbot, you look well. I assume you were not hurt, either?"

"Nothing serious, my lady."

"I am relieved. May my escorts rest in the great hall while Rhoslyn and I visit?"

"Of course." St. Claire nodded to a waiting groom. The men handed the reins to the boy, then followed St. Claire as he escorted Rhoslyn and Elizabeth to the great hall.

"Have you any idea who attacked you, Sir Talbot?" Elizabeth asked.

"I suspect my brother," he replied.

"I assume you are searching for him?" she said. St. Claire nodded, and she added, "Perhaps you should speak with my father. He knows the countryside well, and I know he would be glad to aid in your search. Your brother must be nearby if he planned the attack."

"I would be glad of your father's help, my lady."

They reached the postern door and St. Claire opened the door, letting the ladies enter first. He followed the women, with Elizabeth's men trailing.

"We will go to the bower," Rhoslyn said.

"I will have Mistress Muira bring food and drink," St. Claire said, and Rhoslyn breathed a silent sigh of relief when he headed for the kitchen.

She led Elizabeth up one flight of stairs to the bower. She closed the door and went to add wood to the hearth's smoldering embers.

When she sat down beside Elizabeth on the bench in front of the fire, Elizabeth said, "How are you really, Rhoslyn? Your eyes look drawn."

"I am tired," she admitted. "It has been a trying week."

"And you are no' pleased to be married to St. Claire?"

"How could I be? He is Edward's vassal. He has no affection for Scotland."

"Yours is no' the first marriage between Scot and English."

"These are particularly dangerous times, Elizabeth. Edward is determined to claim Scotland, even if he must take it a piece at a time. And St. Claire is capable of giving it to him. Perhaps even singlehandedly."

Elizabeth laughed. "He is a large man and a skilled warrior, but he is no god."

"I am no' so sure," Rhoslyn said. "You didna' see him in battle. He must have killed half the enemy himself." At the raise of Elizabeth's brows, Rhoslyn added, "Think what ye may. I do not exaggerate. St. Claire is no small ally for Edward."

"Edward would not trust a fool," Elizabeth said. "It is true, he has his eye on the crown, and will pay for the fight from Scottish coffers. But we will no' simply bow down to him."

"He already controls our noble's castles," Rhoslyn said.

Elizabeth waved a hand. "A political tactic. If he dares march an army across the border those same nobles will meet them with drawn swords."

"While St. Claire attacks from the rear."

"He does no' strike me as fool enough to fight a losing battle," Elizabeth said. "At worst, he will encourage the nobles to follow Edward. You must admit, many already favor Edward."

"They are only looking out for their interests in England," Rhoslyn muttered.

"True," Elizabeth agreed. "But we speculate. The most important thing is that Sir Talbot seems kind, and he protected ye against your attackers during the hunting party."

And his brother, Rhoslyn heard the thought. Rhoslyn could hide nothing from Elizabeth.

"He knows how to protect his own," Rhoslyn said, and wished she could accept him based on that fact alone.

"'TIS GOOD TO see ye, Lady Rhoslyn," Malcom said.

Talbot swung the axe down against the tree that had fallen in front of the storehouse door, then yanked it free. Boyd stood opposite him and swung his axe onto the same spot. Talbot flicked a glance at Rhoslyn as she halted beside Malcom, then again swung his axe. This was the first he had seen her since the yesterday's evening meal.

Rhoslyn nodded. "I see last night's wind did some damage. Why was I no' told?"

Talbot swung the axe again. "I was told."

"That doesna' mean I should no' be informed," she said. "Even when Alec was alive I was aware of all that went on in Castle Glenbarr. Why are you chopping the tree, St. Claire? Should you no' have the lads do that?"

He laughed. "Are you saying I am too old to chop up a tree?"

"I am saying ye might have more important things to do, like no' keeping Angus Gair waiting."

"Angus will have plenty to drink while he waits," Talbot replied.

"Alec never made him wait."

Talbot brought the maul down on the tree again. "Perhaps he did not keep as much ale on hand as I do."

She opened her mouth to reply, then her attention fixed on Malcom, who was busy studying the ground, and she closed her mouth. So, the lady was accustomed to having her way. And, Talbot thought with no little surprise, Harper had sheltered her as much as he could. She was strong and courageous. He wouldn't have thought her naive, especially in regards to men. Her gaze shifted past him and a moment later Angus

Gair came strolling into view.

Angus stopped beside her and crossed his arms over his massive chest. "I might have known."

Talbot glimpsed a smirk on Rhoslyn's face before he slammed the axe into the tree trunk. "A man must prioritize, Angus," Talbot said as he worked the axe free.

The big man grunted. "Aye, but ye need a real man to do the job."

Talbot planted his axe head first on the ground and met his gaze. "I assume you mean yourself."

Angus strode to where Boyd stood opposite St. Claire. "Lad, ye are no' doing it right." He took the axe from the younger man, waved him aside, and stepped up to the tree. Half a dozen men on their way to the practice field stopped to watch. "Put your back into it." Angus swung the axe with such force that a large chunk of wood flew from the trunk. "I am surprised your laird didna' teach ye that." He looked at Talbot and grinned.

"I take that to be a challenge," Talbot said.

"I wouldna' want to embarrass ye." Angus' grin widened.

"I do not embarrass easily. The first man to split the trunk?"

"I will even give ye a head start and let you continue with the scratch you made in the wood." Angus lifted his brows in question.

"That will not be necessary," Talbot said.

More men, a mixture of Highlanders and English, gathered around them.

"Unless you feel the need to have the head start," Talbot said.

"That is good of ye, St. Claire, but I will manage."

They took their places at opposite ends of the trunk.

"Malcom," Talbot said, "if you would say the word."

Talbot and Angus gripped their axes. Malcom glanced between them, then shouted, "Go!"

Both men swung their axes, hitting the wood with jarring force. Onlookers began to shout and, with each blow, Talbot noticed the crowd grew. Amidst their cries, bets passed as to who would win. He angled his axe first left, then right, and his gash deepened with every strike. Angus swung over and over, brute strength an advantage Talbot couldn't match blow for blow. But it took more than brute strength to win a battle.

"God's teeth, St. Claire, use some muscle," Rhoslyn shouted.

He flicked a glance her way. She glared as fiercely as the men. But she cheered for him. As the blows fell faster, the shouts grew more intense. Finally, a large crack split the air and for an instant he feared Angus had beat him, but another blow to the wood and his end of the trunk struck the ground with a thud.

Cheers went up and he looked up to see Angus' end had also fallen to the ground. The crowd surged forward, a chorus of voices arguing over whose log hit the ground first. Angus looked at Talbot, grinned, then shrugged. Talbot shifted his gaze toward Rhoslyn. She shook her head as if in reprimand, but he was sure he saw a hint of satisfaction in her eyes.

Angus elbowed his way through the crowd to Talbot and clapped him on the back. "Have ye any rope, St. Claire? We had best show these lads how to haul these logs away."

"You do not wish to cut it yourself?" Talbot asked.

Angus gave a hearty laugh. "Ye have bollocks, lad. Nay, I think we should haul it away from the storeroom, then have a drink and discuss business."

Talbot felt certain his wife would be pleased with that.

THE DOOR IN the private solar opened behind Rhoslyn. "Ye may leave the wine on the table," she said without looking up from the household rolls.

"I did not bring wine. I can fetch some, if you like."

Rhoslyn snapped her head up and met St. Claire's dark eyes. "I thought ye were one of the maids."

"Are you disappointed?"

"Nay. I simply was no' expecting you. Is something wrong?"

"Need something be wrong for a husband to visit his wife?"

Her treacherous heart beat faster. He was calling her wife. He'd begun to make a habit of it: When Elizabeth visited two days past. Yesterday afternoon in the kitchen. Last night in the great hall when she announced she intended to retire. And now today.

"Did ye finish your business with Angus?" she asked. "How many cattle did ye purchase?"

"He will deliver one hundred head over the next year. He has the best cattle in all the Crieff market."

"I hope he didna' demand a high price in revenge for ye beating him at tree chopping."

"Did I beat him? It seems we were evenly matched."

She snorted. "Clearly, your end of the log struck the ground first."

"I am flattered you noticed," he said, and embarrassment washed over her.

"Of course I noticed. I have eyes."

"Aye, you do. Lovely eyes."

Rhoslyn flushed. "Was there something ye wanted, St. Claire? As you must see, I am busy."

He nodded at the household rolls. "Have you always kept the accounts?"

"Since I was seventeen."

Surprise flickered in his gaze. "Where did you learn the skill?"

"Alec taught me." She laughed. "Or I should say he gave into my pestering to teach me." Sadness settled over her with the memory. "Mistress Muira ran his household so well that I was no' needed. I cared for Andreana, but she had a nursemaid, which left me too idle for my liking."

"Most noble ladies spend their days with a needle, or directing the servants, no matter how apt they are spending their husband's fortunes. Do such things hold no interest for you?"

She wrinkled her nose. "Mistress Muira would no' allow anyone to direct her. I was wise enough to know better than to make trouble in my husband's house. As for sewing, I am ashamed to admit even the good sisters at Saint Mary's could no' improve my skill."

"What of spending your husband's money?" he asked.

Rhoslyn shrugged. "How much can a woman spend?"

"Some can spend a great deal."

"Is that what you came to speak with me about, spending my money?"

A corner of his mouth twitched.

"I imagine you consider it your money," she said.

"If it was necessary to pay my men to protect Castle Glenbarr, would you object?" he asked.

"Nay, so long as it wasna' you who started the trouble that warranted the protection. Is there something ye wish to confess? An old enemy who may come calling?"

"I doubt any of them will venture into the Scottish highlands to avenge themselves on me."

One already had. His brother.

His expression sobered, and she realized he was thinking the same thing. "There is a matter we need to discuss."

Apprehension sent a chill through her.

"Would you sit with me near the fire?" he asked.

She rose and crossed to the bench. They sat down and she looked expectantly at him.

"You are looking well," he said, though she knew he meant *you seem to have recovered from my brother's violation.*

"Lady Rhoslyn, I believe it is time we consummate our marriage."

Shock shot through her, followed by fear.

"I do not say this to force you to accept me as your husband," he quickly added. "I say this because I do not wish there to be any doubt that I am the father of your children."

She drew a sharp breath.

"I am sorry. There is no easy way to solve this problem."

She stiffened. "Problem?"

"If a child is born in nine months, some will say the child is not mine. But if you are my wife in every sense of the word, the rumors will be little more than an annoyance."

He had slipped into her bed the morning following their wedding. No doubt, the servants had noticed that they hadn't seen him there since.

"I do not want you—or the child—to suffer that indignation," he said.

Rhoslyn swallowed. "And if the child resembles your brother?"

"My brother looks very much like my father. Why would I care that our son favors him?"

Was he saying what she thought he was saying? Surely, he didn't want to call his brother's son his own. Then she realized the truth.

"It would not have mattered if Melrose had gotten me with child. You would have taken me to wife and called another man's child your own."

St. Claire shook his head. "Nay, it would not have mattered."

She stared. "What manner of man are you?"

"The kind that is tired of war," he replied.

"I have never known a man to tire of war."

"Perhaps the ones you know have not had enough. I have."

"Impossible. Ye are too skilled a warrior. A man such as you does not give up fighting."

Amusement glimmered in his eyes. "A man such as me? What do you make of me, Rhoslyn?"

"Ye are a man who, if your king commands you to fight, you will."

"If I am of more use to him here than at war, he will not ask me to fight."

Suspicion rose in her. "The only way you would be of more use to him in Scotland is if ye put his needs above Scotland's."

"Scotland and England have been at peace for some time," he replied. "There is no reason for what we need to be at odds."

"Now that your king is determined to rule us, that peace is sure to end."

"I do not think William Wallace or Robert Bruce will allow that," St. Claire said.

Had she heard correctly? Did an Englishman—a knight—say that a Scot would not allow the English to rule him?

"Do ye realize you speak treason?" she asked.

He laughed his deep, rich laugh, and said, "Edward knows well enough that Robert Bruce has no intention of letting him rule Scotland."

"You speak as if Scotland will prevail over England."

"Would it be the first time?"

"St. Claire, ye are a traitor."

He shrugged. "I am a realist. Scotland has never willingly bowed to anyone, much less the English. Why should they start now?"

"They named Edward arbiter for the Scottish crown. That is a good start."

"A business deal on the part of the Guardians, nothing more."

She wanted so much to agree with him, to believe their leaders had the situation in hand and Edward would become nothing more than an annoyance. How easy it would be to trust this man. He would protect her—and their children. Their children. What would happen when the peace between Scotland and England ended—as it surely would? Who would their sons fight for? Who would their daughters marry? Perhaps they wouldn't have children. If she couldn't conceive, or if it took years to conceive as it had with Alec, that would allow for time to prepare, to see if…

"Whatever Edward does, I will not risk your happiness," he said. "Any children born to you will be mine. But to ensure that no one challenges me, we must share a bed. You may hate me—"

"Hate you?" She felt heat rush into her cheeks when his brow lifted. "I do no' blame you for what your brother did."

"But neither do you want me," he said.

What could she say? She could want him, and with little urging. But to admit that…to admit that, meant what? Edward could command him to kill Wallace and that would not change the fact he was her husband.

"You are loyal to Edward. I am loyal to Scotland. That fact alone can crush us."

He placed a hand over hers. "I will not let it."

Chapter Fifteen

~

T HE FOLLOWING EVENING, as they passed through the gates at Dunfrey Castle ahead of two dozen men, Talbot half expected Lady Rhoslyn to beg him to take her back to Castle Glenbarr.

"I still say it is convenient that ye allow me to leave Castle Glenbarr when it suits your plans," she muttered.

He hid a smile. "Should we return there and you not be allowed even this small reprieve?"

She shot him a narrow-eyed glare. "And risk the ride back in the dark. I think ye wouldna' agree even if I demanded it."

"Not tonight," he admitted, but knew she had no wish to return, at least not tonight. Once he realized the pain associated with the memories at Castle Glenbarr, he knew he had to bring her to Dunfrey Castle to consummate their marriage.

They passed through the archway from the outer bailey into the inner courtyard and were greeted by a groom. Talbot dismounted and went to Rhoslyn's horse.

"Have you ever visited Dunfrey Castle?" he asked as he helped her from the saddle.

"Once, when I was eleven. Fordyce Galloway lived here. When he died, his wife married a lowlander whose only heir was English. Their son inherited Dunfrey Castle, but he lost the property to Edward."

Talbot tossed the reins to the groom and commanded his men to come to the hall once they'd taken care of their horses, then pressed a hand to the small of Rhoslyn back urged her toward the door.

"He did not pay his taxes, I take it?"

"Nay. The property lay unused until you took possession."

Talbot kept only a small contingent of men at Dunfrey Castle, which left the bailey empty this late in the day. He found he liked the quiet and wondered what Rhoslyn would think of living a more sedate life here.

"Do you like Dunfrey Castle?" she asked.

"I do. The buildings are in excellent condition. The forests support an abundance of game. I plan to build cottages and employ freemen to farm the land."

She looked at him in surprise. "You, a farmer? I canno' imagine it."

"I hope you can imagine it," he said. "How else am I to maintain the fields at Castle Glenbarr if I do not become a farmer?"

"You can leave the running of Castle Glenbarr to me," she said.

"Or we could hire a steward," he said.

"Are ye saying I canna' do it?"

"I am saying you might have more important things to do."

"Like raising your sons?"

He shifted his gaze to her. "They would be your sons as well."

Her expression turned speculative. "How do ye feel about being banished to the Scottish Highlands by your king?"

Talbot repressed a laugh. "Buchan is little different from Kent."

They had reached the castle and walked through the archway at the front door. He pulled the huge door open and Rhoslyn preceded him into the large foyer.

"Ye havena' seen Buchan in the winter," she said as he pulled the door shut. "It is bitter cold. Much colder than Kent."

"I imagine we will find ways to keep warm."

Her brows snapped down. "Are ye telling me you will bed me often in the winter?"

"As often as you let me."

"Let ye?" she said. "You are my husband. You may bed me as often as ye please."

"I am not my brother, Lady Rhoslyn. I do not force a woman, even my wife. I would hope you understood that by now."

Her eyes flew wide. "That isna' what I meant."

"We have many years ahead of us. I would rather enjoy that time with my wife." Talbot urged her forward and up the stairs. They climbed to the third floor where he took her to his chambers. "The rooms are smaller and the furniture not as opulent as Castle Glenbarr," he said, "but I find it comfortable. Would you like a bath?"

She shook her head. "I dinna' want to put your women to work at this hour."

"I agree. I will go down myself and heat the water. The men can carry up the water for you."

Her brows rose. "Ye and your men will prepare the bath? That I must see."

An hour later, the bath sat before the fire filled with steaming water. The last of the men who'd carried up the water left as Talbot poured two goblets of wine. He gave one to Rhoslyn and she emptied it in several gulps. She returned the goblet, then went to the tub and began untying the laces on her gown. Talbot set his wine on the table and crossed to her. She looked up, then froze when he gently moved her hands aside and began loosening the laces. Once loose, he grasped the fabric at her waist and pulled the dress over her head. She stood before him in her shift.

His cock jerked at the glimpse of her breasts straining against the thin linen fabric before he turned. He returned to the wine and refilled their goblets. The rustle of fabric conjured a vision of the shift sliding across her breasts before Rhoslyn dropped it onto the floor. The gentle swish of water against the side of the tub told him she had lowered herself into the tub.

He waited a moment, then turned. She rested, back to him, facing the fire.

"Would you like more wine, my lady?"

"Aye." She picked up a cloth from the table beside the tub, scooped soap from the small earthen jar sitting alongside, and began lathering her arms.

Talbot took the goblets to the tub and set her wine on the table where the soap had been. From the corner of his eye, he saw her slow in rubbing the soapy cloth along one sleek arm. Water lapped at the pink nipple of the breast not hidden by her arm. Talbot turned away and took a drink of his wine. He crossed to the bed, set the goblet down and began taking off his boots. His mail shirt, then shirt, followed before he finished off his wine.

Rhoslyn dipped down into the tub, then came up, hair dripping. She began lathering the long tresses. Talbot went to the tub and knelt on one knee behind her.

She stilled. "Is there something ye want, St. Claire?"

"Aye, but we will begin with your hair."

"My hair?" She twisted, coming face to face with his chest, and jerked back. Water sloshed over the top of the tub.

Talbot grasped her shoulders and her head snapped up. "Unless you wish me to pull you out of this tub before your hair is finished, I suggest you face forward." She frowned, and he lifted a brow and flicked a glance at her breasts.

A blush crept up her cheeks and she pulled free, turning her back to him.

He scooped soap from the jar on the table, then gathered her hair atop her head. She sat stiffly as he lathered the thick mane. Slowly, he worked his fingers through her hair and across her scalp, massaging until she released a slow sigh. He set the soap on the table then instructed her to rinse her hair. She dunked her head, rubbing her hair to remove the soap.

Talbot couldn't tear his eyes from her breasts, swaying with the small waves of water created by her movement. She lifted her head from the water and he handed her a towel. She wiped her eyes, then cast him a quick glance and yanked her eyes back to stare down at the water as she dried her hair. Talbot grabbed the drying cloth from the table and handed it to her. He shoved to his feet as Rhoslyn rubbed her hair dry.

He wasn't sure whether to laugh or worry that she took an inordinate amount of time to dry her hair. She finally rose from the water and quickly wrapped the towel around her. She rubbed her arms.

"Are you cold?" he asked.

"The water had grown cold," she replied.

"I can remedy that." He swept her into his arms.

She cried out and threw her arms around his neck. Talbot sat down on the bench, cradling her on his lap.

"Have ye gone insane, St. Claire? I am all wet."

He grasped her chin and tilted her face toward his. "Are you?"

She frowned. "Am I—*St. Claire.*"

He lowered his mouth onto hers.

RHOSLYN FROZE WHEN St. Claire's lips touched hers. She held her breath, suddenly uncertain what to do. She felt like that fifteen-year-old virgin who had awaited Alec in his bed on their wedding night. But Alec's lips hadn't felt so…full. She shivered. The tense muscle of his arm beneath her fingers belied the gentle brush of his lips against hers—and the thick bulge beneath her buttocks. His arms tightened around her and she knew an instant of panic.

He broke the kiss and buried his face in her hair. "You need never fear me, Lady Rhoslyn. As long as I live, you need never fear anyone."

Tears sprang to her eyes with a sting she hadn't felt since Dougal died. Rhoslyn willed her emotions into subjection. She was being childish. What reason had she to cry?

St. Claire drew back. His gaze moved across her face and he gently brushed aside the wet locks that clung to her cheeks. His eyes then locked with hers.

"Am I so terrible? Can you not forgive me for what my brother did, or is it that you will never be able to stomach an Englishman touching you?"

His fingers rested on her left cheek, warm, gentle…

Rhoslyn could only shake her head.

His gaze sharpened. "Are you saying you cannot stand my touch?"

"Nay," she blurted.

His brows dove downward.

"I mean, nay, that is no' what I am saying."

"Then I am not repulsive?" he asked.

She scowled. "Ye are teasing me."

"Am I?"

"You know full well you are a beautiful man."

Amusement warmed his eyes. "Beautiful? I have not heard that."

"Ye are no' a very good liar, St. Claire. You know you are a braw man."

"Beautiful and braw," he said. "That is a good thing, then?"

"I imagine no woman ever kicked ye out of her bed."

His eyes darkened. "Including you?"

Her breath caught. "You are my husband."

"Aye, but we spoke of this already. I will not force you."

"If I turned you away, ye would go?"

"I would ask at least for a son," he replied. "Perhaps also a daughter."

Her heart began a fast beat.

"Would that be so terrible?" he asked.

Staring into his dark eyes, it seemed as if giving him sons and daughters would be the most natural thing in the world. Didn't a wife want to give her husband children? She shivered.

He lifted a brow. "I am remiss in my duty, my lady. You are sitting on my lap and still not warm."

"Nay," she began, but he rose with her in his arms and strode to the bed. Her pulse raced. He ducked between the curtains and laid her on crisp, clean sheets.

"The towel," he said, "it is wet. Give it to me."

She hesitated. Then yanked the cloth from her body and dragged the covers up to her chin. The chilled sheets elicited another, stronger shiver. St. Claire stepped back and loosened the ties on his breeches, then shoved them and his braies down his hips. Rhoslyn glimpsed his thick erection in the instant before she yanked her gaze up to his face.

He climbed into bed beside her and pulled her close. "The sheets are cool. I should have had the maid warm them."

"It is all right," Rhoslyn said, teeth chattering.

He wrapped his arms around her and pulled her close. Her breasts pressed against with the warm, hard muscle of his chest and desire tightened her sex. Unexpected guilt surfaced. She was doing nothing wrong. Alec was gone. He wouldn't ask her to remain barren and die alone. Yet, she hadn't considered the possibility that she would marry again…that she would desire another man.

A nervous flitter stirred in her belly. She had been nervous with Alec, as any virgin would be with her husband, had cared for him, had desired him, but her feelings hadn't been this intense. And that, she realized, was where her guilt originated. St. Claire had done nothing more than hold her against his naked body, and she trembled. Could he discern her reaction?

His member pulsed against her thigh. Her mouth went dry. Aye, he knew.

They lay, quiet, his heart thumping out a powerful beat against her breast. Why didn't he roll on top of her and enter her? What would it feel like when he did? Embarrassment washed over her and she was glad he couldn't see her face.

"Are you warmer?" he asked.

"Aye."

"What do you think of my hiring men to work the land around Dunfrey Castle? I would have to hire a steward and an overlord. You must know men who I can trust."

Was he asking about business at a time like this? "My grandfather would know men."

"Perhaps, while the steward is learning, you could oversee his work. Ensure that he is honest and knows what he is doing."

What was wrong with the man? It was obvious he wanted her. She had never known a man to talk business while making love to a woman. Unless… Was she nothing more than business to him?

"If ye wish," she replied in a business-like manner. "As you know, I am proficient with numbers."

"And with the servants."

"What?" she said.

"You are good with the servants. They care for you."

"I care for them."

He nodded, his chin brushing the top of her head. He was going to drive her mad.

"You will probably have to hire someone to replace your cousin," he said.

"My cousin—oh, aye. How have ye been getting along without him?"

"He left only the week before you returned home."

"*Returned home,* that is what you call kidnapping me?"

"I saved you. Did you really want Melrose?"

The amusement in his voice pricked her pride. "He would make a good husband."

"He would do as you commanded, you mean."

That is exactly what she'd meant, but said, "A good husband knows when to listen to a wife."

"I shall remember that."

Was he going to talk all night long? Mayhap his desire had waned. She shifted slightly, then froze at the press of his very rigid cock against her thigh.

"Are you all right, Rhoslyn?"

"Are ye going to get this over with or not, St. Claire?"

"You want me to be quick about it?" he asked.

Rhoslyn didn't miss the husky note in his voice.

"How long can a man take to finish the job?" she replied.

"Enough time to ensure the lady is well satisfied."

The brush of his fingers on her arm startled her and she jumped.

He stilled. "How can I think of doing more when a simple touch makes you jump?"

"'Tis no' that. Ye simply caught me off guard."

"Shall I tell you everything I plan to do to you?"

A tremor rippled through her body at the thought of what planned to do to her. If the hardness of his member was any indication…she swallowed.

"First, I want to brush my fingers across your skin." He began again to trace lazy circles along her arm.

Gooseflesh race along her flesh.

"You like that," he murmured.

It wasn't a question.

The finger moved upward across her shoulder, then neck, tickling the fine hair at her nape. She shivered.

"You like that, as well." He slid his fingers into her hair and gently fisted her hair, pulling her head back. "Now I am going to kiss you."

His lips touched hers and she closed her eyes, breathing deep. His tongue flicked at her mouth in warning, then swept inside. She was startled at the sweet taste of him, a combination of the wine he had drunk and something she couldn't quite define.

He released her hair and murmured against her lips, "I am going to touch your breasts."

He flattened his palm on her shoulder, and her heart beat faster as he slid his hand down until the warm palm cupped her breast. He broke the kiss and began nibbling on her ear. Heat pooled between her legs.

"You are very beautiful," he whispered.

With his thumb, he grazed the tip of her stiffened nipple. Pleasure streaked through her.

"Shall I taste your breasts now, my lady?"

The hoarse note in his voice—and the question—made her head whirl. How did she answer such a question? But he waited for no answer, and dipped his head downward. Anticipation tightened her sex. When his warm mouth closed around the nipple she couldn't halt a moan. Then, God help her, he suckled, and she wondered if he would bring her to pleasure that instant.

"I am going to touch you," he said against her breast.

Touch her?

The hand on her breast stroked downward and she realized what he meant. He suckled harder and her senses muddled. He lightly ran his fingers over the sensitive dip in her belly, causing a quiver across her flesh she felt clear to her core. His large hand brushed her curls, then closed over her mound.

"St Claire," she whispered.

"Aye, love?"

"This is strange."

"Do you want me to stop?"

"God no," she blurted, then jammed her eyes shut from embarrassment.

"I am relieved," he said, his voice a bit choked.

He dipped a finger between the moist folds that protected her swollen nub. The digit caressed the delicate bud. Rhoslyn forced back the impulse to clamp her legs together. She was torn between wanting him to touch her and mortification. Alec rarely touched her this way and, in truth, she had wanted him to. St. Claire applied slight pressure and need shot through her. Oh, she was wrong. Alec had never touched her *this way*. She shifted restlessly, wanting the pleasure hinted at in his caress. It had been so long. All those months before Dougal's birth, then the isolation of the convent. Too long.

He shifted his mouth to the other breast and drew on the nipple. Rhoslyn thrust the fingers of one hand into his thick hair and tugged.

"Ahh, you like this, my lady?" He sucked harder.

Rhoslyn moved against his finger. He slid one muscled leg across her legs. The thigh was heavy and so very warm, and she wanted more of him, skin to skin. His caresses intensified. She fisted his hair more tightly. He covered the other breast with his hand. Sweet Jesu, she was drowning.

His warm, moist tongue ringed the nipple. Rhoslyn moaned. Cool breath washed across her flesh and the exquisite pucker of the areola pushed her over the edge. Pleasure rolled over her in a sudden tidal wave that bowed her off the bed. She dropped back onto the mattress and couldn't stop her thighs from clamping around his hand as a second spasm rocked her.

An instant later, she became aware of the firm ridge of his manhood between her thighs, at the entrance to her channel. He poised over her, his form blurred.

"I shall claim you now, Lady Rhoslyn. All will know it, but most of all, you will know."

He entered her slowly, stretching, filling her until his pelvis lay flush with hers. He lowered his head and kissed her, full, sweet, and tender. Then he began to move inside her. A wondrous sensation rippled through her. He pulled back, then pressed his hips against hers again. He at last lowered himself onto her and she melted beneath his weight—she felt certain she would melt altogether, once again lost in rising need. Lovemaking had never been like this with Alec. Guilt resurfaced, but a sudden hard thrust of St. Claire's rod inside her drove away all thoughts of the dead, and she cried out.

Rhoslyn wrapped her arms around his neck. Hard muscle bunched beneath her fingers as he thrust into her, faster, harder, driving her once again toward that bliss that only a man could give a woman. Surging upward into full consciousness and feeling, her release broke free and consumed her in blinding pleasure. He uttered a groan and her climax spiked again and rippled through her in waves that left her with the knowledge that he had, without question, claimed her.

Chapter Sixteen

~

R HOSLYN SLOWED HER walk across the bailey at Castle Glenbarr and covertly watched St. Claire. He stood near the gate talking with two of his men. Today, he wore no mail shirt as he so often did. Instead, a white linen surcoat woven with gold thread hugged his shoulders and hung to his knees. He laughed at something one of the men said and crossed his arms over his chest. The surcoat went taut over his back, and her knees weakened. Sweet Jesu, she'd lost her mind.

This last week, St. Claire had kept her in a daze. Alec hadn't demonstrated as veracious an appetite as some husbands she had heard discussed while St. Claire made even the stories she'd heard seem tame.

As if sensing her scrutiny, he shifted his gaze past the man who stood in front of him and caught her eye. She couldn't pull her gaze away from his. A faint smile played about his full mouth. A satisfied smile. A smile that told her he remembered last night when he laid her down beneath the oak tree under the stars.

The cool grass beneath her and his warm body on top of her, his hard rod—she shut out the memory. To her shame, she broke her gaze from his and hurried away. His gaze seemed to burn her shoulder blades until she entered the castle.

Hand on the castle's door bolt, the door now safely closed behind her, she allowed herself a moment to regain her senses. What was it about him that made her want to melt like butter on a summer day? He was a beautiful man, but that alone wasn't the answer. Surely, that wasn't why the sight of him alone sent a skitter across the insides of her stomach.

Any time now, they would leave for the village, for the games planned for that afternoon. St. Claire said the games were in celebration of their marriage, but she suspected it was an excuse for him to gauge the mettle of the local young men. Either way, she would be spending the afternoon with him. Her traitorous heart skipped a beat at the thought.

The door started to shove open and Rhoslyn jumped aside. St. Claire entered and she nearly bolted for the staircase.

He paused in closing the door, his brow creased in a frown. "Is something amiss?"

She shook her head. "Nay, what could be amiss?" *Other than you being here?*

"It seems strange you are standing at the door."

He would notice that. "You have a suspicious mind, St. Claire."

"Perhaps," he replied. "But it is still strange."

"Did you want something?" she demanded.

The smile reappeared with a hint of amusement. "Are you ready to go to the village, or did you forget?" he asked.

"Forget that ye have ended my imprisonment? Nay, I am no' likely to forget that."

He closed the door and stepped close to her. "Would you prefer to stay at Castle Glenbarr?" He grasped a lock of hair that had sprung free of her braid and rubbed it between his fingers. "We could find something to do."

Heat rippled through her.

He slid an arm around her waist and pulled her close. "Would you like that?"

She would like it very much. Too much. As he well knew.

He dipped his head and kissed her. Already she had grown too familiar with the way his full mouth molded with hers. He swept his tongue inside her mouth. The way he tasted. He slid his free arm around her. The way he held her so tight it nearly took her breath. The way he made her wish they didn't have to leave Castle Glenbarr and that the world would never intrude.

He broke the kiss and nuzzled her ear. "What say you, Lady, would you prefer I make love to you?"

A thrill streaked through her. "Everyone will know," she whispered. As they surely must know after the way she cried out his name last night under the oak. How could anyone not have heard?

He gave a low laugh. "So?"

"Andreana is looking forward to going." She had difficulty concentrating. He nibbled on her earlobe.

"We could send her with an escort."

"The men will be disappointed you did not compete in the games." Sweet Jesu, what was he doing to her earlobe? A shiver traveled down her back.

"They want to beat the Dragon, you mean?"

"Aye," she breathed.

He pulled back and looked down at her. "Would you tame the Dragon, Lady?"

Her cheeks flushed warm. "The games are for men."

"Not the games I would play."

She suddenly felt as if she couldn't breathe.

Rhoslyn pulled back. "We must go. I will fetch Andreana."

He didn't release her. "What is wrong, Rhoslyn?"

She forced herself to meet his gaze, praying none of the panic welling up in her showed. "Nothing is wrong. But we promised everyone we would go. Andreana will be disappointed."

His gaze, once again intense, searched hers. Finally, he gave a gentle smile. "As you wish."

Twenty minutes later, Rhoslyn sat with Andreana on a plaid on the grass beneath a clear blue summer sky that reminded her of days when she was a child and chased butterflies among the heather on the hills beyond. Spectators crowded around the open field where St. Claire and young Colin stood toe-to-toe in readiness for the ball to be thrown into the air for their first game of shinty.

"Sir Talbot seems in good spirits," Andreana said.

"Aye," Rhoslyn said, though she wasn't sure if the sparkle of humor in his eyes represented joy or the surety of a man about to annihilate his opponent. Probably both.

Everyone seemed in good spirits. The entire village had turned out for the festivities, as well as those from ten miles around. Jugglers meandered through the crowd tossing balls, fruit, or knives. Faint plucking of harps and psaltery drifted through the excited chatter. Rhoslyn began to relax. Bright sunshine made the day perfect for the games.

The ball sailed into the air. St. Claire and Colin leapt, sticks tangling, then St. Claire's smacked the ball and it flew toward his teammates. They leapt toward the ball, with him and Colin matching stride with one another. The ball flew in St. Claire's direction and he swung for it. Colin, who matched him in height and weight, shouldered him aside and swung at the ball. Rhoslyn tensed when St. Claire tumbled to the ground. He rolled and came to his feet, laughing as he took off after Colin.

"I will never understand men," Andreana said. "They seem to love a hard tumble."

"Aye, they do." Rhoslyn smiled. "'Tis one of the things we most like about them."

"Are ye saying you like St. Claire?" Andreana asked.

Rhoslyn caught her dry humor.

"'Tis just an observation," she said.

"An observation about your husband."

Rhoslyn ignored the astute remark and watched St. Claire catch up with Colin, who was now surrounded by his teammates as they hit the ball across the grass. St. Claire charged past Colin, jabbing him in the belly with an elbow as he passed. The younger man faltered. The ball whizzed past St. Claire. He changed course and an instant later, reached the ball as one of his opponents and a teammate did. St. Claire dodged in front of his opponent, giving his teammate the chance to hit the ball.

The man whacked the ball while several other teammates raced alongside him toward the far end of the field. The opposing team rushed after them. St. Claire weaved past two of their opponents and shot past his team as they neared the goal. His teammate with the ball hit it toward St. Claire, and he swung hard, sending the ball across the goals as Colin tackled him.

The crowd roared and several men jostled in front of Rhoslyn. She jumped to her feet and pushed past the men in time to see St. Claire clap Colin on the back. St. Claire noticed her and grinned. She shook her head. Andreana was right. Men liked being knocked to the ground.

THE SUN GREW warmer as the day wore on and many of the men stripped down to their kilts. St. Claire wore dark breeches and, like the others, was now bare-chested as they lined up for a footrace. He had refrained from competing in the archery contest, for Andreana had pointed out that he had proven his archery skills by killing the boar that attacked Rhoslyn.

He cast Rhoslyn a grin, and her heart warmed as she smiled back. The man was having as much fun as the boys. She laughed inwardly. He was little more than an overgrown boy himself. His attention returned to his competitors and she allowed her gaze to slide across his chest. A boy with the body of a full grown man. A tremor rippled through her at the memory of that broad chest poised over her as he thrust into her last night.

Lady Isobel stepped into view beyond St. Claire. She stopped in the shade of a large ash tree, her attention fixed on him. Ire flared at sight of her open appreciation. Grandfather was right. Isobel would seduce St. Claire without guilt. As if sensing her scrutiny, the lady shifted her gaze to Rhoslyn. Isobel started forward, and Rhoslyn quickly realized she was headed her way.

Isobel reached them. "Lady Rhoslyn. Lady Andreana." She lowered herself onto the blanket beside Rhoslyn. "Such a perfect day for the games."

Rhoslyn nodded. "It is."

"Sir Talbot is doing well," Isobel said. "His team won the shinty match due much to his efforts."

"He is a skilled athlete," Andreana said, though Rhoslyn noticed her gaze fixed on Sir Baxter, who stood talking with a group of men to their left.

"That he is," Isobel agreed.

"How is Lord Herbert?" Rhoslyn said.

Isobel looked at her, brows lifted. Embarrassment washed over Rhoslyn when even Andreana cast her a curious glance.

"He is well," Isobel answered. "He will be pleased that you asked about him."

He would be pleased if his wife didn't openly pursue another woman's husband.

"The race is about to begin," Andreana said.

They looked at the men.

"The markings on Sir Talbot's arm is a picture of his sister, if I recall," Isobel said.

"Aye," Rhoslyn replied.

"The face puts me in mind of Lady Taresa."

Rhoslyn jerked her head in her direction. "Lady Peigi's mother?"

Isobel cocked her head. "I am surprised ye remember her. She left Buchan before you were born."

"I know her only by name. It is Lady Peigi, I remember. She returned to Buchan when her father died—" Rhoslyn stopped and calculated "—nineteen years ago."

"Aye," Isobel said. "He swore she would no' have his title or his land. In the end, he had his way. She died of a fever not long after he died."

"Why was he so angry?" Andreana asked.

"Because she married against his wishes."

"Then he had a right to be angry," she said. "I will married whoever Grandfather commands me to marry."

"Sir Talbot will choose your husband," Isobel said. "Will you do as he commands?"

"I must," she said.

Isobel laughed. "Then ye need no' worry he will banish you as Lord Baliman did Lady Peigi." Her smile vanished. "When Lady Peigi left, Lady Taresa went to live in one of Lord Baliman's lesser castles in the westernmost part of Buchan. She returned to Narlton Keep when her daughter inherited the title, but left again when Lady Peigi died. She has no' been back since. In truth, I am surprised she did no' return to Spain. I think she stays as far away as possible from the squabbling in the family. They constantly fight over who will be her heir."

"Lord Baliman met her on a pilgrimage?" Andreana asked.

Lady Isobel nodded. "In Galicia, at the Santiago de Compostela. It was quite a love match. Interesting, when you consider that his father was no' more pleased with his choice in a wife than he was his daughter's choice in a husband."

"Who did she marry?" Rhoslyn asked.

"Some untried knight, is what I hear. Lady Taresa does no' speak of her daughter."

"I remember Lady Peigi as a very quiet, withdrawn lady. I saw her father only once. He was loud and full of vitriol."

"Such things matter little to a man as wealthy as he."

Rhoslyn nodded, remembering. "He was wealthier than Lord Lochland."

"Indeed," Isobel said. "It was the dissention amongst the Kenzies that allowed Lochland to rise to power. So long as the family fights over the title, he will remain the most powerful man in Buchan."

Rhoslyn hadn't realized the Kenzies played such a large role in the earl's rise to power.

"Why does Lady Taresa not foster a son?" Andreana asked. "He could put an end to the squabbling."

"An excellent question," Lady Isobel said. "The answer is simple. She plans to let her husband's name die. It is her revenge for him banishing Lady Peigi."

"She is only hurting herself." Andreana said.

"Make no mistake, she is hurting his family. He has no close relatives, and those he does have are not strong enough to hold the land once she is gone." Isobel leaned in closer. "I have heard that she took Sir Derek Camdem as lover and plans for him to have Narlton Keep and her other lands when she is gone."

"A lady does no' take a knight as lover," Andreana said.

"She does if she is sixty-three-years-old and wealthy."

Andreana grimaced. "She is ancient."

"No' too ancient to—"

"*Lady Isobel*," Rhoslyn cut in.

Isobel closed her mouth, but no remorse shone in her eyes.

"Ye seem to know a great deal about the Kenzies," Rhoslyn said with asperity.

"Lady Taresa and my mother are friends."

Rhoslyn wondered if Lady Taresa would appreciate Isobel's gossip.

Shouts went up and Rhoslyn's attention snapped to the racers as they shot forward from the starting line. St. Claire and two other men raced neck and neck ahead of the others.

"Why is Sir Talbot not pulling ahead?" Andreana asked. "He can easily outpace the other men."

"I suspect Sir Talbot is a man who knows how to pace himself." Lady Isobel looked at Rhoslyn. "Is that no' so, Lady Rhoslyn?"

Rhoslyn had had enough. "Beware, Lady Isobel. St. Claire is no' a man to toy with."

One man pulled ahead as the racers reached the halfway mark. St. Claire stayed three paces behind the man, while everyone else strained to keep up with them.

Shouts of encouragement went up, and Rhoslyn listened to bets on who would win. Most favored St. Claire's competitor. The racers neared the finish line and St. Claire shot past the other man and beat him by little more than a nose. The onlookers voiced a great cheer. A cheer for their laird: Sir Talbot St. Claire.

TALBOT DIDN'T KNOW his wife well, but he did know she was pregnant. She hadn't told him. She didn't have to. The last month she had welcomed him into her bed enough nights that he should have felt guilty. But he didn't. He liked bedding her. More than liked. He needed her.

He'd regretted Rhoslyn's decision to return to Castle Glenbarr, but it turned out for the best. She settled into a routine that seemed to please her—and he gleaned interesting tidbits from the servants. It had taken her seven years to conceive with her first husband, and he suspected she believed, and probably hoped, that she couldn't conceive right away, if at all. That would have assuaged her worry that a child born too soon might be Dayton's.

The inability to conceive had to have been her husband's fault, not hers, for since Talbot had begun making love to her, her flux hadn't come. She might be a woman whose flux was less regular, but she had grown short of temper, which told him she was worried.

He'd begun to suspect last week, but now... His head spun with the thought of becoming a father, a dream longed for, and now within sight. Edward loved him much, for Talbot achieved his goals too well, and made himself too valuable as a warrior. Then the Maid of Norway perished and the opportunity to bring Scotland to heel had been Talbot's salvation. Or was Lady Rhoslyn his salvation?

He'd waited, hoping she would tell him about the child, but wasn't surprised by her silence. Another three months and she wouldn't be able to hide the truth. Might she wait that long? She might, but he wouldn't.

Talbot thought to find her in her usual spot this time of afternoon, going over the household rolls in their private solar, but she wasn't there. She wasn't in her chambers, either. He turned from the room and happened a glance out the window. Their chambers overlooked the bailey. East, beyond the stables, grew a large oak tree—which his wife was climbing. Half a dozen women stood at the foot of the giant oak looking up at a cat. He knew that cat.

Talbot spun and hurried down to the great hall and out the door. Moments later, he reached the women. Their chatter ceased and they backed away as he reached the tree. Rhoslyn stood on the second branch, which was level with his chest. Half of her hem draped an arm, revealing a generous portion of leg. She stilled and looked down.

"What are you doing?" he asked.

She scowled. "What do ye think I am doing?"

"I think you are being foolish."

"I am capable of climbing a tree, St. Claire."

"Rhoslyn, come down."

"Not until I fetch Lucifer."

"Aptly named," he said under his breath.

"Mayhap ye should come down, Lady Rhoslyn," Dona said. The cat belonged to the old woman and was as ancient as she.

Talbot took a hold of his wife's ankle. "I do not want you climbing that high."

Her brows dove downward. "Take your hands off me, St. Claire, or I will—"

He seized her arm and yanked. She shrieked and tumbled into his arms.

Talbot stared down at her. "As I was about to say, you can fall."

"Put me down."

He obeyed.

"Ye had better start climbing," she told him.

"The cat will come down when he is ready," Talbot said.

"Have ye ever had a cat, laird?" Dona asked. "They are good climbers, but they often bite off more than they can chew. He will stay up there until he is too weak to climb down, then he will fall. We must bring him down."

Talbot shifted his attention back to Rhoslyn. "I suppose if I do not get him down, you will be up that tree the moment I turn my back."

"Aye," she replied.

Yes, he would never have to wonder what this woman thought.

Talbot hoisted himself up onto the first branch, then climbed until he reached the branch below the cat, who perched halfway out on the limb.

"Lucifer, come," he commanded.

Giggles wafted up to him.

"He is no' a dog, St. Claire," Rhoslyn called. "He will not come on command."

The very reason he disliked cats. With a firm grip on an overhead branch, he eased out onto the limb. Lucifer meowed.

"Easy, laird," one woman called up. "Ye dinna' want to scare him."

He did want to scare the cat. Talbot came within arm's reach of the animal and the branch he stood on creaked. He halted and extended one arm.

"Come, Lucifer."

The cat meowed.

"Come."

Another meow, but the villain didn't move.

Talbot inched out far enough to be able to grab the cat. Lucifer backed out of reach. Talbot looked down at the branch he stood on. Sturdy enough to hold Rhoslyn, no doubt. He considered leaving the task to one of the younger, smaller men, but threw an arm over the overhead branch and crept out farther.

"Careful, laird," Dona called up. "That branch looks thin out there."

The branch was thin. He reached the cat and grabbed its scruff before he could scamper away again. The limb beneath Talbot gave a loud crack and the cat hissed with a guttural meow, digging its claws into the exposed flesh of Talbot's neck. Lucifer twisted and Talbot jerked in an effort to maintain his hold. The limb gave way beneath them as the cat hissed and sank its claws deeper into his flesh. They somersaulted in a tangle of fur and surcoat.

Talbot hit the ground on his side with a thud. The cat leapt from his arms and scampered off with Dona hurrying after him. Talbot drew a stuttered breath and blinked into focus the female faces that encircled him.

"Are ye in one piece, St. Claire?" Rhoslyn asked.

He noted the absence of sympathy.

"St Claire," she said when he didn't reply.

He groaned.

Her brow furrowed in uncertainty. "Surely, you are no' hurt from that short fall."

He'd fallen at least fifteen feet and was lucky he hadn't landed on his neck.

"I dinna' see any blood," one woman said.

He groaned again and closed his eyes.

An instant later, slim fingers gently probed his head. "St. Claire," Rhoslyn said.

This time concern filled her voice, desperate concern, if he wasn't mistaken.

Talbot snapped open his eyes, seized her shoulders and dragged her to him for a sound kiss. Rhoslyn yanked back, mouth agape.

"*St. Claire.*" She tried to twist free, but he pulled her close and kissed her once more, slowly, this time.

"Aye, he is no' harmed," one woman said.

Talbot rolled on top of Rhoslyn, still kissing her.

"I would say he is healthy as a horse," another said.

Rhoslyn finally managed to wedge her hands between them and he allowed her to push him away.

"Have ye lost your mind?" she demanded. "The ground is wet and cold. Get off me."

He looked up at the women. "Do I not deserve a reward for risking my life?"

"I would say ye are risking your life lying on top of Lady Rhoslyn in public," a woman said.

She had a point. Talbot looked down at his wife. Her dark eyes roiled with fury.

"Were you not the least bit worried I had injured myself?" he asked.

She gave a disgusted snort. "Ye should have let me climb the tree."

His amusement vanished. "I can easily survive a fall. You and our child cannot."

RHOSLYN'S EYES WIDEN.

He knows.

"Child?" Edina said.

"Lady Rhoslyn," Molly cried, and they all began to talk at once.

St. Claire shoved to his feet and extended a hand toward her. Her heart pounded. He knew. But how? She wanted to slap his hand away. He lifted a brow. Rhoslyn narrowed her eyes. He shrugged and grasped her hand, pulling her to her feet. The women immediately encircled her, their chatter a muddle of congratulations, advice, and general joy.

"Why did ye no' tell us?" Molly asked.

"The babe has been inside her a mere month," Edina said. "She was probably waiting to be certain." She looked at St. Claire. "But a husband knows."

"Aye," the others agreed, heads nodding in vigorous agreement.

Tears sprang to Rhoslyn's eyes. The women were letting her know they accepted the baby as St. Claire's without question. They began hugging her and laughing and she feared she wouldn't be able to hold back the tears.

"Aye," she managed in a level voice. "I wanted to be certain. As ye can see, St. Claire is going to be too protective."

"Of course," Tira said. "He wants ye and the babe to be safe."

Rhoslyn nodded. "Aye. Now I am a bit tired. Will you walk with me, St. Claire?"

"Go on," Edina said. "Take a nap." She looked at St. Claire. "Ye might want to put your wife to bed, laird." She winked.

St. Claire bowed. "Excellent advice." He turned to Rhoslyn and held out his arm. "My lady."

She cast him a dark look, accepted his arm, and started away. Opposite the stables, out of earshot of the woman, Rhoslyn said, "How did ye know?"

"As the women said, a husband knows."

Rhoslyn snorted.

"No one told me," he said. "I feel certain you told no one."

No, she hadn't. She still didn't half believe it. All those years with Alec she had been so sure it was her fault she didn't conceive. To conceive so quickly now had to mean it was Alec and not her who had been at fault. How many times had she knelt in the chapel, begging one saint after another for a child? Now, she had gotten pregnant within the first month of marriage. Mayhap, the first time.

They started around the stables and Rhoslyn grabbed St. Claire's arm and pulled him around the back of the building. "Why did ye tell the women I am with child?"

"Because it is better they believe we are happy about the babe."

She stiffened. "Then ye are no' happy."

He frowned. "What makes you say that?"

"You say it is better they *believe* we are happy. That implies ye are hesitant."

"I am very happy. It is you who have misgivings."

"Aye, I have misgivings. It is easy for you to say you will love the child no matter what. But when the babe doesna' look or act like ye, anger and resentment will make you think differently."

"Rhoslyn, the child is mine."

"Ye hope it is yours," she shot back.

He grasped her shoulders. "The child is mine."

"Your brother—"

"My brother will never come near my children. *My children.* Do you understand?"

She searched his face. How she wanted to believe him.

He pulled her against his chest. At first she resisted, but he held her tight and rested his chin on her head.

"Lady Andreana is grown," he said. "She will soon marry and leave our house. Do you not want children?"

She did, but what if the child wasn't his? Worse, what if the child ended up buried beside Dougal?

St. Claire drew back, then pulled her against his side and began walking. "We should send word to your grandfather."

"Nay," she said too quickly, then amended, "Do no' tell him in a missive. Invite him to come, then we will tell him in person. But let us wait at least a month."

"Why?"

"Many things can go wrong in the first few weeks."

"Like falling from a tree?"

She slapped his arm.

"Do you not think it better if everyone knows you are having my child?" he asked.

Rhoslyn looked at him. "Do ye believe your brother is still in Scotland?"

"I have no reason to believe he has left. I wrote my father and Edward. If Dayton returns to England, they will send word."

She grew tired of hiding from him within the walls of Castle Glenbarr. Never before had she allowed anyone to bully her. *Never before have you had so much to lose,* a small voice replied.

"I told ye it could be some time before ye caught him," she said. "How long am I to endure being prisoner here?"

"Until I catch him, especially now that you are pregnant. Make no mistake, Dayton will happily claim my son as his if he believes it will gain him your fortune."

"Just as you would claim his," she said more to herself than him.

He glanced down at her, and she glimpsed the hurt in his eyes. The emotion vanished in an instant, but her guilt pierced soul deep.

He looked straight ahead. "Rhoslyn, if you were pregnant with Melrose's child, I would have claimed you as my wife and taken the babe as my own. I suppose my brother and I are much alike."

Denial leapt on her lips. He wasn't like his brother…not wholly. St. Claire had the right to demand that she honor the betrothal. That was the way of things for women like her. When her grandfather betrothed her to Alec she understood her duty and married him. He had been a good man and she loved him. But, in truth, he loved her more than she had him. Her stomach knotted. Hadn't that always been a niggling guilt—one she had managed to ignore until now? St. Claire made her feel... Made her feel what? *Feel.* That was all.

Feeling was everything.

Feeling was dangerous.

Chapter Seventeen

"I OFTEN WONDERED if Alec wasn't at fault for your inability to conceive," Seward told Rhoslyn.

Talbot liked the old baron's honesty.

Lady Rhoslyn shrugged. "It would seem ye were right."

Seward shifted his attention to Talbot. "Edward will be pleased to learn the news."

Talbot shrugged and glimpsed the slight narrowing of Rhoslyn's eyes. She hated it when he did that. She also wasn't pleased that he had contacted her grandfather. She'd wanted a month. He'd given her three weeks.

"Edward might be pleased," Talbot said.

"Ye know he will be glad," Seward said. "But we will worry about that when the time comes. I am pleased."

"That is enough," Talbot said.

"When will the babe come?"

"Mid-spring," Rhoslyn answered.

Seward's gaze swung onto him. "Ye have had no word on the whereabouts of your brother?"

Talbot shook his head. "He seems to have disappeared."

"An adder waiting to strike," Seward murmured.

Talbot had to agree.

"I assume the servants know about the pregnancy?"

"Aye," Rhoslyn said, and shot Talbot a recriminating glance.

"It may no' matter," Seward said. "There is no telling what a madman will do. If we say nothing, Dayton may feel desperate enough to make a move. If we announce the pregnancy, he might become emboldened to make a claim. Either way, I wager he is still in Scotland."

"There is the chance he realizes his folly and has given up," Rhoslyn said. "He may simply be hiding."

"Perhaps," Seward said. "But it is more likely he is waiting for an opportunity."

"Your grandfather is right," Talbot said. "Dayton will not give up so easily."

"Mayhap I should look for him myself."

"Nay," Rhoslyn blurted. She cast a pleading glance at Talbot.

"You can, but it would likely be a waste of time," Talbot said. "I have men searching for him."

"They are no' doing a good job," Seward said.

"You do not know my brother. He is a skilled warrior and hunter. He will not be easy to find. But he will make a mistake, and that is when I will catch him."

The old baron glanced at Rhoslyn, then said to Talbot, "This will no' be over until he is dead."

"Aye," Talbot said. "I know."

TALBOT HAPPENED TO be on the wall when the rider was sighted in the distance, riding at breakneck speed.

"He is slumped in the saddle," Baxter said.

Talbot nodded. He scanned the horizon for other riders but found none. The rider drew closer and a prickle crept up his spine when he recognized the crest on the man's mail shirt.

"Kinsley." Baxter looked at Talbot. "They have barely had time to reach Banmore Castle."

"Open the gate," Talbot ordered, then turned and hurried down the stairs.

He reached the bailey as the man rode inside. Talbot instantly took in the dark stain on his sleeve, and caught him as he nearly fell from his saddle.

"Kinsley," the rider rasped.

Baxter appeared at his side.

"Help me get him inside," Talbot ordered.

Baxter slung one of the man's arms over his shoulder and Talbot did the same with the other, then they brought him inside and lowered him into a chair at the table near the hearth.

"Bring ale," he told a waiting lad, then said to the rider, "What happened?"

"Attacked," he said between gulps of air. "At the gorge."

Talbot looked at Baxter.

"Colliston Gorge is west of us on the way to Banmore Castle."

The man grabbed Talbot's shirt. "They fell upon us—"

The lad appeared with ale and Talbot pressed the lip of the mug to the man's mouth.

He drank greedily, then pushed Talbot's hand away. "Kinsley asks ye for help."

"How many?" he demanded.

"Maybe fifty," the man replied.

"Gather a hundred men," Talbot told Baxter. "We ride within the hour."

LED BY ROSS, Talbot rode hard with his men. Twenty minutes later, they reached the gorge and he knew the attackers were gone. Bodies lay broken and bloodied across the trampled ground. Seward had ridden with twenty men; a dozen lay dead on the road alone, but Seward was not among them. Maybe he had eluded his attackers and reached the safety of Banmore Castle.

Talbot ordered men to check the fallen warriors, then sent scouts to search the area. He hoped Seward's attackers had gotten sloppy. Talbot took a dozen men and began searching for more wounded.

Minutes later, one of his men located Seward. He lay near two of his men, a sword wound through his ribs. Blood darkened the ground beneath him. Talbot dismounted and dropped to one knee beside him and was surprised to discover a faint pulse at his neck. Talbot removed Seward's mail shirt and tunic, then tore the tunic into a long strip and began binding the wound.

Ross appeared on his horse. "We found one of the attackers still alive."

"Is there any clue as to who he and his companions are?" Talbot demanded.

"He wears no crest or identifying marks."

"Beat it out of him, then throw him over a horse and bring him to Castle Glenbarr. If you find any others, bring them as well. Have you any idea who they might be?"

"Your brother comes to mind."

"I cannot think what he would gain by killing Seward." But Talbot wondered if he knew his brother at all. "Take Cullen. He is our best tracker," he said. "Track them, but do not make contact. I want to know who they are. Then I will deal with them myself."

Ross nodded, whirled his horse around and was gone.

Talbot mounted his charger, then had Seward lifted onto his horse behind him and tied to him. The old man moaned, then fell silent. Talbot took thirty of his men and started for Castle Glenbarr. The slow pace he was forced to maintain in deference to Seward chaffed against his desire for speed. They reached the castle an hour later, and Baxter met them in the bailey.

"God's blood," Baxter muttered as he lifted Seward from the saddle.

"Easy," Talbot said.

They entered through the postern door and Mistress Muira hurried toward them from the kitchen. She reached them as they neared the stairs.

Her eyes widened. "Sweet God." She crossed herself, then shouted, "Leanna!" A girl appeared in the doorway. "Bring warm water and clean rags to the laird's chambers." She hurried past them and up the stairs. "None of the other rooms are warm enough," she said as they ascended. "I will have a fire prepared, but until the room is warm enough I will tend him in your private chambers, laird."

They reached the third floor and Talbot laid him down in Rhoslyn's bed.

Mistress Muira sat beside Seward on the bed and surveyed the bandage. "Have ye a knife, laird?"

He gave her the knife strapped to his belt and she made quick work of cutting the knot Talbot had tied in the bandage.

"Where is Lady Rhoslyn?" he demanded.

"The ladies solar."

Talbot motioned Baxter to follow and they entered his private solar.

"Have you any idea who attacked him?" Baxter asked.

"One was found wounded, but alive. God willing, we'll know soon enough."

"Would Dayton attack the old baron?" Baxter said.

"If he thought it would profit him, aye. But I cannot see how it would help his cause."

"Perhaps I should go to the gorge and have a look?" Baxter said.

Talbot shook his head. "Ross is there. He knows the land better than we. If there is anything to be found, he will find it. Add an extra watch to the guards, and send men to scout the land between here, Dunfrey Castle, and Banmore Castle. Keep scouts out until I tell you otherwise. Any news, inform me immediately—especially when the men return with the prisoner. Lady Rhoslyn will demand to be informed as well. Leave her to me."

"Aye," Baxter said, and left.

"LADY BRAE IS but fourteen," Rhoslyn told Lord Davis. "It is no wonder her parents are loathe to let her marry just yet. Did they no' agree that the marriage would take place one year hence?"

"Aye," the young lord replied. "But I love her. I canna' wait."

Beside Rhoslyn on the bench in the ladies solar, Lady Saraid began swinging her feet distractedly. Rhoslyn sighed inwardly. She had clearly been gone too long. All of Buchan must have learned that she had returned home and now stood outside her door. The requests to facilitate marriage proposals and petitions to foster or tutor young ladies would keep her busy until the birth of her own child. She started to cover her belly with a hand, then remembered she wasn't alone.

"Lady Rhoslyn?" Lord Davis said. "Will ye speak with Lady Brae's father?"

Saraid swung her feet harder.

"Sweet Jesu, cease swinging your feet, child," Rhoslyn said.

The girl immediately stilled and Lord Davis's eyes rounded like a doe caught in a bowman's sights.

Rhoslyn released a breath. "Lady Saraid, a lady doesna' act bored when she has guests." Neither does a lady lose her temper with a young girl.

"'Tis impossible not to be bored," Saraid replied.

Rhoslyn had to agree, but couldn't admit that. Lady Saraid was thirteen and wanted to be anywhere but here. "A lady never lets it be known she is bored," Rhoslyn told her.

Saraid's brows dove downward but she remained silent.

Rhoslyn returned her attention to the young man. "Lord Davis, your future bride is still young. Would ye really tear her from her family too soon?"

He frowned. "She *wants* to marry me."

"Of course she does," Rhoslyn said gently. "But she asked you to be patient and understand that her parents were no' quite ready to let her go."

"Aye," he shot back. "They do no' understand she is a woman grown."

Almost a woman grown, Rhoslyn thought. But not quite. "Did it occur to ye that she does not want to hurt her parents?" Rhoslyn asked.

"They canna' hold her forever," he muttered.

"I doubt they want to do that. Do ye plan to have children?"

"Of course. I want many sons."

"Mayhap a daughter or two, as well," Rhoslyn said. "A sweet babe who will grow up into a beautiful woman."

His cheeks colored. "Aye, a daughter would please me."

Would her child be a girl this time? Would St. Claire be happy with a daughter? "Can ye imagine handing her over to a man?" Rhoslyn asked the young man. "Ever?"

His lips pursed.

"Her father has made his decision," Rhoslyn said. "It is best ye abide by it. You are betrothed. You can wait a year for her fifteenth birthday."

The young man looked as if he had been given a death decree, but he nodded. "Thank ye, Lady Rhoslyn."

The door to the solar opened and St. Claire entered. The hard set of his mouth caused Rhoslyn's heart to jump. Something was wrong.

"Ye may go, Lord Davis," Rhoslyn said. "Lady Saraid, work on your needlework. It is on the table where ye left it."

Lord Davis strode to the door. "Sir Talbot," he said.

"My lord," St. Claire said. "It is good to see you."

The young man nodded, then left.

Rhoslyn rose and crossed to St. Claire.

"Will you speak with me in our chambers, my lady?" he asked.

"Aye. Lady Saraid, I will return later."

They left and when they reached their solar, she said, "What is it?"

"Your grandfather, he is wounded."

"Wounded? What do ye mean—Where is he? What happened?" The room spun. St. Claire grasped her arm. "Tell me," she insisted.

"Someone attacked him on his return trip home," he said.

Rhoslyn gasped. "Is he—"

St. Claire shook his head. "Nay, but I will not lie. He is seriously wounded."

"Where is he?"

"In your chambers."

Without another word, she ran across the room to her door and burst into her quarters. Mistress Miura sat on the edge of her bed beside her grandfather. In an instant, Rhoslyn took in the bloody bandages on the table beside the bed and the gash in his ribs.

She hurried to the bed. "How is he, Mistress?"

"He is alive," she replied.

The need to cry tightened her throat. "What can I do?"

Muira instructed her and, together, they finished cleaning the wound, then applied herbs and bound his ribs. What seemed eons later, Rhoslyn sat alone with her grandfather in the dimly lit room.

The tread of booted feet approached from behind.

"What do ye want, St. Claire?" she asked.

"Mistress Muira informed me he is resting well," he said.

Rhoslyn shot to her feet and whirled on him. "With no help from ye."

Surprise flickered in his eyes. "I am the one who found and brought him here."

"How is it ye were with him when he was wounded?" she demanded.

"I was not. Seward sent one of his men back for help. I went immediately."

"Without telling me."

"I took a hundred men. What help could you have offered that they could not?"

"I would have gone, you monster," she snapped.

He barked a laugh. "That I would not have allowed."

"Ye could no' have stopped me."

"Christ, Rhoslyn, had I wasted even a moment, he could have died."

She closed the distance between them in an instant. "Had ye killed Dayton, Grandfather would not be lying in that bed at all."

His gaze sharpened and she was startled to realize her barb had struck home. That was what she'd intended, but satisfaction didn't taste as sweet as expected.

"You believe Dayton is responsible for the attack?" he asked.

"Who else?"

"You are saying Seward has no enemies."

"None who would attack him with such malice."

"Nay?" St. Claire said. "Only a few days ago Roberts intended to kill him."

"Bah! There is a difference in fighting and sneaking up on a man like a dog. This smells like your brother."

"It could be him," St. Claire said. "But to what end?"

"To draw you out, force you away from Castle Glenbarr. God only knows. The man is not in his right senses."

"That is true," St. Claire said. "But he is not a fool when it comes to warring."

"Warring, aye, and ye brought it to us."

"You are overwrought," he said. "I understand your worry. But you know this was not my doing. However, I will find who is responsible and give you his head."

She stared. "His head? What comfort will that be if my grandfather dies?" Rhoslyn turned away and returned to her grandfather's side.

All was quiet for a few moments, then the tread of boots on stone told her St. Claire had left. Only then did she let the tears flow.

AT THE KNOCK on the door, Talbot called, "Enter."

Ross entered. Talbot noted his mud-caked boots and grimy hands and hair—and the blood crusted, gaping hole in his left shirts sleeve.

Talbot laid his quill on the parchment and rose. "Did you find Seward's attackers?"

Ross glanced at his wounded arm and grunted. "We ran into a band of marauders. Fools tried to relieve us of our horses."

"It seems Buchan is riddled with thieves and cutthroats," Talbot observed.

"No more so than England, I imagine," Ross replied without rancor. "I hear ye took one of Kinsley's attackers alive."

Talbot nodded. "He died before reaching Castle Glenbarr."

"I suppose we should be thankful our enemies are no' as hardy as we are," Ross said. "Or mayhap we are better killers."

Talbot grunted. "Did you locate Seward's attackers?"

"Not exactly. There were about twenty men. They split off into three groups. On a hunch, I took Cullen with me and we followed the northernmost riders. Those men broke off and we were able to follow only two men into Elgean. We lost their trail there, but that village falls under the protection of Sir Jason Boyd. I canna' believe thirty men could plan an attack without Boyd knowing."

"Then you believe he is behind the attack?" Talbot asked.

"He at least knew of it," Ross replied. "But beware. That will no' be easy to prove."

Talbot nodded. "If he sent the men but did not go with them, he can claim they were acting of their own accord. And you did not actually find any of the men?"

"Nay. We lost the tracks in the village."

"I imagine that was the plan," Talbot said. "What reason would Boyd have to attack Seward?"

Ross grunted. "Boyd has lusted after Castle Glenbarr since he was a boy. But he hasna' the power to take it alone. His laird is Domhnall De Quincy, the Earl of Maddsen. De Quincy is a rival of our laird Eoghan Neachdan, the Earl of Lochland. De Quincy wouldna' mind tipping the scales of power in his favor. If any of his knights managed to seize Kinsley's power, well," he shrugged, "all the better for him."

"What a coincidence that one of his men chose now to attack."

Ross nodded. "Ye find that odd, as well?"

Now Talbot understood what Dayton might have to gain by attacking Seward.

RHOSLYN REFUSED TO move from her grandfather's side, and the following night, when the door quietly opened behind her, she thought St. Claire had returned as he had last night, to insist she come to his bed.

His bed. A mental picture flashed of lying safe and warm in his arms. Tears pricked, then guilt followed with a hard stab. How could she consider sharing the man's bed who was responsible for her grandfather lying at death's door? She placed a palm over her belly. How could she hate the father of her child?

She started from her thoughts when Mistress Miura appeared beside the bed.

"I am all right, Miura," Rhoslyn said. "Ye need no' worry about me."

"I know well enough to worry about ye, my lady, but that isna' why I come. I thought you should know that Lord Lochland is here."

Rhoslyn looked up sharply. "Here? Now?" Fury rammed through her. "Grandfather is in bed but a day and already Lochland picks the bones." She shoved to her feet, then hesitated.

"Go on," Muira said. "I will sit with him."

Rhoslyn still hesitated. If anything happened while she was away from his side. If he died… She shook her head. "Nay. I canna' leave him."

The housekeeper nodded. "I will let ye know if the men call for you."

Rhoslyn started to sit down on the bed, then stopped. The men would not call for her. They would make their plans, then she would be forced to live with the consequences.

"Muira, wait." Her heart was breaking. "Nay. I must go. If—when—my grandfather awakens and he learns I shirked my duty he will not forgive me. You stay. If you need me for anything—anything at all—you will call me?"

"Aye, my lady. But he is sleeping well. I dinna' think you need worry. He is strong."

Rhoslyn nodded and hurried from the room before she could change her mind. She reached the great hall and found Lord Lochland sitting alone at the table.

He rose as she approached. "Lady Rhoslyn."

She reached him and dropped into a curtsey. "Lord Lochland." She rose. "It is good to see you."

"And you. How is your grandfather?"

"His breathing is strong. We are hopeful he will awaken at any time."

He smiled indulgently and she wanted to scream. Instead, she said in a sweet voice, "Would ye like to come into the bower? We can speak in private there."

"Nay, Lady Rhoslyn, I am here to see your husband."

"Anything that concerns him concerns me," she said.

"Aye, but I think it is better if he and I speak alone first."

"If you fear that I will be upset when you speak of my grandfather, ye need no' worry. I understand the situation."

The postern door opened and frustration bubbled up when St. Claire entered. He strode to where they stood.

"St. Claire," she said, "this is the Earl of Lochland. Lord Lochland, my husband, Sir Talbot St. Claire."

St. Claire canted his head. "My lord, I am pleased to meet you."

Lord Lochland gave a curt nod, then cast a glance at Rhoslyn. "I wish our meeting was under happier circumstances. Can we speak privately?"

"Aye. We can go to the bower." He looked at Rhoslyn. "Will you have wine sent up?"

She nodded. "Aye." Rhoslyn turned, and St. Claire led him toward the stairs.

She secured a tray of wine and two goblets, then took her time approaching the bower. As hoped, she arrived when the men were standing in front of the fire.

They turned as she entered, and Lord Lochland said when she crossed to the table near the hearth, "Lady Rhoslyn, as I said earlier, it is better if I speak with your husband alone."

She set the tray on the table and began pouring the wine. "Why? He will only repeat to me everything you say." That, she knew, was likely untrue. She looked up at the earl. "Surely, there is no need for that?"

Irritation flared in his eyes. "It will no' be easy for ye to hear what I have to say. As much as I pray your grandfather lives, he may not, and I canna' put aside my responsibilities because of sentiment."

She angled her head in acknowledgment. "Of course not. I would not ask it of ye." She picked up the two goblets, went to the men and gave them each a glass.

"Please sit, Rhoslyn," St. Claire said.

He betrayed no anger in his manner, but she'd learned how apt he was at disguising his feelings. They hadn't spoken since their argument. If he was angry with her wouldn't he have ordered her from the room? She sat on the bench before he could change his mind.

The earl turned his attention to St. Claire. "As I was saying, I am hearing rumors that two of Kinsley's enemies are plotting to take possession of his holdings."

"They must know I would not allow that," St. Claire said.

"Aye, they surely know, for anything they take is yours when he dies. But that doesna' mean they will not try, and soon, for they will want to attack while he lies unconscious."

St. Claire nodded. "They may try."

Lochland gave a slow nod. "You can defend Seward's people. Still, I would prefer to avoid a war."

"Have you not the power to stop them?" St. Claire asked.

"I am no' their laird, and their laird is no friend of mine. In truth, he would love nothing better than to gain a foothold in my territory."

"Who are these men and their lord?"

"Their laird is Domhnall De Quincy, the Earl of Maddsen. He rules the land to the south. The two I suspect of plotting against Kinsley are Baron Balcaskie and Sir Jason Boyd."

Something flickered in St. Claire's eyes. "De Quincy would risk a fight with you?" he asked.

"Mayhap ye dinna' understand how powerful Kinsley is," Lochland said. "Within Buchan, he is second only to me. He commands fifteen hundred men-at-arms, and easily that many warriors amongst his tenants, if need be. If they were to gain control of his land, it would be no small matter for me to drive them out." Lochland studied him. "You have the skill to defend his land, but can ye inspire his men to follow ye?"

"If they want to win, they will follow me," St. Claire said.

A shiver snaked down Rhoslyn's spine. St. Claire's confidence recalled the memory of him slicing open the neck of his enemy. Would he view her grandfather's death with the same dispassion as he did fighting an enemy?

Lord Lochland's eyes rested on Rhoslyn. "I should have married De Quincy to your wife. That would have solved this problem."

Marriage to Domhnall De Quincy? Sweet Jesu, that was worse than marriage to St. Claire. Though she would marry De Quincy if it meant her grandfather lived. But she couldn't buy her grandfather's life. God didn't barter. She'd learned that first hand.

Rhoslyn said to Lochland, "If it is true De Quincy wishes to seize your power, then my marriage to him would only ensure war upon my grandfather's death."

The earl gave a slow nod. "Ye are right. Which is why I have decided to betroth Lady Andreana to him."

SHOCK REGISTERED IN Rhoslyn's eyes, then was gone so quickly Talbot almost doubted he'd seen it.

"Ye canno' marry Andreana to Lord De Quincy," she said.

"I can," he replied.

She shook her head. "Forgive me, I am not making myself clear. You canna' marry her to anyone. She is already married."

"Already married? To who?" he demanded.

"To my husband's captain, Sir Baxter D'Angers."

Lochland turned his hard gaze onto Talbot. "Is this true?"

"I am sorry, St. Claire," she quickly replied. "This is all my fault. It was my idea to marry her to Sir Baxter. She is of marriageable age, and I felt it better she marry a man my lord husband knew to be of a good character."

My lord husband? Talbot wanted to laugh. It seemed his wife wasn't above stroking a man's ego when it served her purpose.

"When did the marriage take place?" Lochland demanded.

"Four days ago," she replied.

His gaze sharpened. "I heard nothing of the marriage."

"We had a very small wedding," Talbot interjected before Rhoslyn could reply. "Given the trouble with my brother, I decided against opening our doors to visitors. We had a small ceremony in the chapel." He smiled at Rhoslyn. "After all, that is what Lady Rhoslyn and I did."

The earl's mouth thinned. "I imagine Edward will be well pleased at the progress you have made in so short a time."

"As my wife said, Baxter is of the highest character. I betrothed them to please her, nothing more."

Relief flickered in her eyes, then was gone when Lochland shifted his gaze onto her.

"I am surprised, Lady Rhoslyn, that you would agree to your step-daughter's marriage to an Englishman—even one of high character."

"I am sure you have heard how St. Claire defended us against marauders," she said. "He saved us. I have come to trust his judgment."

Talbot was startled to read true gratitude on her face. Only last night she had accused him of being responsible for the attack on her grandfather.

"Marauders?" Lochland's brow lifted. "I was told the men who attacked were employed by your brother."

"That is what I believe," Talbot said.

"Surely there must be some way other than marriage to Andreana to avoid fighting with De Quincy?" Rhoslyn said. "There is no guarantee he would have agreed to the marriage, anyway."

"He would have agreed," Lochland said. "But it seems your husband will have to deal with him."

Chapter Eighteen

~

WHEN THE POSTERN door closed behind Lochland, Talbot was ready for Rhoslyn as she rounded on him. He held up a hand to quiet her. "A moment, Lady Rhoslyn." Talbot called to a lad waiting near the table. "Find Sir Baxter and send him to my private quarters. Look first on the wall. If he is not there, try the field where the men train."

"Aye, laird," the boy started to turn away.

"Lad."

The boy stopped.

"Come with Baxter to my chambers."

The boy's eyes widened, but he turned and sped from the room.

Talbot turned back to Rhoslyn. "Where is Lady Andreana?"

Rhoslyn shook her head. "I do no' know. She could be in her chambers, or mayhap she is sitting with my grandfather."

"We had better find her and tell her she is married."

Rhoslyn's eyes rounded. "My God, St. Claire, what have I done?"

"Gotten us all hung, if your priest does not agree to forge marriage papers."

"You mean ye really will betroth Sir Baxter to Andreana?"

"You were not sure I would?" He laughed. "If you had doubts, why did you tell Lochland they were married?"

"I could think of nothing else."

"I suppose I should be glad you did not think of me killing him."

"The thought crossed my mind," she replied, and Talbot suspected it was more accurate to say that she considered killing him herself.

"Let us find Lady Andreana," he said.

He strode to the kitchen and ordered one of the maids to find Andreana and send her to his chambers. He returned to Rhoslyn and they hurried to their private quarters.

When he closed the door behind them, she said, "What if Father Crey will no' say they are already married?"

"He will agree if he wants any more contributions from me."

Her mouth fell open. "Ye canna' bribe a priest."

"Aye, but I can."

She shook her head. "He will do it to save her from De Quincy."

"All the better. That will save me silver."

"That is blasphemy," she said, but he caught a hint of laughter in her voice, and relief flooded him. Perhaps she had seen reason and understood he wasn't to blame for her grandfather being attacked.

"It is frugal," he replied.

"We must have witnesses. Mistress Muira will surely agree. My grandfather. Perhaps some of your men as well, St. Claire." Her brow knitted in worry. "Will Sir Baxter marry her?"

"He will do as I command."

"I do no' want him to hate her."

"Rhoslyn, it is a good match for him. He will be pleased. Do not worry."

She snorted. "Ye are a terrible liar. He hates Scotland. I believe he dreams of you and him returning to England."

Talbot regarded her. "There was a time you dreamed of me returning to England. Now you have married your stepdaughter to my captain."

"Your captain is preferable to De Quincy."

"Hmm," Talbot intoned. "So it isn't that you see our redeeming qualities, but simply that there is someone you perceive as being worse than we are."

She stepped closer to him. "Nay. You are wrong. I..." Confusion washed across her features and Talbot read in her eyes fear for her grandfather's life and anger that he had been hurt.

Talbot grasped her chin and tilted her face up toward him. "You..."

She reached for his shoulders, rose on tiptoes, kissed him, then drew back. "I am grateful that you are saving Andreana."

He looked down at her. "Grateful?"

That was a start.

A KNOCK SOUNDED at the door and Rhoslyn jerked free of St. Claire's embrace.

"Enter," he called.

The door opened and Andreana entered. "Ye called for me, laird?"

"Aye, Lady Andreana." He looked at Rhoslyn.

"Andreana, come, sit with me at the fire."

The girl looked from Rhoslyn to him, brows drawn, but she did as Rhoslyn asked.

They sat and Rhoslyn took Andreana's hand in hers. "There is no way to say this save directly."

"What is it?" Andreana blurted. "Has Grandfather died?"

"Nay," Rhoslyn quickly assured her. "Nothing like that. I am sorry.

We didna' mean to frighten you. Andreana, ye are to be married immediately."

Andreana blinked. "Married?" She looked from Rhoslyn to St. Claire. "What has happened?"

"Lord Lochland wanted to betroth you to De Quincy," St. Claire replied.

Andreana gasped.

"Your mother told him you were already wed to Sir Baxter."

Rhoslyn squeezed her hand. "It was the only way. St. Claire says Sir Baxter is a good man. He is preferable to De Quincy, do ye no' agree?"

"Aye," Andreana said slowly. "It is just so…unexpected." She looked again at St. Claire. "What does Sir Baxter think about being saddled with a Scottish wife?"

"He will consider himself fortunate," Rhoslyn interjected.

Andreana gave her a gentle smile. "Sir Baxter has no more wish to marry a Scottish woman than ye did to marry an Englishman."

"Andreana," Rhoslyn remonstrated.

"Do not chide her for understanding the truth, Rhoslyn," St. Claire cut in, then shifted his gaze to Andreana. "It is a good match for him, more than he could have hoped for at least another five years, maybe more. Aside from being intelligent and beautiful, you are an heiress. He will see the advantage in marrying you."

"But you told Lord Lochland that we were already married. How will you hide the truth from him?"

Rhoslyn patted her hand. "Leave that to us."

Andreana shook her head. "I must know, for Sir Baxter and I are to live this farce."

"It is no farce," Rhoslyn said. "You will truly be married. Father Crey will date the wedding's church records four days past."

Her brows rose. "That is a dangerous game."

"The risk is worth keeping you from De Quincy," Rhoslyn said.

Andreana nodded. "Aye." She shifted her attention to St. Claire. "Thank you. This is a terrible risk. I am in your debt."

Annoyance pricked. Rhoslyn had risked just as much as St. Claire, but Andreana acted as if she had nothing to do with saving her from De Quincy. Though, St. Claire hadn't had to go along with the lie. He could have told Lord Lochland the truth and left Andreana to her fate. He did, in truth, have more than Rhoslyn to lose if the earl discovered their lie. Was he doing this to make up for her grandfather's injury? Of course he was, he—Another knock came to the door. St. Claire bade them enter. The lad and Sir Baxter entered the room.

"Sit, Baxter," St. Claire said.

The man's brows rose, but he obeyed as St. Claire strode to the writing table in the far corner of the room. As he wrote something on a parchment, Rhoslyn noticed the furtive glances Andreana cast in Sir Baxter's direction. Rhoslyn recalled the day Andreana returned to Castle

Glenbarr, and her reaction to Sir Baxter when they were introduced, then the way she had watched him during the games. The girl was attracted to him! So this marriage might not be the prison sentence Rhoslyn had feared it might be.

St. Claire rose from the table with the parchment, folded and sealed. He instructed the boy to deliver the note to Father Crey in the village. The lad left and St. Claire faced them.

"Baxter, you will be pleased to know that I have betrothed you to Lady Andreana."

Startlement flickered in the knight's eyes. "Forgive me, my lord, this is somewhat...abrupt."

"Aye," St. Claire said, and recounted to Sir Baxter what had happened.

Sir Baxter gave a slow nod. "I have heard of De Quincy. It is said he does not deal fairly with his tenants."

Rhoslyn snorted. "That is but one of his faults. He would rule all of Buchan, given the chance, and he would do it on the backs of those who work the land. He is a cruel man."

"I suppose it is fortunate, then, that I am free to save Lady Andreana."

The words were sweet, but Rhoslyn was sure she heard bitterness in his voice.

"Aye, it is," St. Claire said. "Father Crey will perform the ceremony immediately, then you and Lady Andreana will leave for England tomorrow."

Andreana gasped and Rhoslyn shot to her feet. "England? But why?"

"As long as Lochland believes his power is in jeopardy he will do anything necessary to protect his position. I can better ensure Lady Andreana's protection if she is beyond his reach."

"If she conceives right away, she will be of no use to the earl."

"Just as you thought you would have been no use to me?" he asked.

Her face heated as much with anger as embarrassment. "There are a dozen other ways you can protect her," Rhoslyn insisted.

"None so well as to send her to England. It is not permanent. Only until your grandfather recovers. Once he is well, he can take his affairs in hand and Lochland will not fight him on this issue. So long as your grandfather agrees with the marriage."

"Ye need not worry," Rhoslyn said. "Lord Lochland needs you as an ally. You saw for yourself, he understood and accepted your decision."

"I saw a man who understands the value of strategy. Do not think he will give up so easily, Rhoslyn. It is not inconceivable that he will ask Father Crey to annul the marriage. Four days is not so long as to make an annulment difficult, and De Quincy would consider the loss of his young wife's virginity worth the power he would gain against the House of Seward." She started to rebut, but he shook his head. "It is not safe for her in Scotland, surely you see that."

"What I see is that it is safer for you if she is away from here. It is less likely Lord Lochland will discover that you lied to him if Andreana is not here."

His mouth thinned. "*We* lied to him, Rhoslyn."

She stiffened. "You would rather I had let her go to De Quincy."

"I would rather you be reasonable. You want her safe. This is the best way. I say again, it is not permanent, only until your grandfather recovers."

"And if he does no' recover?"

His gaze remained locked with hers. "I thought you were unwilling to consider that possibility."

"I was no' willing to consider the possibility that you would send Andreana away."

"Then you should not have married her to Baxter."

RHOSLYN COULD SCARCE believe Andreana was married, even if only for a day. Worse, she couldn't believe they stood at the gate saying goodbye.

"I will be well," Andreana assured her.

Rhoslyn smoothed back a lock of hair that strayed from Andreana's braid. "He has been kind to you. I see it."

Andreana blushed and nodded. "He is kind."

"If you need anything—"

"I will write," Andreana cut in. "I promise."

"Dinna' let those English treat ye badly," Rhoslyn said.

"No more badly than we have treated them," she replied.

"You have grown too wise, Andreana."

"You taught me well."

Rhoslyn had promised herself she wouldn't cry, but a tear slipped down her cheek.

"If ye cry, I will cry, too," Andreana warned. "I think my husband would prefer no' to have a weepy wife on such a long journey."

Rhoslyn swiped at her cheek. "Ye are right." She pulled Andreana into a long hug. Then she let her go.

"MAKE SURE THE men finish this roof today," Talbot told Ross. "The other two can be repaired before—" He broke off at seeing Ross's eyes shift past him. The men working on the cottage had stopped and were also staring at something behind him, as well. Talbot twisted and looked over his shoulder. A woman wrapped in a plaid against the gusting wind rode between two knights, followed by a dozen others.

"God's teeth," Ross said under his breath.

"You know her?" Talbot asked.

"Aye. Lady Taresa Baliman."

"Who is she?"

"She is a very great lady who hasna' been in this part of Buchan for nearly twenty years. I wonder what brings her here now."

"There is only one way to find out." Talbot strode from the cottage toward the lane.

"Back to work," Ross ordered the men, and started after him.

They reached the road as the company neared. Talbot could better see the woman and guessed her to be fifty-five, and still quite striking. Her dark hair, streaked lightly with silver, hung to her shoulders in a pearl beaded hair net. Her almond shaped green eyes—Talbot started. Her green eyes were those of his sister's.

The company reached Talbot and Ross, and stopped.

"Can we be of service, my lady?" Talbot asked.

She regarded him intently and, for an instant, he saw his sister in the same cool expression.

"You are Sir Talbot St. Claire," she said.

The words were not a question and had been spoken with a slight Spanish accent.

"Aye, my lady. I am."

"I have come to speak with you."

A strange chill swept through him. "You are welcome in Castle Glenbarr," he said.

Her eyes shifted past him to the castle, which lay just beyond the village. She seemed to think for a moment, then said, "Perhaps we could sit in one of the cottages?"

"My lady—" the knight to her left began.

"Have no fear, Derek. Sir Talbot will see to my safety inside the cottage. Is that not correct, Sir Talbot?"

"I will guard you with my life," he replied.

She looked at the knight and Talbot noted the softening in her eyes. "You will see that all remains well here."

The man's mouth thinned, but he canted his head in acknowledgement.

"Ross," Talbot said, "will you ask if we might sit in one of the cottages?"

"Aye," he replied, and left.

Sir Derek dismounted and helped the lady from her horse. Ross returned and showed them to a cottage three houses down from their work site.

Talbot seated Lady Taresa in one of the two chairs at the modest table near the hearth, and waited.

"Will you sit?" she asked.

"If it pleases you." He sat in the chair opposite her.

"You have your grandfather's eyes and his hair," she said without preamble.

Talbot tensed. "I did not know my grandfather."

"That is a shame," she replied. "He was a good man. May I see the picture of your sister on your arm?" That caught him completely off guard, but before he could reply, she added, "It is on your arm, I have heard."

"It is, my lady. Might I ask why you want to see it?"

"Is it a secret?" she asked.

"Nay." He waited, but she offered no further explanation. Talbot rolled up the sleeve on his right arm, halting where his shirt covered his shoulder, exposing all but the top of his sister's head.

Lady Taresa leaned forward and traced a finger over her face. "What was her name?"

"Lilas."

She removed her hand and leaned back in her chair. "The face is hers."

Unease lifted the hairs on the back of his neck.

She lifted her gaze to his face. "She never told me she had children."

Talbot rolled his sleeve back down. "You knew my mother."

A sad light entered her eyes. "She was my daughter."

FROM HER SEAT at the window in her private solar, Rhoslyn watched the village, and the riders St. Claire spoke with.

"I dinna' want to look at the accounts," Lady Saraid complained.

"Ye will someday be glad you learned these things," Rhoslyn said without taking her eyes off St. Claire. "Your father will no' be pleased if ye neglect your duty while here at Castle Glenbarr."

"My father is unfair," the girl complained.

If life was fair, her grandfather wouldn't be still lying unconscious in her bed. They fed him broth and wine. Muira refused to allow Rhoslyn to clean him. The housekeeper herself took care of him. Rhoslyn would never be able to repay her kindness.

"Can we not do something else for a while?" Saraid asked.

Rhoslyn squinted in an effort to make out the face of the lady talking with St. Claire. "Your father wants to make sure ye are ready to run your own household."

And he had woefully neglected his duty. He'd let the girl run wild, and now she didn't want to be broken. He'd gotten down on his knees and begged Rhoslyn to take her for six months. She'd not committed at first, but the baron kept sending gift after gift with a plea to help him. Rhoslyn hadn't seen her since she was eight, and was shocked to find she was more boy than girl. Getting her into a proper dress had been a feat.

The knight to the woman's left got off his horse and assisted her from the saddle. Ross returned and he, the woman, and St. Claire began walking. Who was the woman? Frustration swept through Rhoslyn.

"I canna' do this," Saraid whined.

Rhoslyn glanced at the paper. "'Tis simple addition. Take your time."

Ross, the woman and St. Claire disappeared from view between cottages and didn't reappear in any of lanes Rhoslyn could see. What were they doing?

The door to her chambers opened and Mistress Muira entered.

"Has something happened?" Rhoslyn demanded.

"Nay, my lady. I am only getting fresh water to change the bandage. Your grandfather is breathing well. Nothing has changed."

Rhoslyn nodded and released a sigh. Seven days. He wasn't dead. But neither had he woken. St. Claire had mentioned nothing concerning his search for his attackers. She had avoided him these last few days, feigning sleep when he came to bed, sleeping on the large bed as far from him as possible. Still, he would have surely sought her out if he'd found out anything? He'd promised her the attacker's head.

Dayton had to be behind the attack. Couldn't St. Claire see that? She wondered if he had any clues at all to his brother's whereabouts. Fear pricked. What if St. Claire couldn't find him? What if he someday claimed her child as his? What if he was the child's father?

St. Claire had claimed the child. He wouldn't change his mind would he? Her gaze caught on Ross, who stepped out onto the lane and headed toward the cottage he and St. Claire had been working on before the woman's arrival. Who was the woman? Alec would never had entertained guests without her. What was St. Claire up to? He'd said nothing about meeting with a woman. But St. Claire had made it clear he didn't feel he needed to inform her of his business. What business could he possibly have with a woman?

"FORGIVE ME, MY lady," Talbot said. "My mother is dead."

She seemed to slump in her chair. "Yes. Twenty years past. She died of a fever."

He shook his head. "Nay, she died giving birth to my sister."

Her eyes focused on him. "Is that what your father told you?"

"It is the truth," he said.

She reached into a small pouch strapped to her belt and removed a scallop shell. She set it on the table, then produced a small velvet bag from the bag and met his gaze directly. "I am Lady Taresa Baliman, wife of Cailin Kenzie, the Earl of Baliman. I met him in Galicia when he made a pilgrimage to Santiago de Compostela."

She pushed the scallop shell toward him. "He gave me this badge to always remind me that God blessed him on his pilgrimage. He married me and brought me here to Buchan. We had a daughter, Lady Peigi Baliman."

Lady Taresa pulled the string on the velvet bag and, almost reverently, withdrew the contents. Talbot understood her care. She held a miniature painting on wood. She set the picture before him.

"She was your mother."

Talbot looked at the painting. There, on the ivory, his sister's face stared back with soft green eyes. The memory returned on a tide of emotion that took his breath. He'd been nineteen, she had been fourteen. It began with a simple cough and runny nose. A fever followed, then her eyes became so sensitive to light that the curtain around her bed was kept closed and only a single candle burned in her room. The red rash that spread across her body marred her beautiful flesh. Against the wishes of his father and his father's wife, he'd held her the last three days of her life until the fever had grown so hot and the pain so great, her heart gave out.

He released a long-held breath and looked up from the painting. "The resemblance is striking, but she is not my mother. My mother died giving birth to Lilas.

"Do you remember her?" Lady Taresa asked.

He remembered a soft voice, an indistinct lullaby, but said, "Nay."

"You do not think the resemblance between my daughter and your sister is proof enough Lady Peigi is your mother?"

"An unmarried noblewoman would never consent to be a man's mistress," Talbot replied.

Pain filled her eyes and he half expected her to end the meeting.

"Are you ill, my lady?"

"No more than usual," she replied.

"My lady—"

She raised a hand. "It is a sickness of the soul that ails me, not the body. My daughter was a proud woman." A tiny smile touched her lips. "Like me." The smile faded. "Then she met your father."

"My father was—is—an honorable knight," Talbot said.

"In his way, yes. But he fell in love with my daughter, and she with him."

"You know my father, then?"

She shook her head. "I never met him. Peigi would not tell us who he was. But that she loved him, there was no doubt. They were together many years. I did not know until she returned after my husband's death that she bore her lover two children. It is clear he did not cast her aside. I do not doubt that he loved her."

"Then why not marry her?" Talbot demanded.

Lady Taresa met his gaze squarely. "Because he was already married."

Talbot stiffened. "My father would not dishonor a lady so."

Lady Taresa gave a slow nod. "Have you ever been so in love that you would throw all caution to the wind for her?"

He recalled Sally. She had been a wealthy tavern owner's daughter. Well-spoken and educated for a girl of her station. He met her six months after Lilas died and two months later he asked for her hand in marriage. Her father was ecstatic. Talbot's father forbade the union. Talbot swore he would marry her without his father's blessing. Unexpectedly, Sally shunned him. He fought and drank the next six months, until he realized it had been Lilas' death that had motivated him and not the undying love he professed. He had felt that all-consuming love for a moment, no more. But, in the end, it had been a lie.

He thought of Rhoslyn. Would he throw all caution to the wind for her? She was his wife. He would defend her to the death. Protect her and their child, give them everything he had. Was that what Lady Taresa meant?

"I left my home, my family, for Cailin," she said. "I gave up everything for him. Then when Peigi confessed that she had dishonored herself with an English knight and carried his child, my husband demanded to know who the man was, but she would not tell him. He banished her. When she returned after his death, I rejoiced at having her back in my life. But God took her from me less than a year later."

Talbot couldn't stop his gaze from returning to the portrait. "You said she died twenty years ago?"

"Yes."

Twenty years ago, Talbot had been twelve. He recalled vividly a sudden and unexplained despondency his father experienced. It lasted months, and Talbot had often thought he'd never quite been the same afterwards. During that time, he and his father were walking one day when his father told him not to let life pass him by, and not to let the world dictate his life. That was exactly what he was trying to do now—as best as a man in his position could. Talbot laughed inwardly. When he thought he was in love with Sally, he'd reminded his father of those words. *There is a difference in not letting the world dictate your life and throwing it away,*" he had said.

"You are my grandson," Lady Taresa said, "and the heir to your grandfather's title and property. As the Earl of Baliman and Baron Kinsley, you will one day be the richest and most powerful man in Buchan. You will be a force to be reckoned with in all of Scotland."

Chapter Nineteen

~

T HE POSTERN DOOR opened and Rhoslyn jerked her head up from the wine she stared at on the table before her. St. Claire entered the great hall.

At last.

She forced herself to remain seated.

When he reached the table and lowered himself into his chair, she said, "Who was the woman you met this afternoon?"

He frowned. "Do you have spies watching me?"

"I have a window. Who is she?"

"A window? Ah, yes, the solar." He motioned a nearby lad for wine.

"Well," Rhoslyn said.

"She is no one," he replied.

"Is there a reason ye are hiding another woman from me?"

He laughed. "If I intended to bed a woman, I would not meet with her in the village."

"Are ye saying you intend to bed a woman?" Rhoslyn winced. Sweet Jesu, she sounded like a shrew.

"That is not what I said, as you know."

She knew it was jealousy that spoke, but couldn't halt the next words. "What I know is that ye met with a woman and will no' tell me who she is."

The postern door opened and Ross entered.

"St. Claire, I warn you," Rhoslyn said. "I will have my answers."

Ross reached the table and halted. "Good evening, Lady Rhoslyn." He looked at St. Claire. "Lady Taresa sent this back for ye." Ross held up a small, black velvet pouch.

"Lady Taresa Baliman?" Rhoslyn blurted.

St. Claire looked sharply at her. "You know her?"

Rhoslyn realized her mistake and shook her head. "Nay. I know *of* her. She hasna' visited this part of Buchan since I was a child. What did she want with ye?"

"She claims my father knew her daughter."

Rhoslyn stared. Sweet Jesu, was it really possible?

He nodded to Ross. "You could have waited to give me that. Return it to the lady with my thanks. You deliver it, Ross. It is irreplaceable."

"What is it?" Rhoslyn demanded.

St. Claire abruptly rose and strode to the stairs. She watched until he disappeared up the staircase, then looked at Ross to ask what was in the pouch, but he turned and strode toward the door.

RHOSLYN SAW LORD Lochland enter the gates two days later and made sure she was in the great hall when he entered.

"I have come to see St. Claire and will have no argument from ye," he said without preamble.

"As ye wish," she replied. "But the men at the gate must have told you he isna' here."

"He is in the village. Someone has gone to fetch him."

"Will ye sit in the solar?" she asked.

He shook his head. "I will remain in the great hall." He started toward the table nearest the hearth.

She hurried to keep up with his long strides. "I will have wine brought."

They neared the kitchen door and she veered away from him. She secured goblets and a flagon of wine and took them to the table.

"Ye are well, laird?" she asked as she poured the wine.

He grunted. "Well enough." He took the wine she offered and drank half the goblet in two swigs.

Rhoslyn made small talk—much to his obvious annoyance—and she was sorry to see St. Claire arrive minutes later. He must have ridden with the devil on his tail. He probably feared what she might say to the earl.

"My lord," St. Claire said when he reached Lochland.

"I will speak with ye, St. Claire, and I want no interruptions from your wife."

"Rhoslyn?" he said.

She nodded and the earl reached into his tunic, produced a parchment, and set it on the table.

"This is Lady Andreana's annulment. I have betrothed her to De Quincy."

Rhoslyn gasped.

"Dinna' bother arguing, Lady Rhoslyn," he said. "The deed is done. Ye of all people understand duty."

"Aye," she snapped. "I understand duty, and I have been sacrificed for that cause twice." St. Claire's gaze sharpened and guilt knotted her insides, but she ploughed on. "But I will no' hand over Andreana to a cruel man."

"Then it is good ye have no say in the matter." He turned his attention to St. Claire. "You understand the need to honor a betrothal as well as any man, and ye will honor this one. De Angers will be amply rewarded for his trouble."

"Trouble?" Rhoslyn cut in before St. Claire could reply. "A man has his wife torn from him and ye call that 'trouble'?"

"Rhoslyn." St. Claire's sharp voice startled her. He looked at Lochland. "Lady Andreana is not here. Sir Baxter took her to his home in England."

"What?" the earl exploded. "This is a trick. Ye sent her away on purpose."

"I do not deny knowing that you might annul the marriage," St. Claire replied. "But it was Baxter who decided to take his wife back to England. He is not an indentured servant. He is free to do as he pleases."

"Aye," Lochland replied. "He is. Lady Andreana, on the other hand, is not free to do as she pleases. By order of the bishop, she is no' married to Sir Baxter. She will return and honor the betrothal to De Quincy."

"You are free to try and enforce the betrothal, my lord, but I wager Baxter has already confirmed the validity of the marriage with a bishop in England. You may petition King Edward, if you like."

Lochland's face reddened in anger. "Ye know an English king isna' likely to dissolve an English marriage in favor of a Scottish one." He rose. "I will no' be thwarted by a lowly knight."

"Then send an army to take Lady Andreana from Baxter," St. Claire said. "But, beware, that lowly knight is no fool."

"I was no' speaking of him," Lochland snapped. "I speak of you. Ye will obey me, St. Claire."

"I am not disobeying you, my lord. I cannot force Baxter to give up his wife. However, I am under no obligation to obey you."

"Ye are under Seward's rule, and therefore under mine," Lochland said.

"I am not under Seward's rule," St. Claire replied. "I am married to his granddaughter. Nothing more."

"Beware, St. Claire," Lochland said in a low voice. "Ye dinna' have the power to defy me."

"Perhaps not. But neither do I have the power to force Baxter to give up his wife."

For an instant, Rhoslyn expected the earl to leap to his feet, sword drawn.

"In fact, ye do have the power to force Sir Baxter to give up Lady Andreana," Lord Lochland said. "I will send fifty men to Castle Glenbarr. Ye will accompany them to England and bring her back. I expect her here in a week." With that he left.

Rhoslyn waited until the door closed before saying to St. Claire, "He is right. Ye do no' have the power to defy him."

"I am gratified at your confidence in me," he replied.

"Dinna' be a fool. He has twice the men you have, even with my grandfather's men."

"Winning is not always about how many men you have, Rhoslyn."

They were interrupted when the postern door opened and Ross entered. His gaze locked with St. Claire's and he started across the room. Uneasiness prickled at the back of Rhoslyn's nape. Something was wrong. Dear God, was there no mercy from heaven?

Ross reached them and said to St. Claire, "One of our scouts spotted two hundred of Jason Boyd's men north of Colliston Gorge."

Rhoslyn drew a sharp breath and she couldn't halt her hand from going to her belly. The babe was but a month inside her. If Castle Glenbarr was attacked, she could be killed along with her unborn child. Her grandfather, too, she realized with horror. He was in even greater danger, for he could not defend himself.

"Take fifty of my men and escort Lady Rhoslyn to Dunfrey Castle," St. Claire said to Ross.

"Nay," she interrupted.

"Rhoslyn—"

"I would be no safer there than here, and I will no' leave my grandfather."

"She is right," Ross cut in. "Men are riding in the direction of Dunfrey Castle as well."

"Take her to the convent, then," St. Claire said, but she was already shaking her head.

"There is another way," Ross said.

He frowned, then understanding spread across his features.

"Enough men-at-arms to ensure a victory can be here in an hour," Ross said. "Ye need only ask."

Rhoslyn looked from one to the other. "What men? Ye have two hundred men of your own, St. Claire, why can you not defend us?"

"I can," he said. "But I do not want you here."

"I will no' go," she said.

"Aye, you will."

Panic raced through her, but she forced a calm voice. "We must send Lady Saraid home before the men reach the castle."

"Ross, come with me," he said. "You, too, Rhoslyn." He didn't wait for her compliance, but grasped her arm and hurried her to the stairs.

Minutes later, they reached his chambers. He ordered her to sit at the bench near the fire, then sat at the table where his pen and seal were, and began writing. He quickly finished the letter, then sealed it and handed it to Ross.

"If anything happens to me, you know what to do with this missive."

Ross nodded.

"Lady Rhoslyn and her grandfather are to be protected at all costs," he said. "Send fifty men with Lady Saraid. Make sure they are back here within the hour."

"Aye," Ross replied.

"If I didna' know better, I would think Lord Lochland had a hand in this," Rhoslyn muttered.

"Aye," St. Claire said. "But he would not attack until after he learned I had defied him." He grasped Rhoslyn's arms. "I will not see you until the battle is finished."

"Who is the missive for?" she demanded.

"You need concern yourself with that only if I do not return."

"Where are these men ye are getting?" she demanded. "Can you no' command them to come to you? Why are you going after them? It is safer to stay within the castle walls."

"For you, yes," he said.

Then she realized his intent. "Ye mean to attack the men from their rear."

"It is our best chance for success."

"It is madness," she said. "What if they beat you and break through the walls?"

"They will not."

Before she could say more, he kissed her, long, hard and with a hunger that took her breath. He hadn't touched her since her grandfather had been wounded. Her body flared to life and she suddenly wished they were alone. What would she do if he didn't return from battle? She thought of his brother and shivered.

RHOSLYN SAT WITH her grandfather until their attackers were spotted from the battlements. His breathing was strong and even, yet guilt washed over her when she left him and sought out Ross. There was no sign of St. Claire or the men he had gone for, and Ross offered no answers as to who the men were. She kept the household busy, until their attackers neared the trees beyond the castle.

When a young squire skidded into the kitchen, Rhoslyn looked up from the vials of herbs she inspected.

"They are coming," the boy said in a breathless pant.

"Who is coming?" she demanded.

"Sir Talbot and his men. They are riding from the east."

Rhoslyn exchanged a look with Mistress Muira.

"Who are the men?" the housekeeper asked.

"They are flying the banner of the Earl of Baliman."

"Baliman?" Mistress Muira said.

A tremor rippled through Rhoslyn. *Lady Taresa.* Rhoslyn had yet to figure out her connection to St. Claire. Cousin? Aunt? Would a cousin or aunt send two hundred men to save an English relative they had never met? Would a cousin or aunt seek out that relative? Nay. But a mother—or grandmother—would.

"The enemy has demanded we open the gates and surrender," the boy said. "They say two hundred more men are on their way to aid in Castle

Glenbarr's fall."

"Dogs," Muira muttered in unison with Rhoslyn's gasp.

"I am going to speak with Ross," she said.

Minutes later, Rhoslyn stood with Ross at the battlements. Her heart leapt into her throat at sight of the torch light that glinted off the early evening sky as if a great bonfire burned. Beyond, St. Claire and his men galloped toward them. The attackers couldn't hope to breach the castle walls this night, much less before St. Claire arrived.

"They have no idea it is St. Claire who rides to them and not their reinforcements?" she asked Ross.

"No' yet, but it canna' be long before they discover the truth."

A shout went up from one of the men on the battlements and Rhoslyn turned in unison with Ross to see another company of riders approaching from the east.

"Sweet God," Rhoslyn whispered.

"Laird," one of the men cried.

Rhoslyn turned and her heart leapt into her throat at sight of her grandfather, one arm over the shoulder of a warrior, stepping up from the stairs. She raced forward and reached his side an instant later, Ross beside her.

"Grandfather." Tears streamed down her cheeks. "You are awake." Anger shot through her. "What are ye doing out of bed?" She turned a hard stare on the man helping him. "Have ye lost your mind? He is half dead. Take him back to my bed."

"Hush, Granddaughter," her grandfather said in a hoarse voice.

"Grandfather—"

"Hush, or I will have someone take ye to your room." He looked at Ross. "Jason Boyd?"

Ross nodded.

"Help me," her grandfather said.

Ross took the place of the other man and Rhoslyn draped her grandfather's free arm over her shoulder. They helped him to the edge where he could look out over the field. He studied the scene for a long moment.

He nodded to the north and the men St. Claire led. "That is Baliman's flag."

"Aye," Ross said. "St. Claire has sought aid from Lady Baliman."

Her grandfather looked at him. "Lady Taresa Baliman?"

Ross nodded, and her grandfather looked at her. "Your doing?"

"Nay. I dinna' know how she discovered the truth—I am not certain myself what the truth is."

He looked at Ross.

"St. Claire is her grandson," he said.

So she'd been right. Sweet God, St. Claire was the Earl of Baliman. What did this mean? Might he be more closely tied with Scotland than England as a result of inheriting the title? He could virtually do almost anything he pleased, short of claiming the throne. Why hadn't he told her?

She narrowed her eyes on Ross. "Ye didna' tell me this when I asked where St. Claire was getting warriors."

"Your husband instructed me to keep quiet."

"Apparently the order does no' apply to my grandfather."

"Nay, it does no'," Ross replied without hesitation.

Her grandfather croaked a laugh. "This will give Lochland fits." Before Rhoslyn could respond, he said to Ross, "Prepare a horse, I will speak with Boyd."

"Nay," Rhoslyn cried. "Ye are barely able to walk. You can no'—"

"By God, Rhoslyn, another word and I will have you locked in your room until this is over."

This time, there was no hoarseness or tremor in his voice, and Rhoslyn stood aside.

TALBOT SPOTTED HIS scout in the distance and slowed at sight of another rider with him. The men neared and he recognized Ross. Fear swept through him and he spurred his horse forward. The animal lunged, then broke into a hard gallop.

When Talbot reached his side, he pulled up alongside the two men and Ross forestalled any questions by saying, "All is well. Better than ye might think possible, in fact."

"Lady Rhoslyn?" Talbot demanded.

"She is well, as is her grandfather. He awoke at the best possible moment and intervened."

"Intervened?" Talbot repeated. "You mean Boyd's men have gone?"

"Aye, though I dinna' think this is over."

Such things were seldom over so easily. "Does Boyd fear Seward so much that he would leave just because the old man rose from his bed?" Talbot asked.

"Sir Jason knows Kinsley will no' spare a man in the protection of Castle Glenbarr and Lady Rhoslyn. But I imagine the two hundred men the new Earl of Baliman was bringing helped make up his mind."

"He need fear me above all men," Talbot said. "Even Seward."

"Ye are English," Ross said, and shrugged.

"He will learn that this Englishman does not forgive so easily."

WHEN THEY REACHED Castle Glenbarr, Talbot found Rhoslyn sitting with her grandfather in the great hall. "You are looking well." Talbot sat in his chair at the head of the table and motioned a boy to bring wine.

"I have been abed nine days," Seward replied. "I should be in the peak of health."

"Ye were nigh unto death," Rhoslyn said.

"Not anymore," he said, then looked at Talbot. "I understand I now address the new Earl of Baliman."

"Lady Taresa believes she is my grandmother," Talbot replied.

Seward lifted his brows. "The resemblance between your sister and her daughter?"

The remark was a question. Had Ross shared the details of Lady Taresa's visit, Seward would have been more definitive. That could only mean Rhoslyn told him. So she, too, had noticed the resemblance between the two women. He cast a glance her way, but she gave away none of what she was thinking. She would choose now to hide her thoughts. The boy brought the wine and Talbot finished the first goblet in three long gulps.

"Ye dinna' seem overly pleased," Seward said.

"There is nothing to be pleased about," Talbot said. "The resemblance is coincidental."

"I doubt that. And I doubt Lady Taresa will give up so easily, especially after ye asked for her help. Ye know you encouraged her by asking for her help. Why do it?"

"Reports said Boyd had four hundred men on his way here."

"Between the men at Dragon's Lair and the men here, you easily have that many warriors. I would not have thought ye would be afraid of battle," Seward said.

"Do you want your granddaughter and future grandchild besieged in Castle Glenbarr?" Talbot asked.

"Nay. I do no'."

Talbot refilled his glass. "You know as well as I how easily the castle would fall if an enemy discovered the passageway that leads to the chapel." He took another big swig of his wine.

Seward nodded slowly. "Who told ye? Rhoslyn?"

"I did no'," she said.

"As long as no one unlocks the door from inside, ye are safe enough," Seward said.

"I plan to bolt the door permanently," Talbot said.

"No one in this household would open the door to an enemy," Rhoslyn said.

"Do not underestimate my brother's ability to find an ally."

She frowned, then hurt appeared in her eyes and Talbot realized his mistake.

"I did not mean you, Rhoslyn." He straightened in his chair and covered her hand with his. "What I meant is that Dayton will not give up. Do not be fooled into believing he has left Scotland. I would have heard if that were the case. This is why I must stop him."

She nodded, but the hurt remained and Talbot wondered if he should take her upstairs. God, how he wanted to make love to her. Since the attack on her grandfather, she'd kept her distance. He'd lain awake much of the night beside her. She might as well have slept in her own bed instead of inches from him.

"Beware." Seward's voice broke into his thoughts. "Ye might one day regret no' having a way out of Castle Glenbarr. Of course, you could always take up residence at Narlton Keep. That would please Lady Taresa. The great keep alone is half the size of Castle Glenbarr."

"I have no intention of leaving Castle Glenbarr," Talbot said. "This is our home." He looked right. "Is that not true, Lady Rhoslyn?"

Chapter Twenty

~

RHOSLYN WALKED AHEAD of St. Claire into his chambers. She had insisted her grandfather take her bed. He'd acquiesced when she stated that she would sleep on a bench beside his bed if he slept anywhere but in her chambers. She hadn't given thought to the fact that meant she had to continue sleeping in St. Claire's bed. So here she was.

St. Claire closed the door and continued to the bed as he lifted his chainmail over his head. Rhoslyn hurried to his side and grasped the armor as he lowered it. He paused and met her gaze, then let her take the mail. She set it on the bench near the window, then hurried back in time to take his gambeson from him. Rhoslyn set that on the bench with the chainmail, then poured two goblets of wine and gave him one.

He took it, then sat on the bench at the foot of the bed and took a long draw on the wine. He set the goblet on the bench then reached for a boot. Rhoslyn set her goblet on the bench, then knelt and grasped his booted foot. He paused and angled his eyes to meet hers. Rhoslyn gave a tremulous smile and he released his boot and leaned back against the bed.

Gently, Rhoslyn tugged the boot from his foot, then took the other one off. She rose and crossed to the table where a pitcher of water sat and brought it and some clean clothes to the bench. St. Claire leaned against the foot of the bed, eyes closed. Rhoslyn wetted a cloth and began washing his left foot. He started and she realized he'd dozed off. His eyes snapped onto her, then he relaxed and she continued.

"You went to Lady Taresa because of me?" she said.

"Aye."

"You do no' wish to be the Earl of Baliman?" she asked.

"I am not the Earl of Baliman."

"It seems ye are."

"I do not have to be anyone I do not wish to be," he replied. "That is why I came here."

She paused in washing his feet and looked up at him.

He stared into his wine goblet for a long moment, then his eyes shifted to her. "I told you, I tire of war."

"Yet, ye came to Scotland." She went back to washing his feet.

He grunted a laugh. "Aye, mayhap I should question the sanity in that decision."

"A man such as you does no' have the luxury of giving up war."

He lifted a brow. "You think I cannot live in peace?"

"You might *wish* to live in peace," she said.

A long silence drew out before he said, "Does this mean you and I will be at war?"

She dried his feet, then picked up the basin and cloths and crossed to the table. "Our peoples are at war."

"Not so," he said. "We have been at peace for some time."

Rhoslyn brought the pitcher of wine to him and refilled his goblet. "It canna' last, as ye know," she said.

"So you have decided you and I must be at war."

She met his gaze. "What do ye want me to say?"

He rose, towering over her, and leaned close. "I want you to say you do not hate me."

"Hate?" she whispered against a dry throat. "'Tis is a strong word."

"It is a strong emotion."

She could feel the heat radiating off his body.

"I will find the man responsible for the attack on your grandfather. And I will kill Dayton."

His eyes dropped to her mouth and a tremor rippled through her stomach.

"You might as well be sleeping in your bed," he said.

"What?"

"You lay beside me in my bed, but you might as well be in your own chambers."

"Ye are my husband," she said. "I canna' refuse you."

"Will you force me into the role of rapist?"

Her heart began to beat fast.

"Tell me you never want me to touch you again and I will leave you be, Rhoslyn."

"I-I did no' say that," she stammered.

"You did not have to. It is one or the other," he said. "If you demand my brother's head along with your grandfather's attacker before truly returning to my bed, then so be it. But once the price is paid, you cannot renege."

"I never said you had to do any of those things," she said. "I never demanded anything."

"Then you do not care if I let my brother live? You do not care if your grandfather's attacker goes free?"

"Of course I care." She slammed her goblet and the pitcher down onto the bench. "I asked you for nothing."

He grasped her arm and pulled her so close she could feel his breath on her face. "Then nothing I do will change your mind?"

"I do no' blame ye for your brother's actions," she shot back.

"But you do blame me for your grandfather—and you blame me for sending Lady Andreana away."

She hesitated. "Ye were right to send her away." It galled her to admit it. "Had ye no' sent her away Lord Lochland would have married her to De Quincy. I canna' fault you for that."

"Nay?" he said. "Then what do you fault me for?"

For coming here. For ripping me from the peace of the convent. For giving me a child whose father I may always question.

But what would have been Andreana's fate if she had remained at the convent? And what of herself? Lord Lochland would have likely betrothed her to De Quincy and Andreana to someone else just as cruel. What would have been the life of a child born from such a union?

Rhoslyn met his gaze squarely. "I blame ye for being a man."

His brows rose. "Then I am condemned, for I cannot change that. But I can remind you that there are some benefits to my being a man." He stepped closer.

She dropped her gaze to his chest. "My grandfather is in the next room."

"Not the next room." With a finger beneath her chin, he tilted her head upward.

His gaze fixed on her mouth as his head lowered. His lips brushed hers and it seemed as though ages had passed since he'd touched her. Her heart pounded and desire streaked through her. She had the sudden urge to shove him onto the bed and ride him—hard. But he kissed her softly, as if reacquainting himself with her. He slid an arm around her waist and pulled her flush against his body. The tightening of her nipples caused her sex to tighten and she couldn't halt the moan that slipped from her lips.

She didn't wait for him to touch her, but cupped the bulge that pressed against his tunic. He swept her into his arms and strode around to the side of the bed. Rhoslyn threw back the curtain and he laid her on the mattress, then came down on top of her. His weight pressed her into the feather mattress. She wrapped her arms around his back and slid her hands down and over the curve of his muscled buttocks.

"My lady."

His warm breath washed over her ear and the husky note in his voice sent a shiver through her.

He nuzzled her ear. "You are impatient."

"A gentleman doesna' make a lady wait." She kneaded his buttocks.

"Rhoslyn," he said in a hoarse voice.

She pulled her knees up and flattened her feet on the bed to brace herself, then arched her mons against his erection.

"By God, Rhoslyn. If you do not stop I am liable to spend myself in my braies."

"I advise you no' to do that, St. Claire." She grazed her teeth along his neck. "I will make you suffer if ye do not please me."

A growl vibrated from his chest. She squeezed his buttocks again and bit down gently on his ear.

"*Rhoslyn.*"

She arched into him again and ground her sex against him, and again, again, and—St. Claire shoved up onto an elbow and yanked her dress to her waist. Before she realized his intent, he buried his face between her legs. Warm lips closed around her sex and pleasure shot through her.

"Holy God," Rhoslyn cried.

He flicked his tongue against her engorged nub. She tried to shove away from him, but he seized her thighs, holding her in place.

"This is-is indecent," she got out between gulps of air.

Need rose to the surface. Rhoslyn fisted the bedding. When he gently sucked she thought she would lose her mind. Rhoslyn started at the feel of his finger sliding into her channel. He went deep, then pulled out, plunging in and out until the pleasure of his mouth on her mingled with the stroke of his finger.

Her climax came upon her with a fury that caught her off guard. Rhoslyn bowed off the bed. Spots raced across her vision. Another wave rolled over her and she collapsed back on the bed. Then St. Claire loomed over her, driving into her as her sex tightened and pleasure streaked through her once again.

A HARD RAP to the door brought Talbot fully awake.

"What is it?" Rhoslyn demanded in a sleepy voice.

He threw aside the thick bed curtain. Early morning sun seeped in the window.

Another knock. "St Claire," Ross called.

Rhoslyn started to rise.

"Stay in bed," Talbot ordered. He scooped up his tunic from the floor and slipped it over his head, then went to the door and opened it.

"Fifty of Lochland's men wait outside the gates," Ross said without preamble. "They expect to escort ye to England to bring back Lady Andreana."

"Men-at-arms are in the trees as I ordered?" he said.

Ross nodded. "One hundred, as ye said."

Rhoslyn stepped around the bed. A dress haphazardly covered her body. "Tell Lord Lochland that the Earl of Baliman doesna' take orders from him."

"Rhoslyn, I will not—"

"How long will ye fight the truth, St. Claire?" she cut in. "What do you think will stop Lochland from making war on you, if no' this?"

"I can deal with Lochland," he said.

"Mayhap. But ye also have your brother and Sir Boyd to deal with. And dinna' forget you promised me the head of my grandfather's attacker. I expect you to keep that promise." She didn't wait for his answer, but said to Ross, "Off with ye, Ross. Deliver the message as I said."

"I will be down in a moment to speak with them," Talbot said.

Ross nodded, then started to turn, but stopped. "If ye ignore Lochland's command he will challenge ye. It might even mean war. At least think about what Lady Rhoslyn said."

He left, and Talbot crossed to the bench near the window where his mail shirt lay.

Rhoslyn tugged a sleeve to straighten it. "Why are ye so stubborn?"

He paused in slipping the mail shirt over his head. "Is being an earl's wife so important? Or is it that you want your son to have the title?"

She snapped her head up and met his gaze. "I come from a proud line of Highlander's. I do no' need your title—neither does our child."

He pulled the mail shirt over his head. "Then why are you so insistent?"

"Because it is so obviously true."

"The likeness between Lady Taresa and my sister—"

"Is too coincidental to be coincidence," she cut in.

He sat on the bench and began pulling on a boot. "I remember my mother only vaguely. I was five when she died."

Talbot paused in putting on his boot. He was five when his father told him she had died. But if she died when he was twelve as Lady Taresa said... Why would his father lie? If Lady Peigi was Talbot's mother, why not simply marry her after Dayton's mother died? A chill coiled in his belly at the vision of Dayton's tirade when he grew old enough to understand that his father's wife—Dayton's stepmother—was Talbot's mother.

His father *couldn't* bring Talbot's mother home.

Neither could he marry Lady Kelsi Emory while keeping a long-time mistress Talbot realized with a flash of insight that he recognized as truth. Lady Kelsi tolerated her husband's bastard children, but she wouldn't tolerate her husband having—loving—another woman. Talbot's father told him that his mother had died giving birth to Lilas. Did he tell his new wife the same lie? Talbot finished pulling on the boot. Would his father truly dishonor a high-born lady in such a manner? Would he take a woman's children from her? And lie to all those he loves?

"Write to your father." Rhoslyn's voice interrupted his thoughts. "Mayhap he will admit the truth."

"I have written, but do not get your hopes up." He grabbed the other boot, pulled it on, then stood. "He prizes honor above all." The words came out of his mouth an automatic reaction.

"Honor has a way of disappearing when a man wants a woman," Rhoslyn said.

Talbot's chest tightened.

"You, a bastard, can say your father is always honorable when it comes to women?" she said.

Talbot imagined Rhoslyn as a maiden of fifteen and wondered what he would have done had he met her before she married Alec Harper. He would have married her. No, he wouldn't have. Her grandfather wouldn't have allowed Talbot within a hundred feet of her. Just as Talbot's father wouldn't have been allowed near Lady Peigi. Just as Talbot hadn't allowed his men near Andreana.

In truth, a king's decree was all that had stopped Seward from killing Talbot when he married Rhoslyn.

WHEN RHOSLYN WOKE two days later, her stomach roiled. She made a dash for the jakes, reaching it just in time to fall to her knees and wretch into the basin. Warm fingers on her shoulder caused her to jump and she jerked her head up to see St. Claire kneeling beside her.

"Go away," she croaked.

He was sure to avoid her bed after seeing her like this. Her first few months while pregnant with Dougal she had slept half the time in her own bed for fear of waking up in need of a jakes. Alec had been solicitous, but she'd known he was relieved not to witness her bent over the jakes for half a day.

"Drink this." St. Claire lifted a cup to her lips and tilted it up.

Cool water met her lips and she took a large sip, then pushed the cup away. She swished the water around in her mouth, then spat it into the pot.

"Take more," he urged, and wrapped her fingers around the cup.

Rhoslyn drank slowly, allowing the water to soothe her throat and belly. When she finished, he pulled her to her feet. He was dressed, she noted, and the morning sun was bright in the room.

"I overslept," she said. "Why did ye no' wake me."

"Why wake you?" he replied. "If you are tired, you should rest."

"I am not ill," she said, though the way her stomach tilted to one side, she wasn't so certain.

"Perhaps you should rest more," he said.

Rhoslyn shook her head. "This will pass." Though with Dougal she had suffered months of nausea.

She had thought she might escape the nausea with this pregnancy. She had been sick within the first month of carrying Dougal. This was her fourth month. If not for missing her flux, she would have thought she wasn't with child, for she felt no ill effects.

St. Clair stared at her, brows drawn.

"This is what happens when a woman is pregnant," she said. "Go about your business. I have work to do. Lady Saraid is returning today."

"I am surprised her father allowed her to return. He is not afraid one of my enemies will attack?"

Rhoslyn snorted. "I wager he wants to say his daughter is under the protection of the Earl of Baliman. Ye will have many new friends, St. Claire."

"They will be disappointed." His brow furrowed. "It might be best if Lady Saraid does not return to Castle Glenbarr for a while. I recall that she tried your patience."

Rhoslyn grimaced. "The girl is irksome. But it isna' her fault."

He lifted his brows. "Nay?"

She gave him a recriminating look. "She is a child. Her father allowed her to run wild. It is no wonder she needs training." He opened his mouth to say something, but she cut him off. "Go away, St. Claire. I want to wash and I must fortify myself for Lady Saraid's arrival."

Amusement appeared in his eyes and he surprised her by placing a kiss on her forehead and leaving without argument.

The day wore on, and Rhoslyn began to wonder if St. Claire were right. Perhaps she should have waited to allow Lady Saraid to resume her training. Her stomach was fine—so long as she didn't smell food—and the girl was trying her patience more than usual. Saraid clearly thought that being sent home meant her training was over, and she snatched every opportunity to demonstrate her displeasure at being forced to return.

They now sat on a bench beneath a tree in the corner of the bailey nearest the castle, studying a list of herbs. Saraid dawdled and stumbled through the list. Rhoslyn sighed. The day had been long. The gate began to open. Rhoslyn tensed before realizing the guards wouldn't open the gate to Lord Lochland's men. She had been on edge since St. Claire had sent the earl's men back to him with the message that he wouldn't leave Castle Glenbarr until his brother had been apprehended.

St. Claire emerged from the stairs leading up to the wall. Rhoslyn's heart warmed with the memory of how he had tended her this morning at the jakes. Three riders entered and Rhoslyn stiffened at sight of the figure in the lead.

TALBOT OFTEN THOUGHT that women had second sight when it came to female matters. Lady Isobel's visit confirmed that suspicion. He also couldn't help wondering how she timed her arrival to catch him as he exited the wall. He would have melted back into the stairway but, of course, she'd seen him.

"Poor Rhoslyn suffered terribly during her first pregnancy," she said as he escorted her across the bailey. She slipped a hand into the crook of his arm and turned her head against the wind that whipped at her cloak. "I will be happy to help in any way I can."

His mind snapped to attention. Was that an offer to warm his bed?

"I am but a twenty minute ride away, Sir Talbot. Ye can call upon me anytime."

Yes, she was letting him know she would bed him. He hadn't forgotten her open appraisal of him during the games.

"I will keep that in mind," he said.

She slowed, forcing him to slow with her. "Rhoslyn had nausea for three months," Isobel went on. "Poor thing. Alec was at a loss as what to do with her."

Talbot wondered if Isobel had made the same offer to Harper she had made to him.

"She did continue with her duties, however," Isobel said. "But that is Lady Rhoslyn, she canna' stay still for more than five minutes." Isobel laughed, and he noticed the sultry note in her voice—for his benefit, no doubt.

She confirmed the suspicion by leaning in close. The side of her breast brushed his arm. The woman had no shame.

"It is kind of you to ride all the way here to visit my wife," Talbot said.

She looked up at him through her lashes. "We have known one another since childhood. I would do anything for Rhoslyn. This is an especially difficult time for a woman. She needs much rest and should no' be overexcited."

The way he had overexcited her last night? Since she had returned to his bed, she had been insatiable. Her belly had yet to show signs of the babe growing inside, but her breasts were heavier and her nipples had turned a darker rose. Talbot felt himself rousing with the memory of her hard peaks in his mouth. Maybe tonight—No. He cut off the thought. She was ill this morning, and wouldn't be in the mood for lovemaking. Lady Isobel was right. Rhoslyn was entering a difficult time. He would have to curb his desire until…until when, after the babe was born? Months after the babe was born. He glanced down at Lady Isobel. She was a shrewd woman.

TALBOT WATCHED AS, for the third time since they'd sat down to the evening meal, Rhoslyn excused herself and hurried to the kitchen.

"Lady Rhoslyn is no' quite herself this evening," Isobel said. She sat to Rhoslyn's left. "Perhaps it would be best if I stay the night. I can attend to her if she does no' feel well."

Talbot knew Isobel intended to wheedle her way into his bed, but truth be told, he was concerned about Rhoslyn. She seemed in a worse state of mind than she had been this morning when he'd found her leaning over the jakes.

"Women grow moody as their time approaches," Seward said. "This is natural, St. Claire."

"So true," Lady Isobel agreed. "But a woman likes to have another woman around."

"Rhoslyn's time isna' close," the old baron said. "When her time draws near, she may want your help. I canna' see that it is of much use now."

Lady Isobel laughed. "Spoken like a man."

A few minutes passed and Rhoslyn didn't return. Talbot rose and went to the kitchen. Rhoslyn was nowhere to be seen.

"Where is Lady Rhoslyn?" Talbot asked Mistress Muira.

"In her bed by now, I imagine," the housekeeper replied. "She wasna' feeling well."

Talbot glanced at the stairs.

"Dinna' worry," Mistress Muira said. "It is common for a woman to want rest while pregnant."

"I should not have allowed Lady Saraid to return," he said more to himself than to Mistress Muira.

"Dinna' be silly," Muira said. "Lady Rhoslyn can no' do nothing for the next few months. As time goes on, she will need more rest, but she will know when that time comes."

Talbot wasn't so sure. He returned to the great hall and sat at his place. "Rhoslyn has retired for the evening."

Lady Isobel nodded. "Just as I thought."

"You are welcome to stay the night, if you like, my lady," Talbot said.

"Of course," she said, and Seward shot him a speculative glance.

AT A SOFT knock to the solar door, Talbot looked up from the rolls he was studying. He rose, crossed to the door and opened it to find Lady Isobel standing in the hallway.

"Lady Isobel. Rhoslyn is abed," Talbot said.

"You are no' asleep." Lady Isobel slipped between him and the open door.

She passed so close that Talbot got a whiff of rose water. She stopped two paces away and faced him.

Hand still on the door bolt, he nodded toward the hallway. "You may return in the morning when my wife is awake."

She faced him. "Ye are working yourself too hard. I know how difficult things must be for you."

"Put your mind at ease," he said. "I am well. Rhoslyn sees to my needs."

Isobel stepped close and put her arms around his neck. "You need no' worry, Talbot. Alec was discreet. We can do the same."

Talbot reached for her hands—the door to Rhoslyn's chambers burst open. She stumbled forward, pushing through the door and into the room.

"Ye bastard," she said, her voice shaking.

St. Claire grasped Isobel's arms and pulled them from his neck. "You should go, Lady Isobel."

"Aye," Rhoslyn spat. "And dinna' come back."

"Lady Rhoslyn," Isobel began.

"Leave," Rhoslyn said between gritted teeth.

Isobel seemed to consider, then shrugged and left.

Talbot closed the door behind her, and Rhoslyn said, "Three months we have been married and already ye are taking a mistress—and in the room next to mine. Alec never treated me thusly."

So Rhoslyn didn't know her husband's indiscretion. That didn't surprise him.

"Things are not quite how they look," Talbot said. His chest tightened when she swiped at a tear that slid down her cheek. He started toward her.

She backed up. "Stay away. Stay away and never come near me again."

She whirled and he lunged, catching her arm. He swung her into his arms. She beat on his chest. Talbot hugged her close.

"Shh, Rhoslyn, listen to me."

"Release me." Tears streamed down her face unchecked.

Talbot lifted her into his arms.

"Nay," she cried, but he strode into his room to the bed.

She twisted in an effort to break free and he crushed her to him.

"Cease fighting," he commanded. "You will harm yourself and the babe."

"Release me." The words were filled with venom, but she stilled.

He pulled aside the curtain and laid her on the bed. "Do not move," he said. She started to scoot to the far side of the bed. "Rhoslyn, I warn you."

She narrowed her eyes. "Ye promised no' to force me."

"I do not intend to force you. But I will not allow you to injure yourself. Now, stay still."

She didn't move and he went to the table near the window and poured a goblet of wine then returned.

"Drink this." He extended it toward her. She lifted her chin in defiance. "Rhoslyn, do not be foolish. Please, drink."

She didn't move for a moment, and he thought she intended to defy him, then she took the goblet and drank a heavy swig.

Talbot sat on the edge of the bed. "Yes, Isobel had her arms around me."

"You were no' resisting her," Rhoslyn interjected.

"I was, in fact, resisting. Think about what you saw. I was reaching for her hands when you entered the room."

"I saw you earlier in the bailey," she said. "You were walking with her arm-in-arm. Ye were mighty cozy."

"Should I run from her?" he asked.

Rhoslyn snorted. "A man doesna' run from a beautiful woman."

"You are the only beautiful woman I want, love."

Her brows dove downward.

"If I intended to bed a woman, I would not do it in the room next to yours," he said. "I am not that foolish, nor would I disrespect you in that manner."

"That only means ye have a woman I do no' know about, and Isobel wasna' willing to wait."

He shook his head. "It means I did not invite Lady Isobel here. There is no one else, Rhoslyn. I would not have the energy—even if I had the inclination. You please me."

"Until I grow fat with child, then ye will find someone else quickly enough—if you havena' already."

Talbot took the goblet and set it on the table beside the bed. He pushed his braies and hose down his hips and tossed then aside, then got into bed.

"I will sleep in my own bed," Rhoslyn said, but he wrapped an arm around her waist and pulled her close, her back against his chest.

"Your cock is hard as a rock, St. Claire," she said. "Ye canna' tell me ye did not want Isobel. I have no wish to be in bed with a man who prefers another woman." She tried to scoot away from him, but he held fast.

Talbot buried his face in her hair. "It is you I am in bed with, not Isobel."

"Because I interfered," she said.

"Because I choose you," he countered. "Now go to sleep."

He wondered how he would sleep with his bollocks so tight with need they felt as if they would burst. And his cock—he didn't want to think about how good it would feel to fit himself more snuggly against Rhoslyn's arse and slip inside her wet passage.

"Sleep," he whispered into her hair, and couldn't resist a deep inhale of her scent before forcing his thoughts away from the salty-sweet taste of her skin.

Chapter Twenty-One

〜

A BOY SHOT into the stables and came to a skidding halt beside Talbot. "John Comyn is here to see ye, laird," he panted out the words.

"Comyn?" Talbot repeated. "Lord of Badenoch? One of the Guardians?"

The boy nodded, eyes wide. "He is at the gate."

This, Talbot decided, wasn't a good thing. He released the horse's hoof and followed the boy from the stables. He reached the gate to find two men standing with their horses and two guards. The elder, a tall, dark haired man, met his gaze. The thin line of his mouth told Talbot the man wasn't accustomed to being made to wait in the bailey, especially on a day that threatened snow. This was the Guardian.

"My lord Badenoch," Talbot said when he stopped before them. "It is an honor to meet you."

The man gave a curt nod. "Such an honor that ye force us to stand at the gate while we discuss business?"

Talbot looked pointedly at the other man. "This is my cousin Davey," the Guardian said.

"I cannot imagine what business you have with me, my lord," Talbot said.

"The kind I would prefer no' to discuss in public," Badenoch said.

Talbot canted his head in acknowledgement. Comyn tossed his reins to one of the warriors then started toward the castle without waiting for Talbot or his cousin. Talbot fell into place alongside him with Davey on Comyn's left. When they reached the postern door, Talbot stood aside and allowed them to enter first. They crossed to the table near the hearth and sat. Talbot called for wine, then turned his attention to the Guardian.

"I have learned from Lady Taresa Baliman that ye are her grandson," Comyn said.

Talbot started, then caught himself. "Lady Taresa is an old woman who grieves the loss of her daughter."

Comyn barked a laugh. "I have known Taresa for over thirty years. She grieves for her daughter, but she is no fool. Show me your sister's likeness on your arm."

Anger flared, but Talbot rolled up the sleeve of his shirt. He felt Davey's stare when Comyn grasped his arm and examined his sister's face. A lad appeared with a pitcher of wine and two goblets and Comyn released Talbot, then picked up the pitcher.

"Ye are her grandson." He filled the three goblets then set the pitcher down. "Deny it all you like, but everyone will know the truth. Including Edward, in case ye have any doubts." He took a drink of the wine, then said, "Even if there were any doubt, he willna' let ye deny the connection."

That was the very thing Talbot didn't want. "What has this to do with you?" he demanded.

"Ye must know he is Balliol's brother-in-law," Davey said. "We support Balliol. As must you."

Talbot stared at the man.

"As the Earl of Baliman, ye become the most powerful man in Buchan," Comyn said. "In fact, no one in Scotland will ignore you."

"I am English," Talbot replied. "At most, I will inherit Seward's barony."

"Ye are the Earl of Baliman," Davey said.

Talbot didn't like the younger man. A strange desperation laced his tone. It made Talbot wonder how far he would go to attain his goals.

"Enough, Davey," Comyn said, then addressed Talbot. "Edward is sure to remind ye that ye are his English knight, but Scottish blood doesna' take well to servitude."

"I *am* English," Talbot repeated.

Comyn studied him. "Mayhap English and Scottish interests are one."

"What do you want, my lord?"

"I want to see your grandfather-in-law."

TALBOT HAD LEARNED long ago there was no stopping the tide. He called for Seward, who joined them in the great hall. If Talbot didn't know better—and he didn't—he would have suspected the old baron of contacting the Guardian. But it could just as easily have been Lady Taresa who sealed his fate. Then again, it could be as simple as a rumor having reached Comyn's ears. Either way, he was trapped.

"I have no intention of leaving Castle Glenbarr," he told the two men. "Nor do I intend to claim the earldom."

"Ye would do well to claim it before it comes looking for you," Seward said.

Concern, the first true concern since he'd seen Lady Taresa ride into the village, niggled. He fixed his gaze on Comyn. "What have you done, my lord?"

"I am no' your lord. As to what I have done, I need do nothing.

Taresa's relatives will take care of matters."

"They can have the title," Talbot said.

Comyn lifted his brows. "Out of the kindness of your heart, I take it?"

"I have no desire to be a Scottish nobleman."

"You are known for your loyalty to Edward," Davey said. "Where is that loyalty now?"

Seward snorted. "It sounds like Davey is confusing you with your brother, St. Claire."

"At least he would understand the importance of supporting his king," Davey said.

"Christ, Davey," Comyn said. "Ye are making an ass of yourself." Comyn glanced at Talbot. "St. Claire doesna' tolerate fools." The Guardian's expression sobered. "Ye havena' had any luck in finding your brother?"

"If I had, he would be dead."

"He may not be the fool you think he is," Davey said.

Comyn's gaze jerked onto him. "Another word from ye, Davey, and I will whip you here and now."

"Dinna' act as if you do no' want him to support your kinsman," Seward said.

"I have Scotland's interests at heart," Comyn said.

"Ye have your interests at heart," Seward said.

"Will ye squabble over politics now, Hugo?" Comyn shifted his attention to Talbot. "Will your son feel as you do about giving up his birthright? More important, will the Kenzies take your word that ye will never dispute their claim?" He paused. "Will your wife and children be safe when you are gone?"

Anger tore through Talbot. "Even if I claim the title, they will never be safe. You have ensured that."

"Nay, lad. Ye sealed your fate when you immortalized your sister on your arm."

RHOSLYN COULD SCARCE believe it. Her husband had accepted the title as the Earl of Baliman. She nodded for more wine to the boy waiting near the table, then leaned close to Lady Taresa and said in a whisper loud enough to be heard over the din of the evening meal, "Is there anything more ye need, my lady?"

Lady Taresa laid a hand on Rhoslyn's. "Please call me Taresa. Perhaps one day you will call me Grandmother." She hesitated, then added, "Will you allow me to stay with you when your time comes?"

Emotion squeezed Rhoslyn's heart. She didn't remember her mother and the thought of another woman, family, being present during the birth of her child brought the prick of tears. God help her, she was growing weepy.

"Aye, my la—er, Taresa. I would be pleased for ye to be with me when the babe comes."

Sir Derek appeared at the table to Taresa's right, leaned down and whispered something in her ear. She paused, listening, then nodded. He left and she returned her attention to Rhoslyn.

"He is very devoted to you," Rhoslyn said.

"He is." Taresa's gaze shifted onto the knight, who made his way through the crowded hall toward the postern door. "He has served me for fifteen years. I trust him with my life."

And more, Rhoslyn suspected. It was obvious the knight was in love with his mistress. Rhoslyn marveled. She never suspected a love affair could carry on so late in a woman's life and with a man so much younger.

Taresa looked back at her. "I never hoped to have a grandchild, much less a great grandchild," Taresa said. "I am very pleased. I hope you and my grandson will visit Narlton Keep soon."

"St. Claire might come, but not me. At least, not until he finds his brother."

Taresa frowned and Rhoslyn realized she didn't know what had happened. Fear seized her. Lady Taresa didn't know that the baby Rhoslyn carried might not be St. Claire's. Rhoslyn glanced to her right to find St. Claire staring at her. Surely, he hadn't overheard their conversation?

"Forgive me," Rhoslyn said to Taresa. "I am suddenly tired."

It was only half a lie. She found she was tired, and the smell of the food on the table wasn't setting well with her stomach. She rose before the older woman could protest and hurried toward the kitchen. Her gaze caught on Sir Ascot, talking with a group of men near the kitchen door. He stared, brows furrowed. The knight was sure to tell her grandfather she had left the great hall upset.

Rhoslyn slowed, then entered the kitchen. She murmured greetings to the women, then took the stairs. She reached her chambers and lowered herself onto the bench in front of the fire. When St. Claire and her grandfather had come to the private solar accompanied by John Comyn, lord of Badenoch, the shock had been no greater than their announcement that St. Claire agreed to claim the Earldom of Baliman.

Her first thought had been that the title would endear Scotland to him. But the rigid set of his jaw had betrayed his thoughts. He had accepted the inevitable, but was determined to serve only Edward. That, she realized with the same trepidation she'd felt upon learning she was to marry an English knight, meant he would put his now-considerable support behind Edward's efforts to crown John Balliol. St. Claire's allegiance to Edward was the very reason John Comyn had taken note of him. Comyn supported Balliol, and knew St. Claire would as well.

Her grandfather seemed oblivious to the danger. He had planned to set fire to St. Claire's Scottish blood without realizing that St. Claire was as much Spanish as Scottish—and he ignored the fact the knight was English through and through. A tremor rippled through her midsection.

Now, that Spanish heritage sat in her hall celebrating the upcoming birth of a grandchild that might not be hers.

Lady Taresa wouldn't be so willing to witness the birth of a grandchild who might be the result of a rape. Would the lady's attitude affect St. Claire? He had sworn the child was his and, to his credit, he hadn't once made her feel otherwise. But Lady Taresa was his blood, and say what he may, blood made demands that couldn't be ignored. Wasn't that what her grandfather had implied when he'd said St. Claire's Scottish blood would fire in his veins? Aye, but St. Claire was dead set against any Scottish claims on his loyalty.

Tears pressed against her eyes. What would become of their son…their daughters? Would their fates have been less brutal had she married De Quincy? Yes. St. Claire was a good man. He would be a good father. Unlike De Quincy, he would care who his daughters married. He had cared who Andreana married. But what would he do if the command to marry them came from Edward instead of Lochland?

A light knock on the door caused her to jump.

"Lady Rhoslyn."

Lady Taresa.

"May I come in?" Taresa asked.

Rhoslyn swiped at a tear she hadn't realized was slipping down her cheek. If she remained quiet maybe Taresa would go away.

"Please," Taresa entreated.

Rhoslyn rose and went to the door. With a fortifying breath, she opened the door. "My lady," she said.

A moment of silence passed and Taresa said, "May I come in?"

Mortification sent a wave of heat to Rhoslyn's face. "Of course. Please, forgive me." She stood aside and the older woman entered.

"What a lovely room," Taresa said.

"Thank you. Will you join me by the fire?" Rhoslyn asked.

"That would be lovely."

Rhoslyn led her to the bench. "Would you like wine? I can have some brought up."

"No. Please, sit with me."

"Of course." Rhoslyn sat beside her.

She started when Taresa took her hand. "Talbot explained what happened. Can you forgive me?"

"Forgive you?" Rhoslyn said. "Ye have done nothing wrong."

"It was an accident, yes, because I did not know that Talbot's brother had abducted you." Concern furrowed her brow. "You are well, yes?"

"I am well, my lady."

"No. Taresa, remember?"

Rhoslyn nodded shyly. "Taresa. I am well. Talbot saved me before Dayton could take me away from Scotland."

Taresa brushed back a lock of hair from Rhoslyn's face. "Talbot tells me he could not be happier that you are carrying his child."

A lump formed in Rhoslyn's throat. "He said that?"

Taresa's eyes narrowed. "He did not tell you that? *Men*," she said with vehemence. "They can be such fools. We will speak with him."

"Nay," Rhoslyn blurted.

"Do not be afraid, little one, I can deal with him. Remember, he is my grandson." She leaned close. "He does not yet know what that means, but I will teach him."

Rhoslyn laughed. "I am certain you will. But you misunderstand. Tal-St. Claire has assured me how pleased he is we are to have a child."

Taresa studied her. "You are certain?"

She nodded. "I promise. In this, he has done all he should."

"In this?" Taresa repeated.

"Forgive me, Taresa, I do no' mean to speak badly of him."

"But…" the older woman urged.

Rhoslyn hesitated, then realized Lady Taresa was not a woman easily fooled. It wouldn't be long before she understood that Rhoslyn politically opposed her grandson. Would she guess how deep the division ran?

"Talbot has been good to me," she said, and it was true.

"But that is not all," Taresa said.

It should be enough, Rhoslyn mentally replied. But it wasn't. "Do ye know John Comyn?" she asked.

"Of course. He is one of the Guardians."

"He is the brother-in-law to John Balliol," Rhoslyn said.

"Ahh," Taresa intoned. "And you fear Talbot will follow his lead and support Balliol."

"Aye," Rhoslyn replied. "Balliol is too amenable to Edward. Robert Bruce is a far better choice for the crown."

"Indeed?" Taresa said. "Have you forgotten that Robert has been amenable to Edward on many occasions? Not the least of which is agreeing to appoint him arbiter of Scotland?"

Rhoslyn nodded. "Robert hasna' been perfect. Who has? But he is loyal to Scotland. Balliol is nothing more than an English puppet."

"You fear for your country and, perhaps, how your children will be used as pawns?" Taresa said.

"I am sorry," she replied. "I know this is no' the familial harmony ye seek."

Taresa laughed. "I am Spanish, my dear. Familial harmony only means we do not kill one another." A twinkle lit her eye. "We love a good fight. I think you and my grandson will fight well."

That was exactly what Rhoslyn feared.

TALBOT STARED DOWN at Rhoslyn, her back turned to him in her bed. He wasn't fooled. She wasn't asleep.

He sat on the mattress beside her. "Are you feeling better?"

"I am fine," she replied.

"You are not pleased?" he asked. "Your children will be nobility."

"My children will have my noble blood in them," she replied.

So she recognized the reality of the situation.

"John Comyn is pleased," she said.

"Aye," Talbot said.

"What will you do when Edward commands our daughters to marry an Englishman?"

Talbot stretched out on the bed and pulled her back flush against him. "We have no daughters yet, and already you have them married."

"I know what lies in store for them."

"To be cared for by a good man."

She turned in his arms and faced him. "Will you promise me that will be so?"

Staring down into her dark eyes, he could refuse her nothing. "I promise."

"And our sons," she said, "will they fight English wars?"

"We have all fought English wars," he said.

She studied him. "Will they serve an English king?"

"They will serve the King of Scotland."

Her eyes narrowed. "Ye believe Edward will rule, that is why you say that."

"I do not appoint kings," he said.

"Oh, but ye do. The Earl of Baliman has much power."

"I have no interest in choosing kings."

"But you will," she said, and his chest tightened at the sadness in her voice.

RHOSLYN STOOD ON the parapet staring west. What seemed like an eternity passed before she spied several moving specs in the distance.

"Please, Saint George, bring the Dragon home," she murmured.

At last, she discerned the riders and sent up a prayer of thanks.

Ross appeared at her side. "It is St. Claire."

"Aye."

When he and his men neared the castle, the warriors on the wall began the wide swing of the gate and Rhoslyn turned toward the stairs.

"Mayhap ye should remain up here until our visitors leave," Ross said.

"I am safe enough," she told him.

She had no intention of being absent when St. Claire confronted his grandmother's relatives. *His* relatives.

Rhoslyn descended the stairs and stepped onto the ground as St. Claire shot through the gates with his men close behind. He turned his horse to face the half dozen mounted men who waited in the bailey, surrounded by a dozen warriors.

"I am gone from Castle Glenbarr less than a day and trouble enters my home," he snapped.

His gaze caught on her and surprise showed on his face, then his eyes darkened. Ross was right. He wasn't pleased. He gave a sharp nod to one of his men. The warrior moved to Rhoslyn's side, hand on sword hilt.

St. Claire pinned his hard stare on the men. "Which of you is Niall Kenzie?"

"I am." The man riding a dark palfrey urged the horse forward a step.

"What do you want?" St. Claire demanded.

Niall narrowed his eyes. "I want to speak with ye."

"You want to tell me that you are the rightful Earl of Baliman," St. Claire shot back. "I have no time for family squabbles."

"Then ye ought not to have joined our family."

"Lady Taresa appointed me her heir," St. Claire said.

Niall gave a derisive snort. "Taresa is an old lady who will do anything to recover a trace of her lost daughter. She isna' capable of making such a decision."

"And you mean to help her make a decision that names you Cailan's heir," St. Claire said.

"He has more right than an English knight," a young man to Niall's right interjected.

St. Claire shifted his gaze onto the man. "Not when that English knight is her grandson."

"Even if ye are her grandson, ye are a bastard," Niall said.

"You may debate my legitimacy with King Edward."

"Ye mean to make war with us?" Niall demanded.

Rhoslyn didn't like the nasty tone of his voice. Apparently, neither did St. Claire.

"Lady Taresa made her decision. It is you who will not accept it."

"She is no' Scottish." Niall spat the words. "The title belongs to a Highlander."

"If you wish to discuss Scottish law, speak with your lord. He will explain your error."

"'Tis no' I who err, Knight."

"Leave now," St. Claire said, "and do not return until you are ready to swear fealty to me."

"Sweat fealty to Edward's puppet?" Niall sneered. "Never."

"Then never return."

For an instant Rhoslyn thought Niall might draw his sword. Another of the men shifted and St. Claire said, "Beware, Kenzie. If any of your men make the mistake of drawing a sword, I will kill you first."

Niall cursed, then yanked on his horse's reins.

The beast started to turn and St. Claire said, "Kenzie." the man's head jerked in his direction. "Do not harass my grandmother or I *will* make war on you."

The man stared for an instant, then kicked his horse's flanks. The warriors moved aside as the palfrey lunged forward, and Niall's men followed.

When the last man passed through the gate, St. Claire dismounted and strode to Rhoslyn. "My lady." He grasped her arm and started toward the castle.

"You have accepted Lady Taresa as your grandmother?" Rhoslyn said.

"What?"

Rhoslyn nearly trotted in order to keep up with his long strides. "You called her your grandmother. St. Claire, are ye in a hurry?"

He looked down at her. "In a hurry?"

"You are practically running."

"Forgive me." He slowed, but his hold on her arm didn't loosen.

"You called Lady Taresa your grandmother," Rhoslyn said. "That means you have accepted her as your grandmother."

"It means I had to make sure those fools did not try to coerce her into doing what they want."

"You mean you only said that to frighten them."

They reached the castle and he opened the door, then urged her in ahead of him.

"The Kenzies are gone," she said. "Are you no' going to return to Dunfrey Castle? Surely your work there isna' finished. You were gone for only a few hours."

He closed the door behind him and stopped, "What were you doing in the bailey? Those men intended trouble. If a fight had broken out you would have been in the middle of it."

"They were six men, guarded by a dozen of your men. A hundred more are about the castle at all times. I was in no danger."

"Men like Kenzie cannot be trusted. He easily could have reached you before one of my men could stop him."

Rhoslyn heard genuine concern in his voice, and the furrow in his brow deepened. "I didna' come down until you arrived, St. Claire. I was on the wall watching for you."

"Why?"

"Why what?"

"Why were you on the wall watching for me?"

"I thought it odd that they arrived during your first absence in a month. I thought they…"

Her answer seemed to catch him off guard and she thought he might relent, but he shook her and said, "You thought they might have laid a trap for me, then come here so that no one would accuse them of attacking me?"

That was very much what she'd feared.

"Then you understand how dangerous they are," he said. "When there is trouble—of any kind—you are to stay in your room."

He didn't wait for a reply, but released her and pushed through the door without a backward glance. Why had he gotten so angry? Surely he knew she was perfectly safe? Alec had never gotten angry with her. He had never so much as raised his voice. But St. Claire wasn't Alec.

MERRYMAKERS CELEBRATING THE marriage of one of Castle Glenbarr's knights to a baron's daughter filled the great hall and spilled out into the bailey. Talbot had furnished wine, ale, and food for the festivities. With the ceremony barely two hours past and the men well on their way to inebriation, he received word that Lord Lochland waited in the bailey with a dozen men. Enough men to protect him on the road, but a small enough number to assure him that Lochland had not come to fight Still, as far as Talbot was concerned, they'd had too many visitors in the two weeks since he'd accepted the title.

Talbot caught the glance Rhoslyn sent his way when the warrior delivered the message, but didn't stop when he passed her on his way to the door. He reached Lochland, who still sat astride his horse.

"Good evening, my lord," Talbot said. "Have you come to join in the celebration?"

"There is no need to pretend that I am your lord," Lochland said. "I am well aware you are the new Earl of Baliman."

Everyone kept reminding him of that. Talbot canted his head. "I am still growing accustomed to the title. Will you join the party? Your men are welcome as well."

"Come on, then, lads," he said, and dismounted.

The men gave their reins to waiting warriors and Talbot led them toward the castle.

"I suppose ye know this means I canna' enforce Lady Andreana's marriage to De Quincy," Lochland said without preamble.

"Yes," Talbot replied.

"Will you hold against me that I betrothed her to De Quincy?"

Talbot appreciated the man's straightforward manner. "Nay, my— Lochland. You only did what you thought best. You must know that Boyd marched against Castle Glenbarr as you predicted."

Lochland nodded. "I understand Kinsley rose from his bed and dealt with him."

"Aye."

"Ye would be a fool to think that is the end of things with Boyd," Lochland said.

Talbot wasn't fool enough to think that Boyd was finished with him any more than Lochland was. "I expect to see him again."

They reached the castle and Talbot opened the door. Laughter and music poured from the room. Talbot allowed Lochland to precede him, then followed the earl, with the earl's men close behind.

Talbot caught sight of Rhoslyn standing with the bride and several other women near the hearth. Her gaze followed Lochland. Talbot read the obvious satisfaction in her eyes and wondered how long it would take before she vocalized her feelings.

"Will you sit with me?" Lochland asked. "I would like to talk further."

Talbot considered inviting him into the bower where it was quiet, then realized Rhoslyn would follow. Talbot nodded, and Lochland gave his men leave to do as they pleased. Talbot led him to the table and secured drink for them both.

"Comyn paid ye a visit," Lochland said, and Talbot had to wonder if straightforwardness was a Scottish trait. If so, he liked it. "He wants you to advise Edward to appoint Balliol as King of Scotland."

"He did not speak of it to me," Talbot spoke loud enough to be heard, and hoped to guests were too busy enjoying themselves to pay attention to his conversation with Lochland.

"He will," Lochland said, voicing Talbot's thoughts. "It doesna' much matter. Edward plans to make Balliol king with or without Scotland's support. But you will make that decision easier."

"You do not like Balliol?" Talbot said.

"Nay. Neither does your wife. But if Edward supports him, you will follow suit."

"He is my king," Talbot conceded.

"A king who will no' support *you* if ye find yourself surrounded by enemies," Lochland said.

Talbot gave a short laugh. "I am surrounded by more enemies in peace than I was in battle."

The earl chuckled. "Aye, I imagine you are. However, ye are in a position to make good friends who will stand by you when Edward will no'."

"You, for example?" Talbot asked.

He gave a nod. "I am one, but there are others."

From the corner of his eye, Talbot saw Rhoslyn approach. "We can speak more of this later." He knew Lochland would want to discuss it at great length.

The earl's gaze caught on Rhoslyn and a speculative gleam appeared in his eyes.

"I advise you not to involve my wife in this debate," Talbot said. Lochland looked at him and Talbot read his indecision. "I make no decisions based on my wife's political views. I will not consider anyone a friend who uses her in any way."

"She doesna' like me anyway," Lochland said.

"No," Talbot agreed, "she does not."

TO HER CREDIT, Rhoslyn was gracious to Lochland. Talbot detected an underlying desire to throttle him, but instead she took delight in speaking gaily of Andreana and Baxter—and their soon return. It was a fabrication, they hadn't discussed the couple's return, but Talbot allowed her this small satisfaction. He had just begun to relax when Lady Isobel entered the great hall.

Rhoslyn shifted her gaze onto her before the door fully closed. Lady Isobel seemed oblivious to the scrutiny, though Talbot suspected she simply pretended not to notice.

Rhoslyn said nothing. They still sat with Lochland and Talbot guessed she didn't want the earl to know that she had caught her husband in an embrace with the woman. But Talbot wasn't foolish enough to think Isobel would remain unscathed. He considered asking Isobel to leave, but any attention he gave her would be looked upon unfavorably by Rhoslyn. She confirmed the suspicion by turning an accusatory stare onto him.

"I did not compose the guest list, Lady Rhoslyn," he said.

Lochland glanced curiously at her and a faint blush crept up her cheeks.

"That minstrel of yours seems to know only two songs," Lochland said. "Did ye bring him from England, St. Claire? He sings only of your exploits in Wales." The earl rose. "I think I will see if he knows any Scottish ballads."

He left and Talbot braced himself for Rhoslyn's fury, but was saved— if saved it could be named—when Lady Isobel approached.

"I willna' have that woman in my home," Rhoslyn said under her breath.

"Is she a friend to the bride and groom?" Talbot asked.

Rhoslyn snorted in derision. "If she is a friend to the groom it is for one reason only."

Talbot privately agreed.

Isobel reached them and he feared Rhoslyn would leap out of her chair and pummel the lady.

"What are ye doing here?" Rhoslyn demanded.

Surprise flickered in Isobel's eyes. "I am here to celebrate the happy couple's marriage. I have known Lady Sine since she was a child. It would be rude not to come."

"Ye didna' think it was rude to seduce my husband."

Isobel gave her a curious look. "Are ye that naive, Lady Rhoslyn?"

Rhoslyn shoved to her feet. A group standing nearby stopped talking and looked at her.

Rhoslyn said to Isobel under her breath, "Are ye saying my husband is the guilty party?"

"He was a complete gentleman." Isobel looked at him. "To my disappointment."

Rhoslyn took a step closer to her. "Then ye admit ye intended to bed him in the room next to mine."

"It was a kiss. Nothing more." Isobel glanced at him. "I suppose I can understand why ye would complain about sharing St. Claire and no'—"

Talbot came to his feet. "Lady Isobel that is enough."

She lifted her brows, and Rhoslyn looked from her to him. Talbot saw the wheels turning in her mind.

Elizabeth appeared at her side. "Rhoslyn, where did ye find your new cook? The deer stew is delicious."

Everyone looked at her.

She lifted her brows. "I am sorry, am I interrupting?"

She was, and knew it, and Talbot would later express his gratitude.

"Lady Isobel, I have no' seen you in some time," Elizabeth said. "Things are well with you?"

"Things are very good," she replied.

Elizabeth turned her attention to Rhoslyn. "Have you met Lady Sine's cousin Raleigh?"

Rhoslyn frowned. "Who?"

"Lady Sine's cousin. He has come from the Isle of Lewis and brought wool as a wedding present, which he says is the finest is all of Scotland. He is wearing a jerkin made of the wool, and it is magnificent. You must come see."

"What do I care about wool?" Rhoslyn said.

"Ye might be able to talk Sir Talbot into purchasing some of the wool."

"I can purchase my own wool," she answered with a dark glance his way.

Elizabeth laughed. "All the better. Come, you must see the jerkin."

Rhoslyn sent a last dagger-filled look Isobel's way, then allowed Elizabeth to lead her away.

Isobel's eyes remained fixed on her. "She doesna' know."

"Nay. And I would like it to stay that way," Talbot said.

Isobel shifted her gaze onto him. "It is in your interest for her to know that Alec bedded me and you would not."

"It would hurt her," he replied.

"But it would benefit you."

"I do not need to be compared to Alec Harper."

She studied him. "I would say there is no comparison, and if Lady Rhoslyn can no' see that, she is a fool."

Chapter Twenty-Two

～

R HOSLYN SPENT TOO much time in her private solar. At a little over five months pregnant, she felt excellent. But St Claire fussed like a mother hen, and constantly ordered her to rest. She had installed Lady Saraid in the kitchen with Mistress Muira in order to have a moment to review the list of goods they had received two days ago. With the addition of St. Claire's men, they had doubled their supply purchases and she seemed always to be working on the rolls.

Now, however, she stared out her window at the rider entering the courtyard. His shaven face and dark brown hair told her he was English, even without the absence of a kilt. This didn't bode well. She rose from the stool and hurried downstairs. Rhoslyn stepped from the stairs into the great hall as the man entered the postern door ahead of St. Claire.

St. Claire's gaze met hers and she read in his eyes the knowledge of her anxious curiosity. Rhoslyn caught sight of the folded parchment in his hand and her fear mounted. King Edward had sent a missive.

To her relief. St. Claire led the man toward the table set up near the hearth. She crossed the room and met them at the table.

"It has been a long ride for Sir John," St. Claire said. "He would like food and drink."

Rhoslyn nodded. "Go to the kitchen and tell Mistress Muira I sent you. She will feed ye near the fire there, where you may warm."

He bowed, then left them.

"I imagine you want to know what is in this missive," St. Claire said.

"It is from Edward?" she asked.

He nodded and lowered himself onto the bench beside the table. Rhoslyn sat beside him as he slid a finger between the folded edges and broke the seal. She was sure he was intentionally taking his time and had to refrain from snatching the parchment from him and tearing it open. He unfolded the letter and she read over his arm.

Sir Talbot,

My congratulations upon your new title as Earl of Baliman. I could not be more pleased. In the interest of keeping positive relations, I command that you appear before me and, as the Earl of Baliman, swear fealty. As my faithful servant, you will leave with Sir John and come to me immediately.

Your King,
Edward

"The bastard." Rhoslyn shot to her feet. "How dare he command fealty from ye. As the Earl of Baliman you owe him nothing."

St Claire looked up at her. "He is my king. He has every right to demand my fealty."

She stared in shock. "You are the most powerful man in all of Buchan. It is to you that men should swear fealty. Ye demanded that Kenzie bow to you."

"Aye, but I still have a lord. All men have a lord."

"Not Edward," she said bitterly.

"Even him," St. Claire replied.

"St. Claire, I didna' know you were a religious man."

"I am not, but that does not mean I do not believe we all serve someone. It is within Edward's right to demand my loyalty, and you should not be surprised that he wants to control my power. And lest you forget, I am not king. If I do not swear fealty to Edward, then I must pledge loyalty to the king of Scotland."

"Ye live in Scotland. You are a Scottish nobleman. Swear fealty to the king of Scotland." His gaze shifted back to the letter and her blood chilled. "Sweet Jesu, ye mean to return to England as he commands." She couldn't believe it.

"I have never disobeyed his command," St. Claire said.

Her mind raced. She wasn't surprised that Edward was tightening his hold. So what were the consequences within her family of Edward's grab for power? He would insist her sons train in England under English tutors; that they marry English women. Her daughters would become political pawns, married to noblemen selected by Edward to strengthen English alliances.

She hadn't considered any of this when she'd learned that St. Claire was the new earl. Her first thought had been of his strengthened ties to Scotland. Anger whipped through her. Edward would tear him away to prevent that, if necessary.

Rhoslyn sat back on the bench. "Is it safe for ye to leave Castle Glenbarr?"

He lifted a brow. "If I abolished your imprisonment here in Castle Glenbarr, you would be riding out the gates an hour later. Yet when I must return to England, you remind me how dangerous it is for me to leave the castle."

Rhoslyn met his gaze square. "That does no' answer my question. Is it safe for ye to leave us?"

He gave a single shake of his head. "Nay."

She shrugged. "Then Edward will have to wait."

"A king never waits."

"Tell him ye will return once you have captured your brother and dealt with the unrest amongst your people."

"My people?"

She read the humor in his eyes. "Ye said you wouldna' leave Castle Glenbarr to search for your brother for fear of leaving the castle unprotected. Kenzie was here only a month ago." Things had been quiet since then, but she wasn't going to remind him of that. "If ye leave and Jason takes Castle Glenbarr while you are gone, he will claim no' only Glenbarr, but the lands that belong to the Earl of Baliman."

"I doubt Jason has such high aspirations," St. Claire replied.

"Ye do no' know the man," Rhoslyn said. "And dinna' forget Kenzie. He would love nothing more than to wage war on ye while you are away." Anger flickered in his eyes and she knew she'd hit home. "Do you want that?" she pressed on ruthlessly. "Do ye want him taking me and your unborn child?"

His eyes darkened with fury. Unexpected emotion fluttered in her belly.

"It would seem I have a dilemma," he said.

Regret washed over Rhoslyn and she wished she could tell him to go serve his king as the loyal knight he was. What would she do if he didn't return? She would be forced to marry again—for a son needed a father. Nay, it was far worse than just remarrying. Before she could choose a husband, before her son was born, Edward would marry her to another of his puppets. She imagined the message arriving telling of Talbot's death, delivered by the man who bore another royal command from Edward that she marry. Her blood chilled at the thought of another man touching her while she still carried St. Claire's child.

"To leave is a death sentence," she said. "You must know that your brother will seize the opportunity to attack ye." In truth, it seemed half of Scotland wanted him dead. He started to reply, but she cut him off. "I know you well enough to know you would leave a legion of men to protect me and take only a few for yourself. Ye have too many enemies to be riding the countryside without a host of men. I canna' allow you to do it."

He studied her for a long moment. "Why not?"

"Because a son needs his father."

"Only a son?" he asked.

Embarrassment heated her cheeks. "The devil you know is better than the one ye dinna' know," she replied, and to her surprise, he threw his head back and laughed.

RHOSLYN FORCED HER legs into motion and passed through the opening in the low stone wall where lay her family in their eternal rest, then turned right. In the nearest corner, alongside the larger stone that belonged to Alec, stood the smaller stone that marked her son's grave. Her knees weakened, but she kept walking until she stood in front of the two graves.

She stared at the name on her son's headstone. The letters floated before her as if she dreamed. She had held him as he died. Did Alec now protect him? How was it possible the tiny body lay all alone beneath the snow-dusted heather? Her heart jerked. In her absence, someone had placed the flowers over the freshly dug dirt and the seed had taken root.

Rhoslyn glanced at the flowers she gripped. Mistress Muira dried heather and scattered it among the rushes. She had filched a few for the graves. But others, braver than her, had taken up where she could not. Who had visited her son? Andreana? Her grandfather? It should have been her. She should have been there to throw the first clump of moist earth down on him. Now, the ground that covered his small body had settled into packed earth as if no body lay buried beneath.

She started to kneel, then realized it would be difficult to rise. She would have to grasp a headstone to leverage herself back up. Dread chilled her bone deep. It wasn't the dead she feared, but the cold stone of her child's grave beneath her fingers. Anger tightened her insides. She had already deserted him once. She owed her son more than a toss of flowers onto his grave before she fled.

Rhoslyn stepped alongside his stone and grasped the top, then lowered herself onto her knees. Wind whipped the plaid around her shoulders and she pulled the fabric closer about her. With a shaky hand, she brushed snow from the small plot, then carefully arranged the heather on the center of the grave amongst the withered flowers. The pink buds made the grave look almost…alive.

"I am sorry, Dougal," she whispered. She brushed her fingers over the tiny flowers. "Ye are to have a brother. Would you like that?"

The wind whipped again, snapping the edge of her plaid. She shivered. It was cold, so cold. The heather skittered across the grave with another gust of wind. Rhoslyn caught it and set it back on the center. She glanced up at the darkening afternoon sky. A storm brewed. The wind would blow the heather off the grave.

Rhoslyn whipped off her plaid and laid it across the grave.

RHOSLYN HURRIED DOWN the stairs leading to the great hall. Just as the maid had said, Abbess Beatrice sat at the table near the hearth. Rhoslyn nearly flew across the room. She reached the table and Beatrice rose.

Rhoslyn threw herself into the older woman's arms. The abbess enfolded her in a warm hug and, for a moment, she could almost believe that she'd never left the convent. She suddenly longed to be back in her cell, listening to the abbess' Bible stories.

Rhoslyn drew back from the embrace. "I canna' believe ye are here. I am so happy to see you. Had I known you were coming, I would have made preparations."

Beatrice smiled. "Ye can imagine that I prefer to travel without fanfare."

Rhoslyn smiled. "Aye, of course. Have you eaten, are ye thirsty? How long will you stay?"

She laughed. "I see you have not changed. I would no' mind food and drink. As for how long I can stay, a day or two. Will that do?"

"A day or two? How wonderful," Rhoslyn cried. "Come, sit with me in my private solar. I will have food and drink brought up." Rhoslyn turned to see women crowding the doorway of the kitchen, staring. She laughed. "Will you greet my ladies? I believe they are anxious to meet you."

"Of course," Beatrice replied.

The abbess insisted on entering the kitchen, instead of having the women pay attendance to her while she sat on the bench in the hall. Once Rhoslyn finally tore her from the kitchen, they settled in the solar near the fire, with a banquet set out before them.

"You must wonder why I am here," the abbess said.

"I left the convent so suddenly that we had no chance to speak," Rhoslyn said. "I assume you came to see how I fare?"

The abbess took a bite of roasted chicken and nodded. "You look well." Beatrice gave her a penetrating glance. "Marriage agrees with you."

Rhoslyn suspected she meant, 'marriage has salved your hurt.'

Was that true? She thought back to her visit to Dougal's grave. Had going there been any easier because she now enjoyed the protection of a new husband or because she was to have a child that would replace him? Seeing the grave hadn't been easy, but yes, she realized with a start, her grief had lessened a bit.

"God works in mysterious says," Abbess Beatrice said.

Rhoslyn looked sharply at her.

Beatrice laughed. "Your face is an open book. Now, how do you like your new husband?"

Her stomach did a flip with the memory of how St. Claire had touched her last night. The desires of the flesh were not something a nun would understand, and wasn't what the abbess wanted to know.

"I see he pleases you," Beatrice said.

Rhoslyn started. "I-he is adequate," she stuttered.

Beatrice laughed. "From the look on your face, I would say he is more than adequate."

Shame washed over her and Rhoslyn dropped her eyes.

"You have no need to be ashamed," the abbess said. "God intended a man and woman to enjoy one another. The babe growing in your belly is one very good reason why."

Rhoslyn nodded while sending up a fervent prayer that the nun hadn't heard the rumors involving Dayton. But when the older woman said, "All things are God's will, Rhoslyn," she knew the abbess had heard of the kidnapping and assumed the worst.

"Is your husband pleased you are to have a child so soon?" Beatrice asked.

She meant, 'has he accepted the child as his own?' Rhoslyn thought, and said, "He is pleased."

Pleasure filled the older woman's eyes. "I knew he would be."

"You did? But how?"

Her expression softened. "I know such things."

Did God speak to the abbess? Was God finally answering her prayers? Was their child to be a blessing? Guilt washed over her. Weren't all children blessings? Wasn't it the parents who tainted them with their anger and hatred?

The sins of the fathers...

"You can be thankful that St. Claire isna' like his brother." Amusement sparkled the abbess' eyes. "At least when St. Claire kidnapped you, he was only kidnapping his wife."

Rhoslyn started before realizing the abbess would have heard of how St. Claire intercepted her on the way to marry another man. Thankfully, Beatrice didn't wait for a reply, but said, "I understand there is even more reason to celebrate."

Rhoslyn frowned. "There is?"

"Sir Talbot is reunited with his grandmother and has been named the new Earl of Baliman."

"Oh, yes," Rhoslyn said.

The abbess lifted her brows. "You are no' pleased?"

"In truth, I am not as happy as I first was," Rhoslyn admitted.

"Why?"

"King Edward demands that St. Claire return to England to swear fealty to him."

"That is not strange," Beatrice said.

"Nay," Rhoslyn agreed. "But it is obvious he only wants control of St. Claire's newfound power and wealth."

"Did ye expect less?"

Rhoslyn shook her head. "Nay. But Edward must know how dangerous it is for St. Claire to leave Scotland at this time."

"Sir Talbot expects his brother to attack?" Beatrice said.

Rhoslyn couldn't halt the flush of embarrassment to her cheeks.

"Ye are not the first woman to be used as a pawn by men, Rhoslyn. You did nothing wrong."

"I swear, I did nothing to encourage him," she blurted.

The abbess grasped her hand and gently squeezed. "I know you, child. Ye are a good woman, obedient to God's laws."

Rhoslyn forced back the lump that formed in her throat. "Thank ye,

Abbess."

"Now, tell me of your husband," Beatrice said. "I am hoping to meet him."

TALBOT ENTERED THEIR private chambers to discover Abbess Beatrice sitting with Rhoslyn. Rhoslyn's cheeks were flushed with pleasure and his heart warmed when she said, "It is about time ye came home, St. Claire."

Home. This was the first time she'd referred to Castle Glenbarr as his home.

"Forgive me, my lady," he said. "I have been occupied at Dunfrey Castle."

"We have company," she said, then laughed. "As ye can see. St. Claire, meet Abbess Beatrice, abbess of St. Mary's."

Talbot canted his head. "Sister Beatrice."

Beatrice acknowledged with a nod. "My lord, it is good to finally meet you."

"Sir Talbot will do," he said.

The same amusement he'd seen the night she'd visited him now tugged at her mouth.

"Nay, laird. Sir Talbot will no' do. Will ye sit with me? I would like to learn a bit about the man Lady Rhoslyn married."

"If you wish," he replied. "But I must warn you, I have been working, and am not sweet smelling."

"If you smelled of rose water, I would worry." She turned her attention to Rhoslyn. "Will you leave us for a little while, Rhoslyn?"

Rhoslyn cast an anxious glance at Talbot. He tensed. Did she suspected the abbess of being his informer the night she fled the convent? No. She wouldn't have been chatting so freely if she suspected.

"Of course," Rhoslyn said.

When she closed the door behind her, he said, "Perhaps you ought to stay indefinitely, Sister."

"Why is that?"

"Lady Rhoslyn defies Lord Lochland when he orders her to leave, but does not utter a peep when you ask."

"I imagine that did no' please the earl."

Talbot smiled at the memory. "It did not. Now, Sister, what brings you to Castle Glenbarr? Have you come to collect on that favor I owe?"

Her expression sobered. "I am, in fact, here to do you another favor."

"What is the price this time?" he asked.

"I can promise you this news is worth any price. Have you received word yet from Edward to return to England?"

Talbot was surprised by the question. "A month ago," he replied.

She gave a single shake of her head. "Nay, I speak of the letter commanding you to Wales to squash a rebellion."

"Wales?" Talbot said. "I have heard of no trouble there."

"Have ye considered what will become of Rhoslyn if you die in battle?"

Unease caused the hair on the back of his neck to stiffen. "That is not going to happen."

"It is unlikely." She locked gazes with him. "So long as you do no' return to England."

"What are you saying?" he demanded.

"Ye didna' heed Edward's command to return to England and swear fealty to him."

"I cannot leave Rhoslyn."

"Nay, you cannot, and for reasons you may not know."

"Such as?" he asked.

"Such as you no' returning from Wales and Edward marrying her to your brother."

"My brother?" he repeated. "Sister, I owe you a debt, but I will not be manipulated."

A long pause stretched out before she said, "Even by Edward?"

Especially by Edward, he wanted to say, but that was untrue. He, like all knights, was manipulated by his king. But service to Edward provided a better life than he could have hoped for otherwise. A manipulation like this, however—either the Abbess was lying or she was misinformed. Then why he hadn't he heard from Edward in the last month? The sovereign's silence troubled him. At the very least, he'd expected a scathing response. At worst, Edward could have shown up on his threshold with a legion of his men.

Nay. Talbot shoved the thought away. Edward was a king. He did what all kings did to preserve their power, but he didn't send loyal knights to be assassinated.

"I am sorry, Sister. Nothing you say can convince me that my king will have me killed—for any reason."

"I pray, my lord, that you see the light. Otherwise, I fear for Rhoslyn and your child."

STANDING ON THE wall, Talbot stared down at the missive from King Edward.

Talbot,

I understand your fears. We would risk all to protect our wives, even the wrath of our king. For this reason, I forgive your failure to heed my earlier command. However, there is a dire matter which requires your attention and cannot wait. Madog ap Llyweln is gathering forces for a rebellion. You are to leave immediately for Wales, where you will join my army at Gwynedd. Quell the rebellion and bring Llyweln to me.

The five hundred men-at-arms I sent with this letter will accompany you. You need not worry about Lady Rhoslyn. Five hundred more men are on their way to Castle Glenbarr. These, along with your men, will suffice to protect the castle until your return.

Send one of my men back with word that you are on your way.

When you quash the revolt, return to England. You will want to see your father. He is not well.

Talbot froze at the last line. Surely his father's wife would have sent word if something was wrong? Talbot forced reason. This was a ploy—had to be a ploy—on Edward's part to ensure that Talbot went to Wales. Still, worry niggled. His father hadn't written. Considering the trouble with Dayton, their father should have replied to at least one of Talbot's letters. Was Edward preventing him from writing? Had Edward intercepted the letters?

Talbot looked at Edward's signature. He had signed the missive with a simple *'Edward'* as if he and Talbot were close. He shifted his gaze past the battlement to the field beyond where waited five hundred men-at arms. Five hundred men who, without doubt, were commanded to besiege the castle if Talbot didn't leave for Wales.

Edward believed unequivocally in his sovereignty—and believed that everyone should and would accept his authority. Which was why he would never send five hundred men to protect a knight's family, even a knight turned earl. He expected obedience at all costs. Edward was not his friend.

Three weeks had passed since the abbess's visit, with no word from Edward until now. She had told the truth. Edward intended that he die in Wales.

Talbot envisioned Rhoslyn and their son twenty years from now having lived with Dayton as their lord. Rhoslyn would never break, but she would hate the man who manipulated their son in order to maintain control over the earldom. It was highly probable Rhoslyn would kill Dayton long before that. She wasn't a woman to let anyone hurt those she loved.

Edward's letter meant that Talbot had to find Dayton—now. As the Earl of Baliman, Talbot could take a legion of men and upturn every rock until he found his brother. Then he would cut out his heart and send it back to Edward.

Talbot turned to Ross, who stood a respectful distance away. "Take your best man and leave through the secret passageway below the east tower. Send the man to Seward. You go to Lady Taresa. We need every man who can wield arms."

"How long will the English army wait?"

"A day, no more. But that is of no consequence. They cannot take Castle Glenbarr before you return."

He released a breath and looked again at the men who covered the field like ants. He had never run away from a battle. Staying behind, not going to Lady Taresa to gather his men felt like running away. *His men.* Whether by blood or by chance, he was the Earl of Baliman. The men who served Lady Taresa served him. The time was now to proclaim to all, Scottish and English, that this was his place in the world and no one, not a local warlord or the king of England was going to take that from him.

THE DOOR TO the solar opened and Rhoslyn jerked her head up from the parchment she'd been staring at the last hour. St. Claire stood in the doorway. They stared for a long moment, then he entered, closing the door behind him. Rhoslyn sat frozen as he crossed the room.

He stopped beside the table where she sat. "The men will be here within the hour."

She nodded. The knot that had been lodged in her throat since the English army arrived that morning moved higher in her throat.

"You have not forgotten what we planned?" he asked.

She shook her head.

"You will not falter?" he persisted.

She would, but she shook her head.

"Tell me," he said.

How could she say the words?

He grasped her hand and pulled her to her feet.

"Say the words."

She shook her head.

"Please me in this, Rhoslyn."

She understood why he insisted. If she said the words then it would be real. But she didn't want it to be real.

"You promised," he said gently.

"Aye. I promised. But that doesna' mean I have to say it out loud."

"It does. Say it."

She couldn't.

Rhoslyn dropped her gaze. "If ye dinna' return, I will go immediately to Lord Melrose and marry him." The words were out of her mouth, but she couldn't believe her lips had formed the sounds.

With a finger beneath her chin, St. Claire tilted her face upwards. "I plan to return."

She couldn't bring her eyes to meet his.

"Look at me, love."

She forced her gaze upward.

"You are not to leave the castle until I return." *Or you leave to go to Melrose,* she heard the unspoken words. "If I return and find you one foot outside the castle, you will force me to punish you."

Rhoslyn snorted. "Beware, St. Claire, ye might return to find I locked the gate."

A corner of his mouth turned upward. "Good. Now kiss me before I go."

He was truly going. Going into a battle against his countrymen who had come to kill him. If he had agreed to go with them, would he have reached Wales or would he have died on the road by some unseen *robber?* Edward wouldn't care how his assassin carried out the order, he would only care that St. Claire was dead.

St. Claire lowered his head and covered her mouth with his. He pulled her flush against his body and Rhoslyn melted against his solid warmth. The kiss was gentle and too short.

When he lifted his head, she said, "Ye need no' go yet. There is an hour yet before they arrive."

He gave a low laugh. "Aye, but I must meet them, remember?"

Her heart pounded. Why did he have to join the battle? He knew the assassin would seek him out. What if there was more than one? What if all five hundred had been commanded to kill him?

Rhoslyn startled when St. Claire laid a palm on her belly. The warmth of his fingers penetrated the fabric of her dress and she closed her eyes, memorizing his touch.

"He is quiet today," St. Claire said.

"Aye," Rhoslyn replied. *Perhaps he knows his father is leaving.*

"He is growing large."

She flushed. Her girth had increased and she had become embarrassed to disrobe in front of him. But St. Claire wouldn't allow her to go to her room to change. He insisted she stay.

He dipped his head and placed a kiss on her belly, then straightened. "I will see you when I return."

He turned and strode to the door. Rhoslyn took a step after them, then stopped. Growing weepy would only make leave-taking harder for him. She didn't want him worrying about her when he faced the army that had been sent to kill him.

He left without a backwards glance, which, though hurtful, was best, and she was grateful. If he didn't return, she wanted to remember him holding her, caressing her belly and thinking of their child. Not a last look that conveyed…conveyed what? *I'm sorry to leave? I will miss you…I love you?*

She sat on the bench with a thud. St. Claire had never spoken words of love. He cared for her well-being, that much was obvious. But love? That was a different matter. But whether he loved her or not, she loved him.

Rhoslyn closed her eyes and forced back the tears that pressed like a raging tide against her eyelids. Thank God he hadn't looked back when he left. She would have surely blurted the words while crying.

What would happen if he died before knowing?

How would she hide the truth from him if he returned?

Chapter Twenty-Three

～

RHOSLYN LIFTED HER eyes to the Christ in the alcove of the small chapel. "I beg you, Saint George, heed my prayer and save, protect, and defend the Dragon, Sir Talbot St. Claire."

Surely, Saint George would give aid, for St. Claire was fighting to save her and their child. St. George would understand that, this time, the Dragon fought for the right.

She bowed her head and whispered the prayer.

Her knees began to ache, but she pressed on, begging that her prayers be heard. Despite her efforts, her mind wandered to the battle that must be waging outside the castle. Here, within the chapel, she was insulated…as she had been in St. Mary's. Yet, her grandfather's men had shown up in the middle of the night and ripped her from her peace. Would it be St. Claire who appeared in the chapel to tell her all was well or would—Rhoslyn opened her eyes and looked up at the statue of Mary.

"Forgive me." She grasped the ledge of the alcove and pulled herself to her feet.

She stood for a moment, catching her breath. Only a little more than seven months pregnant, yet she felt as if she weighed as much as a horse. Rhoslyn caught her breath and felt her legs steady, then hurried from the chapel and up the stairs to the north tower. Before she'd gone halfway up the stairs, her breathing came in heavy gasps and her legs felt as if she waded through sand. She stopped and rested.

Twice more she was forced to rest before she reached the top floor of the tower. St. Claire had forbade her from leaving the castle, but he could not stop her from watching the battle from the north tower. And she could no longer sequester herself away from the world.

Rhoslyn paused in the doorway, startled by the silence. Sounds of a battle this large would penetrate even the thick stone of the tower walls. She hurried to the window and drew back the shutters. Campfires dotted the field in the darkness beyond the wall. She squinted, but could discern no riders approaching in the distance. Had St. Claire decided to wait until morning to attack? He had said nothing of this to her. But then, he wouldn't. The English army would surely have scouts watching for danger. Wouldn't they know if St. Claire approached?

She placed a hand over her belly and gently soothed as if to quiet the babe. Castle Glenbarr could easily withstand a yearlong siege. St. Claire had seen to that. Not that he'd believed it would be necessary. Lady Taresa had seven hundred warriors, and her grandfather, five hundred. The two hundred men inside the castle walls would stay while those three hundred who lived in the village and on his land would follow him into battle. Altogether, St. Claire would ride with at least fourteen hundred men. They would easily beat the English army back. But none of that guaranteed St. Claire would survive the battle.

Thank God they had discovered Edward's plot to kill him. At least, that way, he stood a chance of surviving. Rhoslyn gave a small gasp upon realizing she hadn't thanked the abbess for warning them of the plot. She murmured a prayer of thanks and one asking forgiveness for her selfishness.

Gratitude brought the desire to cry. The abbess was so kind to deliver the message personally. Rhoslyn could only wonder how Sister Beatrice had heard of Edward's plan, but the abbess was a powerful woman. In the time Rhoslyn spent at the abbey, she had seen some of the Guardians visit. Even William Wallace once came in the early morning hours. Like the wee hours of the morning when her grandfather's men arrived to take her to Lord Melrose.

Rhoslyn had been unlucky enough for the abbess to be away the night the men came for her. How different might things have turned out if she'd been there. Might the abbess have counseled her not to go? Might she have known something that would have better guided Rhoslyn? Had things turned out so badly?

The abbess had said she knew St. Claire would be glad for the baby.

For an instant, Rhoslyn was back in her cell, feeling Sister Hildegard dress her. *"She sent me,"* Hildegard had said of Beatrice. Beatrice *had* been there. Why, then, hadn't she intervened? The appearance of her grandfather's warriors to take her away in the middle of the night in order to avoid marriage to St. Claire was no small matter.

Rhoslyn's thoughts came to a screeching halt. Aside from the men sent to bring her from St. Mary's, only her grandfather and Lord Melrose knew she would be leaving the abbey that night. Her mind jumped forward. Was it possible one of the warriors had betrayed them and sent word to St. Claire? Possible yes, but probable? More probable than the possibility that Beatrice was the one who told him?

Beatrice hadn't seen Rhoslyn off with the warriors because she had left for Castle Glenbarr before Hildegard came and told her the men were there.

It couldn't be. Beatrice would never betray her. Never.

If not her, then who?

Rhoslyn mentally counted through the men who had been there that night. She knew them all. Not a one would betray her grandfather. But one of them had. How could she possibly prove it? St. Claire would know. Maybe. The traitor might have sent an anonymous letter. If Beatrice stayed at the convent, why hadn't she come to Rhoslyn when the warriors arrived? If only she could speak with the warriors her grandfather had sent for her.

Sir Ascot. Her grandfather had left him at Castle Glenbarr to help St. Claire.

Still no signs of St. Claire. Worry tightened her belly. Had something gone wrong? Either way, there was nothing she could do. In the darkness, she wouldn't be able to distinguish St. Claire.

She turned from the tower and hurried from the room. She stopped at the stairs and stared down. The climb back up would be difficult. Rhoslyn glanced back at the room, then turned and started down the stairs.

SIR ASCOT WASN'T in the castle and Rhoslyn was forced to wait as one of the lads fetched him from the wall. She ascended to her private solar and waited. At least once she was done speaking with him, she would be rested for the trip back to the north tower.

He arrived a little while later.

"Sir Ascot, thank ye for coming. Will you sit?" She nodded at the other end of the bench were she sat.

"Nay, my lady. I canna' stay long."

"Of course. Forgive me for calling you here. No signs of St. Claire?"

He shook his head.

"I expected him before this," she said.

"Dinna' worry. I am certain he is safe. It may be it is taking more time than anticipated to gather his men."

That was true. She had no idea how Lady Taresa managed her men. "I am certain you are right," she said.

"Is that all?" he asked.

"Not quite. Can ye tell me, Sir Ascot, the night you came for me at the convent, how long did ye wait?"

"Wait, my lady?"

"Before I arrived."

"It was some time," he said. "I am of the mind that had we left sooner, Sir Talbot would no' have caught us."

Rhoslyn couldn't help a small gasp.

"My lady, forgive me. I did no' mean to blame you. You could not have understood the need for haste. In truth, I didna' believe he would stop us. How could he have possibly known?" Sir Ascot paused, then his gaze sharpened and Rhoslyn realized he'd deduced that she knew something. "Have ye an idea who told him?" He went down on one knee before her. "Tell me and I will deal with the traitor."

Rhoslyn smiled gently. "Sir Ascot, do ye regret our current circumstances?"

"You shouldna' be caught in the middle of someone else's war," he said vehemently.

"And if this war had been Lord Melrose's?" she asked.

He didn't answer.

She laid a hand on his arm. "I understand your fears." *And share them.* "Did my grandfather no' send you here to help my husband?"

He bent his head. "Forgive me, my lady. I am yours to command."

"Continue as ye have," she said. "When you protect St. Claire, you protect me."

He lifted his head and determined glint shone in his eyes. "Aye, my lady." He rose, bowed, and left.

Rhoslyn stared even after the door had closed.

Abbess Beatrice had slipped away from the convent while Hildegard delayed her grandfather's men.

Why?

TALBOT GLANCED PAST the warrior carrying the torch and caught sight of the approaching rider.

The man drew up alongside the torchman and said to Talbot, "There is a company of men, about two hundred, approaching from the rear."

"Who are they?" he demanded.

"They are flying the banner of Lord Lochland."

Talbot exchanged a glance with Seward, who rode to his left. "Have you any idea what he wants?"

Seward shook his head. "Nay."

"They are riding fast," the warrior said.

Castle Glenbarr lay two miles ahead. Talbot found it hard to believe the earl was headed anywhere but there.

"I will take my men and see what he wants," Seward said.

"Nay," Talbot replied. "I do not want to deviate from the plan. We will arrive at Castle Glenbarr together. When Edward's army sees that they are outnumbered three to one, there is a chance they will retreat."

"Ye are still intent on not killing them?" He gave Talbot no chance to reply. "They will only return with more men."

"I will not slaughter my countrymen for obeying their king's command."

"Ye had best prepare to slaughter them, for they may no' retreat," Seward said.

Anger shot to the surface. "Aye," he said. If that happened, he would deal with Edward. "Take your men and circle around behind Lochland," he told Seward. "But do nothing unless you hear us attack."

"I suppose I must obey ye, Lord Baliman." Seward's amused tone took the sting from the words. He called an order for his men to follow, and steered his horse to the right to circle back.

Talbot sent a hundred of his men back around the other side. Then he turned the remaining five hundred men, faced the oncoming riders, and waited.

MINUTES LATER, A lit torch appeared on the road in the distance. The approaching riders Talbot didn't slow, but Talbot knew they had to have seen the torch held by the man to his right. The thunder of horses' hooves soon reached his ears. The men neared, then slowed and finally stopped fifty feet away. Lochland rode forward alone and halted in front of Talbot.

"I am pleased ye had the sense no' to attack me," Lochland said.

"What do you want?" Talbot demanded.

"I understand ye have English visitors," Lochland said. "A few of my men are anxious to meet them."

"I will not trade favors, Lochland," Talbot said.

"Aye, eventually ye will, but I am no' asking it of you."

"Why do this?" Talbot demanded.

"Edward might be a good arbitrator, but he has no right to force any of us to our knees."

"Do you forget that I am English?" Talbot said.

"Nay, just as Edward hasna' forgotten that ye are a Highlander."

The earl was right. Edward was all too aware of his Scottish connection, which Talbot suspected had a part in Edward's plan to murder him. How much did Lochland know?

"What makes you think Edward sent his men to force me to do anything?"

Lochland laughed. "Edward does no' send five hundred men to Scotland to *ask* for anything."

That was also true.

"You will do as I command," Talbot said. "If the men-at-arms retreat peacefully, I will allow them to return to England."

A moment of silence passed before Lochland said, "What will ye do if they return in greater numbers?"

"Kill them."

RHOSLYN ONCE AGAIN stood in the north tower watching through the window when the door behind her opened. She whirled and startled to see Lady Taresa enter. Behind her came Mistress Muira.

Rhoslyn hurried forward. "My lady, what are ye doing here? St. Claire, is he with you?" She hadn't seen them arrive.

Taresa clasped her hand. "No, child. He is not with me. He told me of your secret entrance and Derek brought me."

"Ye should no' have come," Rhoslyn said. "I am surprised St. Claire allowed it."

She laughed. "He has no power to command me. Though he did try. When I told him I was coming and he could not stop me, he instructed Sir Derek on how to enter through the secret passageway. It was necessary I come."

"It isna' safe," Rhoslyn insisted.

"It is quite safe," she replied. "The English army has no interest in me. I could have passed through their ranks and entered through the front gate, but to open the gate was too risky."

Rhoslyn shifted her attention to the housekeeper. "How did you know I was in the north tower?"

"Ye were no' in your apartment. It was an easy deduction."

Rhoslyn nodded, then said to Lady Taresa, "Come, let us sit in my solar."

Taresa's gaze shifted to the window. "You can see the battlefield from here?"

"You can see the men. The battle hasna' begun. St. Claire has yet to arrive."

"Then we should stay and watch."

"Nay," Rhoslyn urged. "It is cold and drafty."

She ignored Rhoslyn and crossed to the window. "You are wrong, child." Taresa looked at her. "Talbot has arrived."

TALBOT SENT LOCHLAND to the west and Seward to the east. Sir Derek caught up with Talbot after delivering Lady Taresa safely to Castle Glenbarr. Her stubborn determination to join Rhoslyn reminded him of his sister. *"Determination runs in our family, Talbot,"* Taresa had said, and he'd half wondered if she'd read his mind.

She had pointed out that he would need Sir Derek to lead the men from Narlton Keep, so it would be easy for Derek to deliver her to Castle Glenbarr first. Talbot intended to refuse, to the point of locking her in her room, until she reminded him that Rhoslyn was very pregnant, and it would be a comfort to have family nearby while he dealt with the English.

Talbot sent Sir Derek south, while he approached from the north. Beside him, rode the warrior carrying the only lit torch amongst their ranks. As expected, when they neared the castle and the English camp, men mounted horses and met them before they reached camp.

Talbot brought his men to a halt.

"Who goes there?" called a man.

Talbot recognized the voice of the captain, Sir Ronald. "It is I, Sir Talbot."

Ronald urged his horse forward. He drew near and squinted at Talbot. "You did not leave through the front gate, St. Claire." The man's voice dripped with accusation. "Who are these men?"

"My men," Talbot replied. "Go back to England, Ronald. Tell Edward I know of his plot."

"Plot? What plot?"

The man's surprise sounded genuine. Talbot could easily believe Edward hadn't chosen his captain as his assassin. If Talbot refused to return to England, Ronald would try to force him, while the assassin waited for an opportunity to kill him. That doubled Edward's chances of making sure Talbot left Scotland.

"Return to England," Talbot said.

"I cannot leave without you."

Talbot glanced at his warrior holding the torch and nodded. The man lifted the torch high above his head. Three companies of men emerged from the trees beyond the field, from the shadows beyond the camp. They seemed to bleed from the darkness.

Shouts went up in the camp.

"You had better stop them," Talbot said. "You do not stand a chance against my army."

Sir Ronald stared at him for an instant, then called, "Evan, return to camp. No man is to draw a sword."

Evan turned his horse. The beast lunged forward, then broke into a gallop.

"How many?" Ronald demanded.

"Sixteen hundred," Talbot replied.

"You could be lying."

"I am not. When the sun rises you will see."

"Why not kill us?" Ronald asked.

"If you do not leave at dawn, I will."

"IT HAD TO have been St. Claire." For the dozenth time, Rhoslyn stalked to the window in her solar, despite knowing she could see little of the men camped beyond the wall.

After the two groups of riders met and talked, the English returned to their camp, and the riders followed, then camped beside them.

"Why is he staying out there?" she said.

"You did not think the English army would leave because he asked nicely?" Taresa said.

Rhoslyn looked at her. "Ye think they mean to fight?"

"No. I think they mean to wait until the light of day to be sure they are outnumbered. It will not be easy for them to tell King Edward they did not raise a single sword. They will have to be certain they are vastly outnumbered."

Rhoslyn glanced at the window. "But ye do think they will leave quietly?"

"Everything is quiet, Rhoslyn. Have faith in Talbot. He does not want to fight his countrymen. He is giving them every opportunity to leave peaceably."

"That does no' mean they will."

"Come, sit with me." Taresa patted the bench beside her. "You do not want to overexcite yourself."

Truth be told, Rhoslyn was tired. But she couldn't think of sleeping.

"Come," Lady Taresa urged. "Talbot will not be pleased if he returns to find you overwrought."

Rhoslyn did as she asked and sat beside her.

"It is kind of you to come to me," Rhoslyn said.

"You are my family. I would not be anywhere else." She smiled. "Family is what matters, yes?"

"Aye," Rhoslyn agreed. "There is nothing more important."

"Tell me," Taresa said, "have you and Talbot decided upon a name for the baby?"

Rhoslyn shook her head. "St. Claire has said nothing."

Taresa snorted. "Men. Never mind. Have you a name in mind?"

"We could name him after his father."

"Talbot is a fine name," Taresa agreed.

"My grandfather's name is Hugo. My father was named Henry."

Taresa's brow rose. "You are certain it is a boy? What if you have a girl?"

"I do no' know. St. Claire seems to want a son."

"All men want sons. But they love daughters, as well. An older sister will keep her brother in line."

Rhoslyn laughed. "No' if she is like me. I was always in trouble."

"Not you," Taresa said in a teasing tone.

"Aye." She recounted the tale of how she had left Banmore Castle in search of her puppy. The animal had gone missing and Rhoslyn was sure he'd gotten lost outside the castle.

The evening wore on, and Rhoslyn at last was forced to give into Lady Taresa's insistence that she sleep. Her eyes grew heavy, and despite her best efforts to continue watch through the solar window, she knew it was best for the baby if she rested.

"If ye hear anything, you will wake me?" Rhoslyn asked of Taresa, once she'd agreed to retire.

"I promise," the older woman said. "But let us hope it is Talbot who wakens you in the morning, and not me."

"Ye dinna' have to go." The words were out of her mouth before she could catch herself and she dropped her gaze.

"This bed is certainly large enough for two," Taresa said. "Would you mind very much if I stayed with you?"

Rhoslyn lifted her eyes. "I would be very pleased for you to stay with me."

Taresa leaned close and said, "It will teach Talbot a lesson if he decides to visit you in the middle of the night. He will think twice about leaving you alone, yes?"

Rhoslyn laughed and hugged the woman.

"YOU LOOK AS if you need sleep," Talbot said to Seward.

The old baron didn't look up from campfire he stared at. "Ye worry about yourself, St. Claire. I am well enough."

Morning light nipped at the edges of the east horizon. None of them had slept. Some men lay sleeping, some talking in low tones, but Talbot listened to noises from the English camp. The sounds suggested men rousing and tending their horses. Unless Sir Ronald intended to attack, his men were preparing to leave. Talbot wasn't a religious man—Rhoslyn was religious enough for the two of them—but if he thought praying would speed Edward's army on their way, he would have passed the night on his knees.

Talbot glanced at the castle. From here, he couldn't see Rhoslyn's room or the chapel. He hoped she'd had sense enough not to spend the night in the chapel. If Lady Taresa directed any of her determination upon Rhoslyn, she might, at some point, have gotten his wife to go to bed.

"If they leave, it isna' the end," Seward said.

"Nay," Talbot agreed.

"It seems ye have taken a stand against your king, after all," Lochland said. He lay on the ground on the other side of the fire. "I wonder why."

"That does not mean I betrayed him," Talbot said.

"Despite the fact he betrayed you?" Lochland said.

Talbot looked sharply at him. It was an obvious guess, but caught him off guard nonetheless.

"Do ye consider it a betrayal to protect yourself?" Lochland asked.

"Nay," he said, but the knowledge didn't stop the sting.

"Good."

Seward remained silent, but Talbot knew the man still seethed. Edward's desire to grab power by forfeiting a loyal knight's life confirmed his worst beliefs about the English king.

"It has been a long night," Lochland said.

"You and your men are welcome in Castle Glenbarr once Sir Ronald and his men leave."

The earl grunted. "'Tis the least ye can do."

They fell silent as the sun lifted slowly and dawn finally made an appearance.

Lochland broke the silence. "We have company." He stared at something beyond Talbot.

Talbot twisted and looked over his shoulder to see Sir Ronald approaching with one of his men. Talbot rose and turned as they neared. Lochland and Seward stepped up alongside him.

"We are preparing to leave," Ronald said, when they reached Talbot. "You know what Edward will do when I return without you."

"Would you prefer to fight now?" Talbot asked.

"So you can slaughter my men?" he sneered. "Have you any message for Edward?"

"As I told you last night, tell him I know of his plan."

Sir Ronald hesitated. "Think of what you do. This is treason."

"Is that what Edward told ye?" Seward interjected.

"Quiet," Talbot commanded.

Ronald looked from the old man to Talbot. "I would speak with you alone."

"Ye can go to the devil," Seward growled.

"I must speak with you," Ronald insisted of Talbot.

"Dinna' be a fool," the baron said. "Ye know what a snake Edward is."

"Enough," Talbot said. He nodded at Sir Ronald and started away from the two men.

"Remember your duty to my granddaughter and great grandson," Seward called after him.

"Remember your vow to me," Talbot replied. He hoped Seward kept his word and didn't tell Lochland or anyone else about Edward's plan to kill him.

They walked until they left the larger clusters of men behind. Up ahead, Ronald's army prepared to leave, though, to Talbot's frustration, they seemed in no hurry. Some were saddled and mounted while others still saddled their horses. Others still sat in groups talking.

"You are Sir Talbot St. Claire," Ronald said. "You have been Edward's favorite from the beginning. What have these Scots done to turn you against him?"

"Return and deliver my message," Talbot said.

"Return with me, I beg you. Whatever has happened, Edward will forgive."

"Edward will forgive?" Talbot shot back. "You know nothing of what Edward has to forgive."

Ronald stepped closer. "He is our king. *Your* king."

"Aye," Talbot said. Just as Talbot was his knight. But that hadn't stopped the pontiff from trying to kill him—all so he could seize Talbot's newfound power. "Have your men ready to leave within the quarter hour." Talbot started to turn, then stopped and added, "Tell Edward this. I will be sending him my brother's head."

Shock shone on the knight's face, then his gaze shifted past him. Talbot glanced over his shoulder. Seward and Lochland approached.

"I beg you not to listen to them," Sir Ronald said in a low voice. "They have poisoned you."

"It is not them who poisoned me," Talbot said in a growl, "but the faithless king you say I serve."

"Faithless? You speak treason."

Seward and Lochland reached them.

"Your wet nurses have come to lead you home," Ronald said. "I suppose I should not be surprised that you are allowing me and my army to leave instead of fighting. You have turned craven, St. Claire."

"This one doesna' know good fortune when it stares him in the face," Lochland said. "If ye have an itch to fight, my men will oblige."

"While Sir Talbot stands aside and watches," Ronald sneered. "You are not afraid we will attack when you return to Castle Glenbarr? I was certain you would ride with us clear to Edinburgh just to be sure we left. Or is there an army hidden somewhere along the way to ambush us? Or is it that the Scottish whore has bewitched you into betraying your king?"

"Is this how English knights speak of a man's wife?" Lochland demanded.

"Nay," Talbot said. Then he thought of Dayton.

Dayton was a master strategist—a strategist who would have a secondary plan. When he saw the army Talbot was able to amass, he would realized that Talbot had no intention of leaving with Edward's army. And he would have set into motion his secondary plan.

Talbot took two steps and stopped inches from Ronald, "Tell me where my brother is and I will let you return to England unharmed."

Surprise flashed across the knight's face.

Seward swore. "By God, the whoreson has hatched a plot."

"Tell me now," Talbot demanded. "What Dayton has planned is not in accordance with our law. He intends to kill me then take my wife and child."

"I obey my king, not you," Ronald snapped.

"Take him," Talbot ordered Lochland. "Then surround his men. Kill any who lifts a sword."

Lochland stepped up to Sir Ronald. "Raise the alarm and I will slaughter every last man with you."

Talbot whirled and strode back toward his camp. Seward fell in alongside him. Neither man spoke, but Talbot knew the old man was thinking the same thing he was: Rhoslyn.

She was safe within Castle Glenbarr. She had sworn she wouldn't set foot outside the castle. His men wouldn't allow her to leave. No one had entered since he left yesterday.

Excerpt Lady Taresa through the secret passageway.

His heart began to pound. If anything was wrong, Ross would have sent word immediately.

They reached the horses and Talbot leapt into the saddle. He dug his heels into his horse's ribs and shot forward before Seward could mount. Seward caught up with Talbot as he veered around a group of men and headed toward the east tower.

"Where are ye going?" Seward shouted once they'd left the camp behind.

"The east tower," Talbot replied.

Minutes later, they reached the heavy brush that hid the secret passageway two hundred feet beyond the rear of the castle. Talbot jumped from his horse with Seward close behind. A shout went up at the wall as he plunged into the thick foliage. No torch burned within the passageway, so they were forced to slow. Talbot felt his way along the damp stone walls. When a glimmer of light came into view up ahead his blood chilled.

They reached the door to find it ajar. The guard he had left lay on the ground. Talbot dropped to one knee and surveyed the bloody gash in his forehead. He felt for a pulse and found a strong heartbeat. Talbot rose, hurried forward, and was met at the stairs by Ross and half a dozen men.

"Where is Lady Rhoslyn?" Talbot demanded.

"In her chambers," Ross replied. His gaze fixed on the man lying on the floor. "What happened?"

"My brother," Talbot said. "Damn him. See to the man."

Ross ordered two of his men to bring the wounded warrior upstairs, then followed Talbot. They reached Rhoslyn's room and found it empty. Talbot looked in the solar and his room, but she wasn't in either place.

"Where might she be?" he demanded.

"In the kitchen?" Ross replied. "Your grandmother stayed with her last night. I havena' seen either of them this morning."

Talbot cursed. He knew he should have been more forceful when Lady Taresa insisted on coming to Castle Glenbarr.

They checked the kitchen, but they weren't there and the women hadn't seen them.

"Get Cullen," Talbot ordered Ross. "He can track for me. He and I will ride ahead. Seward, gather five hundred men and follow."

"Ross can gather my men. I am going with ye."

"I dinna' understand," Ross said. "If a stranger entered the castle and went to Lady Rhoslyn's room, someone would have noticed. Your brother could no' have gotten inside the castle undetected."

"Aye," Talbot agreed, "but he could have found someone willing to bring Rhoslyn to him." And when that traitor found the women together, he took the two of them instead of killing Lady Taresa. What were the chances Dayton would consider that a good idea? Her death furthered his interests. That gave Dayton control of the title once he married Rhoslyn.

"They canna' have gotten far," Seward said. "Do ye think your brother would chance returning to Stonehaven? You have a mighty big price on his head there."

Talbot had a big price on his head in all of Scotland. Dayton couldn't hope to outrun Talbot while burdened with Rhoslyn, who was heavy with child. He wanted the baby almost more than he wanted Rhoslyn. Where would he go? Then Talbot knew.

"Seward, you remember John Comyn's cousin, Davey?"

"Aye," he replied, then understanding dawned on his face. "Your brother doesna' plan to leave Scotland."

"Why leave when I will be dead any day?"

Seward nodded. "Then he will emerge from whatever rock he has hidden under—married to Rhoslyn."

A man entered through the postern door. Sir Derek. He crossed to the staircase where they stood.

"What has happened?" Derek demanded. "Ye have surrounded the English army."

There was no avoiding the truth. "Lady Rhoslyn and Lady Taresa are missing."

"Missing? How is that possible?"

"My brother must have taken them."

Derek stepped toward Talbot. The three men with Talbot surged toward Derek.

"Hold," he commanded, and they stopped.

"Why did the kidnapper take Lady Taresa?" Derek demanded.

"Maybe he found them together and preferred that to killing her," Talbot said. "I do not know."

"She was under your protection," Derek snarled.

"You can aid in finding her or stay," Talbot said. "Either way, I am going."

Derek stared for a long moment, then gave a curt nod.

Minutes later, Talbot stood with Cullen, Seward, and Derek beside the secret passageway's door.

Cullen inspected the floor. "Two men," he said. "Though only one ascended the stairs."

They went outside. A warrior waited with horses for Cullen and Derek.

Cullen took only a moment to study the tracks. "Four horses. They rode north."

"Is Davey's home north?" Talbot asked.

"Nay," Seward said. "But what do ye wager the tracks turn east toward his home?"

Two riders. His brother and the traitor who let him in. Guilt rolled over Talbot. He sat in the camp on the other side of the castle while someone entered and kidnapped Rhoslyn and Lady Taresa.

"I should have blocked the passageway before I left," he muttered.

"Why did ye no'?" Seward demanded.

Talbot vaulted into the saddle. "Because I am a fool."

TO THEIR SURPRISE, the tracks turned west. When they reached Colliston Gorge, Talbot realized why the riders had gone that way. The tracks were lost amongst the rocky terrain and even Cullen couldn't be certain which way they'd gone.

"East," Seward said. "I feel it in my gut."

Talbot felt the same. His instincts had served him well in the past, but he couldn't afford to be wrong. "Cullen, you will wait here for the men Ross is bringing. Send him east with half on my trail, and you lead the other half. Study the tracks, follow the freshest trail you can find."

Cullen nodded, and Talbot headed east with Seward and Derek.

Seward had told Talbot that Davey's keep was well fortified and would withstand a siege long enough for Rhoslyn to birth their child. Once cornered, though, Dayton would be more dangerous than he already was. They had to catch them before they reached Davey's home. Talbot kept his gaze on the ground and prayed they picked up the trail again.

They found tracks an hour later. Another hour passed before Talbot glimpsed a red silk half-hidden by calf-high grass. Sir Derek cursed and shot ahead. Talbot caught up with him and, together, they reached the spot at the base of a hill where Lady Taresa lay.

Talbot dropped to one knee beside her, Derek opposite, as Seward reined up beside them and dismounted. Derek slid an arm beneath her back and gently lifted her upright. That's when Talbot saw the blood that coated the grass beneath her.

Her eyes fluttered open.

"Where are you hurt, my lady?" Derek said.

A gentle smile touched her mouth. "I knew you would come," she whispered, her soft accent marred by a raspy breath. Her eyes shifted to Talbot. "And you, my grandson." She lifted a hand and he took it. "Find your wife and my great grandchild."

"I will." Talbot's heart thundered. "Are they well?"

She gave a tiny nod. "He has not harmed them."

"He?" Talbot repeated. "My brother?"

"He is one. The other is Bret Carr."

"I know him," Seward said.

"He came to Rhoslyn's room." Lady Taresa swallowed. "You would have been proud. Your wife is brave."

Talbot's blood chilled at the thought of how Rhoslyn's *bravery* must have put herself and their child in danger.

"They ride fast," she said. "It is not good for Rhoslyn." Taresa released a shuddered breath.

"I will take you back to Castle Glenbarr," Derek said.

Her eyes shifted to him. "No. I will not be returning."

"My lady," he began.

"Derek." He went silent and she returned her attention to Talbot. "I am so happy to have found you."

"And I you," Talbot said. "But save your strength. Sir Derek will take you back to Castle Glenbarr. I will find Rhoslyn. Do not fear."

"There is a small village twenty minutes north," Seward said. "They have a healer."

Lady Taresa shook her head. "They are not far ahead. Find them,

Talbot." She looked at the knight. "Derek." The word came out so weak Talbot thought it had to be her last.

"My lady," Derek replied.

She motioned with her hand for him to come closer. He bent his head and she pulled him close so that his ear touched her mouth. Talbot couldn't hear what she said, but Derek's "Nay, my lady," told him the knight was hearing the truth he couldn't accept. Taresa released him and he lifted his head and looked down at her.

"There is a healer twenty minutes away. You are strong. I will take you there."

She grasped his arm. "Swear."

"*Taresa.*"

Talbot heard the raw plea in Derek's voice and exchanged a glance with Seward, who gave a tiny shake of his head.

"Derek." The strength in her voice startled Talbot and for an instant he thought she might survive her wound. Then she coughed a wet cough he knew went soul deep.

"Swear," she insisted, then added in a gentler tone, "my love."

Derek bowed his head. "I swear."

Relief washed over her features and she turned her face toward Talbot. "Tell Rhoslyn I am sorry I could not see my great grandchild born."

Talbot considered telling her all would be well, she would be there, but he saw the light dimming in her eyes and the plea that her request be honored. She did not want her family to forget her.

"She will understand, Grandmother."

Her mouth parted in surprise, then relaxed into a weak smile. "Remember, you are my grandson. Our family does not accept defeat."

She closed her eyes and released her final breath.

Chapter Twenty-Four

D EREK SURPRISED TALBOT when he gently laid Taresa back on the ground, then rose and stepped into his saddle. He kicked his horse's ribs and said not a word when Talbot and Seward caught up with him. What was there to say? Derek was right. Taresa was under Talbot's protection. She'd been in his home, where she should have been safe.

They rode twenty minutes in silence when a curl of smoke came into view, rising from the wooded hills ahead.

"Whose land is this?" Talbot asked. They had left Glenbarr's property half an hour ago and now rode through unfamiliar territory.

"The far eastern edge of my land," Seward replied. "The cottage belongs to David Morrison. He tends cattle for me. It is another four-hour ride to Davey's. Mayhap your brother stopped to rest."

"If he did, he will have killed your man. Does Morrison have a family?"

"His wife, Diana."

Guilt washed over Talbot when he realized he hoped Dayton had stopped there.

They crested the next hill and Talbot glimpsed a cottage amongst the trees. Three horses stood before it, heads hung low, reins tied to a nearby tree.

A low growl emanated from Sir Derek's chest and he leaned low in the saddle in readiness to ride hard.

"Hold," Talbot commanded.

The knight's head snapped in his direction.

"They have not seen us," Talbot said. "When they do, Dayton will threaten Morrison and his wife. We have the element of surprise." Talbot recognized the cold fury in Derek's eyes and said, "I will slay you where you sit, Sir Derek."

Defiance flashed in the man's eyes, but he said, "As you say, laird."

They left the horses out of sight below the crest of the hill, topped the ridge, and crept downhill, keeping to the trees. At the side of the cottage,

Talbot motioned for Seward and Derek to stay, then he inched around to the front window and peered through the window frame. Inside, a woman pulled a kettle off the fire. She appeared at ease. Had Dayton presented himself as a friend? Rhoslyn might not sound the alarm for fear of causing harm to the man and woman. A man came into view at the hearth and Talbot recognized Carr.

Where was Rhoslyn? Where was his brother?

He returned to Seward and Derek.

"They are inside. I did not see Rhoslyn or Dayton."

Seward glanced past him and Talbot saw in his eyes the same impulse to storm the cottage.

"If we wait until they leave," Seward said, "We may avoid harm to the women."

Talbot nodded. "Is there another window in the cottage?"

"The other side. Where the bed is."

"Stay here."

Talbot crept around the cottage to the other side. A fur covered the window, but the shutters stood open. He reached in and slid a finger between the curtain and frame. The hairs on the back of his neck stand on end an instant before the cold steel of a sword point pricked his neck.

"You should have gone with Sir Roland."

Dayton.

His brother's voice carried not a hint of emotion, which meant Dayton would kill him without thought, without remorse.

Talbot spun. The sword point drew a line from the back of his neck to his jaw. He ducked. Dayton brought his sword down in a wide arc. Talbot yanked his sword from its scabbard and swung upward. Steel clanged against steel an instant before Dayton's blade would have cleaved his skull.

Dayton swung and lunged, forcing Talbot back. His shoulder crashed into the cottage wall, but he jabbed. Dayton leapt back. Talbot pressed him into retreat. Dayton parried.

"The child is mine," Dayton said.

Talbot feinted left, then swung right and pierced the skin between arm band and chain mail. Dayton cursed. A man appeared around the side of the cottage, sword in hand. *Carr.*

Talbot slid right to keep the man away from his back.

"Get him, fool," Dayton shouted.

"You cannot face me on your own, craven," Talbot snarled at Dayton.

Carr charged Talbot's left side.

Boot falls pounded and, an instant later, Seward and Derek burst into view. Both men held swords at ready. Carr whirled to face them. Talbot blocked a left, then right parry from his brother.

"This one is mine," Derek shouted. The knight brought a hard blow down on Carr, who blocked, but fell back a pace.

Talbot sidled forward, jabbed low, then parried left. Dayton dodged the blow, but Talbot saw the opening and rammed his sword tip into Dayton's collarbone. Dayton leapt back, narrowly dodging the sword, and Talbot swung a sideways arc that sliced the top of Dayton's sword arm.

Dayton howled, a wounded animal's cry, then brought his sword down in a bone-jarring blow that cut a gash in the sleeve of Talbot's chain mail. From the corner of his eye, Talbot glimpsed Rhoslyn and the woman standing beyond the fighting. Seward hurried to the women.

Dayton swung his sword low. Talbot deflected the blow as Dayton spun and brought his sword around to Talbot's left. He dodged the weapon and skittered back several paces. Talbot thrust, ripping a hole in Dayton's leg below his chain mail. Blood spurted, but Dayton pressed his attack. Talbot blocked a heavy blow and dodged behind a tree as Dayton's sword narrowly missed his midsection and split a gash in the wood.

A man's shriek broke through the clash of steel, but Talbot's focus didn't waiver. Dayton rushed him, swinging left, then right, then left and right. Talbot gave one mighty push and shoved back with the next blow. Dayton stumbled to the side, but regained his feet, then brought a heavy blow down across Talbot's left arm. His chain mail protected his arm, but the shock of the blow reverberated through his arm. He gritted his teeth against the pain as Dayton landed another hard blow. Steel slid against steel until the hilts collided and they strained nose-to-nose.

"You are not a St. Claire," Dayton said. He breathed heavily, but his voice still held no emotion.

Talbot shoved him away, then allowed his sword to falter, as if the blow Dayton had landed on his arm had weakened him. Dayton lunged, and Talbot thrust his sword into the opening at his brother's jugular. Dayton's head snapped back, then his eyes riveted onto Talbot's. Talbot yanked his sword from his brother's neck and he fell face down onto the ground at this feet.

Talbot leaned a palm against a tree, breath coming in heavy gasps. Dayton's blood pooled around him like thick syrup. Talbot felt nothing. Not even relief.

What would his father say?

RHOSLYN SHOOK LIKE a leaf, but managed to dig her heels in and stop her grandfather from forcing her back into the cottage.

"Help St. Claire," she ordered.

His brother was driving him back toward the trees.

"Your husband can handle himself," her grandfather said. "After all, he is—was—Edward's favorite knight."

Rhoslyn looked at him in horror. "You wager with his life? He is the father of your grandchild."

"If I interfere he will only kill me in punishment."

"She is right, Kinsley," Diana said. "Ye must help him."

Rhoslyn's heart leapt into her throat when Dayton's sword swung perilously close to St. Claire's face. "Sweet God, Grandfather, I beg you." She grasped his arm and yanked.

"Have faith in your husband, Rhoslyn."

Tears welled up in her eyes. "He might die. At least help Sir Derek."

Her grandfather snorted. "Carr is no match for him. See," he said when Sir Derek's sword slashed through the flesh on the man's wrist.

A wave of pain washed over Rhoslyn and she jerked.

Her grandfather looked sharply at her. "What is it?"

She shook her head.

"Granddaughter," he said in a stern voice.

Steel clashed in a succession of blows as St. Claire and Dayton disappeared behind a tree. St. Claire stepped into view, retreating in quick steps as his brother drove him backwards with quick parries of his sword.

"Rhoslyn."

She jerked at the harsh note in her grandfather's voice.

"Is it the babe?" he demanded.

"She was in labor when they arrived," Diana said.

Brent Carr cried out and Rhoslyn's gaze snapped onto him in time to see him fall to his knees, blood gushing from his leg.

He threw his sword down. "I yield."

"Yield?" Sir Derek snarled.

He reached down and yanked something from the man's left wrist. Sunlight glinted off red jewels. The ruby bracelet Lady Taresa had worn. Sir Derek rammed his fist into the man's face. Rhoslyn started. Brett dropped to the ground and Sir Derek drove his sword through his neck.

Bile rose in Rhoslyn's throat as another wave of pain washed over her.

TALBOT WALKED FROM the trees and he took in Carr lying on the ground face up, blood trailing from the wound in his throat. Sir Derek had killed him in almost the same fashion Talbot had Dayton. Derek hadn't severed Carr's head as Talbot had Dayton's, however.

He caught sight of Rhoslyn leaning against Seward with the woman, Diana, clutching her arm. Rhoslyn's gaze met his and her mouth parted in surprise. There was something else in her eyes. Was it relief? He crossed to the group.

When he reached them, he saw Rhoslyn's tears. Before he could assure her he was well, she gave a deep groan and stumbled. Talbot lunged and caught her close to him.

"All is well, my lady," he started to assure her. Then she tensed in his arms. He looked sharply at Seward. "What is wrong?"

"The babe is coming," the woman said. "Quickly, bring her inside." She hurried around the cottage.

"The babe is coming?" Talbot repeated.

He lifted her into his arms and carried her inside. Diana stood beside a bed separated from the rest of the room by a thin curtain.

He crossed to the bed and gently laid Rhoslyn on the mattress. "Why is the baby coming now? It is too soon. She is not yet eight months pregnant." Unless he counted the two weeks between when bedded her and Dayton's rape.

Diana pulled the blanket up over Rhoslyn's belly. "Sometimes that is long enough."

"How long has she been in labor?"

"An hour, maybe longer," she replied. "She was laboring when they arrived. That is why they stopped."

Talbot whirled to face Seward. "Why did you allow her to stay outside?"

The old man snorted. "Do ye know my granddaughter at all?"

"She might have—" Talbot broke off, suddenly at a loss.

Seward's brow rose. "Might have what?" Talbot didn't reply and he added, "Birthed the babe then and there while still ordering everyone about?"

"Sweet Jesu, St. Claire," Rhoslyn said in a strained voice, "cease bullying my grandfather."

Sir Derek appeared in the cottage doorway. "Keep a watch, Sir Derek," Talbot ordered. "And bring our horses around. I do not want any unwanted visitors." The knight nodded and Talbot sat on the mattress beside Rhoslyn. He took her hand and clasped it tight. "Are you well, my lady?"

She lifted her free hand and touched his jaw where Dayton's sword had cut him. "You are bleeding."

"'Tis a scratch," he said.

Diana appeared at the bed, a basin of water in hand and clean clothes slung over her shoulder. "Go on now," she ordered.

"Have you birthed a child?" he asked.

"Aye," she said. "Twice before."

"Have you a midwife?" he asked. "We can fetch her."

"She would only arrive to see your wife suckling the babe at her breast."

"Are you sure—"

"Laird," she cut in, "unless ye plan to bring this baby into the world, let me be. Now, shoo."

Rhoslyn tensed again and gave a deep grunt.

"I will stay," he said.

The woman's mouth fell open in shock. "A man doesna' stay in the birthing room."

"Midwives always have help," he said. "You may have need of me."

She glanced at Rhoslyn, indecision in her eyes, when Rhoslyn began panting heavily. Diana's attention came back onto him. "As ye say. I may have need of you. But you will do as I say, and willna' move from her side unless I tell you otherwise—no matter what. Do you understand?"

"Aye."

Talbot soothed Rhoslyn, fetched more water and clean cloths as Diana ordered. When Sir Derek came to report that a company of men had arrived, led by Ross, Talbot had to admit relief. He had expected his child to be born surrounded by the protective walls and fighting might of Castle Glenbarr. Here, only the flammable walls of the cottage separated them from the dangers of the world. He ordered Sir Derek to secure the bodies and have the men surround the cottage to keep watch until they left for Castle Glenbarr.

The day wore on toward evening as Rhoslyn labored. When the sun set, Talbot heard the door creak open beyond the closed curtain.

"Diana," the man called. "Kinsley, what are ye doing here?"

Seward quietly explained to Morrison what had happened.

MORNING CAME AND Talbot feared Diana would collapse from exhaustion. He and her husband had forced her to lie down, but she had slept little more than an hour before she returned to Rhoslyn's side.

"Are you sure we do not need the midwife?" Talbot asked.

"Why would we need a midwife?" Rhoslyn demanded.

He looked at her. "Rest, my lady." The labor pains were coming too quickly and he could see the fatigue in the droop of her eyelids. He wanted to ask Diana what was wrong, why the baby was taking so long to come, but feared worrying Rhoslyn.

"Mayhap ye should get some rest, laird," Diana told him.

He shook his head. "I will stay."

"Ye look tired," she insisted.

"Not as tired as my wife. Should not the babe have come by now?"

"Ah, so that is it," she said. "Ye fear something is wrong because the baby hasna' rushed into the world to meet you."

Frustration wore jagged on his nerves. "You need not worry, my lady wife."

"Lady wife, is it?" Rhoslyn croaked a laugh.

Diana wrung out a cloth with cool water and mopped her brow.

"Your lady wife is well enough," Rhoslyn said. "St. Claire, ye know nothing about birthing babies. He will come when he is ready. Some come quickly." She stiffened and groaned with another contraction. When the pain passed, she said, "Some take their time."

This child took another four hours. But at last Rhoslyn could no longer resist the urge to push, and Diana told her it was time.

What seemed eons later, Diana cried, "I see the head."

Talbot jerked his gaze in her direction and froze at sight of his son's dark hair peeking out from the sheets that covered Rhoslyn's midsection and thighs.

"Push again, my lady," Diana ordered.

Rhoslyn's jaw tightened.

"Harder," Diana cried.

Rhoslyn groaned with effort. In the next instant, the baby came free with a wail that brought a tightening in Talbot's chest as Rhoslyn collapsed back onto the pillows.

"Well, well," Diana said. "It seems ye have a daughter, laird."

Talbot broke from the spell. "What?"

Diana held up the baby. "A daughter."

A daughter.

Diana cleaned the baby, then wrapped her in a small blanket and lay her in Rhoslyn's arm. "Ye must feed her."

Talbot sat on the bed beside Rhoslyn. He watched transfixed as Rhoslyn guided their daughter's mouth to her nipple. The babe fumbled for an instant, then latched on as if starving.

Diana laughed. "There is a lass who knows what she wants."

A few minutes later, Talbot became aware of Diana cleaning up the bedding and cloths. He lifted Rhoslyn and the babe and held them while she spread clean bedding. His chest tightened when Rhoslyn leaned into him and fell asleep with the baby at her breast.

A daughter. He had expected a son. It only made sense they would have daughters, but he had been so sure their first child would be a son. What did a man do with a daughter? Would she always be so...fragile?

Diana finished and he gently laid Rhoslyn and their daughter back on the mattress.

Rhoslyn woke and looked at him. "I know ye wanted a son, St. Claire."

He tore his gaze from the small bundle and sat on the mattress beside her. Had she been reading his mind? Nay, he never thought he didn't want a daughter. What in God's name did a man do with a daughter?

He shook his head. "I wanted our child. Nothing more."

"But ye talked of nothing but a son."

"As did you," he said.

Rhoslyn shifted and held the baby out toward him. He didn't move.

"Ye should hold your daughter," she said.

Suddenly, his heart quaked and it seemed every fiber of his being shook. He allowed Rhoslyn to cradle the baby against him, the small head resting in the crook of his arm. He didn't move.

The women laughed.

"She willna' break," Diana said.

"She is so tiny." He smoothed a tiny lock of hair away from her face. "She has my father's dark hair." He looked at Rhoslyn and was startled to see tears in her eyes. "What is amiss?" He sat on the bed beside her, then stood again and looked around for Diana.

Diana rolled her eyes. "Sit beside your wife." She gave him a gentle shove and he sat down.

"What is wrong, my lady?" he asked Rhoslyn. "Are you ill?"

She shook her head, her eyes on the baby. "She doesna' have your fair hair."

Then he understood. Talbot leaned forward and brushed a kiss on Rhoslyn's sweat soaked forehead, then whispered, "I see a hint of your red hair. She is beautiful." He placed the baby in Rhoslyn's arms and was reminded of Lady Taresa's words. *"Have you ever been so in love, that you would have thrown all caution to the wind for her?"*

And he understood.

"If ye dinna' let me see my grandchild, I will kill you, St. Claire," Seward called from the other side of the curtain.

Diana pulled the curtain back and Seward entered. Sir Derek stood beyond, near the hearth, staring into the fire as if none of them existed. Something he held glistened in the firelight and Talbot realized it was a length of gold and ruby jewelry.

Seward stopped beside Talbot. "A daughter?" he said.

Talbot shifted his gaze to the baron. "Aye."

"Give her to me," Seward said. "She needs to know her grandfather."

RHOSLYN AWOKE TO a squalling baby.

"She is hungry again." Diana laid the baby at Rhoslyn's breast.

Rhoslyn tugged down the top of her shirt and the baby latched onto the exposed nipple.

"She is a lusty one," Diana said. "Have ye named her yet?"

Rhoslyn looked at St. Claire. He stood at the side of the bed, staring down at the baby with the same dazed look he'd had since she placed the baby in his arms. It seemed that becoming a father had reduced the mighty warrior to mush.

Rhoslyn unexpectedly remembered her intention to ask St. Claire about Abbess Beatrice. What would have happened had the abbess not told him of Rhoslyn's flight from the convent? She would be in Longford Castle married to Jacobus and waiting for their child to be born. No, St. Claire said he would have razed the castle, then brought her home.

She smiled. "What say you, St. Claire? Have we a name?"

He shook his head.

"Mayhap we should name her after your mother."

"Aye," he said, but she knew he wasn't really listening.

"Peigi," she urged.

His eyes shifted to her face and understanding glimmered. "I did not know her. Perhaps Taresa? Taresa Peigi?"

A lump formed in her throat. Beyond the alcove, Sir Derek stood near the table at the hearth. She had seen him come and go earlier, seen the sorrow that haunted his dark eyes. She understood that sadness. When

Lady Taresa had fallen after Brett Carr's sword pierced her midsection, Rhoslyn had raced to her side and dropped to her knees beside her.

"*Be safe, Rhoslyn,*" she had said. "*Love him. He is a good man.*" Rhoslyn thought those were to be her last words, but she added in a whisper. "*Tell him I love him. Tell them both.*"

Rhoslyn shifted her gaze to St. Claire. They both had to know Lady Taresa was gone, for she was not with Rhoslyn. But they didn't know what had happened.

"I did no' tell you. Taresa—" Sir Derek took a step toward the alcove. Tears choked her throat.

St. Claire sat on the bed beside her and covered her hand with his. The baby's mouth fell from her breast. She had fallen asleep. Rhoslyn pulled her shirt up over her breast and nestled the baby in her arm, then looked at him.

"She loved ye." Rhoslyn looked at Sir Derek and said in a louder voice, "She loved you both."

"What happened?" St. Claire prodded.

"Come closer, Sir Derek," Rhoslyn urged. He hesitated, then came as close at the invisible line created by the curtain. "Taresa gave her life for us. For all of us." It took a moment for Rhoslyn to be sure she could speak. Then she said, "Lady Taresa could see the hard pace Dayton set was taking its toll on me. It was clear your brother had no intention of stopping for anything short of death. Lady Taresa rode with Brett Carr. The bastard," Rhoslyn added under her breath.

"We approached a small forest and she insisted she had to relieve herself. At first, Dayton refused to stop, but she told them she had no qualms about soiling herself and Brett in the bargain. We stopped and they allowed me to dismount. Under the guise or her helping me—which was no lie—we went behind a bush where she showed me a dirk hidden in her boot."

"She had a blade?" St. Claire said. "Why did she not use it before you left the castle?"

"Because Brett threatened her with a knife to my throat."

Fury flared in St. Claire's eyes. "I would kill Dayton twice, if I could."

"And I would watch." *But that wouldn't bring Taresa back.*

"Ye will have to reattach his head first," her grandfather said.

Rhoslyn stared at her husband. "Ye severed his head?"

"I promised you his head."

"And you keep your promises. I assume ye plan to send the head to Edward—once I have had a look?"

"Aye."

"I wish I could deliver is myself," she said, then quickly added when St. Claire's eyes darkened, "Never mind. So, Lady Taresa told me to cry out as if I was in labor. I didna' want to do it. But she insisted. She had a way of getting her way."

Sir Derek smiled the first smile Rhoslyn had seen from him.

"I did as she commanded," Rhoslyn went on, "and the two men hurried over to us. Lady Taresa stepped back and drove her blade down onto Brett when he faced me. I wish it had been Dayton instead, but Brett was closer. He turned in the last instant and deflected the blow. Your brother was furious. He was nothing like the first time he kidnapped me."

"Dayton can be unstable," St. Claire said. "Even as a boy he would lose his temper for something small, while maintaining an unnatural detachment."

"His fury died as quickly as it came," she said. "He was almost emotionless when he told Brett to kill Lady Taresa."

Sir Derek cursed.

"Forgive me," Rhoslyn quickly put in. "I…" She slumped against the pillows. "There is no easy way to tell this story."

"Would you rather leave?" St. Claire asked Sir Derek.

He straightened. "Nay. I would hear it all."

St. Claire gave her a nod.

"There is little else to tell. Brett obeyed." Rhoslyn grasped his arm. "St. Claire, we must find her. She must have a Christian burial. I remember where they left her."

"I have already commanded that to be done." Sir Derek looked at St. Claire. "I assumed you would want her cared for, laird."

"Aye. I am grateful," St. Claire replied.

"You know where she is?" Rhoslyn asked.

"We found her."

"Sweet Jesu," Rhoslyn whispered.

"She was alive," St. Claire said. "We were with her until the end."

Gratitude rushed through Rhoslyn. God hadn't completely deserted her. "Then she told you."

"Told us what?"

"That she loved you." Rhoslyn looked from St. Claire to Sir Derek. "And you, Sir Derek. She wanted you to know that she loved you."

"She said the words?"

Rhoslyn's heart wrenched at the hoarse plea she heard in his voice. "Aye, she said the words."

His gaze shadowed, as if far away. "She never said the words."

"Her last thought was of you."

His eyes focused on her. He nodded. "Just as her last words to me were of you and the babe." He took three steps to the bed, then came down on one knee. "She commanded me to take this from her killer and give this to her great grandchild." He held out the gold and ruby bracelet Lady Taresa had been wearing.

Rhoslyn gave a small gasp.

He laid the bracelet on the blanket beside the baby. "Her last command was that I should ensure the safety of her great-great grandchild. If you will accept a humble knight's service, I will protect the new Lady Taresa with my life."

"Just as your Lady Taresa commanded," Rhoslyn murmured. She looked at St. Claire.

"This was what she whispered to you in those last moments?" he asked.

"Aye," Sir Derek replied.

St. Claire gave her a small nod, and she said to Sir Derek, "I appoint you our daughter's protector. She will be your Lady Taresa."

Startlement shone in his eyes. Then gratitude. He bowed his head once more. "So long as I breathe, you need never worry for her safety."

To Rhoslyn's surprise, St. Claire picked up the baby and rose. She voiced a small cry, then quieted in her father's arms.

"Rise, Sir Derek, and meet Lady Taresa Peigi St. Claire," he said.

The knight rose and gave a stiff bow to the baby. Both men stared down at her, and Rhoslyn was reminded of St. Claire's words when he'd first brought her to Castle Glenbarr. *"What man knows peace when he takes a wife?"* Yet he looked perfectly at peace now. Was this what he had sought?

He looked up from the baby and met her gaze. Then he smiled a dazzling smile that said all was right with the world. He looked back down at their daughter and Rhoslyn realized her daughter needed a brother to complete the trio.

WHEN THE DOOR opened behind her, Rhoslyn looked up from the rolls she was reading. St. Claire entered. He crossed to the table where she worked and stopped beside the cradle that sat beside Rhoslyn's bench. At six months old, Lady Taresa Peigi St. Claire had finally begun sleeping through the night.

"It has begun to rain," he at last said.

"Does that mean John Comyn will be staying?" she asked.

"Aye. We were the last he was to visit."

Rhoslyn lifted the quill from the parchment. "Are you going to tell me what he said?"

"Edward appointed John Balliol as king."

She closed her eyes. God help them.

"I am commanded to appear before him."

Rhoslyn looked sharply at him. "Before John or Edward?"

He stared down at her and her heart began to pound wildly. What would Edward do to St. Claire if he was forced to return to England?

"You say there is no difference between the two men," he said.

"You cannot return to England," she said.

"You told me I must obey my Scottish king."

Sweet God. And he would obey.

Would their new king—or his liege lord—force St. Claire from their home? Rhoslyn placed a palm over her belly. Would he be present for the birth of their son?

THE END

FROM THE AUTHOR

I hope you enjoyed Talbot and Rhoslyn's story as much as I enjoyed writing it. I suspect the future holds more for these two and their clan. I have included a sample of My Highland Love, the first book in the Highland Lords series.

Live long and prosper.
Tarah

MY HIGHLAND LOVE

How does a woman tell her betrothed she murdered her first husband?

Elise Kingston is a wanted woman. Nothing, not even Highlander Marcus MacGregor, will stop her from returning home to ensure that the man responsible for her daughter's death hangs.

Until she must choose between his life and her revenge.

Chapter One

America
Winter 1825

"*THE LORD GIVETH and the Lord taketh away.*" Or so her eulogy would begin.

The heavy gold wedding band clinked loudly in the silence as he grasped the crystal tumbler sitting on the desk before him. He raised the glass in salutation and whispered into the darkness, "To the dead, may they rot in their watery graves." He finished the whiskey in one swallow.

And what of that which had been hers? He smiled. The law would see that her wealth remained where it should—with him. A finality settled about the room.

Soon, life would begin.

Solway Firth, Scottish-English border

ELISE JUMPED AT the sound of approaching footsteps and sloshed tea from the cup at her lips. The ship's stateroom door opened and her grip tightened around the delicate cup handle. Her husband ducked to miss the top of the doorway as he entered. He stopped, his gaze fixing on the medical journal that lay open on the secretary beside her. A corner of his mouth curved upward with a derisive twist and his eyes met hers.

With deliberate disinterest, Elise slipped the paper she'd been making notes on between the pages of the journal and took the forestalled sip of afternoon tea. She grimaced. The tea had grown cold in the two hours it had sat untouched. She placed the cup on the saucer, then turned a page in the book. As Robert clicked the door shut behind him, the ship's stern lifted with another wave. She gripped the desk when the stern dropped into the swell's trough. Thunder, the first on the month-long voyage, rumbled. She released the desk. This storm had grown into more than a mere squall.

Robert stepped to her side. "What are you doing?"

"Nothi—" He snatched the paper from the book. "Robert!" She would have leapt to her feet, but her legs were shakier than her hands.

He scanned the paper, then looked at her. "You refuse to let the matter lie."

"You don't care that the doctors couldn't identify what killed your daughter?"

"She is dead. What difference can it possibly make?"

Her pulse jumped. *None for you. Because you murdered her.*

He tossed the paper aside. "This has gone far enough."

Elise lifted her gaze to his face. She once thought those blue eyes so sensual. "I couldn't agree more."

"Indeed?"

The ship heaved.

"I will give you a divorce," she said.

"Divorce?" A hard gleam entered his eyes. "I mean to be a widower."

She caught sight of the bulge in his waistband. Her pulse quickened. Why hadn't she noticed the pistol when he entered?

Elise shook her head. "You can't possibly hope to succeed. Steven will—"

"Your illustrious brother is in the bowels of the ship, overseeing the handling of the two crewmen accused of theft."

Her blood chilled. When her father was alive, he made sure the men employed by Landen Shipping were of good reputation. Much had changed since his death.

"One of the men is wanted for murder," Robert said.

"Murder?" she blurted. "Why would a stranger murder me?"

Robert lifted a lock of her dark hair. "Not a stranger. A spurned lover." He dropped the hair, then gripped the arms of her chair and leaned forward. "Once the board members of Landen Shipping identify your body as Elisabeth Kingston, the stipulation in your father's will shall be satisfied and your stock is mine."

The roar of blood pounded through her ears. If he killed her now, he would never pay for murdering their daughter. And she intended that he pay.

Elise lunged for the letter opener lying in one of the secretary compartments. The ship pitched as her fingers clamped onto the makeshift weapon. As Robert yanked her to her feet, she swung the letter opener. Bone-deep pain raced up her arm when the hard mass of his forearm blocked her blow. The letter opener clattered to the wooden floor.

She glimpsed his rage-contorted features before he whipped her around and crushed her to his chest, pinning her arms to her sides with one powerful arm. He dragged her two paces and snatched up the woolen scarf lying on the bed. In one swift movement, he wound it around her neck.

Robert released her waist, grabbed the scarf's dangling end, and yanked it tight around her neck. Elise clawed at the scarf. Her nails dug into the soft skin of her neck. Her legs buckled and he jerked her against him. His knees jabbed into her back and jolts of pain shot up both sides of her spine. She gulped for air.

His breath was thick in her ear as he whispered, "Did you really think we would let you control fifty-one percent of Landen Shipping?" He gave a vicious yank on the scarf.

No! her mind screamed in tandem with another thunder roll. Too late, she understood the lengths to which he would go to gain control of her inheritance.

The scarf tightened. Her sight dimmed. Cold. She was so cold.

Amelia, my daughter, I come to you—the scarf went slack. Elise dropped to her knees, wheezing in convulsive gasps of air. Despite the racking coughs which shook her, she forced her head up. A blurry form stood in the doorway. *Steven.*

The scarf dropped to her shoulders and she yanked it from her neck. Robert stepped in front of her and reached into his coat. *The pistol.* He had murdered her daughter—he would not take Steven from her. Elise lunged forward and bit into his calf with the ferocity of a lioness.

Robert roared. The ship bucked. Locked like beast and prey, they tumbled forward and slammed against the desk chair. The chair broke with the force of their weight. The secretary lamp crashed to the floor. Whale oil spilled across the wooden floor; a river of fire raced atop the thin layer toward the bed.

Steven yanked her up and shoved her toward the door. Robert scrambled to his feet as Steven whirled and rammed his fist into Robert's jaw. Her husband fell against the doorjamb, nearly colliding with her. Elise jumped back with a cry. Robert charged Steven and caught him around the shoulders, driving him back onto the bed.

The ship bucked. Elise staggered across the cabin, hit her hip against the secretary, and fell. The medical journal thudded to the floor between her and the thick ribbon of fire. Her heart skipped a beat when Robert slammed his fist into Steven's jaw.

She reached for the open book and glimpsed the picture of the belladonna, the deadly nightshade plant. Fury swept through her anew. She snatched up the book, searing the edge of her palm on the fire as she pushed to her feet. Elise leapt forward, book held high, and swung at Robert with all her strength. *May* this *belladonna kill you as your powdered belladonna killed our daughter.* The crack of book against skull penetrated the ringing in her ears. Robert fell limp atop Steven.

The discarded scarf suddenly blazed. Elise whirled. Smoke choked her as fire burned the bed coverings only inches from Robert's hand. Steven grabbed her wrist and dragged her toward the door. He scooped up the pistol as they crossed the threshold and they stumbled down the corridor to the ladder leading up to the deck.

"Go!" he yelled, and lifted her onto the first tread.

Elise frantically pulled herself up the steep ladder to the door and shoved it upward. Rain pelted her like tiny needles. She ducked her head down as she scrambled onto the deck. An instant later, Steven joined her. He whirled toward the poop deck where Captain Morrison and his first mate yelled at the crewmen who clung to the masts while furiously pulling up the remaining sails and lashing them to the spars.

Steven pulled her toward the poop deck's ladder. "Stay here!" he yelled above the howling wind, and forced her fingers around the side of the ladder.

The ship heaved to starboard as he hurried up the ladder and Elise hugged the riser. A wave broke over the railing and slammed her against the wood. She sputtered, tasting the tang of salt as she gasped for air.

A garbled shout from the captain brought her attention upward. He stared at two men scuttling down the mizzen mast. They landed, leapt over the railing onto the main deck and disappeared through the door leading to the deck below. They had gone to extinguish the fire. If they didn't succeed, the ship would go down.

Elise squinted through the rain at Steven. He leaned in close to the captain. The lamp, burning in the binnacle, illuminated the guarded glance the captain sent her way. A shock jolted her. Robert had lied to the captain about her—perhaps had even implicated Steven in her so-called insanity. The captain's expression darkened. He faced his first mate.

The ship's bow plunged headlong into a wave with a force that threw Elise to the deck and sent her sliding across the slippery surface. Steven shouted her name as she slammed into the ship's gunwale. Pain shot through her shoulder. He rushed down the ladder, the captain on his heels. Another wave hammered the ship. Steven staggered to her side and pulled her to her feet. The ship lurched. Elise clutched at her brother as they fell to the deck. Pain radiated through her arm and up her shoulder. The door to below deck swung open. Elise froze.

Robert.

He pointed a pistol at her. Her heart leapt into her throat. Steven sprang to his feet in front of her.

"No!" she screamed.

She spotted the pistol lying inches away and realized it had fallen from Steven's waistband. She snatched up the weapon, rolled to face Robert, and fired. The report of the pistol sounded in unison with another shot.

A wave cleared the railing. Steven disappeared in the wash of seawater. Elise grasped the cold wood railing and pulled herself to her feet. She blinked stinging saltwater from her eyes and took a startled step backwards at seeing her husband laying across the threshold. Steven lay several feet to her right. She drew a sharp breath. A dark patch stained his vest below his heart. *Dear God, where had the bullet lodged?*

She started toward Steven. The ship listed hard to port. She fought the backward momentum and managed two steps before another wave crested. The deck lurched and she was airborne. She braced for impact against the deck. Howling wind matched her scream as she flew past the railing and plummeted into darkness—then collided with rock-hard water.

Cold clamped onto her. Rain beat into the sea with quick, heavy blows of a thousand tiny hammers. She kicked. Thick, icy ribbons of water propelled her upward. She blinked. Murky shapes glided past. This was Amelia's grave. Elise surfaced, her first gasp taking in rainwater. She coughed and flailed. A heavy sheet of water towered, then slapped her against the ocean's surface. The wave leveled and she shook hair from her eyes. Thirty feet away, the *Amelia* bounced on the waves like a toy. Her brother had named the ship. But Amelia was gone. Steven, only twenty-two, was also gone.

A figure appeared at the ship's railing. The lamp high atop the poop deck burned despite the pouring rain. Elise gasped. Could he be— "Steven!" she yelled, kicking hard in an effort to leap above another towering wave. Her skirts tangled her legs, but she kicked harder, waving both arms. The man only hacked at the bow rope of the longboat with a sword. "Steven!" she shouted.

The bow of the longboat dropped, swinging wildly as the man staggered the few steps to the rope holding the stern. A wave crashed over Elise and she surfaced to see the longboat adrift and the figure looking out over the railing. Her heart sank. The light silhouetted the man—and the captain's hat he wore. Tears choked her. It had been the captain and not Steven.

Elise pulled her skirts around her waist and knotted them, then began swimming toward the boat. Another wave grabbed the *Amelia*, tossing her farther away. The captain's hat lifted with the wind and sailed into the sea. She took a quick breath and dove headlong into the wave that threatened to throw her back the way she'd come. She came up, twisting frantically in the water until she located the ship. She swam toward the longboat, her gaze steady on the *Amelia*. Then the lamp dimmed... and winked out.

Chapter Two

~

Scottish Highlands
Spring 1826

ENGLAND LAY FAR behind him, though not far enough. Never far
enough. Marcus breathed deep of the crisp spring air. The scents of
pine and heather filled his nostrils. Highland air. None sweeter existed.
His horse nickered as if in agreement, and Marcus brushed a hand along
the chestnut's shoulder.

"It is good to be home," Erin spoke beside him.

Grunts of agreement went up from the six other men riding in the
company, and Marcus answered, "Aye," despite the regret of leaving his
son in the hands of the Sassenach.

He surveyed the wooded land before him—MacGregor land. Bought
with Ashlund gold, held by MacGregor might, and rich with the blood of
his ancestors.

"If King George has his way," Erin said, "your father will follow the
Duchess of Sutherland's example and lease this land to the English."

Marcus jerked his attention onto the young man. Erin's broad grin
reached from ear to ear, nearly touching the edges of his thick mane of
dark hair. The lad read him too easily.

"These roads are riddled with enough thieves," Marcus said with a
mock scowl. His horse shifted, muscles bunching with the effort of
cresting the hill they ascended. "My father is no more likely to give an
inch to the English than I am to give up the treasure I have tucked away
in these hills."

"What?" Erin turned to his comrades. "I told you he hid Ashlund gold
without telling us." Marcus bit back a laugh when the lad looked at him
and added, "Lord Phillip still complains highwaymen stole his daughter's
dowry while on the way to Edinburgh." He gave Marcus a comical look
that said *you know nothing of that, do you?*

"Lord Allerton broke the engagement after highwaymen stole the dowry," put in another of the men. "Said Lord Phillip meant to cheat him."

"Lord Allerton is likely the thief," Marcus said. "The gold was the better part of the bargain."

"Lord Phillip's daughter is an attractive sort," Erin mused. "Much like bread pudding. Sturdy, with just the right jiggle."

A round of guffaws went up and one aging warrior cuffed Erin across the back of his neck. They gained the hill and Marcus's laughter died at sight of the figure hurrying across the open field below. He gave an abrupt signal for silence. The men obeyed and only the chirping of spring birds filled the air.

"TAVIS," ELISE SNAPPED, finally within hearing range of the boy and his sister, "this time you've gone too far and have endangered your sister by leaving the castle."

His attention remained fixed on the thickening woods at the bottom of the hill and her frustration gave way to concern. They were only minutes from the village—a bare half an hour from the keep and safely on MacGregor land—but the boy had intended to go farther—much farther. He had just turned fourteen, old enough to carry out the resolve to find the men who had murdered his father, and too young to understand the danger.

Bonnie tugged on her cloak and Elise looked down at her. The little girl grinned and pointed to the wildflowers surrounding them. Elise smiled, then shoved back the hood of her cloak. Bonnie squatted to pick the flowers. Elise's heart wrenched. If only their father still lived. He would teach Tavis a lesson. Of course, if Shamus still lived, Tavis wouldn't be hunting for murderers.

Those men were guilty of killing an innocent, yet no effort had been made to bring them to justice. The disquiet that always hovered close to the surface caused a nervous tremor to ripple through her stomach. While Shamus's murderers would likely never go before a judge, if Price found her, his version of justice would be in the form of a noose around her neck for the crime of defending herself against a man who had tried to kill her—twice.

Any doubts about her stepfather's part in Amelia's death had been dispelled a month after arriving at Brahan Seer when she read a recent edition of the London *Sunday Times* brought by relatives for Michael MacGregor. She found no mention of the *Amelia's* sinking. Instead, a ten thousand pound reward for information leading to the whereabouts of her *body* was printed in the announcements section.

Reward? Bounty is what it was.

The advertisement gave the appearance that Price was living up to his obligations as President of Landen Shipping. But she knew he intended she reach Boston dead—and reach Boston she would, for without her body, he would have to wait five years before taking control of her fifty-one percent of Landen Shipping. She intended to slip the noose over his head first.

Elise caught sight of her trembling fingers, and her stomach heaved with the memory of Amelia's body sliding noiselessly from the ship into the ocean. She choked back despair. If she had suspected that Robert had been poisoning her daughter even a few months earlier—

"Flowers!"

Elise jerked at Bonnie's squeal. The girl stood with a handful of flowers extended toward her. Elise brushed her fingers across the white petals of the stitchwort and the lavender butterwort. She was a fool to involve herself with the people here, but when Shamus was murdered she been unable to remain withdrawn.

"Riders," Tavis said.

Elise tensed. "Where?"

"There." Tavis pointed into the trees.

She leaned forward and traced the line of his arm with her gaze. A horse's rump slipped out of sight into the denser forest. Goose bumps raced across her arms.

Elise straightened and yanked Bonnie into her arms "It will be dark soon—" Tavis faced her and she stopped short when his gaze focused on something behind her.

Elise looked over her shoulder. Half a dozen riders emerged from the forest across the meadow. She started. Good Lord, what had possessed her to leave Brahan Seer without a pistol? She was as big a fool as Tavis and without the excuse of youth. She slid Bonnie to the ground as the warriors approached. They halted fifteen feet away. Elise edged Bonnie behind her when one of the men urged his horse closer. Her pulse jumped. Was it possible to become accustomed to the size of these Highland men?

She flushed at the spectacle of his open shirt but couldn't stop her gaze from sliding along the velvety dark hair that trailed downward and tapered off behind a white lawn shirt negligently tucked into his kilt. The large sword strapped to his hip broke the fascination.

How many had perished at the point of that weapon?

The hard muscles of his chest and arms gave evidence—many.

The man directed a clipped sentence in Gaelic to Tavis. The boy started past her, but she caught his arm. The men wore the red and green *plaide* of her benefactors the MacGregors, but were strangers.

"What do you want?" She cursed the curt demand that had bypassed good sense in favor of a willing tongue.

Except for a flicker of surprise across the man's face, he sat unmoving.

Elise winced inwardly, remembering her American accent, but said in a clear voice, "I asked what you want."

Leather groaned when he leaned forward on his saddle. He shifted the reins to the hand resting in casual indolence on his leg and replied in English, "I asked the boy why he is unarmed outside the castle with two females."

Caught off guard by the deep vibrancy of his soft burr, her heart skipped a beat. "We don't need weapons on MacGregor land." She kept her tone unhurried.

"The MacGregor's reach extends as far as the solitude of this glen?" he asked.

"We are only fifteen minutes from the village," she said. "But his reach is well beyond this place."

"He is great, indeed," the warrior said.

"You know him?"

"I do."

She lifted Bonnie. "Then you know he would wreak vengeance on any who dared harm his own."

"Aye," the man answered. "The MacGregor would hunt them down like dogs. Only," he paused, "how would he know who to hunt?"

She gave him a disgusted look. "I tracked these children. You think he cannot track you?"

"A fine point," he agreed.

"Good." She took a step forward. "Now, we will be getting home."

"Aye, you should be getting home." He urged his horse to intercept. Elise set Bonnie down, shoving her in Tavis's direction. "And," the man went on, "we will take you." The warriors closed in around them. "The lad will ride with Erin. Give the little one to Kyle, and you," his eyes came back hard on Elise, "will ride with me."

The heat in his gaze sent a flush through her, but her ire piqued. "We do not accept favors from strangers."

His gaze unexpectedly deepened.

She stilled. *What the devil? Was that amusement on his face?*

"We are not strangers," he said. There was no mistaking the laughter in his eyes now. "Are we, Tavis?" His gaze shifted to the boy.

"Nay," he replied with a shy smile. "No' strangers at all, laird."

"You know this man?" Elise asked.

"He is the laird's son."

"Marcus!" Bonnie cried, peeking from behind Elise's skirts.

Elise looked at him. Marcus? *This* was the son Cameron had spoken of with such affection these past months? It suddenly seemed comical that she had doubted Cameron's stories of his son's exploits on the battlefield. She had believed the aging chief's stories were exaggerations, but the giant of a man before her was clearly capable of every feat with which his father had credited him.

Prodded by the revelation, she discerned the resemblance between father and son. Though grey sprinkled Cameron's hair, the two shared the same unruly, dark hair, the same build... and... "You have his eyes," she said.

He chuckled.

Heat flooded her cheeks. She pulled Bonnie into her arms. "You might have said who you were." She gave him an assessing look. "Only that wouldn't have been half as much fun. Who will take the child?"

His gaze fixed on the hand she had wrapped around Bonnie and the small burn scar that remained as a testament of her folly. His attention broke when a voice from behind her said in a thick brogue, "'Tis me ye be looking for, lass." She turned to a weathered warrior who urged his mount forward.

Elise handed Bonnie up to him. Stepping back, she bumped into the large body of a horse. Before she could move, an arm encircled her from behind, pulling her upward across hard thighs. A tremor shot through her. She hadn't been this close to a man's body since—since those first months of her seven-year marriage.

Panic seized her in a quick, hard rush. The trees blurred as her mind plunged backward in time to the touch of the man who had promised till death do them part. Her husband's gentle hand on their wedding night splintered into his violent grip the night he'd tried to murder her—the movement of thighs beneath her buttocks broke the trance as Marcus MacGregor spurred his horse into motion. His arms tightened around her and she held her breath, praying he couldn't hear her thudding heart.

The ambling movement of the bulky horse lifted her from Marcus's lap. She clutched at his shirt. Her knuckles brushed his bare chest and she jerked back as if singed by hot coals. Her body lifted again with the horse's next step and she instinctively threw her arms around Marcus's forearm. His hold tightened as rich laughter rumbled through his chest.

"Do not worry, lass. Upon pain of death, I swear, you will not slip from my arms until your feet touch down at Brahan Seer."

Elise grimaced, then straightened in an effort to shift from the sword hilt digging into her back.

"What's wrong?" He leaned her back in his arms and gazed down at her.

She stared. Robert had never looked so—she sat upright. "I've simply never ridden a horse in this manner."

"There are many ways to ride a horse, lass," he said softly.

Elise snapped her gaze to his face, then jerked back when her lips nearly brushed his. She felt herself slip and clutched at his free arm even as the arm around her crushed her closer. Her breasts pressed against his chest where his shirt lay open. Heat penetrated her bodice, hardening her nipples. A surprising warmth sparked between her legs. She caught sight of his smile an instant before she dropped her gaze.

ABOUT THE AUTHOR

Award winning author Tarah Scott cut her teeth on authors such as Georgette Heyer, Zane Grey, and Amanda Quick. Her favorite book is a Tale of Two Cities, with Gone With the Wind as a close second. She writes modern classical romance, and paranormal and romantic suspense. Tarah grew up in Texas and currently resides in Westchester County, New York with her daughter.

Website:
http://www.tarahscott.com

Facebook:
https://www.facebook.com/TarahScottsRomanceNovels

Twitter:
@TarahScott

Blog:
http://tarahscott.tarahscott.com/

ALSO BY TARAH SCOTT

Highland Lords Series
My Highland Love
My Highland Lord

Lord Keeper
A Knight of Passion
The Pendulum: Legacy of the Celtic Brooch
When a Rose Blooms
Labyrinth
An Improper Wife
Hawk and the Cougar
Double Bang!
Born Into Fire

Coming Soon
Death Comes for a Knight
My Highland Chief

A MacLean Highlander Novel
The Highlander's Courtesan

Award Winning Titles
Lord Keeper
Golden Rose Best Historical of 2011
First place in the 2004 RWA CoLoNY Happy Endings contest
Third place in the Greater Seattle Chapter RWA's 2003 Emerald City

My Highland Love
Indie Romance Convention Best Readers Choice Awards 2013

AS T.C. ARCHER

Sasha's Calling
Fontana's Trouble
For His Eyes Only
Full Throttle

Kirsoval Scourge Series
Winter in Paradise
Yeoman's Paradise

Sin Series
Sin Incarnate

Coming Soon

Phenom League Series
Behind Enemy Lines
Desert Fox

Sin Series
Sin Revisited
Sin Reborn

Texas Rangers: Special Ops Series
Abducted
Reconnaissance Team

Made in the USA
Middletown, DE
08 October 2016